SECRETS

Katharine Marlowe

Young Emma Bellamy is newly widowed and struggling to redefine her personal and professional life. She is shaken, however, when her husband's lawyer receives an extremely suggestive letter that she signed, but has no recollection of writing. Soon she learns that more of these alarmingly truthful missives have been sent to every important person in her life.

Who is out to destroy her reputation? Who wants to alienate her friends, stepchildren, and colleagues? She can't think of anyone that mean and spiteful, but she vows to discover the truth even if it has surprising—and terrifying—consequences.

Other *Leisure Books* by Katharine Marlowe:
HEART'S DESIRES

SECRETS

KATHARINE MARLOWE

LEISURE BOOKS NEW YORK CITY

A LEISURE BOOK®

May 1993

Published by special arrangement with Donald I. Fine, Inc.

Dorchester Publishing Co., Inc.
276 Fifth Avenue
New York, NY 10001

For further information, contact: Donald I. Fine, Inc., 19 West 21st Street, New York, NY 10010.

The name "Leisure Books" and the stylized "L" with design are trademarks of Dorchester Publishing Co., Inc.

Printed in the United States of America.

Prologue

With a sigh she pulled the sheet of stationery from the typewriter. After scanning it she signed with an initial at the bottom, then folded the page into the envelope. A stamp, then it went on top of the pile of other letters.

She replaced the cover on the Selectric, switched off the light and got up. Carrying the half dozen or so envelopes she went down the stairs and out through the front door to walk the length of the driveway to the mailbox. She placed the letters in the box, raised the red flag to signal the mailman there was post to be collected, then walked back up the driveway to the house.

She went to the kitchen, put the light on, then had to stop, staring at Calla. The little dog's head had lifted alertly the instant the overhead light had gone on. Emma smiled, then looked around, trying to think why she'd come downstairs.

"I must want tea," she told the dog. "Isn't it absurd, Calla? I've come down, but I can't for the life of me think why. Do I want a cup of tea?"

The dog cocked her head to one side, eyes on Emma.

"Now that I'm here," Emma said, bending to stroke the Jack Russell's pleasingly shaped head, "I'll put the kettle on. Then," she said, straightening, "perhaps I'll remember what I was after down here. It's chilly in here," she said, rubbing her bare arms under the robe before reaching for the kettle. Her feet were cold too. If she hadn't known better, she'd have sworn she'd been out-of-doors.

Chapter One

After the telephone call from Richard Redmond, she went out the back way, letting Calla run free. Watching the little dog go bouncing through the tall grass as if on springs, Emma tried to focus her attention. It was very difficult. In the seven months since Will's death she'd found herself unable to concentrate for long on anything. She began each day determined to take control—of her life, of her work, of the household—but within minutes she'd be sliding away to a hushed interior place where time was of no consequence. Hours seemed to get lost in the corners, like dust collecting into small furry clots. She lost not only time but ideas and impulses. It was distressing to return to the present to find her brain as vacant as a suburban railway station at three A.M.

Calla arrived at the water's edge and stood with her head cocked, as if wondering why

Emma was taking so long. Such a remarkable little dog, Emma thought, quickening her pace. Almost human in her intelligence and sensitivity, Calla kept her linked, however tenuously, to the world; her minimal needs prevented Emma from taking up permanent residence in that silent place that beckoned so enticingly during her waking hours.

She stroked Calla's smooth, well-shaped head then seated herself on the pebbly shore as the dog gamboled off to investigate a chunk of driftwood twenty-odd yards away. The telephone call, Emma reminded herself. Richard Redmond, sounding strained and slightly peculiar, as if a fish bone were caught in his throat.

"Emma, there's a matter I'd like to discuss with you. I'd prefer not to go into it over the telephone. I thought if it's convenient I'd stop by this evening after office hours."

She'd been intending to reply to his most recent letter regarding the estate, but, like so many other chores she'd neglected since Will's death, she hadn't yet got around to it. Everything seemed like too much of an effort. Her only significant accomplishment in recent months had been to answer all the condolence letters. She'd spent a week at that, quite soon after the funeral. This onerous chore completed, she'd felt at liberty to sit—in the house, or here on the beach—for periods of unknown duration, contemplating the previous seventeen years of her life and searching for some incentive to go forward.

She felt old. This was due partly to her having lived for so long with a man twenty-six years her senior, and partly because, with his death, she'd lost all momentum. She'd been left not only a widow but somehow an orphan, too. It was admittedly absurd to think of herself in these waiflike terms, but, inescapably, it was how she felt.

Calla was digging energetically in the damp sand to one side of the driftwood, her compact brown and white body quivering slightly. The air was warm enough for mid-September, but thick with dampness. Emma wrapped her arms around her knees and looked out at the water. A sailboat quite far out was braving the chop. For some minutes she tracked its spasmodic progress across the horizon. Then the air and shore sounds thinned and she was viewing the perfectly preserved London scenes once more. It seemed she was obliged always to start at the beginning in order to remember details she might previously have missed. It was time-consuming and enormously frustrating. She'd have preferred to be able to leap forward and enter, say, in the middle. She longed to get to the end, convinced that when she'd completed this review she'd be able to pick up the primary threads and continue weaving whatever future she might have. But her mind invariably turned right back to the very beginning, as if to the first page of a lengthy novel whose plot kept changing.

With a sigh she surrendered, her mind speeding in reverse. And she was eighteen again, living in that room on the fifth floor of the house in South Kensington, with the bath and toilet one floor below. It was a cozy, elongated room, with an oversized wardrobe occupying the entire wall to the left of the door as one entered and the narrow bed filling in the space below the window on the opposite wall. There was a hot plate and a basin, a chair, a desk with her typewriter, and her books in a row on the mantel over the bricked-up fireplace.

A pay telephone was situated in the entryway on the ground floor, with extensions on every landing. The calls she got were primarily from the agency for which she'd been doing temporary secretarial work since leaving school five months earlier, or from her mother. She'd met several young men in the course of her newly won freedom but, without exception, after a few dates she began to begrudge them the time they took away from the writing she did on evenings and at weekends. Quite quickly they'd stop calling. She wasn't bothered.

Since the age of eight she'd dreamed of being a writer. Her father and many of her teachers had encouraged her to believe she had the talent and the determination necessary to succeed. Her mother, though, had always considered it a frivolous aspiration. By the time she was fourteen Emma had learned to withhold her enthusiasm—about most things—because to confide in her mother was to become embroiled in a lengthy argument. Her mother was the self-appointed arbiter of what was or was not suitable for her two daughters.

Since Vivian, her older sister by three years, had proved herself to be completely intractable in every area, Mrs. Dalton chose to direct her critical attention to the more placid, generally less difficult Emma. When Vivian left home at the age of seventeen after a screaming row lasting several days, her mother became even more critical and insidiously demanding. Emma endured the almost daily incursions into her privacy until she completed her schooling. Then she too escaped from the house in Richmond.

Being on her own was wonderful. She tolerated her mother's frequent telephone calls, and every few weeks made a Sunday-afternoon duty visit home, primarily to see her father, who grew animated at the sight of her. While he managed to make it clear that he loved her and missed her, he was never willing to disagree openly with his wife's strongly stated opinions regarding most things but especially with respect to their daughters. Vivian was impossible, beyond redemption. And Emma was, despite her visible self-reliance, on the road to ruin.

The visits and the carping inquisitional one-sided telephone conversations were a small price to pay for being at liberty to come and go as she chose, to provide for herself via the secretarial jobs, and to write as late into the night as she wished. She had several short stories going the rounds of the magazines, and a novel better than halfway finished. She'd already received a number of printed rejection slips, but a few encouraging notes from editors too. She didn't at all mind the rejection slips. They constituted proof that she was finally working at what mattered most to her. She felt productive and positive and knew if she persevered and kept working, one of her stories would be accepted for publication. Then she'd be truly on her way as a published author.

When Brenda from the agency rang her just before Christmas regarding a three-day assignment, Emma was quick to accept even though Brenda sounded somewhat hesitant.

"It's all perfectly legitimate," she'd assured Emma, "but it is at a hotel, and I'd understand if you preferred to turn this one down."

"Why?"

"Well, you are very young," Brenda had said. "And some of our girls get a bit nervy about executives in hotel suites. Not," she'd added quickly, "that we've ever had any problems. It's just that we usually send along our older girls. You understand. But what with Christmas being so close, we're rather short-staffed."

"I don't mind," Emma had told her. "I could use the extra money."

"In that case," said an audibly relieved Brenda, "let me give you the details."

The next morning Emma had gone to the Savoy, arriving early as she did for every appointment, to do three days' secretarial work for an American named Willard Bellamy. She'd stopped at the desk and asked them to ring up to announce her, then accepted directions from the clerk before heading for the elevator.

Calla was barking. Drawn abruptly back into the present, Emma looked over to see the feisty little bitch angrily confronting an intrepid seagull in a minor territorial dispute. Calla put an end to it with a springing leap that sent the startled bird aloft with an indignant squawk. Calla's head lifted to follow the bird's flight, then, apparently satisfied with the outcome, she gave herself a shake, executed a smart turn and trotted back to nudge Emma's knee with the side of her head.

Emma reached into her cardigan pocket for one of the biscuits she always carried for Calla and held it out on the palm of her hand. Calla looked at the bone-shaped biscuit, then at Emma, awaiting permission.

"Good girl," Emma said. "Eat, Calla." The dog ducked her head to Emma's palm, took the biscuit between her teeth, then settled on the sand to eat it.

Absently smoothing Calla's back, Emma looked again at the horizon. The sailboat had gone out of sight. She wondered what Richard Redmond had to say that couldn't be discussed over the telephone. She was under the impression that the estate could at last be settled, now that two of Will's four children had given up threatening to contest the will. It had been an unpleasant although fairly predictable skirmish, with a frantic flurry of telephone calls and visits. Susan and Edgar had each come several times to the house to assure Emma of their full support, and to berate their sister and brother for attempting to deny their stepmother what was, by all rights, hers. While she very much appreciated these displays of loyalty, Emma had been unable to do more than sit and listen while she gazed at their faces, mutely marveling over being, at thirty-five, stepmother to a quartet of adults ranging in age from thirty-three to thirty-seven. It heightened her sense of having aged a year for each of the twenty-five months of Will's illness.

Seventeen years of turmoil. Emma rhythmically caressed Calla's solid, warm body. Nothing had turned out the way she thought it would.

Will had warned her. She had to admit that. But she'd been far too young to take anyone's advice seriously. She'd been in love and unable to imagine that everything wouldn't work out perfectly.

She thought with sad fondness of her youthful conceit, of her notion that people would respond positively once they came to know her and they understood that the considerable age difference was irrelevant in the face of hers and Will's emotional commitment to one another.

"It shouldn't matter," he'd said often over the years. "But somehow it does. They see a middle-aged man with someone young enough to be his daughter and they react every time with a knowing smirk. People are never going to understand. It'll never be easy."

Well, a few people had understood, or at least they'd accepted the situation. Willard had been forty-four, the divorced father of four, and on that morning when she knocked at the door to his suite at the Savoy she was expecting nothing more than three days of dictation and transcribing work before heading home to Richmond to celebrate Christmas with her family. She was hoping there'd be no scenes, that they'd be able to get through the three days peacefully.

Will. He'd opened the door and, looking amused, asked, "You're Miss Dalton?"

"Yes, I am," she'd confirmed.

"I'm sorry," he'd said, stepping back from the door to allow her to enter. "I was expecting someone—older."

"Why?" she'd asked with a smile, watching him close the door. An attractive man, tall, with fair, graying hair and lively bright blue eyes. She'd found him immediately intriguing. Americans fascinated her, not just their accents but their enviable self-assurance. They seemed so much freer, so much less inhibited about so many things than the British.

"I don't know," he'd said. "You're supposed to be forty-five, with gray hair, glasses, and a brisk businesslike manner. Care for some coffee?"

"Yes, please. I am brisk and businesslike," she'd said, following him across the room to a table where there was a tray with cups and a large carafe of coffee.

As he poured, he said, "Take off your coat, have a seat. D'you take dictation?"

"Yes, I do."

"Well, good. I've got a couple of meetings. I'll want you to take notes."

"All right." She'd stood holding her coat and bag, waiting for instructions.

"At the risk of appearing rude," he'd said, carrying two cups across to the sofa, "might I ask how old you are? Come sit down. Just leave your coat anywhere."

"I'm eighteen," she'd answered, draping her coat over the back of a chair before seating herself at the far end of the sofa.

"Still in school?" He lit a cigarette, then thought to offer her one.

"No, thank you. I don't smoke. I left school five months ago."

"That'd be about right, wouldn't it?" he'd said. "I have twins your age who graduated high school in June. Susan and Shawn are in college now. Are you planning to continue your education?"

She took a sip of the coffee before answering. "Actually, no. I believe life itself offers one all the education one might need. What sort of business are you in?"

"Publishing."

"Oh! What sort of publishing?"

"General. Does that interest you?"

"Yes, very much. I'm a writer. I mean to say, I'm trying to be a writer."

Again he'd looked amused, asking, "And what have you written, Miss Dalton?"

"I've got some short stories going the rounds. And I'm better than halfway through a novel."

He'd looked at her appraisingly for a long moment before gulping down some of his black coffee. "Think they're good?" he'd asked.

"Well, naturally I would, wouldn't I?" she'd answered without sarcasm. "One must believe in oneself."

"Oh, absolutely. Couldn't agree more. Coffee okay?"

"Yes, thank you."

He'd looked at his watch, then said, "Might as well get on with it. The hotel's organizing a typewriter. It should be here any minute. In the meantime, I've got a few letters that need to go out today. Then there's an eleven o'clock meeting where I'll want you to take notes, and another one at three. Sound okay?"

"Yes, fine."

"Would you like to show me some of your work?" he'd asked unexpectedly.

Thrown, she'd stumbled over her answer. "I'm not . . . I mean . . . I don't know."

"I'm always looking for new writers. You think about it," he'd said kindly. "Now, did you happen to bring a steno pad with you?"

"I did, actually."

"Good." He'd set down his cup, reached for an address book on the table and began flipping through it.

Like lint on the lens of her private projector, Richard's telephone call began to interfere with the mental film. Why was he stopping by the house? Visitors enervated her. They had such clearly defined expectations, wanting one to be attentive, to observe certain amenities. Beverages were to be offered, ashtrays and glasses and places to sit; attention was to be paid, polite queries as to the state of one's health and well-being. A tiresome gavotte of wordplay. She'd managed all these months to keep practically everyone at bay, dealing almost entirely by telephone. She didn't as a rule mind dealing with letters—from Richard, from old friends of Will's, from her publishers, from fans—but quite a stack of them sat unanswered beside the typewriter. She kept adding to the stack, promising herself she'd take a day to get caught up, but she hadn't yet got to it. She could control telephone conversations, keep them brief and to the point; she could control correspondence even more successfully—if she ever got round to tackling the ever-growing number—but she could scarcely control a visitor. She felt as if she'd lost whatever social skills she'd once possessed.

Before Will's illness she'd liked having people around. Most weekends at least one of the guest rooms had been occupied, and often all three. Now she and Bernice were alone in the house during the week, and Bernice left every

Saturday at noon and didn't return until Monday morning. She went off to stay with her son and daughter-in-law and grandchildren in White Plains. Emma kept expecting her to announce she was leaving, that she'd accepted a position in a household where meals were served three times a day, and people came and went regularly; where there were conversations and laughter, even arguments. Someplace with more to offer than an uncommunicative widow and her clever dog. She dreaded the idea of losing Bernice but could think of no enticement that might induce the woman to stay, should Bernice announce that it was her intention to go. Not that she'd be likely to respond to anything Emma might offer her. Bernice was very much her own person, and she'd do whatever she believed to be right. Still, Emma grieved at the thought of her going. Bernice was kind and sensible, a good friend.

A cold edge to the breeze now, Emma pulled the cardigan closed and let her chin rest on her knees as she looked up the beach. This hundred-odd-yard scoop of private terrain at the water's edge seemed at some times like her personal prison. At other times she felt inordinately privileged now to be its sole owner. Of course no one could actually own anything, especially not an actual piece of the earth. This land was on loan to her—or, more accurately, to whomever resided in the house—rather like an improbable overscale terrarium in which all manner of things flourished. The tide daily brought unlikely gifts, depositing them in a tangle of seaweed and fast-food wrappers: bits of driftwood, sea-glass, bivalve shells with purple interiors, floats that had come free from fishermen's nets, bottles and boxes and feathers.

If she could, just once, get from the beginning through to the end of this retrospective perhaps she'd be able to work again, to live again, to view for example this beach with a reasonable degree of equanimity, instead of staggering along under the need to put her mental stockroom in order. She wished Richard hadn't called, hadn't announced his intention to stop by. She'd been well along, but now she'd have to start again, back in that room on the fifth floor of the house in South Kensington.

Despair creating an ache in her chest, she let her eyes return to the horizon, the splash of the incoming waves dissolving to silence.

It was a cozy, elongated room, with an over-sized wardrobe occupying the entire wall to the left of the door as one entered . . .

Chapter Two

"Good evening, Bernice."

"Good evening, Mr. Redmond. Miz Bellamy expecting you?"

The woman smiled pleasantly, and Richard wondered why Emma hadn't let the housekeeper know he was coming.

"I believe so," he answered. "I gather she didn't tell you."

"She's not herself these days," Bernice said quietly. "Probably forgot. You say anything to her yet about those letters?"

"You mean there were others?"

"Looked to me like as if she had a whole handful of 'em when I saw her going up the driveway in nothin' but her robe and slippers. Here it is almost midnight and I see someone walkin' up the driveway, so I take a look out the window and it's Emma. Kinda gave me the willies.

She's not herself," Bernice repeated with concern. "I'm hopin' you can maybe get her back to seein' sense."

"To be truthful, if you hadn't called and I'd simply received that letter . . . I honestly don't know *how* I'd have reacted. You're quite sure she's unaware of having written them?"

"Mr. Redmond," Bernice said patiently, "I've been after her every day for better than two months to answer that big pile of letters up in her office. And every day she says to me, tomorrow; says she doesn't have the energy to bother with writing letters, can't face it; she knows she should but she just can't get to it. You go on ahead. She's in the solarium. See if she admits to sending you any letter. I don't mind telling you she's got me real worried."

"All right," he said somewhat doubtfully. "Thank you, Bernice."

Bernice headed off to the kitchen and Richard stood for a moment gazing down the hallway. Then he glanced into the large living room to his right, noting that black fabric still concealed the mirrors. There was something very unsettling about those shrouded shapes. He'd been hoping to find the house back to normal.

Bernice was out of sight. He cleared his throat and started toward the rear of the house. As he went past the kitchen he could hear water running, and the faint sounds of a radio playing. With Willard's death the house seemed to have lost its center, its pulse. Where once it had fairly throbbed with energy, now it somehow made him think of Queen Victoria—black-clad and outsized, with her back turned to the sea. Richard had several times suggested that Emma sell the house and buy something smaller and more manageable. So far, she hadn't responded in any way to the suggestion.

He paused in the wide doorway to the solarium. Emma was seated in one of the rattan armchairs, with Calla curled up on the terra cotta-tiled floor at her feet. Emma was turned slightly to one side, chin resting on the palm of her hand, staring fixedly out the window wall that overlooked the Sound.

He said, "Good evening, Emma," and she started, looked over at him, then got to her feet.

"Hello, Richard."

He crossed the room to shake her thin cool hand, asking, "How are you?"

"A drink, Richard? Tea or coffee, or perhaps something stronger?" She looked over at the ornate rattan trolley just inside the door. She saw that Bernice had dusted the bottles, and the glasses looked freshly washed. The ice bucket, though, was empty. Emma had neglected to mention that Richard was stopping by; one more thing she'd forgotten.

"I wouldn't mind a Coke, or anything soft."

"Of course." She went to the intercom and asked Bernice please to bring a Coca Cola for Mr. Redmond. Then she said, "Come sit down, Richard," and returned to her chair.

While they waited for Bernice—Emma bending to pat Calla's head with a long slender hand—Richard wondered why he forgot from one visit to the next how very pretty Emma was. Perhaps it was because they conducted most of their business over the telephone and through the years had met in person only occasionally. The bulk of their meetings had taken place during the past two and a half years. He'd last seen her some six weeks earlier. And now that he thought about it, he'd been surprised then as well.

She was indeed very pretty, with pale translucent skin and dark, deep-set eyes. Her fair hair was cut in an extremely short, side-parted style that was remarkably flattering to her delicate features. She was taller than average and despite the full cut of her long-skirted cotton dress he noticed that she'd lost even more weight since he'd last seen her.

"How are you, Emma?" he asked again, wondering if she might be in the throes of a breakdown. The idea of that saddened and alarmed him.

"The same," she answered in her pleasantly soft clear voice, sitting back, her long hands gripping the down-curving arms of the chair. "Last night I dreamed Will took a frightful spill, but I was too far away to help him. It was terribly real. He was so frail, so helpless." She shook her head and looked out the window for a few seconds. Then, making an effort to maintain some acceptable form of dialogue, she said, "I expect it will take some time before my dreams and I become accustomed to his death."

"Undoubtedly," Richard said sympathetically. "I know how rough it can be."

"Yes," she said slowly, her eyes narrowing slightly as if to assist her recall. "Your mother died not very long ago, didn't she?"

"It's been three years."

"Really? I thought it was more recent." Again

27

she turned to look out the window and Richard studied her thoughtful profile, the graceful length of her neck, the silvery wisps of hair at her temples. Her looks, he'd long since learned, were entirely deceiving. The pale pastels and tiny prints of the rather old-fashioned dresses she invariably wore contributed to a first impression of insubstantiality. She looked the least likely woman to write the kind of books she did, those intricately plotted, psychologically incisive voyages through the minds of murderers. He'd read all seven of her books and sincerely admired not only her writing skill but her insights.

In fact, the moment she began to speak, the impression she gave of being a dreamy lightweight was at once shattered and one was forced to recognize the acuity and intelligence shining in those round brown eyes. She was one of the brightest women he'd ever encountered, and from their first meeting he'd readily understood why Willard had fallen so hard for her. He'd actually been mildly jealous of Willard's having had the good fortune to win her. Of course that had predated Richard's own marriage, and back then he'd viewed women somewhat differently and always from the vantage point of his personal requirements, which had since undergone radical alteration. All those years ago, he'd been an eager 25-year-old lawyer pegged to become an associate, and being assigned to handle Willard Bellamy's legal affairs had been a small coup.

Willard had made an appointment to rewrite his will and had brought along his new wife. Richard doubted he'd ever forget that meeting.

Willard had been charming, easygoing, candid. His new wife had looked no more than sixteen, the very essence of a latter-day flower child with an Indian cotton scarf tied around her forehead, its ends trailing over her long hair; she'd been clad in a bulky patchwork coat, which she removed to reveal a voluminous pinafore dress, her feet encased in what looked like mukluks, large silver loops in her pierced ears. Richard had tried to keep his surprise from showing as he shook their hands in turn, then invited them to sit down.

Emma had actually taught him a valuable lesson that day: do not judge people by their looks. A cliché of course, but something that had served him well over the years, particularly when it came to dealing with women. It had been his experience, beginning with Emma, that appearances too often belied the personalities they concealed. Now, sixteen years later, he was being taught the lesson once again, and by his original teacher. But did she still have her original faculties, or were they being eaten away by grief?

"Are you aware that you're staring at me?" she said quietly, expressionlessly, as Bernice came in carrying a tray with Richard's Coke and a cup of tea for Emma.

A few moments and Bernice was gone and Richard was apologizing. "I'm sorry. It's been a long day."

"Every day is a long day," Emma declared, holding the cup of tea with both hands, her eyes on his. Richard had not only sounded odd over the telephone, he was also behaving a bit oddly. And he looked uncomfortable, as if he'd

29

sat down to discover the seat cushion was wet. "Is something wrong?" she asked. "The chair's not wet, is it?"

"The chair?" He shifted to one side to touch the cushion, said, "No," and looked down at Calla, wondering if the dog was in the habit of soiling the furniture. The idea was so absurd he laughed aloud, then felt ridiculous. "I thought," he tried to explain, "maybe you were warning me that Calla has taken to . . . Never mind." He was on edge and in many ways wished there'd been no need to come here.

"This conversation's taken a somewhat surrealistic turn," she said, and smiled. He was further thrown, unable to recall when last he'd seen any evidence of her lighter side. Was this sudden change of mood indicative of a mind out of balance?

He returned the smile, drank some of the Coke, then said, "I know I've suggested it before, and at the risk of being repetitious, have you given any thought to selling this place?"

"I have thought about it, Richard," she said, the smile vanishing as she looked around the room. "I think about a great number of things, but the thoughts seem to get lost in the corners. Which is very likely why I haven't been able to work. I am completely bereft of ideas. My publisher is anxious to have a new book. His recent letters have pointedly referred to certain payments made upon my signing of the last contract. Perhaps I should return the money . . ." She trailed off, her head turning toward the window as if drawn by some powerful force.

"Maybe a change of scene would help," he offered, anxious to keep her attention.

"It might," she allowed, her eyes at last returning to him. Having this man taking up space, expecting her to answer questions, was jarring. It would have been nice simply to look at him without any need to speak. His face was appealing and she'd always found his smile quite beautiful. She liked Richard. He was essentially a calm man. There wasn't the slightest hint that he harbored any doubts about his identity or his motives. She raised the cup to her lips and drank some of the tea. "Is there some problem regarding the estate, Richard?"

"No, no." He set down his glass intending to open his briefcase, decided to wait, and said, "It should be all wrapped up by the end of this week. I'd be sad, you know, to think you're not going to keep on writing, Emma. I really enjoy your books. I took forward to each new one."

"It isn't that I wouldn't like to. I would, very much. But I have nothing to say. I'd never have finished the last one if Will hadn't kept on at me, if he hadn't insisted."

"He wouldn't have wanted you to stop now."

"No," she agreed. "He wouldn't have wanted to die, either, given a choice in the matter. Did you know, Richard, that there was a rumor that I was nothing more than a front, that it was actually Will who wrote the books?"

"I didn't know that," he answered, thinking the idea was ridiculous. No one who'd known both of them would ever have found it remotely credible.

She nodded soberly. "It's true. People found it hard to believe I could have written such quote mature unquote prose at such a young age. To be honest, it was Will who pointed me in the right direction. When we met I had half a novel done and he persuaded me to let him have a look at it. He read it that same night and the next day said he thought it would make a good mystery, and pointed out all the reasons why. After deliberating, I decided he was right. I trusted his judgment. He was an established publisher, after all. For the next little while I read dozens of mysteries, got a feel for the plotting, the characterizations, the moods, the settings and so forth, then I began rewriting. On his next trip to London he read the fifty or so new pages, made suggestions, and subsequently I sent him five or six chapters at a time and he wrote back with more suggestions, comments. Eight months later, when the book was completed, he put me in touch with the agency in London. At his urging they took me on and made a sale quite quickly."

She looked over at him, and he said, "So that's how you started."

"That's how Will got me started," she amended. "And that's how we worked right up to the end. I'd give him half a dozen chapters and he'd point out what worked and what didn't. We'd argue now and then, or rather I'd argue, but he was usually right. I've never published anything that didn't have his imprint on it."

"That doesn't mean you couldn't."

"No, but I'm not feeling especially confident just now. Why am I telling you all this?" she wondered aloud.

He had no answer and covered the moment by reaching for his glass, eyeing her over the rim as he drank.

"I'm very angry with Will," she said, giving

voice to the thought as it occurred to her. "It compounds my guilt. He shouldn't have forced me to be so dependent on him. Now that he's gone I feel . . . disqualified, as if he actually was the one who wrote the books." She bent abruptly and lifted the sleeping dog onto her lap.

"You were very young," he began.

"I was also very independent," she cut in. "I savored my independence. I took great pride in providing for myself. It was a mistake to turn myself over to him so completely, as if I were some sort of package he claimed from the lost property office."

"Don't you think," he said, choosing his words with care, "that it was what the situation required?"

"Perhaps," she sighed. "I no longer know. All I do know is that it's seventeen years later and now that I'm on my own I find it difficult to remember how to function effectively. I sound so self-pitying," she said with annoyance. "I'm not. I'm simply angry."

"Have you been out of this house since Willard died?" he asked.

"I take Calla down to the beach every morning . . ."

"No, I mean *out*."

She shook her head. With a touchingly open expression, she said, "Where would I go?"

Thinking this would be a good way to take the sting out of what he'd come here to do, he said, "Let me take you to dinner this weekend. Or brunch on Sunday. You're too young to be moldering away in this house."

"Is that why you've come here this evening, to rescue me?" For a second time she smiled, this time with amusement.

"I didn't know I was going to invite you out," he said truthfully. "It suddenly seemed like a good idea. No," he said, knowing the moment had come to reach into his briefcase and bring out the letter. "I came to discuss this." He got up, crossed the room, handed her the letter, then returned to his chair.

She looked at the envelope front and back, then lifted the flap and removed the page inside. She began to read, and a deep flush spread upward from her throat all the way to her hairline. Even the rims of her ears turned red. Her mouth opened slightly. One hand rose to curl itself against her lips.

Dear Richard,

I've decided I want to sleep with you. As I know it's an idea you've entertained more than once during the years of our acquaintanceship and as I also know you'd never risk approaching me, I thought I'd make my feelings on the matter known to you.

It's been almost two years since the last time I made love. I've always been fond of you and I imagine you've suffered some degree of sexual uncertainty since your divorce. It can't have been easy losing your wife to another woman, just as it hasn't been easy for me trying to come to terms with my new status as a widow.

I am alone in the house each weekend from Saturday afternoon until Monday morning. No one need ever know. I sleep in the nude and lately when I touch myself

I've imagined it was you. I've felt your hands and mouth on my body, felt you inside me. Your weight, your thrust, are already familiar. Call me. E.

She read the letter twice, noticing during the second reading that her hands had begun to tremble. She was painfully aware of Richard waiting for some explanation and of her own profound embarrassment.

"Richard," she said, but had to stop and drink some of the tea to ease her desiccated throat. The cup rattled in the saucer as she put it down. "I didn't write this letter," she told him, forcing herself to meet his eyes. "It's obviously my stationery, and it certainly looks like the typeface of my typewriter. But I didn't write this. Oh, good God!" she exclaimed softly. "Is this why you're inviting me out to a meal?"

It was his turn to be embarrassed. "Not at all," he insisted. "That was purely spontaneous," he said, trying to explain. "And I really didn't think this was something to be discussed over the telephone."

"No," she agreed, looking again at the envelope and the postmark, then at the encircled "E" at the bottom of the letter. "Who would do a thing like this? Why?"

His shoulders lifted and fell in a shrug meant to indicate his inability to comment. He felt a small twinge of disappointment at her denial. The letter had actually aroused him. It was like a fabulous fantasy, that an attractive woman would invite him to make love to her. But after his telephone conversation with Bernice he'd known it was merely a fantasy and had come to the house tonight with that idea fixed firmly in his mind.

She thought for a few moments. "Quite a number of people had access to my desk, you know, Richard, especially at the last. Everyone knew Will was failing. So many of his friends came to see him. Then there are the children. Well, Susan and Edgar primarily. They stayed here those last few days. Shawn and Janet came several times but only to harass me. Still . . . After the funeral . . . I have no idea how many people were here. Dozens." She felt as if the air in the solarium had turned liquid and she was drowning in it, her lungs going heavy, her heart laboring. What made the letter all the more hateful and alarming were the elements of truth it contained. It had been nearly two years since she'd last made love. She did sleep in the nude; she was alone on the weekends. And, most damning, during her last visit to Richard's office, she'd taken a close look at him and had been shocked to realize she found him appealing. He must have been mortified by the reference to his ex-wife. Had she known about that? She couldn't recall if she had.

"We'll forget about it," he said, anxious to clear the air.

"I'm terribly sorry, Richard. I can't think why anyone would want to embarrass either one of us in this fashion."

"We'll forget it," he repeated. No harm had been done, after all. Although, according to Bernice, there were other letters. The other recipients might not be so fortunate. It was impossible to say what elements were operating here, with a woman who claimed to have no knowledge of having written the letters in the first place. She appeared genuinely, deeply disturbed by what she'd read. And while it was one thing to lie, it was another to blush at will. He'd never known anyone capable of that.

"May I keep this?" she asked. "I'd like to look at it again when I'm calmer, see if I can't get some clue as to who could have written it."

"Of course," he said. "I made a copy, just in case."

"In case of what?" she asked somewhat fearfully.

"In case there are more letters," he said quickly, unable to think of anything else halfway reasonable.

"Oh, no! You don't think . . . ?"

"It's possible." It *was* possible, he thought. From her point of view, this could be seen as some sort of poison-pen letter. Christ! He was beginning to feel a vine-like tangle collecting around his ankles.

"People will think I've gone mad!" She protested so strongly that Calla stirred, opened her eyes and looked up at her.

"Let's not anticipate," he said quietly, more and more convinced of—in a sense—her innocence. Perhaps she'd hatched an alter ego who'd taken to writing letters late at night. Perhaps she'd . . . who knew? He couldn't begin to imagine what might happen when a mind as clever as Emma's took an unexpected turn. "It may come to nothing."

She shifted to look out the window. It was beginning to get dark. All at once she had the feeling that people were outside, looking in at her. She wanted to get up and close the curtains but suspected it wouldn't help.

"I'd still like to take you to dinner. You need

to get out of here," he said. The only thing he knew for certain was that in no way could it be healthy for her being housebound in this stone mausoleum for seven months.

Another flush was spreading upward from her chest. Bewilderment was like a sticky coating on her flesh. "I truly did not write that letter," she said, closing her eyes for a few seconds.

"It's forgotten. Which evening would you prefer, Friday or Saturday?"

"Why?" she asked, venturing to look again at him.

"Maybe there was some degree of truth in that." He pointed at the letter she was still clutching in her right hand. "And maybe I just think it's a good idea on general principle."

"You're asking me out on a *date*," she said incredulously. "Are you aware how limited my experience is in this area? Do you realize it's been more than seventeen years since I . . ." *Shut up!* she told herself. *Don't go on with this dreary recitation.* "Would you be doing this if you hadn't received this letter?"

"Probably not," he conceded. "It woke me up, in a way. And I thought, Why not? It's perfectly legitimate. No harm, no foul."

"What does that mean?" she asked with a frown. "What is it, a reference to baseball or something?"

He laughed. "To tell you the truth, I don't know. I've never been much for sports. It's merely an expression that serves the purpose now and then. Which night?" he persisted. Now that he'd extended the invitation he refused to be deterred. He also couldn't believe she wasn't in her right mind. Somewhat disturbed perhaps, but not mad. Not Emma.

"I can't think." She rubbed Calla's head, thinking. "Friday, I suppose."

"Good!" He took hold of his briefcase and got to his feet. "I'll be running along now."

Removing Calla from her lap, she rose to walk with him to the door, aware of his height and breadth as they walked side by side; he pushed the air aside, creating invisible eddies that washed over her, bringing with them his particular scent and a hint of bay rum.

Upon arriving in the foyer they shook hands with their accustomed formality. She opened the door, casting about for something to say. "If you change your mind, I'll understand perfectly," she told him, looking at his sleek automobile parked at the apex of the driveway.

"Emma," he said gently, drawing her eyes back to him. "I'm not going to change my mind. And I hope you won't either. You *need* to get out of this house." He looked up at the stone facade. Now that he thought about it, it really did feel as if he were rescuing her. He was going to have to find some way to convince her to get the hell out of this house.

"Perhaps I do," she said, also looking at the house. "Goodbye, Richard."

She stood waiting until he installed himself in the car, fastened his seat belt and started the engine. This was all very strange, she thought, as he waved and drove off. Strange and alarming.

Chapter Three

"Bernice, do you know how to type?"

The woman removed her reading glasses and put down the newspaper. "Do I what?"

"Type. Do you know how?"

Bernice folded her arms in front of her on the kitchen table and regarded Emma with an expression bordering on astonishment. "I knew how to type, you think I'd of been cleaning up for people coming on twenty-seven years now?"

"No, I expect not."

"Nine years I've been here, all of a sudden you're askin' me do I type?"

"I'm sorry if you find it an unreasonable question," Emma said apologetically.

"I don't know about unreasonable," she said. "Peculiar, definitely. You hungry? I know you said not to fix dinner, but you should eat something. Way you're goin', the next thing anyone knows

40

you'll wind up in the hospital gettin' fed through a tube. I got some nice roast beef, well done the way you like it. I could fix you a samwich."

Emma pulled out a chair and sat down. Calla was curled up in her basket beside the stove. Bernice was waiting for an answer. "Thank you. I will have a sandwich."

Bernice smiled with satisfaction. "Good." She got up and went to the refrigerator. "Good," she repeated, pulling out the roast beef, mayonnaise, lettuce. "Kind of bread you want? I got whole wheat and rye."

"Rye, please."

"Wanna cup of tea with it?"

"I'll put the kettle on," Emma volunteered.

"So how come you didn't tell me Mr. Lawyer was comin' by?"

"I forgot."

"Uh-huh. No more problems about Mr. Willard's money, I hope," Bernice said, wondering if Emma would mention that business about the letters.

"No, no further problems regarding the estate."

"Shawn and Janet, they've always been a couple of real sweethearts, hatchin' plots, lookin' to make trouble." Bernice shook her head as she swiveled the lid off the Hellmann's jar. "The nerve of those two! Tryin' to make out like as if you're not entitled. So what'd he want?"

"Richard?" Emma took a moment to decide how much she wanted Bernice to know. "He asked me to dinner Friday evening."

"You don't say!" Bernice's eyebrows lifted. "You goin'?"

"I accepted," Emma said, a jolt of renewed guilt and embarrassment causing her to study

Bernice's reactions closely.

"Well, good! It's about time you got out some."

"You think so, do you?"

"Yeah, I think so. How come you're actin' so prissy? *You think so, do you?*" she mimicked with an affectionate laugh. "Ease up, woman. Nobody's gonna give you a hard time about goin' out to eat with Mr. Lawyer."

"Nobody has to. I feel guilty as it is."

Bernice got a plate from the cupboard, put the sandwich on it, then said, "Sit back down and start on this while I do up the tea. You want bags or the loose stuff?"

"The loose, please," Emma answered, resuming her seat at the table but continuing to study Bernice as she moved about, getting the tea caddy, pouring hot water into the teapot to warm it, the way Emma had shown her when she'd first come to work for them.

Bernice liked to say she was one-quarter black, one-quarter Iroquois, one-quarter English and one-quarter American mongrel. She was 45 years old, short and plump, with skin almost as fair as Emma's, green eyes, a wide, appealingly youthful face, big healthy teeth, and a halo of frizzy brown curls. No matter what the circumstances might be, Emma was always glad to see Bernice. It had to do with Bernice's consistent warmth, with her easy smiles, and with the fact that Emma believed Bernice genuinely cared about her. In the past few years Emma had surrendered herself often into Bernice's motherly arms, seeking a consolation the woman never appeared unwilling to give. And there was undeniable comfort to be derived from being clasped to Bernice's softly yielding warmth. She'd had more mothering from Bernice in the past two years than her own mother had given during the first eighteen years of her life.

Bernice and her husband, Joe, had put all three of their children through college by cleaning houses as a team twelve to fifteen hours a day, six days a week, every week of the year. When Joe had died of a coronary nine years earlier, Bernice took Willard up on his offer to be their live-in housekeeper. With her two oldest away at college at the time, and her youngest in his last semester of high school and already accepted by the college of his choice, she saw the offer as an opportunity to take life a whole lot easier.

Up to that point she and Joe had worked for the Bellamys for several years and had found them to be decent, likable folks, unlike some she could've named. So the transition from three-times-a-week help to daily live-in was fairly painless. She had her own place— what had once upon a time been the guest house out back—with plenty of room for all her furniture and for the kids when they were home from college and, later on, the grandkids. The Bellamys had never minded her having the kids or the grandkids to stay. While her own three were at college, Mr. Willard, and Emma especially, used to take time to talk with them about their interests. And they'd both written references for the kids when it came time for them to go out into the working world.

Right from the day she came to stay, despite the fact that she was nowhere near old enough, she'd played mama and big sister to Emma.

There was something about her that got to Bernice. She was smart as could be when it came to high-toned conversations with those publishing people who were always up visiting from the city. But when it came to everyday things, like dealing with Mr. Willard's kids, she just got lost. So Bernice helped her out, giving advice here and there, letting Emma have the benefit of her experience. Emma had a sweetness and a kind of innocence that made Bernice want to look out for her, especially where that Shawn and Janet were concerned.

In her opinion, Mr. Willard had kept Emma from growing up properly, kept her young so he could go on showing her off, year after year, to all those friends of his who probably thought the marriage would last no time at all. Emma was his prize, his little-girl bride, who wrote them clever books and talked real well with her nice English accent; she was his pride and joy— so long as she kept on needing him and didn't decide one day it was time she took to acting and dressing her age.

When Mr. Willard got sick, Emma started coming to the kitchen most evenings to sit for a spell, drinking tea and talking quietly about the latest the doctors had to say, about the sickness he got from the medicines, and about how the worst thing she'd ever known was having to watch the man dying day after day. It was as if Emma finally began growing up in a big hurry, because she knew she was going to have to make her own way in the world and she'd better learn fast.

By the time the end finally did come, Emma had pretty well caught up to herself. She did everything that had to be done and showed she had real grit. But once Mr. Willard was in the ground and all the mourners went on their way, Emma started forgetting all kinds of things and gave up talking. There were days when she didn't speak a single word but just sat out in the solarium looking through the window or went down to the beach with the dog and stared at the water. She didn't even say much when those two nasty children of Mr. Willard's started making a fuss over the will. She only sighed and said, "Richard will take care of it. He's a good lawyer."

Bernice didn't doubt for a minute that Mr. Redmond was a real good lawyer. Oh, he'd been a bit on the overanxious side when he'd first started doing the legal work for the family. But he'd grown up a lot since then. That divorce a few years back took a good deal of the starch out of his sails. He wasn't nowhere near so rush-rush and impatient as before. Nowadays he was calmer, slower, nicer. He was also a fine-looking man who'd do the right thing by Emma and wouldn't go taking advantage of her. Bernice thought if anybody could get through to Emma, he'd be the one.

"I'll tell you what I think," Bernice said, bringing the proper china teacups to the table.

"What's that?" Emma ran her fingertip back and forth over the edge of the plate upon which sat the thick sandwich.

"First off, I think you better get some of that food in you."

Emma pulled the plate closer but couldn't, for the moment, get herself to touch the food. "What were you going to say?" she asked as

Bernice brought over the teapot and milk jug and sat down.

"I think," Bernice said momentously, "it's foolish, you feelin' guilty. The two of you could use each other's company. You can't keep on sittin' around here day after day, not doin' a thing, not sayin' a word to anyone. And when're you gonna start back to workin', anyway? Or is it your plan to sit idle the rest of your life?"

"I have no plans." Reluctantly, Emma picked up half of the sandwich.

"Well, make some!" Bernice poured milk into the cups before lifting the teapot. "You're still a young woman. Plenty of things you could be doin'."

"You like him, don't you?" Emma said, as she bit into the sandwich.

"Mr. Lawyer? I like him fine, and he ' sure is easy on the eyes. D'you ever wonder about that wife of his? I see Ruby that cleans for him at the market sometimes. Way she tells it, he don't do much more than you since Mrs. Lawyer up and left. Just goes to work, stays late, then comes home an' sits around. Sounds like the two of you ought to get on like a house afire."

"Why are you talking this way?" Emma asked, having trouble swallowing. "I'm not the least bit interested in what Richard's cleaning woman has to say, and I can't imagine why you think I would be. For two years I was on twenty-four-hour call. I still wake up most nights thinking Will's calling me. I'm trying to adapt myself to . . . to what I've got left, which doesn't appear to be very much."

"Well, excuse me if I upset the grieving widow!" Bernice snapped. "I was just passing along what I *thought* was a little useful information. To my way of thinkin', it helps to know as much as you can about people. But what do I know? You got you a bee in your bonnet, actin' like you're the only one ever lost her husband. And now, on top of everything else, there's all kinds of stuff you don't want to hear about. It's time you snapped out of it, Emma, before you go peculiar in the head."

"I hope you're not thinking of leaving," Emma said in a rush. "I don't know what I'd do if you left . . . I didn't mean to criticize you. But I don't feel sorry for myself. Primarily, I'm confused. And angry, for a number of reasons, but mostly because it's as if I'm stuck in one spot and can't move out of it . . . I didn't know he was . . . I can't think why I agreed to go to dinner with Richard. I wish I'd refused. I feel guilty enough as it is without compounding it by going out with another man."

"Will you *listen* to this?" Bernice addressed the walls, before returning her attention to Emma. "Why do you keep on with this 'guilty' business? You talk like as if you're plannin' to cheat on your husband when here the man's been dead seven months. You think he'd have wanted you holed up in here day in and day out with only that dog for company? And when're you gonna get yourself up them stairs and back to work? You're startin' to make me mad. You know that?"

"I have no idea what Willard would've wanted for me," Emma replied heatedly. "All I do know is that I can't work. Believe me, I'd love to. It would give me something aside from my endless bloody mental peregrinations to think about."

"Perry-*whats?*"

"Navel inspecting. All right?"

"Oh! Is that what you've been doin'?"

"In practical terms, yes," Emma answered, an idea taking root in her brain. She slipped her hand into her cardigan pocket. The letter was still there. Fingering the envelope, she felt the old familiar sizzle of excitement in her head, the sudden expanding euphoria in her chest that heralded the genesis of a new book. There was an unsuppressible tingle of urgency accompanied by a sense of well-being that gave her all at once a tremendous appetite. She took a healthy bite of the sandwich then washed it down with a gulp of tea. God almighty! She had an *idea,* and already it was growing, feeding on itself, breeding, spawning plot lines.

Bernice blinked several times, trying to figure out how it had happened. Here they'd been sitting talking, and just like that everything changed. From one minute to the next, with not a hint of warning, Emma came marching back to the land of the living. *I'll be damned!* she thought, not sure she should even take her tea for fear of sending Emma back over the line. *What d'you make of that?* she mused, seeing the light back on again in Emma's eyes. *Maybe I should've taken her to task a whole lot sooner,* she thought, gratified.

After wolfing down the sandwich and two quick cups of tea, Emma gave Bernice a hug, saying, "I know I've been tiresome these past months. You've been wonderfully patient and I do appreciate it. You're not thinking of leaving, are you?"

Bernice hugged her back. "I'm not gonna go leavin' you, so don't worry about that. And don't go feelin' guilty cause you're still alive and said you'd go out with Mr. Lawyer. Just go and try to have a good time. It's no sin to eat out with a man, you know."

"I expect you're right. I'm going to go up now." Emma moved away, her hand delving into her pocket. "I'll see you in the morning."

"Bit early for bed, isn't it?"

"I have a few things I want to do."

"You gonna start writin'?"

"Why do you ask that?"

"You got the look," Bernice said with a grin. "I know that look."

Emma smiled. "I want to make a few notes."

"Yeah," Bernice nodded, the grin holding. She'd been right to call Mr. Lawyer after all.

Emma left the kitchen then tore up to her office on the second floor. She was desperate to get started, but was momentarily halted as she looked first at her old IBM Selectric, then at the Smith Corona lap-top word processor that had been Will's last gift to her. "Use it," he'd insisted. "It'll make a world of difference in the way you work." He'd read aloud to her from the manual and gone step by step through the functions with her, his determination overcoming her skepticism. She knew how the thing worked but had never actually used it. She'd been too busy helping Will die. Now she was confronted by something that supposedly would free her from the need to type draft after draft. For purely practical reasons she thought she'd put the machine to use when it came time to begin the actual writing.

She looked at the typewriter, which she'd last used months ago to answer the condolence letters, then again at the tidy laptop, the urgency singing in her ears. All right, all right. She turned on the table lamp then opened the drawer for a package of index cards, took a new Pilot Fineliner from the box, and on the top card wrote *Secrets*. Pleased and excited, she began making notes on the cards and worked without pause until she'd filled more than a dozen. Then she recapped the pen and read the character outlines and plot ideas. It would be her first novel without a murder, a venture into psychological suspense that wasn't too far removed from her previous efforts. Satisfied, she turned out the light then sat for a few moments thinking.

In bed she read the letter again. Seeing it now not as a device to be used by a character in a novel, but as an indirect, very personal attack, she was mortified anew at the explicit sexual references. Who would want to do this to her? And why? She hadn't really suspected Bernice but had felt compelled to question her nonetheless. Bernice was incapable of so malicious a deed. But any number of other people were eminently capable: in particular Janet, Will's oldest child, and Shawn, one of the twins; the pair who'd thought to contest their father's will. There were undoubtedly other candidates but she was too tired to attempt making a mental list.

And how, she wondered, had the author of this poison-pen letter managed to obtain some of her stationery? Setting the letter on the bedside table, she switched off the light and stretched out.

She'd placed her last order more than a year ago. Anxious at the time about being away from Will for too long, she'd gone to the usual shop with samples of her envelopes and paper and simply ordered more. In previous happier times, she'd enjoyed going through the various books, deciding on the styles, ink and envelope liner colors. She'd long believed that letters were representative of the sender. She favored heavy stock in pale shades, embossed with complementary ink and clean, uncluttered type. Her current letterhead was peach with deep blue printing, simple but distinctive.

After the funeral anyone could have wandered upstairs and taken a supply of her paper and envelopes. Dozens of people had come to the house that afternoon. There was no possible way she could know who'd been up and down the stairs.

And something else, she thought, turning onto her side, something that had occurred to her every time she'd gone into that shop: anyone at all could place an order for personalized supplies and give any name they chose. You weren't required to show proof of identification in order to buy stationery. If you paid cash and said you were going to be out of town, you wouldn't even have to leave a telephone number. You could simply say you'd stop back in three or four weeks to collect your purchase.

Feeling slightly dizzy, she closed her eyes. She had no way of discovering who, or how, or, most importantly, why. How frightening to think one's life could be so easily invaded! Sitting up, she reached for the Panasonic microcassette recorder on the bedside table, checked to see if the batteries were still good, then spoke into it. "Remember to discuss purchasing the stationery."

At a strategic point the villain would casually, confidently go into an establishment and, after all due deliberation, order precisely the same stationery as the victim. Then, in due course, the villain would have the weapon of choice right at hand.

She put the recorder down and again closed her eyes, able to see ideas darting about like tracer lights on the darkened screens of her eyelids. Wasn't it wonderful! she thought. Just when she'd all but given up hope, she was actually taking the preliminary steps toward a new novel. It felt so good to be tired in this way. She'd never written a book entirely on her own. Will had always been nearby to help her shape the work. But that didn't mean she couldn't do it. She could. She'd already started.

While she tidied the kitchen Bernice kept an ear open but didn't hear the typewriter going. Later, passing the office on her way to the master suite to turn the bed down, she glanced in and saw Emma at her desk, head bent, writing on cards. The cover was on the typewriter. Maybe there wouldn't be any more letters. Maybe it didn't mean anything at all. Emma had just finally answered some of those letters that had been sitting there for months.

Well, Bernice thought, at least Richard was going to get the woman out of the house. And high time, too. Be good for both of them.

Secrets

*   *   *

Richard got the Xerox copy of the letter from his briefcase and read it again. Then, with a slow shake of his head, he crumpled the page and tossed it into the wastebasket.

Chapter Four

When Emma awakened the next morning the energy and excitement were gone. She looked at the letter on the bedside table and was afraid. Why was it, she wondered, that daylight so often dulled the clarity with which one was able to view things under cover of night? Here was another morning and she contemplated with dismay the day to come.

After a brief stop in the kitchen for a cup of coffee, she called to Calla and opened the back door to go down to the beach. Calla went springing off through the tall damp grass and Emma watched her go, envious of the small dog's ability to take pleasure simply in freedom. She herself was free, and knew logically that she should have been able to enjoy it. But she couldn't. She wasn't even sure she knew how.

For a few hours the previous night she'd relo-

cated her sense of herself—at least as a writer—
and had once again been the willing channel
through which ideas traveled on their way to
tangibility. She wanted it to continue, wanted to
feel purposefully directed, but knew better than
to attempt to force creativity. It had to volunteer
itself. If she tried to work without the necessary
inner urging she'd only be shuffling words. Past
experience had taught her it was pointless to go
to the typewriter simply for the sake of putting
in time. Invariably, what she wrote during these
obligatory stints got thrown out at the next legiti-
mately inspired session.

Gathering her skirt under her, she sat on the
pebbly sand as Calla played tag with the incoming
waves, trotting to the water's edge as the water
washed back, then turning to race ahead of the
next wave foaming in.

Years ago words and ideas had come to her
in waves and she'd hurried to keep up with the
flow, writing constantly. She'd carried small ruled
notebooks with her as she rode the buses or the
underground to her temporary jobs. And in that
room on the fifth floor of the house in South
Kensington she'd typed until the ribbons had to
be replaced.

Willard Bellamy had said, "Would you like to
show me some of your work?" and she'd gone
home that evening to look through her half-
completed novel, trying to read it with Willard
Bellamy's eyes. Perhaps he'd think it was good;
perhaps he wouldn't. But if she was going to be
a writer she couldn't afford to pass up an opportunity that might never be duplicated. A publisher
was interested in reading her work. She'd be mad
to refuse.

The next morning, when she arrived at the suite at the Savoy, he greeted her warmly, and she said, "I took you at your word. I've brought along my manuscript for you to read."

"Good for you!" he said so enthusiastically that she felt sure she'd done the right thing.

She took the brown envelope containing the 135 pages and placed it on the coffee table, feeling as she did a sense of momentousness. She was giving this American the power to influence her future. It was frightening and thrilling. If he liked her work, he could in all likelihood be of great help to her. If he disliked it, her dreams might very well be crushed. The direction of the rest of her life lay in this man's hands.

"Scary, isn't it?" he said kindly, correctly interpreting the expression on her face.

"It is a bit, actually," she admitted. "But I thought it over last night and decided it'd be foolish not to show it to you."

"You're right. It would be. Help yourself to some coffee," he said, reaching for the envelope and weighing it in both hands. "I've got a hunch about you," he told her as she lifted the lid of the carafe to breathe in the steamy fragrance of the coffee. "Do *I* scare you?" he asked.

"No," she said after a moment. Not only did he not scare her, she'd gone to bed the night before picturing herself dancing, of all things, with him. "I dreamed last night I was dancing with you." She smiled to show how silly that was. But instead of smiling back at her, his expression turned sober.

"Sit down here for a minute," he said, "and talk to me."

She sat with her cup and saucer balanced

on her knee and waited to hear what he'd say. She was most intrigued by him, had never encountered anyone at all like him. He seemed to have a set of interior barometers and gauges that told him how to handle situations. She'd watched him during the previous day's meetings and had admired his restraint, his way of waiting to hear everything others had to say before putting forth his own opinions in a concise, no-nonsense fashion that rang with quiet authority. She'd also observed the others at the meetings and had seen the deference and respect he'd aroused in them.

Although some of the terminology had been alien, she couldn't help but be aware—as were the others—that this was a man who knew what he was on about. When he spoke of wholesalers and distributors, of unit costs and discounts, his associates had nodded in recognition of his knowledge, his obvious business acumen. And when he'd talked of building certain mid-list authors, of planning campaigns to increase sales and achieve name-brand recognition for this author or that—names that meant nothing to Emma—he'd succeeded in generating a tangible excitement among all present. Seeing him at work had been the major factor in her decision to show him her manuscript.

The other factor was his personal appeal. He had good eyes, very blue, very direct; he had a strong nose and square chin; he smiled often with great warmth; his skin was smooth and fair; he wore expensive, well-tailored suits and a wonderful spicy scent. Unlike the English men she'd worked for, he wore black silky-looking socks that didn't end at his ankles, and his shoes weren't the traditional ungainly lace-ups but sleek, comfortable-looking loafers. He was altogether different; he was foreign, fascinating.

"I think I mentioned to you that my twins, Susan and Shawn, are your age," he said. "But they're nowhere near as mature as you are."

"Everyone's different," she said. "We don't all grow at the same rate. I've always been rather too serious for my age. I expect it's because I look so much younger than I am, and people rarely give much consideration to what one has to say when one looks young. I want to be taken seriously. Just because I'm young doesn't mean my thoughts don't have value."

"Of course," he concurred. "Tell me about yourself," he said, shifting to face her more squarely, one arm extended along the back of the sofa.

"Isn't there work to be done?"

"We'll get to it. Right now this is more important. Tell me," he said again. "Where are you from? What's your family like?"

She sketched in her background and quick portraits of her parents and sister, and he listened intently.

"I'm very interested in you," he told her. "Not just your writing, but you. If that upsets you in any way, I'll understand and that'll be the end of it. I'm very direct," he smiled. "I know that's not the way over here. In England things are suggested rather than stated. But I've never been good at obliquity. You strike me as atypically English in that regard, probably because of your age. I like it," he added. "It's easier to deal with people when all the cards are on the table."

"I agree. And what you said doesn't upset me." To the contrary, his expression of interest was very exciting. She perceived it as a compliment to her maturity, and couldn't help feeling her life was about to change dramatically.

"I'm a great deal older than you," he said. "I've been divorced for three years and have four children roughly your age. My former wife wanted a new life and there was no place in it for her children. That's been rough on the kids but mainly a relief to me. We hadn't been getting along for years before the split finally came. We married young, had our kids fairly early on, then discovered we no longer had anything but the children in common. I love my work, always have, so it wasn't hard to redirect my energy to the job. I wanted to avoid the complications that were bound to crop up in becoming involved with another woman.

"Yesterday when you turned up it came home to me pretty forcefully what I've been missing. I felt more alive all day than I have in a long time. I saw the way people react to you, and I realized I was proud to be with you, proud of the way you handle yourself. Naturally I know it's not my right to feel that way, for all kinds of reasons, not the least of which is that I'm almost old enough to be your grandfather." He gave a self-deprecating laugh and paused to allow her time to react. She didn't say anything but waited to hear him out. "I have a couple of meetings today and that's it for my business here. I'll be flying back to New York tomorrow. But I'd like to spend my free time between now and then with you. Would you like to have dinner with me tonight? Or are you offended that an old man finds you attractive?"

"I'm not offended," she said quietly. "I am sorry though that you'll be leaving tomorrow. You're really not that old, are you? And I'm not that young." Hoping to clarify matters and also to prove she was not without experience, she said, "I have dated several men. I mean to say, I'm not . . . ignorant." She felt herself flushing with awkwardness but didn't lower her eyes. "I find you very attractive, too."

He looked at her then with such overt approval that the flush seem to double in intensity so that it felt as if her entire body was glowing with a bright red light.

He smiled and said, "Unless you go running for the hills, Emma Dalton, I think I'm going to marry you."

His image faded. She returned to the present to see Calla still engaged in her game of tag with the waves. Emma folded her arms across her knees, lowered her head onto her arms and wept.

"What's the matter?" Bernice asked from the stove where she stood with her arms folded over her ample breasts.

Emma shook her head. Bernice could see that she'd lost the light again, she couldn't keep it on. "You need to get out," she said. "You want to go shoppin'?"

"Shopping?"

"Yeah," Bernice smiled. "Let's go buy you a nice new dress to wear out on Friday night."

Emma spread her hands over the front of her skirt, saying, "You don't like my clothes?"

"The truth?" Bernice said, her head tilting to one side.

"Yes." Emma straightened and let her hands drop to her sides.

"I think it's about time you started dressin' your age."

"I think you're right," Emma replied unexpectedly.

"Saks, in the Stamford Town Center," Bernice decided. "They've got nice things."

"Fine. I'll get my handbag and we'll go."

"You mad about something?" Bernice asked in the car.

Emma glanced over. "It would be safe to say I'm angry at just about everything, but not with you."

"Oh!" Bernice nodded and sat back. Emma didn't say another word throughout the drive to Stamford.

In the designer dress department, Emma was at a loss. She had no idea what might or might not suit her. As the saleswoman approached, she couldn't help wondering why she'd agreed to this venture.

Bernice, meanwhile, was looking at price tags and thinking she might just keel over. Eight hundred dollars for a skimpy little black shirt. Twelve hundred for a pair of slacks. Who bought this stuff? she wondered, turning to see how Emma was making out with the saleswoman.

Seeing Emma floundering, Bernice walked over and said, "She needs something to wear out for dinner. Nothing too fussy."

"Yes," Emma said gratefully. "Something simple."

"All right," the saleswoman said, sizing Emma

up before making a circuit of the room. Judiciously she selected four dresses, then said, "The fitting rooms are this way."

Bernice hung back. Emma signaled to her to come.

"I'll leave you to try them on," the woman said, and went out.

Bernice looked at each of the dresses, checking the price tags, before removing one from its hanger. "Try this one first. This is sharp."

A clear red silk, the dress had long sleeves, a close-fitting bodice with a rounded neckline, a slightly flared skirt and a button-down front.

"Course you'll have to get shoes to go with it, you buy that one," Bernice said as Emma stepped out of her old cotton dress. "And a decent slip . . ." She lost track of what she'd been saying at the sight of Emma's body, clearly defined beneath her white slip. She'd never seen Emma undressed, never seen her in anything that gave any hint of her figure. For Bernice a lot of things she'd wondered about were answered simply by being allowed to see this woman without benefit of her usual shapeless dresses.

Despite her recent weight loss, Emma had the kind of body that women envied and men noticed. Long shapely legs and slim hips, a narrow waist and high round breasts. Her skin was pearly with a faint blue tinge to it. Viewing her all of a piece now, Bernice decided the short hair was flattering to the shape of her head and to her unadorned face. Emma was a powerfully attractive woman who had no idea of this fact. No wonder Mr. Willard had kept her close by him, had never encouraged her to change the kinds of clothes she wore or to make the best of her appearance. If he'd ever done that, Emma might have discovered her appeal, might even have left him.

Emma was preoccupied, avoiding the mirror, something she'd done for the seven months since Will's death. She'd covered all the mirrors in the house and thought she might never have a reason to uncover them. A low-grade fear was creeping through her limbs just being close to one now. But if she didn't make some pretense of looking at herself, Bernice would think it peculiar. So, being careful not to look at her face, she gazed at the glass. Seeing her body, she thought of the last time she and Will had tried to make love. The chemotherapy—those diabolically potent drugs waging war against his diseased cells—had robbed him of his ability to perform. She'd felt sluttish for having tried with her body to distract him from his pain.

That vile letter suddenly came to mind, bringing with it an image of her infrequent furtive efforts to relieve herself of some of the accumulated tension, those abysmal dead-of-night, self-induced climaxes that left her feeling exhausted, depressed, and even more alone.

"Dress suits you," Bernice stated.

"It's very bright," Emma said doubtfully, turning to study the dress in the triple-paneled mirror as she fastened the buttons. Someone had, for Richard Redmond's edification, put down on paper one of her darkest secrets. Who? And why did someone wish to shame her?

"I like it," Bernice declared. "Gives you some color, shows off your shape. First thing I ever seen you put on showed you *got* a shape."

"You don't think it's too vivid?" Emma shifted

to one side, then to the other, pushing away her speculations.

"Buy it!" Bernice told her. "Then we'll go to Macy's, where the real people shop, and get you some everyday things."

"I'll have to buy shoes," Emma reminded her, taking a final look, relishing the feel of the silk against her skin, before undoing the buttons. What was she doing? She'd never have the courage to wear this garment in public. "And a slip, too. It might help if I change from the outside in," she thought aloud, returning the dress to its hanger.

"Help what?"

"I have to do *something*, Bernice. I can't keep on the way I have been. After Joe died, did you feel as if you weren't sure anymore who you were?"

"That how you feel?"

"In part."

"Emma, me and Joe we grew up together. You understand? I was sixteen, he was nineteen when we got married. We were both kids. It wasn't like with you and Mr. Willard."

The saleswoman returned. Bernice handed her the red dress and said, "We'll take it." The woman went off with the dress and Bernice said, "You follow what I'm sayin' to you?"

Tiredly, Emma nodded. "I'm not a child, Bernice."

"Not now, you're not. But that's only cuz of the way things turned out. He hadn't of got sick, things'd still be the same, wouldn't they?"

The saleswoman popped back in asking, "Will that be on your Saks card?" and without turning, Bernice said, "We'll be out in a minute.

Could you leave us be, please?"

The woman recoiled as if Bernice had struck her, sniffed and turned on her heel.

"I can't answer that."

"He kept you a child," Bernice said with feeling. "Maybe he never meant no harm—that's not for me to say—but he didn't let you grow up."

"I loved him," Emma said weakly, as if that justified everything.

"People need to be able to stretch out some, you know."

"And you don't think he allowed me to do that?"

"Sure doesn't look that way."

Emma sighed and looked at her three-way reflection. "What is love, anyway?" she asked rhetorically. "When I was eighteen I thought I knew. At eighteen I thought I knew everything." Her eyes shifted to Bernice, and she gave her a smile that was the equivalent of a shrug. "I'm a long way from eighteen now. We'd better go out and pay for that dress."

"You ought to call up some of your friends, start seein' people. It's time."

"Yes," Emma agreed. "Perhaps I'll ring Linda this afternoon."

As they walked toward the cashier, Bernice said, "You plannin' on keepin' the house?"

"Yes, I think so. I like being on the beach. I like the house. It's my home. I have nowhere else to go. Why do you ask?"

"Just wondering. Kind of a big place for a person alone."

This time Emma did shrug. "I know it is. But I don't want to move. At least not now.

Maybe not ever. I have to go one step at a time, Bernice. And it seems there's a tremendously long way to go."

"To get where?"

Emma took a moment. "To get to me, I suppose." She gave the saleswoman her American Express card, then with a sudden smile said to Bernice, "I feel quite wicked buying this dress."

"Why don't you get real wicked and buy a few more things," Bernice suggested. "Do you good to spend a little of your hard-earned money."

"We could have lunch in one of the restaurants upstairs," Emma said. "Would you like that?"

"Sure. That'd be fine. And after lunch, we could have us a look round the cosmetics department in one of these stores."

"All right," Emma said a little giddily. "Let's do that."

Like a lost child, Bernice thought. Like as if a trip to the mall was the most exciting thing that'd ever happened. Sad fact was, it was damn nearly true. There were all kinds of things Mr. Willard had never left her free to do. Well, Mr. Willard be damned! The time had come for Emma to start living in the world again, to start back to working, to see some of her friends, to stop spending every day of her life just staring into space, forgetting half the time what she'd been saying or doing. And Bernice intended to do her best to see that Emma did.

Chapter Five

Emma stood surveying the landscape of her bed. She had never bought so many things at a single time: the red dress, shoes, tinted hose, several silk slips, two sweaters, some blouses, and the blue jeans Bernice had persuaded her to buy.

She'd enjoyed herself. Bernice was good company, and Emma had insisted on getting her a brilliant green oversized shirt she'd admired. Bernice hadn't wanted to accept it, but Emma had persisted, finally winning her over.

Anxious to perpetuate the renewed motion in her life, she sat down on the side of the bed to call Linda. Perhaps they'd make a date to have dinner or see a film.

"Hello, Linda. It's Emma."

"Well, you've got some goddamned nerve!"

Taken aback, Emma said, "I beg your pardon?"

"I said you've got some goddamned nerve!"

Katharine Marlowe

"I'm afraid you have me at a disadvantage," Emma said lightly, wondering if Linda was acting out her upset at Emma's failure not to have been in touch sooner.

"Why am I talking to you?" Linda asked. "I ought to hang up right in your ear."

"Look, I'm sorry it's been so long since I've called. I should have, I know, and I've been meaning to, but . . ."

"I can't believe you've actually got the balls to phone me, after the things you wrote in that letter!"

A sudden bitter taste in her mouth, Emma asked, "What letter?"

"Oh, come on! Don't play dumb! The letter I got the day before yesterday telling me in no uncertain terms exactly what you think of me."

"Linda, I did not write to you."

"Hey! I've got the thing right here."

An unpleasant ache now in her chest, Emma said, "You may have received a letter, but I did not write it." Her voice dropping, she said, "This is dreadful."

"Wait a minute," Linda said, doubt taking the sharp edge off her tone. "Are you trying to tell me somebody else wrote this vicious little missive?"

"My lawyer also received one." Emma blotted her damp face with her sleeve. "You really must believe me when I say I haven't written you a letter."

"I don't know," Linda said slowly. "It sure reads like you."

"Linda, we've known each other for years. In all that time, have I *ever* written to you?"

"After the funeral . . ."

"Aside from that. Have I? Ever?"

"Well, no. What the *hell*, Emma?"

"It's as much a mystery to me as it is to you. If the letter you've received is as vile as the one sent to Richard, I can well understand your upset. But I promise you it's not my doing."

"It's pretty hateful," Linda confirmed. "I've been stewing over how to deal with it, trying to decide if I was going to write you back and tell you to go fuck yourself or drop by and say it to your face."

"I think perhaps I should see it if you still have it."

"Oh, I've still got it all right. In fact, I made a couple of copies in case I decided to use it in one of my books. You never know when a good piece of venom'll come in handy." She laughed, as if at her own eccentricity.

"Linda, may I come over?" Emma got to her feet, as if the move might impel her friend to agree.

"What, now?"

"Yes, if I may, if you're not working."

"Who could work with this thing in the house?" Linda emitted another brief laugh, then sighed and said, "Sure. Come on over. I'll put on some coffee and you can tell me what the hell's going on."

"I wish I knew," Emma said fervently. "I'll leave now." She hung up and stood for a moment staring at the telephone. She was wet with perspiration, the underarms of her dress saturated. Another letter. *Why* was this happening? She felt as if she'd been struck between the shoulder blades; her knees wanted to buckle. Linda was her best and dearest friend. They'd met soon after the American publication of

Emma's first book when Linda had come to interview her for the Stamford *Advocate*.

At the time a free-lance journalist, Linda had been friendly and funny and exceptionally well-prepared for the interview, with a lengthy list of intelligent questions. Emma had liked her from the outset and the scheduled hour-long session stretched into four. After her ninety-minute tape ran out, Linda had turned off the recorder, lit a fresh cigarette and said, "Okay, I've got more than enough for the piece. Now tell me. Are you really only twenty, or is that just PR bullshit?"

After assuring her that actually was her age, Emma had asked, "Do you like your work?" which got Linda going on the subject of her ambition to write a novel. The free-lance work kept her so busy she hadn't managed to get more than a few chapters done. She was also involved in a heated affair with a married man whose visits were, of necessity, during lunch hours and an occasional evening.

Linda was then twenty-seven and in one of her stringent diet phases, so she was into her size-nine wardrobe. About five foot five, she had a mane of unruly hennaed curls, heavily made-up hazel eyes, a prominent nose, and a generously lipsticked full mouth. When in one of her thin phases she favored bold prints, patterned stockings, and singularly ugly footwear. Oddly enough, it all worked. She was strikingly attractive, wildly energetic, and slightly manic.

When in one of her heavy phases, however, Linda culled from her size-fourteen wardrobe formless drab tops that she wore over tight black pants. She left off the makeup for the most part and allowed her curly hair to return to its natural light brown. The overweight Linda tended to be lethargic, thoughtful and somehow even more attractive. Her weight was a sure indicator of the state of her love life. If she was into the size nines, there was a man on the scene. If she was snacking constantly, she was between affairs.

In the years since they'd met, Linda had published six hugely successful commercial novels. Emma eagerly read the first one and was nearly sick with disappointment. Linda wrote what Emma privately thought of as "designer label" novels, about wealthy, vacuous women who traveled extensively, primarily for the purpose of shopping, who took up with the wrong men for a time but who, in the last few chapters, experienced an epiphany that enabled them to recognize the good men who'd been patiently waiting. The characters were paper-thin, the situations clichéd, and the writing pedestrian. The books were crammed full of crudely explicit sexual scenes that were utterly devoid of emotion.

Rather than lie to her, Emma had avoided altogether any mention of Linda's novels. Instead, she listened to Linda tell of her skyrocketing advances and the generally scathing reviews her books got; about her periodic affairs and the shortage of decent men in the world; about her klutzy cleaning woman who was forever breaking things but who was too sweet to fire; about her frequent and hilarious visits to various spas; or about her nieces and nephews, to whom she was devoted. What

Emma liked best about Linda was her unflagging sense of humor. Nothing ever really got her down for long. She had an inner core of resilience that allowed her to find something funny in almost every situation. And if you could laugh, she always said, you could keep on going.

With the income from her first two books, she'd bought a charming two-story condo in Southport. After the condo came a Mercedes sports coupe and a pair of mink coats, one for each of her wardrobes. Every July she left for six weeks' travel in Europe, meeting up with friends in London or Paris or Amsterdam. And upon her return every August she started another book, having gathered enough new material to churn out one more best-seller.

Linda was the most generous person Emma had ever known. She never allowed anyone to pick up the tab for a dinner out; she returned from her annual trips with expensive gifts for all her friends; she lavished attention and presents on the men who came and went through her life; she was paying the college tuition for three nieces and two nephews as well as having made substantial gifts of money to her two brothers; and she gave large sums to a variety of charities. Through the years a fair number of people had taken advantage of Linda's generosity. But not for long. The moment Linda sensed someone had latched onto her, hoping to get a free ride, Linda turned off and the invitations to dinner and the gifts abruptly ceased. She had a finely honed instinct for self-preservation and was far more intelligent than her books would have led one to believe.

As she drove toward Linda's place, Emma tried to imagine what the impostor could possibly have written in this latest letter. She hated the idea of losing Linda's friendship even if she had neglected her since Will's death. She'd been neglecting everyone, but she'd been so bound up in her scrupulously detailed review of the years with Will and so anxious to get to the end of it that she'd been unable and unwilling to see anyone for fear that it would delay her. She could see now that she was either going to have to find some way to accelerate the process or to abandon it altogether. And since she doubted she could abandon it, she had no alternative but to push forward. If she didn't, she risked alienating the few friends she had.

She parked in front of Linda's double garage, got out and walked through the gate of the fence that enclosed the narrow tidy garden at the side of the duplex. Through the sliding glass doors to the kitchen she could see Linda at the counter, eating ice cream directly from the container. She waved and Linda put down the ice cream and came to open the door.

"Jesus! You're a goddamned stick," Linda said with an accusing smile before giving Emma a hearty hug. "Get the hell in here and tell me what's going on!" She grabbed Emma's upper arm to tow her inside as she slid the door closed. "Sit down," she said, going over to the counter to jam the lid back on the Häagen Dazs container, then shoving it into the crammed freezer.

Emma sat down at the big round table in the kitchen's spacious dining area and watched

73

Linda light a Marlboro. Linda was between sizes, so it wasn't possible to tell if her weight was on the way up or down. The ice cream offered no clue since Linda consumed at least three pints a week regardless of her emotional condition. Häagen Dazs was, she liked to say, her one true passion and she bought half a dozen each of Chocolate Chocolate Chip and Vanilla Swiss Almond every month.

"Coffee?" Linda asked, checking to see if her Braun coffee-maker had finished dripping.

"Yes, please."

"Don't look so nervous," Linda said, squinting against the smoke from the cigarette held between her teeth. She thought Emma had scarcely aged in fifteen years. Sitting stiffly with her hands folded in her lap, with her short hair somehow accentuating the vulnerable length of her neck, and one of her familiar voluminous Laura Ashley dresses, she looked young and worried. Her tiny wrists and slender ankles added to the impression she gave of extreme fragility. Linda had always felt much more than seven years older, and considerably more worldly. Yet Emma invariably surprised her because, despite her appearance, she was very well informed and remarkably perceptive when it came to the whys and wherefores of people's behavior. She was also wonderfully truthful and utterly nonjudgmental. Through the years she'd listened to Linda's tales of romantic woe and been consistently sympathetic while refraining from offering the kind of self-aggrandizing advice so many other women couldn't resist spouting. "I won't get out the heavy artillery unless you fail the polygraph test," Linda said in the hope of easing Emma's visible apprehension. She was glad now she'd taken the time to give Richard Redmond a quick call at his office. Their conversation had prepared her for the likelihood of Emma's denial of having written the letters. Recalling Richard's advice to go slowly and, "Be gentle with her—she seems honestly convinced someone else is writing them," Linda was curious to see for herself how Emma would handle the situation. She also wanted to make sure Emma wasn't actively in the process of losing her marbles.

"It's very upsetting," Emma said, glancing at the palms of her hands before drying them on her skirt. "For reasons I can't begin to imagine, someone's decided to write letters on my behalf."

"Mine's a doozy, that's for sure." Linda opened the cupboard and reached for two handsome glossy black mugs. She poured the coffee, added Equal and cream to hers and carried them over to the table. Setting the black coffee in front of Emma, she reached for the ashtray, then sank with a sigh into her chair. "You know how long it's been since I saw you?" she asked, wanting Emma to realize she not only valued their friendship but also that she'd missed her. It was only now, in fact, that she realized just how much she'd missed her.

"I know," Emma said softly.

"Since the funeral, that's how long. What the hell've you been doing all these months?" Linda asked.

"Thinking," Emma answered. "I've been going day by day over every last thing I can remember since I first met Will."

"What for?" Linda looked nonplussed. "What's the point?"

"It seems to be something I have to do before I can go on." Emma looked at her friend, trying to determine which phase she was in. Her hair was wild as always but with gray streaking the brown. She had on somewhat less eye makeup than usual but no lipstick. Tight black pants but with a vividly printed Hawaiian-looking baggy short-sleeved shirt, bare feet.

Linda grinned. "Can't figure which way I'm headed, huh?"

Emma smiled. "You seem to be mid-mode."

"You got that right. I've been hanging at 118 for nearly six months now. Curious?"

"Very." Emma had to ask herself how she could have forgotten how much she enjoyed Linda's company. It made her wish even more fervently that she could get to the end of the damned retrospective.

Linda put her cigarette down on the lip of the ashtray, folded her arms on the table and leaned forward over them. "You know something?" she said. "I'm scared shitless to tell you anything. I got that letter and the roof fell in on me. I've always counted on you, Emma. I've had more freeloading assholes go through my life than I care to mention, but you've been a constant. Oh, I know Willard couldn't stand me. You don't have to pretend about that anymore. You never let him influence you, though, and that impressed me. It did. I don't know too many women who'd be that loyal, especially when it came to going up against a husband for the sake of a friend. In fact, you're about it. And I know you've been having a lousy time since he first got sick, so you don't have to explain why I haven't seen you. I understand that, even if I have missed the hell out of you. But I have to tell you, when that letter arrived I felt as if I'd lost the only friend I've ever had who's been loyal no matter what. You say you didn't write it, okay. We'll let that go for the moment. Do you *know* how goddamned glad I am to see you? I am, you know. Are you a teensy bit glad to see me?"

"Of course I am. Very."

"Okay." Linda reached into her shirt pocket, pulled out the folded letter and slapped it down on the table. "Go ahead and read it," she said, retrieving her cigarette from the ashtray. "Then we'll talk."

Her hand trembling slightly, Emma picked it up. Another sheet of her stationery, another envelope, postmarked the same as Richard's. She looked over at Linda, who was waiting patiently for her to get on with it. Much as she disliked it, she had no alternative but to unfold the page and read the typewritten words.

Dear Linda,

I've decided it's time to be honest with you, as honest as you've always been with me. It isn't that I've been dishonest so much as I've withheld my opinion for fear of being hurtful. And now that I think about it, I can see I have perhaps done you a disservice by failing to be as forthcoming with my thoughts as you've been.

I read your first book and could scarcely believe someone with your intellect and ability could write such meritless rubbish.

I waited and read the second one, hoping you'd put to good use your talent and humor. But you didn't. What a pity that you'd waste your gifts with such profligate piffle! Plastic people with expensive clothes they're all too eager to remove in order to engage in sexual acts of unrelenting and tiresome sameness. The characters in your novels are brainless marionettes with limitless funds who do nothing, say less, and about whom no reasonably intelligent reader could possibly care.

You have wasted time and valuable energy on work that is unworthy of you. You've indulged your appetite for overpriced ice cream and overrated men instead of using your admirable discipline to produce quality prose, which would give you, instead of a bulging bank account, the self-esteem you crave.

If I didn't care very much for you, and didn't greatly value your friendship, I wouldn't have said any of this. E.

By the time she got to the end of the letter, Emma's face, neck and ears were on fire. She carefully put the letter down on the table then drank a little of the coffee to ease the dryness in her throat.

"You know what really pisses me off about that letter?" Linda said, stabbing out her cigarette and at once lighting another.

"What?" Emma asked thickly.

"Every last fucking word of it is true," Linda said.

"Oh, I don't . . ."

"Every last fucking word," Linda said, cutting her off. "You think I don't know the books are garbage? You think I haven't always known what you think of them?"

"But I didn't write that . . ."

"It doesn't matter!" Linda cried, anxious to get to the crux of the matter. "*Somebody* wrote it. And whoever it was, they've got your style and vocabulary down to a T. All these years I've been waiting for you to say something, anything, give me an opening so we could really talk. But you never did. I think you thought you were being kind, avoiding the subject of my books for fear of offending or hurting me. If you'd ever, just once, said something, I'd've jumped in with both feet and we'd've had a big laugh over it. It's the one thing I've always held against you. You know that? That we've been friends, that you wouldn't even let your husband come between us, but you didn't care enough about me to tell me what you really thought."

"You're acting as if you believe I wrote that." Emma pointed to the letter. She felt as if she were on trial and bound to defend herself without benefit either of counsel or knowledge of all the facts.

"Well, whoever wrote it did us a favor, in a way. I've finally got that opening I've been wanting, that chance to clue you in to the fact that I'm not stupid, Emma. You know how many best-sellers I read before I figured out that good writing doesn't sell worth spit? Dozens! You know how many manuscripts of mine got turned down before I decided to go for the gold and to hell with impressing a handful

of reviewers and selling five hundred copies?
I did four gorgeous books, just crammed full
of insight and wonderful characters. Agents
couldn't have cared less; editors couldn't have
cared less. So I sat down and wrote what they
wanted. I get probably the worst reviews in
the entire Western world. I've sold somewhere
around nineteen million copies so far. And right
now we're negotiating a two-point-five-million-
dollar contract for the hard-soft rights to my
next two books. So who's crazy?"

"Certainly not you," Emma said, meeting her
eyes.

"You're damned right! So don't think for a
minute that I couldn't sit down and write something that'd curl your toes, because I could.
But I like eating regularly and having a little
something in the bank, so I write dreck. I have
no illusions, Emma. It's about time you knew
that."

"But I've never thought you did."

"Emma, you think I'm a no-talent bimbo
who's forever taking up with the wrong men."

"That's simply not true!"

"I don't take up with the wrong men, Emma."
Linda forged ahead, determined to take advantage of this singular opportunity to clear the
air once and for all. "I take up with the absolutely right men, the ones who're never going
to be able to come through for me because
the idea of having some guy around full-time
gives me the shakes. I like my life just the way
it is, thank you very much. I have no interest
in having some jerk leaving hair all over my
nice marble bathtub or expecting me to do his
crummy laundry. All I've wanted since I was a

kid is the wherewithal to live exactly the way I want, without having to answer to anyone."

"I envy you," Emma said quietly, cowed. "I don't expect you'll believe that, but I truly do envy you."

"Give me a king-sized break!" Linda said, disbelieving. "You with the adoring husband, the oh-my-God reviews, the safe secure life. You envy me?"

"I had no idea at nineteen when I married Will that I was giving up what mattered most to me."

Her features softening, Linda asked, "What?"

"My freedom," Emma whispered. "The right to my own life."

Linda stared at her for a long moment. "Shit!" she said. "I never thought of that. Why didn't I ever think of that?"

"Now I have it again but I can't seem to remember how to use it," Emma said without the slightest hint of self-pity, but with authentic confusion.

Linda sat staring at her for a few more seconds then got up, walked across the room, opened a drawer, grabbed two spoons, got two containers of Häagen Dazs from the freezer and came back to the table. "Here!" she said, giving Emma a spoon and the Vanilla Swiss Almond. "I think we both need this."

Emma blotted her eyes with her sleeve and laughed.

"You'd better stay for dinner," Linda said, prying the lid off the Chocolate Chocolate Chip. "We've got a lot to talk about."

"Yes," Emma agreed. "I'll just ring Bernice to let her know."

Chapter Six

"I'm in the mood for chicken fingers," Linda announced. "Sound okay to you?"

"Yes, fine, thank you."

Linda cocked her head to one side with a half smile. "Every time you say, 'Yes, please,' or 'Yes, thank you,' I can just see you as a kid. Course," she went on, pulling two packages of filleted chicken breasts out of the refrigerator, "you're not much more than a kid now. Not compared to me, anyhow. Do you realize I'm going to be *forty-three* in a couple of months? Jesus! How did that *happen?*"

"It's not all that old," Emma said.

"Hah! Easy for you to say. What're you now, thirty-two, -three?" Linda looked appraisingly at Emma. She still looked too young for her life, too young to have put up with Willard Bellamy's arrogance and possessiveness, his politely concealed determination to direct every area of her life. She'd always been impressed by the way Emma quietly resisted him; she didn't look like a woman who'd have the kind of inner strength she had.

Emma had a number of qualities one wouldn't have expected, including a streak of stubbornness she displayed when it came to defending what she believed to be right. And while not an especially humorous woman, she was a terrific audience, loved to laugh. Linda had always liked making her laugh because when she lost some of her reserve and let herself unbend Emma was great company. She was critically incisive when it came to books and writing, and probably the most precisely articulate woman Linda had ever met. She was also a pleasure to look at, and had little if any vanity. Which was a damned good thing in view of the fact that she'd been blessed with a body Linda would've killed for and a face that was right out of a Botticelli painting.

"I'll be thirty-six in February," Emma was saying.

"A baby." Linda positioned herself behind the island, pulled over the cutting board and opened the packages of chicken. "So," she said, taking a long-bladed knife from the drawer, "are you ready to hear all the latest poop?"

"Absolutely." Emma sat up straighter in the chair. Just like an attentive schoolchild, Linda thought, giving her a fond smile. Maybe Emma wouldn't admit to writing the letters, but no way was she losing her marbles. It would have showed in her eyes, and it didn't. Maybe Redmond was mistaken, and someone else actually was writing them.

"Okay." Quickly, deftly, Linda began slicing the breasts into strips. "The reason I've stayed at 118 for nearly six months is because of my latest fella. I'm into what I've dubbed the Cher Memorial Youth Brigade. Next thing anyone knows, I'll be getting tattooed in sensitive places." With a laugh she looked over and Emma smiled at her. "Do you sense what's coming?" she asked teasingly.

Emma shook her head. "I've been fairly out of touch with the world for the last two and a half years."

"His name is Chris," Linda said. "He's twenty-four."

"Twenty-four?" Emma's smile grew wider, a glint brightened her dark eyes.

"He's so young his dough hasn't finished rising," Linda laughed. "Never mind. He thinks I'm Venus on the half shell, which has done my poor ravaged ego a world of good. Plus, he's one of the new breed whose mothers have taught them that women are to be respected as equals. So he takes out the garbage without being asked, loads the dishwasher, cleans the tub after he's used it, and is an equal opportunity orgasmitron."

"*What?*" Emma laughed.

"If it's no good for me, it's no good for him. Bliss in Reeboks. And just guess what he does!"

"Student?"

"Graduated, got his degree at U. Conn. Guess again!"

"Editorial?"

"He's a *chef!* A chef, for chrissake! The man *cooks* for me. Hence the new mid-mode look." Linda, knife in hand, did a little spin that sent her long wild hair flying. "Emma, he's adorable. He makes great money and takes *me* out to dinner so he can check out other chefs in the area. He listens when I talk and actually hears what I'm saying. I have to stop myself from taking bites out of him."

"How did you meet?" Emma asked, folding her knees up under her skirt and winding her arms around them.

"Oh, this is good!" The breasts now all in strips, Linda floured them, got two eggs and beat them in a bowl, dumped in the chicken, then poured an inch-thick layer of bread crumbs on a plate. "I was out for dinner with my brothers and their wives. You've heard me talk about what a pain in the ass Alan's wife Lee is. This particular evening she outdid herself." Linda began dipping the egg-covered chicken strips into the bread crumbs. "She orders this elaborate fish salad and when it comes she has a fit because it's got squid or something in it. The waiter comes over to see what's wrong and Lee's giving him a hard time because he didn't tell her there was going to be squid or whatever in the salad.

"Well, this being one of those expensive, terribly subdued restaurants with terribly subdued young waiters, he quietly, politely asks Lee if she'd care to order something else. She makes a great to-do about having another look at the menu, orders tournedos or a fillet—I forget— and off goes the waiter back to the kitchen with the fish dish.

"To make it short, the steak wasn't the way she wanted it. By this point, the rest of us have finished eating and she's getting on our nerves. The waiter wants to kill her but he's been trained not to attack the customers, so he takes the steak away to cook it some more or uncook it, whatever, and five minutes later out comes this adorable young man all in white with his chef's hat and brand new Reeboks, not so much as a smudge on them. He personally presents goddamned Lee with her food and she's so impressed by all this attention that she finally shuts the hell up. The chef introduces himself, shakes our hands, and asks if the rest of us enjoyed our meals.

"By the time he got around to my side of the table, I had one of my cards out and slipped it to him when we shook hands. Without so much as a blink he went off back to the kitchen, and had already left a message on my machine by the time I got home. I phoned right back and he came over after work that night. He's been coming over three or four times a week ever since. I'm crazy about this guy!"

"He sounds lovely," Emma said, happy for her. She'd never seen Linda quite so effervescent.

"My baby boy." Linda grinned, getting a large jar of Hellmann's from the fridge, then going to the cupboard for honey, English mustard and curry powder. "You know, you haven't denied any of what was in that letter," she said cannily, glancing over at Emma while she measured out of a cupful of the mayonnaise. "That's because you agree with all of it, don't you?" She watched Emma's eyes closely.

Emma wet her lips, not sure what to say. She hated being put on the spot in this fashion, yet she was also tempted to admit she did agree.

"Come on! Admit it!"

"Well," Emma said carefully, "it does have some degree of truth."

"You *hate* my stuff! Why won't you just come right out and say so?"

"This is very awkward," Emma said, feeling her face growing hot. "Couldn't we put it aside?"

"You'll feel a lot better once you say what you really think." Linda added three tablespoons of honey to the mayonnaise, then a half teaspoon of the powdered mustard and the same amount of curry powder. Bringing the bowl and a fork over to Emma, she said, "Here. Mix this up. Profligate piffle," she quoted with a chuckle. "I kept wondering where I'd heard that before, so I went back through every one of your books and found it on page seventy-six of *Strangers*. Whoever's writing these letters is going to a lot of trouble to sound just like you."

"Why do you want to do this, Linda?" Emma asked sadly.

"Because it's about time," she said simply. "Because we're friends, and friends are honest with each other."

"I really can't do it," Emma said apologetically, looking down to see the mixture in the bowl turning a pleasant yellow color as she stirred. The situation reminded her of the countless confrontations with her mother, those one-sided rows when her mother always managed to become the wronged party. "The truth can sometimes kill you. It's safer not to say anything at all," she said, her voice low, her heart rate quickening.

"That's a hell of a philosophy." Linda placed

an electric skillet on the countertop, poured in some corn oil, then adjusted the thermostat. "How'd you happen to come to that conclusion?" she asked, sprinkling dill weed and garlic powder over the chicken, then regarding Emma with a pang. She'd never pushed at Emma this way, and Emma was obviously troubled by it, but certainly not to the point where she seemed unable to cope, and Linda had to persist.

"It has to do with my parents," Emma said, keeping her eyes on the bowl. "Ancient history."

"Okay," Linda relented, seeing Emma starting to shrink. "I'll drop it. So," she said, placing the chicken strips in the sizzling oil, "what've you been reading lately? You have been reading, haven't you?"

"Most of every night," Emma told her, "when I can't sleep. My only real outings have been to the bookstore. What have I read?" she asked herself, unable to recall any specific titles. All she could see were the two stacks in the den, one of new purchases, the other of those she'd already read. "This and that, quite a few biographies."

"Have you read *Glass Houses*?" Linda asked casually as she reached for a spatula and began turning over the pieces of chicken.

"I have, actually," Emma said with enthusiasm. "A lovely book, beautiful writing."

"You liked it, huh?"

"I more than liked it. Bits and pieces keep coming back to me."

"They do, huh? What, for example?"

Linda seemed to be challenging her again.

They often argued over books, especially the ones that garnered the best reviews. It was Linda's contention that if the critics loved a book it was either garbage or doomed. "The death of the grandmother in particular," Emma said, recalling the lyrical, unsentimental prose, its spare effectiveness, its impact. "I wept buckets over that."

"You don't say." Linda looked peculiarly gratified, as if a long-held theory of hers had been proved right.

"I take it you didn't like it."

"No, no," Linda said. "I was crazy about it. I loved it, *adored* it." She tore several pieces of paper towel and laid them down on a plate. "As a matter of fact," she said with a fiercely knowing look, "I wrote it."

"Did you?" Emma asked softly, her voice belying the jolt this information gave her. "Did you really?"

"Oh, yes," Linda said flatly. "Sent it out as an unsolicited manuscript with my mother's maiden name on the title page. I didn't even tell my agent, didn't want anyone to suspect I had anything to do with it. I got seven rejections. On submission number eight a very nice, very gung-ho young editor fell in love with it, went in to do battle with the powers-that-be and got them to buy it.

"They gave me a thirty-five-hundred-dollar advance. They did a three-thousand-copy first printing, with a whopping five-thousand-dollar advertising budget. So far, despite the glowing reviews, it's nowhere near close to selling out the print run. Kind of proves my point, doesn't it?"

"I rather think it proves you really do have great talent."

"See!" Linda pounced, pointing an accusing finger. "You believe every last word of that fucking letter! Now will you admit it?"

With a sigh, Emma got up and placed the bowl on the counter, then put the fork in the sink. "Tell me why you did it, Linda."

"To prove I could, naturally."

"But if no one knows you're the author, to whom are you proving anything?"

"To myself, and to you, Emma. If you'd told me you hadn't read it, I'd've made up some story and given you a copy under some pretext or other to get you to read it. I knew you thought I'd sold out for the money. This was the only way I could think of to show you that good rarely equates with success."

"That's dismal," Emma said skeptically.

"Couldn't agree more. But it's also the truth. Now tell me I'm wrong!"

Seeing there was no way out, Emma crossed her arms under her breasts, leaned against the counter, took a deep breath and said, "Not one of those six books you've published under your own name lived up to your abilities." She could feel her pulse beating furiously in her throat. "I was so excited when you signed that first contract. I begged for an advance copy of the book and rushed straight to the solarium to read it. It broke my heart. I so wanted it to reflect you, your humor, your wonderful eccentricity. I couldn't find you anywhere in it. Even the author photo on the back looked like someone else."

"A three-hour makeup and hair session."

"Someone else, as I've said. I dislike this, Linda," Emma said almost pleadingly.

"I know you do," she said with sympathy, then turned to begin swiftly removing the finished pieces of chicken from the pan, depositing them on the paper towel-covered plate. After switching off the frying pan, she turned back. "The thing is, it's not a bad thing to do, Em. The truth does *not* kill people. As a matter of fact, it can go a hell of a long way toward cementing an iffy friendship."

"Is that what we've been, iffy?"

"For a little while now, uh-huh. You were wrong to let so much time go by without getting in touch. I thought of calling you fifty times a day but after a couple of months I decided maybe you were mad at me for some reason. I don't know. And how come you didn't disagree when I came right out a short while back here and said Willard didn't like me? Which, as we both know, is a gross understatement."

"I never understood why he took such exception to you," Emma admitted. "Especially when I was so very fond of you right from the beginning. We had an epic row about you. He tried to forbid me to see you." She shook her head at the memory, her eyes shifting away from Linda to focus on the far wall. "It was as if he thought he was addressing one of his children." Again she shook her head. "I told him I'd choose my own friends, that it was not his ordained right to determine who was or was not suitable to be a friend of mine. And in view of the dreary fact that I hadn't any friends who weren't his by rights, I refused to back down. If he didn't like it, I told him, well . . . He was quite shocked by my vehemence. He'd never really seen me angry, or defiant. But of course he was unaware of how often I'd had to do battle with my mother. I might have been young, but I wasn't unprepared or unwilling to defend myself. It was the one and only time he ever attempted to make that sort of decision for me." At last she returned her eyes to Linda's.

"That sort," Linda said. "But not other sorts."

"I haven't yet reached that part of my review," Emma said warily.

"What does that *mean?* You can't comment on the marriage until you've gone back over every last detail of the entire sixteen years? What kind of bullshit is that?"

"Seventeen years in total," Emma corrected her. "And unfortunately it would appear it's the bullshit I have to get through before I can lay both hands on my life again. I am sorry if that sounds dreary and pretentious, or however it sounds to you. I'd love not to be doing it but I seem to be well and truly trapped in it." Despairing of the way she sounded and desperate to change the subject, she said, "I do have an interesting bit of news I think you'll appreciate."

"So give. What?"

"I'm having dinner tomorrow evening with Richard Redmond."

"Are you kidding?" Linda exclaimed, surprised. He hadn't mentioned that during their brief conversation. "You're going out with that *hunk?* You *are* talking about the lawyer? Guy about six-two, great build, gray at the temples, neat little moustache, killer smile. That Richard Redmond?"

"Yes." Another awful flush had turned her overheated. Their conversation reminded her of those she'd had with Vivian before Vivian had left home; whispered late-night confessions Vivian made about boys and the things she'd done with them, the things she'd allowed them to do to her.

"You're going out to dinner with *him?* Jesus! I need a drink. You want a drink?"

"No, thank you."

Linda got a bottle of gin from one of the cabinets, then stood holding it, staring at Emma. "You ever been with anyone but Willard?"

"There were three or four young men I dated before he came along."

"Dated, yeah. But did you ever sleep with any of them?"

"Actually, I made love with two of them."

"Well, thank God for something."

"Sorry?"

"Think what kind of lousy shape you'd be in right now—not that you're in such great shape—but think where you'd be if Willard had been your one and only. I mean, it's a long time ago and all that, but at least you've got some frame of reference. You'd be in serious trouble. I mean, you'd be comparing every guy who came along to Willard. Although that'll probably happen anyway. It's inevitable after spending almost half your life with someone. Boy! I can't get over this! You going out to dinner with Richard "The Hunk" Redmond. That last party you guys had. Remember? Redmond was there, one of the ambulatory amputees cuz he just split up with his wife. Remember?"

"Vividly."

"I asked him if he'd like to have dinner sometime. He looked at me with this completely inscrutable expression, didn't say yes, no, or fuck off. Just smiled and turned to talk to somebody else. The smile saved it from being one of my life's more humiliating moments."

"You never told me that," Emma said.

"Hardly something I'm going to brag about. Sure you won't have a drink? Sun's well over the yardarm."

"Perhaps a glass of wine, if you have any."

"Of course I do. Red or white?"

"Red, please."

Linda opened a bottle of red wine, poured a glass for Emma, fixed gin and tonic for herself, then said, "Don't you feel better, having everything out in the open?"

"About the books, you mean?" Emma thought for a few seconds, then said, "Yes, actually, I do. I'd never want to hurt you, Linda. And I couldn't possibly have known your feelings on the matter. Most writers would actively defend their work."

"I'm not most writers. I'm somebody who wanted to break in, but I couldn't. I wrote my heart out, but nobody wanted the books. So, I sat down and studied the market, took a good look at what sold and what didn't. Then I gambled and created a pastiche of what it seemed to me publishers wanted. And it worked. So now I can afford to subsidize Margaret McGarry's books. I told you I'm not stupid. My philosophy has always been if you can't go in the front way, find a side door or a window."

"It's a sensible philosophy," Emma said with admiration.

"Give me a hug," Linda said, crossing over from the island to put her arms around Emma. "I love you, you know, Em."

Emma hugged her back, feeling oddly purged. "I love you, too," she said. "And I'm sorry if I let you down."

Linda pulled back and looked at her with dismay. "You didn't let *me* down, Em. Don't you get it? You've been letting yourself down."

Chapter Seven

With the second letter in hand, and that electric sizzling in her head again, upon returning home from visiting Linda Emma went directly upstairs to her office. Getting out the index cards, she looked over her notes then began adding to them. She was very close to the point where she'd start the actual writing. The opening was already clear in her mind, as were her central characters. She'd chosen a villain but couldn't decide upon a motive, and that worried her. There would have to be a very good reason why someone would decide to interfere in a person's life by writing letters. But what could that reason be?

She pushed her chair back from the desk and sat looking at the typewriter. It was a simple enough matter to buy a Selectric element to match someone else's typeface. There were only a certain number of elements and ribbons available. Given the resources, and the time, one could drive or take the train into Manhattan, say, and purchase everything that was needed. And given that one had already obtained the stationery—having either ordered it somewhere or stolen a supply—there was nothing to stop one from writing letters (taking care, of course, to sound as much like the victim as possible) and then dropping them into a mailbox where they'd be given the appropriate postal cancellation stamp.

What could the culprit hope the net effect of these letters would be? He/she might be seeking to discredit the victim. Or, if the victim were already in the throes of some private turmoil, he/she might be bent on pushing her over the brink into a breakdown. Or he/she could be trying to drive the victim mad. Given that enough people received these letters and reacted negatively, the campaign could work to isolate the victim by alienating her from her friends and family. But why? To what end?

Was someone trying to drive her crazy? she wondered, shifting from hypothetical theorizing to direct questioning. And if they were, why would they think sending letters would accomplish that? Or were the letters only the start of a campaign that might escalate in any number of directions? This thought killed off her creative energies and aroused her fear. Instinctively she'd eliminated both Bernice and Linda from her list of suspects. That left Shawn and Janet, possibly even Susan and Edgar. Who else?

Switching off the desk lamp, she got up and went to the master bedroom to find that Bernice

had turned back the bedclothes and put away
Emma's purchases. Emma opened the dressing
room door, put on the light and saw that the
red dress had been placed on a quilted hanger
and covered with a plastic dry-cleaning bag. The
blue jeans had been folded over a hanger, the
sweaters inserted into individual plastic bags and
stacked on the shelf with her other sweaters; the
blouses had been ironed and hung away, the new
shoes positioned at the near end of the shoe rack.
Bernice was the essence of efficiency. She'd taken
care of everything.

Removing her dress, she put it and her undergarments in the hamper, returned her flat-heeled
shoes to the rack, then, carrying a nightgown over
her arm, turned out the light and went into the
bathroom.

When the tub had filled she eased her way into
the hot water and stretched out, letting her head
rest against the rim. The heat released the tension in her muscles as she closed her eyes and
returned to the matter of the letters. It appeared
that Richard had been the first to receive one.
Linda was the second. If the culprit was mailing
several at a time it would be impossible to establish the chronology. Perhaps she'd soon discover
that everyone she knew had been sent a letter.
Good God! This truly was horrendous. Could the
point of the exercise be to shame her so thoroughly that she'd have to leave the country? Linda had,
typically, elected to be reasonable. And Richard
had responded in a most civilized fashion. Other people might not choose to be quite so fair-
minded. Richard had from the outset shown himself to be scrupulously evenhanded. It was one of
the qualities she'd long admired in him.

She'd been married to a man who'd zealously and most possessively overseen almost every aspect of her existence. If Will had ever, even for a moment, suspected that she liked Richard Redmond's firm but gentle manner, or that she felt rarely rewarded by the exceptional appeal of his smile, he'd have made it a point, under some pretext or other, to secure the services of another attorney. Yet the truth was she'd always been drawn to Richard. He was as bookish as she and enjoyed discussing the attributes or flaws of whatever he'd read most recently. And he'd never shown any qualms about quibbling with her over details in her own books. He'd also been happy, on a number of occasions, to supply her with legal information she required for one of her manuscripts.

Sleepy and susceptible, she found herself slipping away to that hushed interior place where her memory was stored. Her brain wanted to slot itself into that beginning groove, but she fought it. Go forward! she willed. Forward to the point where she'd left off.

Yes.

"Unless you go running for the hills, Emma Dalton, I think I'm going to marry you." He made this declaration with such stunning confidence that she could only believe it was foreordained.

So convinced was she that her future was in this man's hands that throughout their dinner together she was anticipating the moment when he announced it was time they made love. She wasn't especially looking forward to that. The buildup to her few previous sexual encounters had been considerably more stimulating than the lovemaking. She'd felt acted upon rather than involved. But she'd allowed two very different young men to see her naked and to touch her because it was all part of staking a claim on her independence. She was a grown woman who'd engaged in a variety of adult activities: demonstrating her reliability by being punctual and doing good work, paying her rent on time each week, and using her free hours to perfect her writing skills. Adding sexual emancipation to this list was only sensible. Not particularly rewarding in fundamental terms, but gratifying in that it represented one less barrier standing between her and her ultimate right to proclaim herself a full-fledged adult.

To her surprise, Willard Bellamy made no overtures before or during their dinner together in the Savoy Grill. As she felt their allotted time together trickling away, she decided she'd have to make it clear to him that she had no objection to allowing him to see and touch her. That didn't mean she wasn't very nervous at the prospect, but she believed in honoring her decisions. And she'd decided not to return to her room in South Kensington that night unless and until she'd made her disposition clear.

He was promising to read her manuscript right away and to telephone her in the morning before he left for the airport, and she felt suddenly panicky, sensing he'd very shortly send her home. She tried to think of some subtle way to tell him she was willing to accompany him upstairs to his suite, but short of blurting out a remark that might embarrass them both, she couldn't think of how to say it.

Fortunately he saw she was struggling to say something, and gave her an opening. "Is anything wrong?" he asked.

"I thought perhaps you'd like me to stay the night with you," she said boldly and watched his face blossom with surprise, while she felt heat rising into her face.

His eyes widened, he smiled involuntarily, and gave a shake of his head as if not quite sure he'd heard correctly. "Is that what you were expecting?" he asked, leaning toward her across the table.

"I don't know that I've been expecting it," she answered. "But I have been thinking about it. You did say you thought you'd marry me. Not that I've taken you literally, but one would assume making love with me was something you'd considered and decided you'd like to do."

"If you don't beat the band," he said delightedly, sitting back to drink some of his brandy and eying her as he did. "I'm flattered, Emma." He put the glass down and lit a cigarette, watching her all the while. "What about you?" he asked finally. "You've thought about what *I* might like to do. What about what *you'd* like to do?"

"Oh, I'm quite amenable," she told him, despite the fact that she'd previously found the experience to be messy and fairly pointless. It seemed to be something men needed to do, and she was not averse to accommodating them. She was taking birth control pills, had been for close on two years, so there was no risk involved in that particular area.

Willard Bellamy continued to gaze at her for several more moments before abruptly signaling to the waiter for the check. After he'd signed for the dinner, he got up, took her firmly by the hand and walked her back through the lobby to the elevators. He didn't speak until

they were inside his suite with the DO NOT DIS-
TURB sign hung on the outer doorknob. Then he
put his hands on her shoulders and said, "Are
you doing this to prove some point, or because
you're hoping to influence my reading of your
book?"

"No. I don't expect I could influence you,"
she answered. "And I can't think what point it
would prove."

"Why, then?"

"Well," she faltered, "you said you're interested in me. I'm also interested in you. And isn't
lovemaking what two people do when they're
interested in one another? It's been my experience that it is."

"Your experience?" One hand left her shoulder to cup her chin. "Eighteen years old and
you talk about 'experience.' You're adorable."

She simply gazed at him, losing her ability to
read him from one moment to the next. She
was any number of things, she knew, but adorable wasn't one of them.

"I have to confess I'd like nothing more than
to take you into the bedroom. But I keep thinking I'm taking advantage of you."

"How?"

"Because I've got twenty-six years on you.
Because it doesn't feel entirely legitimate even
to be having this conversation with you. And
because for all I know you're in way over your
head."

She frowned, becoming weary. "If you'd
rather I left," she said, and looked over at the
door, "I'll quite understand."

"Jesus Christ!" he said. "Enough of this."
Again taking her by the hand he led her into

the bedroom, asking, "Would you like to use the bathroom?"

She said, "Yes, please," and went to close herself into the marvelous art deco room with ornate tiles and brass fittings. Trying to ignore her nervousness, she undressed and folded her clothes neatly, then washed her face before using the bidet. Ready for whatever was to happen, she took the deepest breath possible, then opened the door.

Willard Bellamy had turned off all but the bedside light. He was sitting on the side of the bed wearing only his boxer shorts and looked up sharply as she came out of the bathroom. He murmured something she didn't catch, held out his arms and said, "Come here."

Close to two hours later, as she was riding home in a taxi whose driver Willard Bellamy had prepaid, she understood that until that night she—or, more appropriately, her two young lovers—had known precious little about lovemaking. Now, sitting somewhat glassy-eyed in the back of the cab, she was dazed by the discovery of her considerable appetites. Willard Bellamy had, in the space of roughly one hundred and twenty minutes, introduced her to her own body in precise, intimate detail. He'd induced in her an animalistic craving that he'd then satisfied so thoroughly and in such a variety of ways that she could scarcely walk properly. After climbing the five flights of stairs to her room, she struggled out of her clothes, collapsed into bed and was asleep in seconds.

Very early the next morning, he telephoned to say, "I want to see you. I'll be leaving here in about twenty minutes. I'll have the driver swing by and pick you up. You can ride with me to the airport. We've got to talk."

She said, "Very well," and hurried to dress.

When the limousine pulled up out front, she was waiting and hurried into the back where Willard sat smiling.

Taking hold of her hand, he said, "Sorry if I sounded brusque on the phone. I just had to see you before I leave. I've got a hell of a lot of things I want to say to you. But first things first. I read your manuscript last night. It was all I could do not to call you at three-thirty this morning, I was so anxious to discuss it with you. Emma," he said earnestly, "you're so good, your writing's so goddamned good. I'm still in a state of shock. How the hell can you be only eighteen?" he wondered aloud, searching her eyes. "Are you okay?" he thought to ask belatedly.

"I'm very well, thank you."

"You're sure ?"

"Quite sure, yes."

"Okay, good. Now, listen. What I wanted to say is this: I'd like you to think very carefully about taking a different direction with this book. You've got such a powerful eye for detail, such a gift for narrative drive that you could turn this into a first-rate mystery. I'm not talking run-of-the-mill whodunit, but something more elegant, finer. A psychological mystery, an interior investigation. Does that interest you?"

"I don't know. I would have to think about it."

"Is this your only copy of the manuscript?" he asked.

"I have a carbon."

"Good. Would you let me hang on to it? I'd like to go over it again, make more detailed suggestions. That is, if you wouldn't mind. I think once I break it down a bit more for you, you'll get a better feel for what I'm trying to say."

"You truly think I'm good?" she said, starting to become very excited.

"Oh, dear girl," he smiled, giving her hand a squeeze. "You're better than good. You're a born writer, a natural. I'm so in love with everything about you I can hardly see straight. I wish to hell I didn't have to leave. But I promised the kids I'd be home for Christmas."

"I quite understand."

"I don't see how you can when I hardly do myself. But never mind that!" he said impatiently, taking a quick look out the window as if to gauge how much time they had left. "Listen, you'll be hearing from me. That's a promise. And I'll be back over in February. The thing is, I want you to have plenty of time so you're sure of what you're doing—in every area. I never want it said that I hustled you into anything, that I pushed you before you were ready."

"I think actually I rather pushed you," she said with a smile.

"I'm not promising anything, but I'm pretty confident I can get you lined up with a good agent here. Your age is going to be a big factor in selling this book. Not that it isn't going to take a lot of work. But I know you can do it. Maybe you won't have a best-seller, but you're going to get off to a damned good start, and I'm going to help you. Does that sound fair?"

"Oh yes, very. And I don't mind the work."

"As for the rest of it, I spent most of the night going over the pros and cons and I've come up with what I think is a decent plan. I propose that we give it a year. I'm back and forth regularly, and we'll be seeing each other whenever I'm here. In between times, you can count on hearing from me. If you still feel the same way a year from now, then we'll make some more concrete plans. Fair enough?"

"I'll still feel the same way," she said buoyantly, wishing they could make love one more time before he left.

"You're very, very young," he said, giving her a kiss on the cheek. "You may not think it or act it, but facts are facts. And the fact is you're eighteen. I want you to have plenty of time to make up your mind, to be absolutely sure about what you're doing."

"Have you made up yours?" she asked, thinking he didn't look as if he'd been up all night. His eyes were clear; he seemed very fit and brimming with energy.

"Pretty much," he replied, running his forefinger over her lips. "It's going to cause no end of fuss. Do you know that?"

The bathwater had gone cold. She sat up, pulled the plug and reached for a towel. No end of fuss, he'd said. No end of it. Stepping out of the tub, shivering in the cold air of the room, she wrapped herself in the towel, her eyes on the concealed mirror. She'd gone to the fabric store and bought an entire bolt of black cotton. Then she'd covered every last mirror in the house. She'd had to use masking tape and several lengths of the cloth to cover the mirrored bathroom wall.

All of it because she couldn't bear to see herself, loathed the very sight of herself. How could anyone possibly understand? Only someone who'd lived through each minute of every hour of every day of those seventeen years could make any sense of it. Much as she loved Linda and understood what it was she'd been trying to do, Linda was wrong. The truth could very definitely kill you. Perhaps not literally. But there were all kinds of ways to die.

Chapter Eight

"So how's Miss Linda?" Bernice asked, setting a plate of scrambled eggs, crisp bacon and whole wheat toast in front of Emma. "Been a long time since you seen her."

"She's splendid," Emma said, so anxious to get to work she wasn't sure she wanted to eat.

"How come you're lookin' at the food like that? Go ahead and eat." Bernice poured two cups of coffee before sitting down, pointedly staring at Emma's plate. Later on this morning, when she got a chance, she'd make a call to Miss Linda.

Common sense taking precedence over her craving to be at work, Emma picked up her knife and fork. "I thought since I'll be out for the evening you might care to go down to Cedric's tonight instead of waiting until tomorrow."

With a bright smile, Bernice said, "Well, that's a nice idea. I'll phone him up, see if that suits."

"You might as well spend the time with your family," Emma said reasonably.

"You excited about tonight?" Bernice's green eyes were alight with anticipation. She looked, Emma thought, very happy.

"I haven't given it all that much thought, really." It was the truth. Since she'd awakened, her brain had been racing, leaping from point to point, eager to begin committing ideas to paper. Her body wanted to be hurrying up the stairs to the office. She ate mechanically, only vaguely aware of the taste of the food.

Bernice shook her head indulgently. "I can see you're in one big rush to get to that typewriter." Emma looked up, and Bernice said, "Your eyes get like you're watchin' this movie nobody else can see. Might as well be talkin' to the wall." She said this with affection and even, Emma thought, quite possibly with pride.

"Have you ever read one of my books?" Emma asked her, taking a bite of the toast.

"Course I have! You think I don't have some curiosity' bout what you get up to hours on end in that office? Read every last one of them, and so've the kids. You use a whole lot of five-dollar words but they're real good books. I liked that one with the crazy schoolteacher best. Had me a teacher just like that in the seventh grade."

"Did you?" Interested, Emma said with a smile, "I hope she didn't kill anyone."

"Looked like as if she could've," Bernice said. "We all were scared silly of her. You have a teacher like that?"

Her mouth full, Emma shook her head.

"Sure seemed like as if you did. They're *real* good, your books," she declared judiciously.

"It's amazing how you do it. I always wonder how you think up all those things."

"I sometimes wonder that myself," Emma said. "I look at my books on the shelf and think,'How on earth did I write seven books?' I have no idea. I made up my mind years ago not to question it. It's simply what I do. And I'm sufficiently superstitious to believe that if I question it too closely I might lose the ability altogether."

Bernice nodded. "Faith," she said seriously. "Some things a person just has to accept. Like believin' there's a God."

"That's true," Emma concurred. "Have you ever read any of Linda's books?"

Bernice smiled widely, showing her teeth. "Sure have."

"What did you think of them?"

"They pass the time. Course if you've read one, you've read them all. I get 'em mixed up, can't remember one from the other."

"I have a book I think you might enjoy," Emma said, blotting her mouth with a napkin. "Come up to the office and I'll find it for you."

"You haven't finished eating," Bernice protested.

"I'm afraid I have. Come with me," Emma said, picking up her coffee to take along.

Emma found *Glass Houses* in the stack of books she'd already read. Soon she'd have to make another trip to the hospital to donate them. Bernice looked doubtfully at the cover. "Read it," Emma told her. "I'm interested to know what you think of it."

"I'll give it a try. Okay if I pick up in the bedroom now?"

"Certainly." Eyeing the word processor, Emma turned off the ringer on the telephone, then opened the desk drawer for a package of DataDisks and the manual, in case she'd forgotten some of the machine's features.

"Hey!" Bernice said from the doorway, Emma's nightgown in her hands. "When you'd decide to start dressing for bed?"

"It was a bit chilly last night," Emma said, centering the lap-top on the desk. That letter to Richard had made her self-conscious about continuing to sleep in the nude.

"Uh-huh." Bernice draped the gown over her arm and went back to the bedroom.

The excitement fueling her, Emma switched on the machine, inserted a disk, followed the lap-top's prompts to prepare it, then returned to the main menu. She pressed number 1— Create, View or Edit Text—and was presented with a blank screen. She coded the machine to Center and typed *Secrets*: CHAPTER ONE, returned twice, then turned to look over the index cards. The opening sentence taking form in her mind, she placed her fingers in position on the keyboard and began.

The room was on the fifth floor of a house in South Kensington, with the bath and toilet one floor below. It was a cozy, elongated room, with an oversized wardrobe occupying the entire wall to the left of the door as one entered and the narrow bed filling in the space below the window . . .

Bernice knew better than to interrupt when Emma was working, knew not to offer food even.

But when it got to five-twenty and Emma was still clickety-clacking away at that little writing machine, Bernice went upstairs to knock quietly on the open door.

Her eyes way off somewhere, Emma turned to look over, and Bernice said, "You gotta start gettin' ready soon. Mr. Lawyer called a while back to say he'd be here at a quarter to seven."

Emma stared blankly at her for several seconds. Then she said, "All right. Let me just finish this bit."

"I'll go set out your clothes," Bernice said, and went along to the bedroom, feeling somewhat guilty at going behind Emma's back to talk to her friends. But having learned from Linda that she'd also had one of those letters, Bernice felt obliged to talk to Mr. Redmond about that. Since Emma wasn't telling all that was going on, Bernice had little choice but to try to stay in close touch with Emma's two friends in the hope that, between them, they could sort things out.

Emma grabbed a notepad and her pen and quickly jotted down points she wanted to remember for the next chapter. Then she looked at the screen for a moment before going to the main menu. Keying in number 2—Set Margins, Tabs, and Format—she positioned the left and right margins, changed the pitch to 12, adjusted to double spacing, then moved the cursor to the bottom line of the right-hand column—Reformat? . . . No—pressed the space bar, and the screen went blank except for the word "Reformatting." When the message changed to "Reformatting Complete," she returned again to the main menu and keyed in number 4—Store Text to DataDisk.

She entered the document name as Chapter One, pressed the return button and the laptop informed her it was storing Chapter One. And in boldface cautioned **Do NOT Remove DataDisk.**

Amazing! Following the instructions in the manual she also stored her personal word list that included the character and street names.

"You're gonna be late!" Bernice warned from the doorway.

"All right. I've finished here." Emma ejected the disk, wrote *Secrets*, Ch. 1 on the label, then put the disk, index cards and her notes in the top drawer of the desk.

She looked, Bernice thought, like someone in a trance as she switched off the desk lamp, then stood up and headed for the bedroom. It always took her a good while to come back from wherever it was she went off to when she was writing. If you tried to talk to her, she'd look at you with those blank eyes and you knew you were wasting your breath. You just had to wait until she tuned back in before you'd get anywhere telling her anything. About the most she'd respond to were questions with yes or no answers. It was different from the way she'd been going blank all these months since Mr. Willard died. Those times she didn't respond at all, to anything. And that'd been real scary, but Bernice had learned to wait. But the way she was now was a good sign, like old times, and Bernice was encouraged.

"Bath or shower?" she asked.

"Shower," Emma said from the dressing room.

"Okay. I'll check back." Bernice waited for a

moment to make sure Emma had begun undressing then went downstairs to fix a cup of coffee to help wake her up some.

Standing under the shower, Emma's attention slowly shifted from her heroine walking down a wet London street to the present. Her neck and shoulders were stiff from the eight uninterrupted hours spent in front of the keyboard. She'd have to book some appointments with Mark, her chiropractor. When she was working she usually saw him at least three times a week.

After scrubbing herself and shampooing her hair, she did the neck-stretching exercises Mark had taught her, then made the water hotter, adjusted the shower head to a driving pulse and let the water pound rhythmically on her knotted neck and shoulder muscles. It wasn't until she was toweling dry that she zeroed in on the fact that she was preparing to spend an evening with Richard Redmond.

A sudden quivering in her belly signaled her misgivings, made her very aware of her body. She should have refused, but now it was too late, and she felt as if she were readying herself for another funeral. Reaching for the hairbrush, she shaped her hair, having perfected by touch this one act of grooming she did daily without benefit of a mirror.

In the dressing room she was daunted by the sight of the red dress, the new slip, pantyhose and shoes, all of which Bernice had laid at the ready. Bernice had also left a cup of coffee on top of the built-in drawer unit and Emma gratefully drank some before starting to dress.

This is bizarre! she thought, pulling on the

sheer hose, then letting the new pink slip slither over her head and settle around her body. Every item felt strange, cool to her skin. Even applying deodorant struck her as abnormal. She stepped into the dress, its redness assaulting her eyes. A second layer of silk draped over her flesh. Strange, strange, she thought, as she fastened the small covered buttons one after another all the way down the front.

Bernice knocked on the outside door and Emma asked her to come in.

"Looks real good," Bernice said appraisingly, looking Emma up and down. "You need earrings and maybe a bracelet."

"Pick something," Emma said, stepping aside so Bernice could look in the jewelry box.

Bernice deliberated, then selected a pair of gold hoops, handed them to Emma, then picked up a heavy gold bangle, saying, "I never saw this before."

"Will gave it to me on our first anniversary. I've only worn it a few times."

"Wear it now," Bernice decided. "You need some kind of bag, and something to keep out the chill. Getting cold, these nights." She found a black cashmere shawl Willard had brought back from one of his trips to Europe and a black patent leather clutch bag he'd also bought. "These're good, go with the shoes," Bernice said. "You don't think maybe you should put them shoes on?"

"I don't feel at all like myself," Emma complained, obediently stepping into the shoes. "I'm not used to such high heels," she said doubtfully.

"Those aren't high. Not more'n two inches.

You want to see *high*, you oughta see some of what my Marla wears. Now those're high. Well," she said, backing into the bedroom to take another look. "You look fine. Don't forget to take your keys and some what-if money."

"Yes, all right," Emma said, taking a few experimental steps. "This is ridiculous." She gave Bernice a smile. "I can scarcely walk."

"You'll do okay. Everything's closed up. Calla's had a walk and I filled her bowls. You spend the whole weekend up here in the office, just don't forget to feed the poor dog. Hear?"

"I won't forget."

"Okay. I'll wait till Mr. Richard comes, then I'll be going. Anything you want?"

"I don't believe so, thank you."

"You think of anything, I'll be in the kitchen the next little while."

Emma went to sit on the side of the bed and looked down at her feet. It had been seventeen years since she'd worn high-heeled shoes. They looked very sleek, very adult. Remembering, she opened the drawer of the night table to lift out the bag of cosmetics Bernice had encouraged her to buy. There was mascara, eye shadow, powdered blush, and lipstick. Feeling all at once like a child readying herself to attend a fancy dress party, she opened the eye shadow and looked at the two pristine cakes of light and dark brown, the sponge applicators. She hadn't worn any form of makeup since that February in 1975 when Will had returned to London.

She'd wanted to buy a new dress for the occasion but had been unable to afford one. So she had her favorite dress cleaned, got her best shoes resoled and polished, and used the small

amount of spare money she had to buy new
stockings and some makeup. Will telephoned
soon after his arrival to say, "How soon can
you get over here?" and she'd gone flying out
to catch a bus to the tube station, fifty-eight
rewritten pages in an envelope under her arm.

He came to the door of his suite and took
a long critical look at her before grasping her
hand and drawing her inside. Then, pulling out
a handkerchief, he'd tilted her face to the light
and carefully wiped off the eyeshadow, lipstick
and the bit of color she'd applied to her cheeks.
"You don't need any of this," he said, frowning
as he refolded the soiled handkerchief, then
wiped away the last trace of pale pink lipstick.
"It detracts from your natural appeal."

She'd felt inept and cheap and foolish. And,
for as long as it took him to strip away the
effort she'd made to render herself as attractive
as possible for him, she'd hated both of them—
him for the heartlessness of this rude greeting, and herself for having believed him to be
accepting of her. But then, when her face was
once again to his satisfaction, he'd kissed the
tip of her nose, spotted the envelope under her
arm, and said, "Is that your rewrite? Let's have
a look," and she'd put aside her hurt because
the work was more important than her bruised
ego. She'd helped herself to a cup of coffee
from the ever-present carafe while he sank into
a chair to read the new beginning of the manuscript.

With time she learned to anticipate his reactions and tried to spare herself additional hurt
by resisting the temptation to brighten her features with the help of harmless glosses and

powders, and by accepting his suggestions as the orders they really were. It was he who'd first taken her to a Laura Ashley shop to buy one of those quaint printed full-skirted cotton dresses, and he who'd taken her to the Vidal Sassoon salon in Manhattan soon after her arrival in America to have her long hair cut off. It was Will who'd suggested the plain flat-heeled shoes, the clear rather than tinted nail enamel on shorter nails. He'd arrived home with packages of expensive hand-embroidered white cotton undergarments that made her feel as if she were back in school and once again compelled daily to don a uniform. But she acquiesced because Willard Bellamy was a man who knew what he was about, and she was too young, too grateful, too indebted, and too in love to dispute the majority of his decisions.

Now Willard Bellamy had been reduced to ashes and scattered into the wind and she was in possession of a dress he'd have hated and a cache of cosmetics he'd have angrily insisted she didn't need.

Picking up the applicator, she applied the sponge tip to the dark brown powdered eye-shadow and with the aid of the small mirror in the box lid darkened the crease of her eye-lids and then put brown mascara on her pale lashes. Pleased with the effect, she brushed a bit of color onto her cheeks and, finally, with a laugh, uncapped the lipstick and redefined her mouth. Because the mirror was tiny she had to move it in a slow circle in order to gain some overall impression of her handiwork. Satisfied she hadn't been too heavy-handed, she dropped the lipstick into the clutch bag, returned the other cosmetics to the drawer and stood up just as the doorbell rang.

Six forty-five exactly. Richard was always prompt. It was something else they had in common. Will had been chronically late. He'd been forever racing to get on planes after the final boarding call, in a mad dash to get to meetings that were scheduled to begin when he was just leaving his office. There wasn't anyone Will hadn't kept waiting, with the sole exception of the undertaker. He'd actually been early for that particular appointment.

The shawl over her arm, she dropped her keys, American Express card, and fifty dollars into the bag, tucked it under her arm and, still somewhat awkward in the shoes, made her way to the stairs.

Bernice met her at the bottom, murmuring conspiratorially, "I was just comin' to fetch you. Mr. Lawyer's waitin' in the livin' room. You look beautiful, Emma. Go have yourself a good time." She gave Emma's hand a squeeze, lifted her chin to indicate Emma should straighten up, then turned to go, saying, "I'll see you Monday morning. You need me, Cedric's number's right on the board beside the kitchen phone."

Emma said, "Thank you," then looked down to be sure all her buttons were fastened and nothing was out of place before crossing to the living room.

Richard was standing by the fireplace looking at the photographs on the mantel.

"Good evening, Richard," she said, and he turned abruptly, saying, "Good evening," before he'd completed the turn.

She enjoyed his reaction. Initially he looked

very surprised, blinking quickly several times. Then his face was transformed by one of his wonderful smiles, and he said, "Emma! You look . . ." He couldn't seem to find an appropriate word to describe how he thought she looked, and visibly worked at it for a second or two before saying, " . . . fantastic!"

"It's a new dress," she said with what she knew was childish pleasure.

"It certainly is," he agreed, crossing the room toward her. "I'd say it's a new you altogether. If you're ready, we might as well go."

"I'm ready," she said, feeling lightheaded.

She was intrigued to see he appeared to be nervous as he hurried to open the car door for her. She reached to fasten her seatbelt as he slid in behind the wheel and started the car before putting on his seatbelt. Music suddenly surrounded them and she listened for a moment, before saying, "That's lovely. Is it the radio or a tape?"

"Tape," he answered. "Bill Evans, 'Waltz for Debby.' If you like it, I can make you a dub. You like jazz?"

"I think I must do," she replied. "This is a very nice automobile."

"It's my divorce present to myself," he said, heading around the circular top of the driveway to the road. "I wanted something major for serious consolation; so I wrote the biggest check of my life and bought this. It's three years old now."

"One would never know it."

"I know. I hate to think I fall into some sort of macho stereotype having to do with cars being sexual icons. I happen to like BMWs and

I decided to go for broke and get the 750 IL. I don't spend my weekends washing and waxing it, or anything like that." He smiled over at her. "I just like being comfortable in my old age."

"You think of yourself as old, Richard?" she asked with interest.

"Sometimes."

"So do I," she said.

"You? You're not old, Emma."

"Neither are you, Richard. At least not chronologically. Why do you think of yourself as old?"

"All kinds of reasons," he said. "Too much work and too little play, life's nasty tricks, gravity, gray hair, indigestion."

She smiled.

"Why do you?" he asked.

"I don't think I can answer that with anywhere near your efficiency. Where are we going?"

"Greenwich. Is that all right?"

"Certainly."

"It's a small French restaurant I thought you might like."

She let her head rest against the soft leather seat, listened to the moody piano music, and breathed in the pleasingly spicy fragrance of his bay rum, her nervousness gone. In its place was a wonderful sense of quite heady anticipation.

Chapter Nine

Emma set aside the menu, took a sip of her wine and looked over at Richard, who was still deciding what to order. She felt as if she'd been transported to some parallel world, one where the old rules didn't apply and new appetites were permissible; she felt like a distilled version of her usual self, with a heightened awareness of sight, sound, and sensation. Enclosed in weightless red silk, her legs slippery in the unaccustomed sheer hose, she was another Emma, unencumbered by guilt, anger, grief, or the need to ruminate over the minutiae of her prior life. This other Emma was most curious about the man seated opposite and she took advantage of his occupation with the menu to look closely at him, noticing the tidy conformation of his ears, the pleasing arch of his eyebrows, the healthy hint of color in his cheeks, the slight upturning of the corners of his well-shaped mouth. He had, in fact, the most perfectly formed, completely symmetrical mouth she'd ever seen on a man. His eyes were a golden brown and long-lashed. His nose appeared to have been meticulously sculpted by an artist of exceptional skill. He was indeed, as Bernice had said, a fine-looking man.

He raised his eyes suddenly and smiled at her, and she felt his smile penetrate her belly and puncture her lungs. Will's bracelet was all at once a manacle weighting down her arm. Allowing her hands to fall to her lap, she slipped the bangle off her wrist and slid it into her handbag.

"What're you in the mood for?" he asked, trying to decide what, aside from the dress, was different about her this evening. She looked brighter, her features more clearly defined. He was aware for the first time of the length of her eyelashes and the arch of her cheekbones, the enticingly youthful curve of her lips. His eyes were drawn to the swell of her breasts, the milky expanse of skin sloping gently back from her breasts to melt into the long column of her throat. Circles of gold touched against the angled upturn of her jaw, swaying slightly when she turned her head. She looked young and both mentally and physically healthy, and he had to wonder for a moment if the letter-writing wasn't some kind of ploy, something she'd done consciously but which, for some reason, she was refusing to acknowledge.

"The duck, I think." She picked up the menu to refer to it again. She had to look away from his approving eyes, busy herself taking another sip of wine. Her social skills were restricted to editorial conferences and at-home parties, conversations with Bernice or Linda or her longtime editor, Kathy. They did not extend to dinner *à deux* in a discreet French restaurant with a most attractive man she really only knew professionally.

"The dress is very becoming," he said, wondering why she'd been so relaxed in the car but was so visibly on edge now.

"Thank you, Richard." She put down the menu and crossed her legs, the flesh of her thighs sensitive to the slight rasp of the slippery hose. She had to force herself to look at him, her eyes fixing on his mouth as he said, "If it helps any, this seems kind of strange to me, too."

"Does it?" His saying that did help. Looking now at his eyes, she asked, "Why?"

"I haven't gone out much since the split with Dell. It's funny the way you can lose the knack of socializing once you've been married then find yourself on the loose again. After spending ten years with someone, you get used to the way they do things. Then all of a sudden you've got to get used to doing things differently, doing them alone, for the most part."

"But surely after all this time," she said, "you must be acclimated."

"To some things, not to others. I think I tend to fall back on memory, maybe even aping the behavior of whomever I'm with—present company excepted, of course."

The waiter presented himself at the table, asking, "Are you ready to order?"

"I believe so," Richard said. "Emma?"

"The duck, please."

"Anything to start, madame?"

"No, thank you."

Richard asked, "Are you sure? How about a

salad? Would you like to share one?"

"Yes, all right. Thank you."

"We'll share a house salad," Richard told the waiter. "And I'll have the *cervelle*."

When the waiter had gone, Emma smiled spontaneously, saying, "You're very brave. I could never eat brains."

Smiling back at her, he said, "Why not? They're delicious."

"I already feel like a vampire. Eating brains would be going too far."

"A *vampire*?" He leaned on the table, his smile holding. "Care to elaborate?"

"Instead of drinking people's blood, I steal their thoughts, appropriate their comments and observations, rework them to suit my prose."

He made a face. "You don't think that's possibly overstating matters a bit?" Was she perhaps just the slightest bit mad? From one moment to the next his impression of her kept changing.

"Perhaps. I've always thought it would make a good horror novel: a character who gets close to people, sucks every last idea from their brains and leaves them appearing catatonic."

"Surely you don't think of yourself that way?"

"Not really." She wrapped her fingers around the stem of her wineglass. "Are you still recovering from the breakup of your marriage?"

"In some ways." He laid his hands one over the other on the table and contemplated them for a moment. Regardless of the confusion she inspired in him he was fascinated by her directness, by the atypical turns of her thinking; he was also flattered by her obvious interest. "In other ways," he went on, "I'm glad to have everything resolved. I was very confused for a long while. And upset, too. Despite Dell's insistence that none of it had anything to do with me, that it'd just taken her a long time to discover her preferences, I couldn't help but feel it had to have something to do with me. After all, I was her husband. We'd been sharing a bed for a long time. Maybe I was naive, but I don't think so. There's no possible way to be prepared for your wife sitting you down one evening to announce she's been living a lie, that she's been unfaithful to her true instincts, and that she's finally discovered herself. And the self she's discovered is in love with her best friend, who just happens to be another woman." He tapped one finger on the face of his wristwatch, then looked over at Emma. "I felt duped, as if I'd been living under false pretenses. All that time I'd believed I was more or less like any other man—trying my best to be sensitive to my wife's needs and my own, paying attention to our marriage, trying to do my share to make it worthwhile."

"It must have been shattering," Emma said softly, readily able to imagine the blow to his confidence. "I expect it made you question your own sexuality."

"I'm still working on that," he said candidly, wondering what it was about this woman that prompted him to reveal so much of himself. "I'm not someone who could lay it all off on the other party and accept her argument *verbatim et literatim*. It's only human to feel you must have contributed in some way. Maybe I was a sexual dolt, deluded, or oblivious, or . . . something.

Who knows what? I'm willing to believe her now, but that doesn't mean I don't keep going back over the ten years of our marriage and the eight months of seeing each other before that, trying to spot clues, hints, innuendos I missed the first time around."

"It's what I've been doing every day since Will died," she said sadly. "Such a tedious exercise, so pointless really. One can't change anything, and the endless retrospection merely highlights any number of things best forgotten."

"True," he agreed. "But I think some of us are natural-born analysts. We can't help digging in the hope that the lightbulb will one day go on and we'll see exactly where and how we screwed up—whether or not we actually did."

"Do you blame yourself?" she asked, resting her chin on her upheld palm.

He took the time to think about that before answering, "Truthfully, no. I believe I did my best. More's not humanly possible."

"That's good." She looked around the dimly lit restaurant with the pronounced feeling that she was being watched. Her eyes met those of a silver-haired, well-dressed man on the far side of the room. He at once averted his gaze, and she looked back at Richard. "In view of what you've told me, that letter seems even crueler now," she said.

The only thing he thought it safe to say was, "Never mind. It's not important." But it was important, because he didn't know what he was dealing with, didn't know the intent behind the letter. Still, here they were out together, and he was actually enjoying her company. "At least," he said with a smile, "it prompted me to do one positive thing."

"So you did invite me out this evening because of it," she said, feeling something twist painfully inside her.

"I'm not sorry, and I hope you're not, either,.." he said sincerely. "I haven't really talked to anyone in a hell of a long time. I don't know about you, but it's helping my perspective. I mean, hearing myself say some of these things out loud makes me see how unimportant they really are, certainly not worth the amount of time and gray matter I've invested in them."

"And that's why you've ordered brains!" she laughed, finding this very funny. Mentally, she observed herself as if from a distance, in awe of this rare outburst. She was fascinated by the woman in red silk, and by the interaction between her and this most attractive man.

"Maybe so." He laughed with her, interested to see how she was altered by the laughter. She lost her stiffness, the rigid line of her shoulders softened, color heightened her prettiness. "It's good to see you laugh, Emma."

"I find so few things funny lately. I can remember myself laughing often, years and years ago. I was on my own, living in a tiny rented room, doing temporary work for an agency and spending my evenings writing. I was young, and my freedom was this extraordinarily delicious sponge cake I took huge bites of every day. Nothing truly bothered me. I had a potent, heady sense of my own power, and it grew greater every day. I'd rush into some café on the way to my temporary job and buy a custard tart and eat it as I flew along the street.

Those tarts were the finest things I'd ever tasted, creamy and rich with a hint of vanilla, lovely flaky pastry. I'd attack every new job zealously, turning out flawless letters, perfect year-end reports, whatever needed to be done. I'd breeze into the agency office to see Brenda, my supervisor, and collect my wages. I was so in charge of myself, so filled with the conviction that I was on my way to an immense and splendid future. Then Will came along." She sat back in her chair and drank some of the wine. "And everything changed." She looked down at the contents of her glass, then across the table. "Had you hoped to have children, Richard?"

"Dell never wanted them. And we were the two halves of a whole. So I compromised. What about you?" he asked, his curiosity about her boundless. It was the first time he'd ever had an opportunity to ask her direct personal questions.

The waiter arrived with the salad and positioned it on the table between them, set small plates in front of them both, asking, "Shall I divide it, or do you prefer to serve yourselves?"

"We'll serve ourselves, thank you," Emma answered. The waiter left and she explained to Richard, "I couldn't possibly eat half of all this. I'll just nibble, if I may."

Richard picked up his fork, repeating the question. "Did you want children, Emma?"

"Shall I tell you an ironic story?" she asked.

"Definitely." He speared a piece of tomato and popped it into his mouth. As he chewed, he waited expectantly to hear what she'd say.

"I like the way you eat," she told him.

Katharine Marlowe

He swallowed, then laughed and said, "Thank you. That's the first time anyone's ever complimented me on my table manners."

"Wouldn't it bother you," she asked, "to have to dine with someone who had atrocious eating habits? It would me. When I was young, I vowed never to eat with anyone I didn't like. Eating is such an intimate act in some ways. Don't you agree?" Without waiting for his answer, she said, "For years I dutifully took birth control pills. Never missed a single night. The last thing I did before I went to bed each night was take one of the twenty-one little pills in the container."

"Please have some." He pushed the plate of salad slightly closer to her, wondering if Emma's madness might be so subtle as to go undetected except by those accustomed to dealing with the brain-sick members of the general population.

She reached out and with her thumb and forefinger picked up a piece of Belgian endive. "I like the slightly bitter taste of endive," she said, biting off the pointed tip. "So," she continued, liking not only the unhurried way this man ate, but also the way he listened with his eyes as well as his ears. "Will, as well you know, had four children. The last thing he wanted was to start a second family when he was already forty-five and his children were adults. I, however, was nineteen and of the opinion that, with time, things would sort themselves out and I would have a child. I had always thought I would," she explained. "The issue of giving birth is, I believe, a consideration at some point for every woman. Whether or not one chooses to become a mother has everything to do with the individual. I was an individual convinced I would have this profound experience in the foreseeable future. My husband was bound to change his mind. Amazing how graphic the mind of a 19-year-old can be!" She smiled and took another bite of the endive. "It has to be obvious to you that he did not change his mind."

Richard nodded, paying close attention. She was again making perfect sense, sounding entirely rational.

"After five years of marriage, I was nurturing a small seed of discontent. After ten, I was plotting rebellion. Twenty-nine seemed to me a benchmark age. Once one reached thirty all sorts of complications could be factored in to the birth process. So it had to be done, if it were to be done at all, very soon." She licked a bit of vinaigrette dressing from her fingertips and looked to see how Richard was responding to the narrative.

"Go on," he said, experiencing something very like a minor electric shock watching her lick her fingers. "And please have some more salad."

She gave a slight shake of her head. "I stopped taking the pills. For the first month or two I felt positively criminal. But he'd had his way in so many, many things. It was only fair I have my way this once. Well, suffice it to say, nothing happened. After six months of fruitless fornication, I made an appointment and went off to have myself checked out like a laboratory rat—poked, prodded, pummeled, x-rayed, the lot. All in a good cause, I told myself, skulking home with a bandage in the bend of my elbow concealing the tiny puncture where they'd taken several very large tubes of blood, and my overall anatomy in a highly offended state." She paused and then laughed again. "All for naught, as my father used to say. The result of that embarrassing palpating and perscrutation was the revelation that I was utterly and profoundly infertile. Barren, sterile, fallow. And I'd taken those bloody pills faithfully twenty-one nights a month, every month for more than twelve years. *That* is ironic."

"It's a shame," Richard commiserated, suddenly terribly sorry for her.

"Yes, I rather thought so." She took a slice of cucumber and bit it neatly in half.

"You could've adopted," he offered.

"Hardly, given that I'd been planning to defraud my husband in the first place. I've never told anyone this story," she said. "It struck me as too sordid to bear repeating."

"Did you tell Willard you couldn't have children?"

"I didn't wish to give him that satisfaction. And I promise you it would have been to his satisfaction."

"So you would've got yourself pregnant and he'd've had to live with it?"

"I expect he'd have insisted I have an abortion," she said matter-of-factly. "He wasn't a man who changed his mind, once it had been made up."

The waiter returned, shifted the plate of salad to one side and set down their entrees, asking, "Would you care for more wine, sir? Madame?"

"Emma? Will you have another glass?"

"Why not? Yes, thank you."

"Two more glasses of red, please."

"Very good," said the waiter and left the table.

Richard looked at his dinner, then at Emma. She downed the last of her wine, and met his eyes as she returned the glass to the table.

"I think you're shocked, Richard. I don't think you'd expected to hear me speak of Will this way."

"You're probably right."

"I didn't know I was going to," she told him. "I've never discussed my marriage. But you've been so truthful . . . I hadn't expected you would be. Perhaps I'm trying to reciprocate. I'm not honestly sure. Have I given you a bad impression of me?"

The waiter delivered two fresh glasses of wine, took the empty ones, and asked if they'd care to have fresh-ground pepper. Both Emma and Richard refused, their eyes locked.

"Do you care what kind of impression I have of you?" he asked incisively.

She looked off to one side, asking herself, Do I care? What *do* I care about? The wine had turned her loquacious, and she was actually relishing this unique opportunity to talk openly. "I think I must do," she answered. "You and I have only ever discussed abstracts or legal matters. It's . . . I don't know what it is. I've never talked in quite this way with a man."

"What about Will? Surely the two of you talked?"

"How do I explain this?" she asked herself aloud, cutting into the breast of duck in an orange glaze. "Will . . . *expounded* primarily. He was didactic, offering reasons to substantiate his mandates. That's not to say he wasn't complimentary at times, and affectionate in his way. But his mind was firmly set, Richard. It had been for many years before I ever knew him. And I was so bloody young. People shouldn't be allowed to be as young as I was." She smiled ruefully and tasted the duck.

"Good?"

"Mmm. Delicious. How are your brains?" she asked, emitting another light peal of laughter.

"Going directly to my sadly depleted store," he quipped. "You have the damnedest vocabulary," he said. "Next time we go out I'm going to have to bring along a pocket dictionary."

"You'd like to go out again with me, Richard?" She looked startled.

"Yes, I would," he said without hesitation, realizing it was the truth. "Wouldn't you like to?"

She flushed but didn't avert her eyes. "I think perhaps I would. I like talking with you . . . very much."

"It's mutual. And ironic," he said, "when you think about it. Two people whose careers depend almost exclusively on words, but neither of us seems to have done any talking for a hell of a long time."

"That's true, isn't it?"

"Tell me some more about your life in London," he said. "You lit up, talking about it."

"Did I? I suppose it's because I was happy then. There really isn't very much more to tell. I had five months on my own before I met Will. From that point on I was indentured, so to speak."

"You asked me about my impression of you

a while back," he said, displaying his lawyerly ability to keep track of points he wished to pursue. "The overall impression I'm getting is that the marriage wasn't quite what it appeared to be."

"What did it appear to be?" she asked.

"Successful, I guess. With all that that implies."

"Oh, it was successful. But success has a different definition for everyone. By Will's standards it was a complete success."

"And by yours, Emma?"

"I'm afraid I'm not yet able to comment. I've not yet finished the retrospective, you see."

"I can understand that."

Taken aback, she looked at him assessingly. "Can you, Richard?"

"I think so. After all, I've spent most of the past three and a half years working on my own purview. Tonight's the first time I've volunteered any opinion on my marriage to Dell, or on my feelings about it."

"Was it very unpleasant, the divorce?"

"As a matter of fact, it was relatively painless. She didn't want anything except one or two pieces of furniture, refused alimony or a financial settlement. She was determined we'd be friends."

"And are you?"

"It was hard as hell for me at first. Here was this woman I thought I knew, but not only did I not know her at all, she made me doubt everything about myself. To pretend to a friendliness I didn't feel would have been just too hypocritical. Seeing her hurt too much. I couldn't be a good sport when she'd left me shot full of holes.

135

It's easier now. We talk occasionally on the phone. She fills me in on what she's doing. And I've managed not to be bitter, even if the experience left me so doubtful about my abilities with respect to women that I've preferred to be alone rather than put myself at risk again by dating. Does that spoil *your* impression of *me?*"

"Oh, not at all. If anything, it allows me to feel more comfortable with you," she told him. "It's sad, though, when someone we love manages to render us less than we were before we invested so heavily in that person. I'm sure you must wonder, as I do, how something posited to be so fulfilling, so beneficial, ends up being so damaging. It's bound to make one very cautious in emotional matters."

"I'd say that sums it up exactly. So . . ." He smiled. "Here we are, two of the walking wounded, comparing notes. I have to tell you this is a hell of a lot more productive than my year and a half of therapy." If she was crazy, he decided, her madness was utterly compelling.

"You went to an analyst?" she asked eagerly. "I've thought so many times this past year of doing that."

"It didn't help much."

"No?"

"Sorry, no. It could've been the analyst, but I tend to believe it wasn't what I really needed." He hadn't, until tonight, been able to pinpoint what it might be that he did need. But looking at Emma, talking to her, hearing her speak of herself and her marriage, he was beginning to feel he was closing in on some answers. It was an unexpected bonus.

"That's a pity," she said. "Another door closed."

"Not necessarily. Maybe you've just saved yourself some time. But then again you might luck out and get someone decent. I've been told you've got to shop for analysts just the way you do new clothes, or a set of dishes."

"But you felt it was a waste, did you?"

"Somewhat." He tore a round of French bread in half and dipped it into the black butter that was all that remained of his dinner. Then he wiped his mouth and hands with his serviette and watched her eat the last of her duck. It was so pleasurable to look at her he could happily have sat for hours observing the way her eye-lashes cast slight shadows on her cheek, or the way the silk went taut across her breasts as she aligned her knife and fork on the plate and sat back in her chair. His desire to touch her was so sudden and so powerful it took him complete-ly by surprise. It had been so long since he'd allowed himself even to think about women that he'd almost forgotten the exquisite ache of undi-luted lust. The contents of the letter came back to him word for word: *It's been almost two years since the last time I made love . . . I sleep in the nude and lately when I touch myself I've imag-ined it was you . . . I've felt your hands and mouth on my body, felt you inside me . . .*

There was a subtle change in his expression, in the way he was looking at her. She saw it, could even feel a corresponding visceral response. Of its own volition her body began readying itself to receive, her cells collecting, shrinking then expanding. She uncrossed her legs and pressed her knees tightly together as she drank some more of the wine. So very many ways to die. Countless, unthought-of ways. Why was freedom so illusory a state, such a nebulous condition? Why wasn't it something tangible one could grasp with both hands and keep?

Chapter Ten

Richard was fairly sure he knew what had happened but couldn't understand why, or if they shared equally in the responsibility. For every action, he thought, there's the good old reaction. A sparking synaptic connection got made in his brain and somehow Emma had picked up on it. Not an actual action, not an actual reaction. Two brains uniquely engaged in a fairly unprecedented communication. It was unfortunate that the conversation just prior to the moment when it all fell apart had prompted the first spontaneous physical response he'd had to a woman in several years. As if possessed of supernaturally sensitive antennae, she'd picked up on it, had known instantaneously that his interest in her had taken on sexual overtones. And their conversational ease had dried up, disappeared. They were all at once like two strangers at an airport both waiting for a flight, attempting to prove their civility to one another but privately wishing they didn't have to.

Neither of them wanted dessert. They drank their coffee in near silence, making polite comments about the quality of the food, the ambience of the restaurant. While the previous two hours had passed all too quickly, the fifteen or so minutes they spent over coffee before he signaled to the waiter for the check seemed interminable. He felt defective, and wondered if there wasn't something about him after all that repelled women. Doubt settled over him like an ashy mist. He tried to think of what he could say, what might regenerate their former ease, but all he could think of was his own deformity. He was, in some fashion visible only to women, horribly flawed, and he'd been indulging in gratuitous egotism to believe it could go unnoticed. Emma couldn't even look at him now, and he was having difficulty pretending everything was all right. Perhaps instead of worrying over the issue of her sanity he should have been worrying about his own.

In the restaurant parking lot, he unlocked the passenger door and waited for her to seat herself, scrupulously avoiding looking at her legs as she swung them into the car. It was entirely possible his eyes communicated a menace of which he was unaware. His every action had become suspect.

Once behind the wheel with the engine running he made one last valiant effort to save the evening and to resurrect his confidence. "Would you like to go somewhere to hear some music?" he asked, fastening his seat belt.

"I think I'd like to go home please, Richard,"

she said quietly, without looking at him.

"Of course." He released the hand brake. His inclination was to floor the accelerator, get Emma back as fast as possible to that hulking pile of gray stone on the waterfront. But he drove carefully, watching the speedometer, irritated now by the Bill Evans tape. Why the hell had he let down his guard? He knew better than to trust appearances, to take at face value what merely appeared to be acceptance by a woman, especially a woman who'd taken to writing letters and then denying their authorship.

"It isn't your fault, Richard," she said, as if reading his mind. "I like you very much. You mustn't think you've said or done anything wrong. I have certain . . . thoughts . . . There are things that come back to me . . . I can't . . . I'm sorry." She swallowed and turned to look out the side window, despising herself for ruining a fine evening and upsetting this kind, very sensitive man.

He couldn't think of a thing it would be safe to say. Despite her effort to absolve him, he still felt deeply and hideously flawed. He upped the volume slightly on the speakers, knowing he should respond to her, but not able to get past his renewed self-doubt.

She looked out at the night, dots of light here and there, hopelessly grounded by the futility of her optimism. Willard Bellamy would never die. He was more alive in her too-malleable brain than he'd ever been in reality. Those ropy gray coils inside her skull bound him to her in ways she'd never have believed possible. Will's body was dead but his essence permeated her being. And what he'd failed to accomplish in life, he'd managed to do in death: he'd taken her over completely. His occupation was so absolute, in fact, that she had to wonder what point there was to her continuing efforts to live. It would be infinitely less painful simply to accede, to swim away into merciful darkness and find peace in oblivion. She could go to a place where no demands were made, where the souls of the dead were left to float for eternity.

He pulled in and coasted to a stop at the apex of the circular drive, still searching for something to say that might end the terrible silence. He knew it was childish, but he wanted to protest the unfairness of what was happening. Emma was someone he genuinely liked, someone he found intriguing, and touching; a woman whose thoughts were as exciting to him as her face and body. Despite the curious business of the letters, she was rewardingly forthcoming at some moments, enigmatic at others; she was unpretentious, charmingly candid, and had offered him glimpses of her interior life that appealed to him tremendously. She'd given him a strong intimation of her losses and he recognized her as a fellow traveler—both of them picking their way through the rubble of past history.

As he shut off the engine he could see peripherally that she'd removed her seat belt and was sitting forward, ready to get out of the car. Swallowing his pride, temporarily rejecting the image of himself as incurably flawed, he undid his own seat belt then turned toward her. Feeling very much out of his depth, he spoke her name and reached over to take hold of her hand. Her fingers closed tightly around his and she fell back against the seat as if she'd been shoved in the chest. Falling, she cried out "Oh!" as if in sudden pain.

She was caught between the anticipated relief of an end to fighting and the fear that she might be making the final foolish capitulation in a lengthy series. But every time she managed to take a small step forward either Will's legacy of control or another cruel letter arrived to send her into retreat. Now, miraculously, Richard was struggling past his own uncertainty to offer her reassurance. He'd broken through the invisible barricades Will had erected all around her; he'd succeeded in penetrating her isolation and, by pure instinct, was giving her what she needed most: a palpable human connection.

Her hand going even tighter around his, Richard watched her head turn stiffly, saw her agonized expression, saw her breasts rising and falling as if she were struggling to breathe, and he prayed he wasn't misreading the urgent signals she was sending. He leaned across to kiss her, and everything went immediately, almost violently, out of control.

Her need was so immense it left no room for anything else, not even the resident ghost. She was free to touch someone alive, to feel the baby-soft flesh behind his ear, to press the flat of her hand to his chest and feel the drumming there, to take her hands over him while he held her face between his hands and kissed life back into her mouth. She stopped her frenzied attempt to learn the breadth and depth of him just long enough to kick off her shoes, reach up under her dress and drag off the hose. She knelt on the seat and tugged at his clothes, then lifted her knee across his lap, and fed him into her body in one rending motion.

Astounded by her rapacity, he followed her lead, too aroused by her sudden utter accessibility even to think. He was, without warning or any preliminary gesture, lodged in the depths of her body. In an unparalleled manner, he'd been taken in by this bewildering woman. And he needed, more than anything else, ever, to go wherever she chose to take him.

She remained motionless, her hands gripping his shoulders as he unbuttoned her dress, lowered the slip, and spread his hands over her breasts. Her softness lulled his brain like a dream-inducing narcotic. He had to press his lips to her neck, feeling the fluttering pulse there, her life humming under his tongue.

Every gesture, every slight touch, was another shock of discovery. He wasn't Will. The texture of his hair, his skin, his lips, were different. The set of his shoulders, the span of his hands, the taste of him and his touch were all different. His manner, his breathing, his scent, were new. The feel of him, even the configuration of their fit, was foreign but overpoweringly right. He filled her absolutely, leaving no room for the ghost. Swaying slightly, she loosened his tie, pulled it off over his head, then worked to open the buttons of his shirt. She ran her hands over the smooth terrain of his chest, shaken by the realization of what was happening. She was actually making love with a man other than Will, and he was allowing her to lead; he wasn't insisting on taking over the control of what she'd initiated. That in itself seemed nothing short of astonishing.

She arched back, her hand directing his, indicating the degree of pressure. There. Intense, grinding pleasure, rippling upward in waves. She closed her eyes and gave in to the delirious instinctive motion, her hips rolling to a primal rhythm. Caught by the inner insistence, she came forward, buried her face in the spicy fragrance of his neck, and let it take her. The ferocity of all the accumulated passion seeking an outlet thundered through her, emerging from her throat in a burst of triumphant laughter.

She shuddered in his arms, gave a deep jubilant laugh, kissed him three, four, five times quickly on the mouth, then, without warning, was overtaken by sobs. She folded against his chest and wept so plaintively he could only shelter her with his body while he stroked her spine, seeking to soothe her.

He was overcome by so many emotions, not the least of which was a welling affection, even love, for this fragile yet incredibly complex woman. His only concern was perpetuating the compelling emotional connection the two of them had somehow managed to make. He held her and caressed her, and waited for her tears to subside. He believed she would, one way or another, explain herself. And, moved, he realized he was beginning to understand her. They *had* made a connection, a highly significant one.

After a time, she lifted her head and asked, "Have you a handkerchief, Richard?"

He found it and pressed it into her hand. "Are you all right?" he asked, watching her dry her face and nose, his arm around her waist, his feeling of protectiveness toward her even more heightened. He was only beginning to know her, but he very much wanted to continue the process.

She couldn't answer; she had no idea whether or not she was all right. She marshalled her senses to take stock. They were still joined. She was sitting half naked on his lap and he was rubbing his cheek against her breast, his arm holding her securely. This man was capable of selflessness, of great caring. She'd behaved inexplicably all evening, but he'd accepted her without criticism, had followed her lead even at great possible risk to his emotional equilibrium. "I do apologize for this," she said, "for performing like a slattern in your splendid automobile."

"Don't apologize," he said quietly. "Don't do that."

"Thank you, Richard. You're very kind." She bent to kiss him very softly, merely letting her lips rest against his.

"Please, for God's sake, don't thank me, Emma," he said hoarsely. "Don't let's either one of us do any of that. It has no place here, not now."

"I imagine we make quite a picture," she whispered, so close she could feel his lips curve into a smile, could feel his relief at her ability to find some humor in the situation.

"Any chance Bernice might be looking out the window?" he asked, his fingertips making patterns on her spine.

"None whatever. She's gone to her son's for the weekend."

"I wouldn't have cared," he confided. "So much for observing the proprieties."

"Nor would I." She breathed deeply, slowly,

appreciative of his gentleness. His touch hadn't once been less than respectful. "I must go in," she said, not moving.

"Want me to go away?" he asked.

"I can't bring you into the house. That's in part why this happened as it has. It's . . ."

"Ssshh!" He placed a finger across her lips. "You don't have to say anything." It was true. He understood.

"I can't cook, you know, Richard. Not proper meals. But I can make breakfast. Would you like to come back in the morning? It'll be all right then. And after breakfast, you could come with me down to the beach to give Calla her run."

"What time?"

"Is eight too early?"

"Eight's just fine. I'll be here."

"Richard, you're a lovely man. Please don't ever feel responsible for the peculiar conduct of the women you meet. Some of us are simply peculiar. It's nothing you inspire." Reluctantly, sadly, she broke the connection. Then, in a gesture that moved him very nearly to tears, she tenderly cleaned him with the handkerchief. It was an act somehow more personal than their lovemaking, the gesture of a woman not only comfortable with her own sexuality but in no way inhibited about displays of intimacy. These brief ministrations revealed more of her than anything they'd so far said or done together.

Turning aside she raised her skirt and without the least self-consciousness wiped the tops of her thighs. "I'll launder this," she said, keeping the handkerchief.

147

Needing to reciprocate, he drew her slip back up, then lifted the dress onto her shoulders. He would have fastened the buttons but she covered her hand with his and said, "Don't bother." She sat looking at him, breathing slowly and steadily, her lips slightly parted.

"I wish I could tell you," she began, then stopped. It was impossible. How could she explain any of it to him when she hadn't yet managed to come to terms with everything herself? His uncommon tolerance drawing her to him, she went close to kiss him again, then sat back thinking to leave, only to discover she had to touch him one last time, kiss him just once more.

"Will you be all right?" he asked, stroking her short silky hair. "Do you want me to see you inside?"

"I'll be quite all right," she assured him, running her thumb over his eyebrow, then down the side of his nose. "Safe home, Richard," she said, and opened the car door. Quickly collecting up her things, she closed the door and went barefoot up the front walk to the door.

He waited until, with a wave, she'd gone inside and closed the door. Unable for the moment to move, he sat and gazed at the front of the house, blinking as the majority of the exterior lights went off. It wasn't until the chill of the night reached through the car to wrap itself around him that he shifted and began to straighten his clothing. He couldn't help smiling at the thought that he'd just made love to Emma Bellamy in his car, of all places. At last, he turned the key in the ignition, glad to feel warm air come pushing out of the vents.

Before turning onto the road he looked back at the house. The downstairs lights had been switched off, and those in several of the upstairs rooms had been turned on. He imagined her going from room to room, traveling past the shrouded mirrors and unoccupied bedrooms. Emma all alone in that huge house with only a small dog for company. What did she do in there, month after month, alone? Was she going to sit down now and write more letters? Had she another personality of which she was unaware? Or had Bernice made a mistake?

Calla didn't need to be walked. She'd undoubtedly taken herself out through her private little door cut into the lower panel of the back door. Emma refilled the water bowl, added more food to the second bowl, then bent to scratch behind Calla's ears. "Good girl," she murmured. "Such a good girl."

Calla trotted along after her as she went back through the house and climbed the stairs to the second floor. She waited while Emma got undressed then followed her into the bathroom, where Emma ran her hands slowly over her breasts, down her sides, across her belly, then over her buttocks. She was swollen and could still feel faint after-tremors at the base of her belly. Calla came close, circling Emma's legs, sniffing. Emma turned on the water in the shower stall, then put one hand between her legs. Sticky seepage, physical evidence, proof that what they'd done had been real. Calla could smell it, could identify Richard's scent on her flesh. She shared all her secrets with Calla; Calla would never betray her.

"I took another man into my body," she whispered to the little dog. "I allowed him to fondle me, explore me. I encouraged Richard Redmond to touch me anywhere he chose. Yes, I did, Calla. You can smell it on me, can't you? I let him see me come. Will called it that. *Did you come?* Couldn't he tell? Where was he that he couldn't see? It was wonderful, thrilling. Wicked."

Richard had known without her having to put her orgasm into words for his enlightenment. He'd held her as if he knew where she left off and he began, not as if they were without beginning or end; not as if she'd become his grafted appendage, his performing toy, his compliant automaton. Richard had inflicted nothing on her, but had bestowed pleasure and had given his trust into her hands without exacting either payment or an explanation that was shaped to meet his satisfaction. Richard hadn't judged her actions, hadn't found her deficient or substandard.

"He accepted me as I am, Calla," she whispered. "Just as I am."

What an extraordinary gift! How generous he was with himself! He'd managed to survive with his best instincts intact. Perhaps she too would survive, after all.

Chapter Eleven

Emma was up at five and at work in the office half an hour later, a cup of coffee going cold beside the lap-top. Having recalled the first chapter from the disk, she quickly read it through, then, satisfied, began Chapter 2.

Referring to the two letters and her annotated index cards, she described the heroine's reaction to the receipt of the first letter by her old friend Edward, then cut away to the series of secondary characters and their activities.

Her eyes on the blue letters appearing on the screen, her fingers moving steadily over the keyboard, she directed people to move, to reveal themselves by their words and gestures, their physical appearance, their quirks. Turns of phrase, certain preferred expressions, mannerisms and particular habits; the pitch of a voice, the set of a head, attitudes; all the small details that went to comprise a complete character were carefully set down. It was deeply satisfying work, layering qualities on the skeletal frames to create unique individuals possessed of hopes and fears, memories and secrets.

At seven-forty she stored the partial chapter on the disk, shut off the machine and carried the half cup of cold coffee down to the kitchen. She stood by the sink for a few minutes, making an effort to pull her attention into the immediate present, away from the events of her paper world. It was always with great reluctance that she left that world and the singular opportunity it afforded her to control absolutely everything. Returning to reality was inevitably a letdown, and she wondered as she had so many times before if other writers experienced the same sort of deflation at having to relinquish, however temporarily, their hold on the sphere of their own creating. With a sigh, she rinsed the cup, then set about organizing breakfast.

She had the coffee-maker going and bacon under the broiler when the doorbell rang. Richard, precisely on time. She wiped her hands on a paper towel and hurried to the door.

He was mildly disappointed to see her in one of her typical long cotton dresses. It was admittedly arbitrary but he'd halfway expected her to be wearing something more in keeping with last evening's red dress. This bulky dress was, to him, emblematic of the Emma he'd known before, not the Emma she was revealing herself to be. Nevertheless he had to smile at the sight of her, fondness for her flowering in his chest.

"Good morning, Richard. Please come in," she said. And he stepped over the threshold, wanting to touch her hand or kiss her cheek, acknowledge in some way the closeness they'd attained the night before, but he could tell simply by her posture that any physical display on his part would create difficulties.

Daylight, she thought, altered everything, placed constraints on one's spontaneity. "Come along to the kitchen," she said. "I've got breakfast underway." She turned and started through the foyer, and he followed, the aroma of bacon awakening his hunger.

"Please, do sit down. Will you have some coffee?"

"I'd love some," he said, remaining on his feet, watching her open a cupboard to get cups. "How are you?" he asked, wondering if she was regretting what had happened the previous night.

"Oh, I'm fine," she said, pouring the coffee.

"Everything's all right?" he asked doubtfully.

"Yes, fine. You take cream, don't you?"

"Thanks." She got cream from the refrigerator while he took several steps across the room, wishing he had less doubts about so many things. He'd always been reasonably cautious but since the split with Dell he'd become far more so. The only way he could be certain Emma was being truthful was by reestablishing contact, no matter how minimal. So he approached the counter and touched her on the arm.

She turned and looked at him questioningly.

"*Are* you all right?" he asked.

She took hold of his hand, saying, "Yes. Are you all right, Richard?"

"Me, I'm fine. I was just worried . . ."

"There's no need to be." She smiled, both her hands now holding his. "I'm rather inhibited here. You understand."

"Sure."

"I think the bacon may be burning," she said suddenly, and grabbed a pot holder as she looked into the oven. "I'm hopeless at trying to organize food. Will actively discouraged me from cooking."

Carrying the cups to the table, he sat down asking, "What did you do when you lived on your own?"

Using tongs to place the shriveled strips of bacon on a paper towel, she said, "I had a hot plate. I heated tins of soup, spaghetti, that sort of thing. We weren't really meant to cook in our rooms, although everyone did." Depositing the broiler pan in the sink, she ran hot water over it, then leaned against the counter. "My next-door neighbor cooked quite elaborate meals on her single burner. I remember climbing the stairs and breathing in wonderful aromas. A truly singular woman. I never knew what precisely she did. She was older, in her late forties, I should think. And she kept irregular hours. Rather round, on the shortish side, quite an appealing, very good-natured woman. She'd stop to talk if we encountered one another on the stairs or in the hallways. She had short curly hair, and a jolly face, very intelligent eyes. She wore black predominantly, but I think only because it suited her. From her voice it was evident she'd been to a good school. I could never decide, nor did she ever say, why she was living in a small—not nearly so small as mine, but not very much bigger—bedsitting room with little that I could see in the way of possessions. I quite often wonder what ever became of her. I liked her very much, although I can't for the life of me remember her name. Is the coffee drinkable?"

"Perfectly," he said.

"I tend to make it too strong," she said. "I hope you like scrambled eggs. Since I invariably break the yolks, it seems only sensible to scramble them."

"I'll be happy to make the eggs, if you like."

"You can cook?" She looked prepared to be impressed.

"I don't know about cook, but I can definitely do eggs. Shall I?"

"Please. I'll fix the toast."

He found a griddle in the drawer under the stove and started on the eggs while she dropped four slices of bread into the toaster, marveling at the novelty not only of being allowed to fiddle about in her own kitchen but of seeing Richard only a few feet away helping prepare the meal. Will wasn't going to come striding in to frown disapprovingly and suggest she leave the cooking to the housekeeper who was paid, after all, to do it.

Here was Richard, looking very nice in gray flannel slacks with a navy sweater over an open-necked white shirt, brown loafers, navy socks, smelling pleasantly of bay rum. She felt like an imprudent schoolgirl whose parents were bound to return home at any moment and reprimand her for taking liberties. Calla pushed in through her plastic door and came over to sniff at Richard's trouser cuffs.

Emma dropped down to stroke the dog's head, certain Calla had now made the unequivocal connection between Emma's scent of the night before and Richard's scent this morning. Calla slid out from beneath Emma's stroking hand and butted her head gently against Richard's calf. He half turned, smiled and bent to take hold of Calla's muzzle, saying, "How's the pooch, huh?"

Emma watched him play for a few moments with the dog before going back to the eggs. Will had ignored Calla, hadn't liked her, hadn't wanted Emma to buy her. But she'd insisted. And Calla, as if to demonstrate her understanding of where her loyalty lay, had never gone to him for attention. A very clever little dog. The toast popped up, causing Emma to jump. Her hands unsteady, she reached for the butter, opened the drawer for a knife.

"If you've got a couple of plates," Richard said, "we're all set here."

She put the plates beside the stove, then carried the toast and a jar of raspberry jam to the table. Distractedly she sat down and drank some of her coffee. "Where do you live, Richard?" she asked as he came over with the food. "This looks very nice. Unblemished yolks."

"I rent a condo in Norwalk. After the divorce, we sold the house, and I split the proceeds with Dell so she'd have enough to buy another place." He picked up a strip of bacon and took a bite. "I couldn't be bothered looking at properties. Besides, I wasn't sure what I wanted, or where I wanted to be. A friend of mine lives in the complex and told me about the apartment. I drove over after work one evening. It looked all right, so I signed a lease."

"And is it all right?"

"The apartment itself is fine. Plenty of room, a fireplace, two bedrooms, two bathrooms. But the noise is phenomenal. I don't think the contractor put one shred of insulation in the walls or ceilings. Fortunately, my upstairs neighbor travels a lot. He sells something or other, so he's only home one or two weekends a month. When he is home I can hear every step he takes. I can hum along to his stereo. I can even hear him talking on the phone, although, fortunately, I can't actually make out what he's saying. Speaking of the stereo." He pulled a boxed cassette out of his pocket. "I made a dub of the Bill Evans tape for you."

She accepted the tape and looked at his neat printing on the box liner. "How very kind of you, Richard!" She smiled at him, then looked up at the ceiling. "There are speakers all over the house. Perhaps you could put it on."

"Glad to. Where's your stereo?"

"Will's stereo is in the library. I don't know how to work it. He didn't allow anyone to touch it. Shall I show you?"

She got up and led the way to the library, pointing out the components housed in a built-in bookcase.

"Why wouldn't he let anyone touch it?" Richard asked, taking a look at the sleekly black Bang & Olufson tuner, CD and cassette players, graphic equalizer and turntable.

"I expect he thought I'd damage it," she said from the doorway.

He flicked the power switch, inserted the cassette, adjusted the levers of the graphic equalizer, then the volume. "It's an expensive system," he said as they returned to the kitchen, "but not all that easy to damage." He was getting a revised picture of Willard Bellamy, one he didn't much admire. "I'm beginning to wonder just what kind of man your husband was."

"Exacting, specific, inflexible, generous, clever," she said, as if reciting from a list, "and old. Not just chronologically but almost in an historic sense. He was *old*. I find it close to impossible to discuss him, Richard. Aside from causing me to feel appallingly disloyal, I begin recrudescing."

"Pardon?"

"It's a fresh outbreak of oozing sores at a point when you've thought the disease was quiescent."

"Christ!" He automatically reached across the table to take hold of her hand.

"I do apologize," she said stiffly. "This is hardly an appropriate moment to be quite so graphic. I hope I haven't spoiled your appetite."

He glanced down at his half-eaten meal then back at her, giving her hand a squeeze. He was about to speak when suddenly a figure erupted into the room. Startled, they both looked up. Everything happened so quickly that neither he nor Emma had time to say or do anything. The figure flew across the kitchen and delivered an open-handed blow to the face that nearly knocked Emma sideways out of her chair.

Leaping to his feet, Richard grabbed the woman by the arm, exclaiming, "What the hell do you think you're doing?" The woman's face was so twisted by anger that it took him several seconds to recognize her as Janet, Willard's oldest child.

Tall but overweight, clad in a dark green track suit and Nikes, Janet stood glowering at Emma, breathing heavily. She had her father's strong features and blue eyes, with shoulder-length medium brown hair. She would have been attractive had it not been for the pronounced frown lines between her eyes and the deep parenthetical indentations on either side of her mouth that made her appear considerably older than thirty-seven. He recalled seeing her at the funeral and thinking her ravaged appearance at the time was due to grief. He could see now that the look was permanent.

Stunned, her hand rising automatically to her cheek, Emma righted herself, trembling as adrenaline surged through her bloodstream and sent her heartbeat wild, rendering her briefly incapable of speaking.

"Isn't this *cozy!*" Janet snapped contemptuously at Richard, trying to free her arm from his grip. "The little widow and her latest boyfriend. Let *go* of me!"

"Are you okay, Emma?" he asked, releasing Janet but taking care to position himself between the two women.

Rising to her feet, her cheek livid from the blow, Emma said, "What's wrong, Janet? And how did you get in? I don't believe I left the door open."

"How dare you say such things!" Janet cried, pitching a crumpled letter at Emma. "It just proves what I've always believed about you. Pretending you give a damn. You've never fooled me for a minute."

Oh hell! Richard thought. Another letter. How many had been written? And why? Emma seemed completely mystified. He simply didn't know what to think, or how to react. But he was impressed by the dignified fashion with which

Emma was handling the situation.

"Janet," Emma said, trying to reason with her, "I have no idea what you're talking about. Why not sit down and have some coffee. We'll all calm ourselves, and you can tell me what's upset you so. Perhaps I can help."

"Help by staying out of our lives!" Janet snapped. "You can't have everything you want! I won't let you come between Laurie and me."

"I'm not trying to come between you," Emma told her. "I'm very fond of Laurie, as you well know. But you're his mother and always will be. No one can take that away from you, Janet."

"You can't drop the pose, can you? Playing the injured party, behaving so reasonably, making it look like I'm the crazy one."

Emma, feeling wearied, studied her step-daughter's contorted features. Janet's anger was so formidable and so deeply entrenched that Emma doubted if she'd know how to live without it. Emma had, from the very first, made a special effort to be friends with all Will's children, but Janet, even then, had been very wary of her as well as overtly resentful. To Janet's mind, Emma had deprived her of her father's love and attention, and nothing Emma could ever say or do would convince her otherwise. Janet had very conveniently managed to bury the real facts, finding Emma a fitting target for her pent-up frustrations.

Emma still believed Janet had got herself pregnant with the idea of arousing her father's sympathy. Instead, for reasons Will took with him to the grave, he'd chosen perversely to refuse to allow Janet's boyfriend to see or speak to her. And when Janet pleaded with him for permission to have an abortion, he'd refused that, too. His behavior had been so cruelly incomprehensible that Emma had secretly offered to help Janet in any way she could. For a few moments in Janet's bedroom that evening, only two months after coming to live in this house, they'd almost attained a closeness. Janet had looked at her with an expression of such naked fear and bewilderment that Emma had been ready to believe they'd finally made contact. Then, her face closing down, her voice laden with contempt, Janet had said, "Your goddamned permission isn't worth shit! You're not even legally an adult. Just get the hell away from me. Okay? Leave me alone and stop trying to win me over. It'll never happen."

"Janet, I'm sorry you're upset," Emma now said, resisting the impulse to touch her smarting cheek again. "I'd like to help, if I'm able."

"You wouldn't have a child of your own, so you think you can have mine. Maybe you can fool Susan and Edgar, but you don't fool Shawn and you sure as hell don't fool me. Always so sweet, always so willing to *help*. Well, you're not having my son!" Janet cried insistently. "So keep away from him, I'm warning you."

"I have no wish to take Laurie away from you. I never have had. Do you have a key to the house, Janet? You must." How had she managed to get one? Emma wondered, looking at the crumpled paper on the floor. Another letter. It and Janet's unrelenting anger made her feel progressively wearier. She couldn't enumerate the times she'd had ugly confrontations with this unhappy, angry woman. Now someone had embarked upon a letter-writing campaign that was responsible for yet another nasty scene. Why was this happening?

"Perhaps you should leave." Richard again reached to take Janet's arm.

"Won't you please sit down and let's try to see if we can't reach some understanding," Emma said.

"You can't quit, can you?" Janet ducked around Richard, saying, "Yes, I have a key! You want it? Here! Have it!" She threw out her fist and with all her might stabbed the point of the key into Emma's upper arm. She hesitated for no more than two seconds, the expression on her face a warring mix of raging self-justification and disbelief at her own actions. For just a moment, Emma thought Janet might capitulate and give in to her visible dismay. But she didn't. She whirled around and tore out of the room. The front door slammed so hard it seemed to shake the entire house.

The only color in Emma's face was her reddened cheek. The trembling fingers of her left hand hovered over her injured right arm as she stared at Richard. Then, very abruptly, she sank to the floor and lowered her head to her knees, whispering, "I feel faint."

Breaking into a sudden sweat while simultaneously thoroughly chilled, she tried to make sense of what had just transpired. But she couldn't think. Her focus was entirely on her arm, on the pain that seemed to boil outward from the wound.

Distraught, wishing he knew what on earth was going on, Richard grabbed a handful of ice cubes from the freezer, wrapped them in a tea towel, then held it to the back of Emma's neck, saying, "Hold this steady if you can while I have a look at your arm."

Emma obeyed, and he lifted her sleeve, cautiously peeling shredded fabric out of the way to inspect the wide blood-filled wound.

"Where do you keep your first-aid supplies?" he asked, sickened by the sight of the injury and the rivulets of blood running down her arm.

"Hall bathroom," she whispered. "Under the counter."

"Don't move. I'll be right back."

When he returned, she still had her head down and was now holding the makeshift ice pack to her forehead.

She didn't say a word while he cleaned the wound, but gasped—tears springing to her eyes and her body going rigid—when, with apologies, he sluiced it with iodine. After applying a liberal amount of antiseptic cream, he covered the jagged puncture with a gauze pad, then wound a length of gauze bandage around her upper arm and gingerly taped the end in place.

"You should probably have a tetanus shot," he said, retrieving the crumpled letter and the key from the floor and putting them, along with the small medical kit, on the counter. "Let's get you up into the chair." He helped her, asking, "Are you okay?"

She nodded, blotting her face on her sleeve.

"Emma," he said, sinking into the chair beside her, "what the hell was that all about?"

"I don't know," she answered, letting her head slowly come to rest on the tabletop. "God! I don't know. Another bloody letter."

"Mind if I have a look at it?"

Her mouth dry, she said, "No." Obviously something in the letter had pushed Janet right over the edge.

He got it from the counter, smoothed it open on the table and read it quickly. "Want to hear this?" he asked, bending to pick up the towel of ice cubes and hold it against the back of her neck. This letter, like the one he had received, sounded strongly like Emma; it had her phrasing, her preciseness. She had to have written it. Yet nothing in her behavior indicated the slightest awareness. He felt a quick darting pain in his temple and wondered if it was the precursor to a headache.

"No. Not now." She couldn't possibly take it in. She was fighting not to faint, her hairline prickling as if from a cold draft, while sweat streamed down her sides, between her breasts. She had to keep swallowing as fluid repeatedly filled the floor of her mouth. In the aftermath of the attack she felt terribly afraid.

"Is there anything I can do for you?"

With a visible effort, she lifted her head. Her face was still devoid of color, except for her cheek, which would likely show bruising. "Would you please take me out of here?" she asked almost inaudibly. "I really cannot bear to remain in this house just now."

"Where would you like to go?" he asked her, mildly alarmed by her waxy pallor and by his growing sense that he, and she too, were caught up in some escalating madness. The question was, whose?

"Anywhere."

"You need to change out of that dress first, Emma. It's got blood all over it."

"Richard, I'd be most grateful if you'd fetch some clothes from the dressing room. The keys are on the chest of drawers, and my handbag's there as well."

He went to do as she'd asked and she twisted her head to look at her bandaged arm. The pain radiated in heated throbbing waves up into her shoulder and down to her fingers. The smell of her scarcely touched breakfast made her stomach rise menacingly. Calla was sniffing at the blood spatters on the floor, her body quivering. "You were frightened, weren't you, Calla? Come here. Good girl." Using her left hand, Emma hefted the dog into her lap. Calla nuzzled her head against Emma's belly, settling. "Poor Calla. Don't be frightened," Emma crooned. "No one will harm you." She sat with her left elbow propped on the table, her clammy forehead resting in the palm of her hand, concentrating on not being sick.

Richard came back and Emma said, "Would you mind if Calla comes with us? She's upset, and I hate to leave her."

"Sure. That's fine. What'll we do about the dishes?"

"We'll leave them. I'll clear up later."

"Okay." He scooped Calla up from Emma's lap. "Feeling any better?"

"Marginally." She took the letter from the table, pushed it into the pocket of her dress, and said, "I'm ready. Let's go."

Wondering why she'd taken the letter, Richard reached into his pocket for the car keys.

At the front door, she stopped. "I've got to code the alarm system." She pressed a series of numbers in the panel to one side of the door.

"Now," she said as they left the house, "any other surprise visitors will have to deal with the police."

The only sensible place he could think of to go was his apartment.

Emma stood at the top of the living room and slowly looked around while Calla went directly to the terrace doors and gazed out as if admiring the view.

"I just grabbed the first things I saw and put them in a bag," Richard said. "If you'd like to change, you could use my bedroom, or the bathroom. How about some coffee?"

"May I lie down, please?" she asked, wondering if the handsome, well-made furniture reflected his taste or that of his ex-wife. The paintings, she was willing to wager, had been Richard's choice. Two quite large, finely executed abstracts of soft billowing forms in subtle pleasing colors.

"The bedroom's this way."

The king-size bed with a heavy brass headboard had been neatly made, the blankets folded back, the pillows squared. Her eyelids were very heavy and her arm seemed to be throbbing now in syncopation with her heartbeat. With her awkward left hand, she tried to unzip the dress.

"Here," he offered. "Let me help."

"Thank you, Richard." She stepped out of the dress, then her shoes, and lay down on the bed. "I'm very sorry for involving you in this frightful mess."

"I involved myself," he said, drawing the blankets over her. "As it happens, I'm glad I was there to prevent it from being any worse. The woman was completely out of control. Try to rest now.

166

I'll take Calla out for a walk."

Her heavy eyelids anxious to close, she said, "I'll feel better in an hour or so. I'm sorry, but . . ."

"Shh. Go to sleep."

Returning with Calla from their half-hour walk, he slid the terrace doors closed quietly, then tiptoed down the hall to look in on Emma. She hadn't moved, but slept exactly as he'd left her. He crept away and went to the kitchen to make some coffee, then sat down on the sofa to read the *Times*, with Calla curled up at his side.

Turning first to the business section, he took a swallow of coffee, started scanning the Friday Dow-Jones closing averages, then lowered the paper, thinking how different, how much more occupied the apartment felt with a woman asleep in the bedroom. Then he reviewed that brief ugly incident in Emma's kitchen, wincing as once more he witnessed Janet driving the pointed end of the key into Emma's arm. It had been one of the most murderous scenes at which he'd ever been present. He meant it when he'd said he was glad he'd been there. He strongly suspected Emma might have sustained even more serious injuries had he not been. And he dreaded the idea of anything happening to her. Crazy or not, he wanted nothing bad to happen to her. He was beginning to believe she'd been through enough unnecessary unpleasantness. Her marriage to Willard was anything but the perfect pairing he—and a lot of others—had imagined it to be. Had Willard driven her beyond reason? Based on his own dealings with the man, he could readily envision how difficult Willard had been capable of being.

His hand extended to pat the small dog, he realized that he cared very much about the woman sleeping in his bedroom. And he wondered how so much had managed to change in so short a time. He hoped to God she wasn't in the throes of a breakdown. But if she were, he already felt fairly committed to seeing her through it.

Chapter Twelve

She opened her eyes and looked around the room, remembering where she was. Then she noticed the clock radio on the parson's table beside the bed and saw that it was twenty minutes past twelve. She'd slept for close to three hours. She got up and went into the en suite bathroom.

Richard was an orderly man but, she was relieved to note, not obsessively so. While everything was clean, and the towels were folded, the lid was off his shaving cream and his razor had been left in the soap dish. Silly perhaps, but she liked the fact that the toilet roll was positioned so the paper rolled forward rather than pulled from underneath.

Carefully avoiding her reflection, she opened the medicine cabinet, found a bottle of aspirin, and took three. She rinsed her face and mouth with cold water, squeezed a bit of toothpaste onto the tip of her finger and rubbed it over her teeth. Richard's robe was hanging on the back of the door. Her arm protesting, she slipped it on and went out to the living room.

Upon seeing her, he put aside the book he'd been reading and stood up, asking, "How do you feel?"

"Much better, thank you. I hope you don't mind my borrowing your robe."

"Of course not. Are you hungry? There's fresh coffee, and I could fix you something to eat."

She came across the room and leaned against him, resting her cheek against his chest. "I would like some coffee, thank you."

He smoothed her hair, asking, "Not hungry?"

"Not just at the moment."

"How's the arm?"

"Sore. I probably should see my doctor, have an injection as you suggested."

"Sit down and I'll get you some coffee."

"Who selected the furniture?" she asked, trailing after him to the kitchen.

"Dell did."

"Yes, I thought that. But you chose the paintings, didn't you?"

He looked over. "Why do you think that?"

"They're the sort of images I expect you'd like."

With a smile, he said, "You're right. Now, would you like to hear some of my deductive reasoning?"

"Certainly."

"My guess is you picked out the furniture in the solarium."

"I most likely would have, had I been given that option. Unfortunately, you're wrong. I'm afraid everything in the house predates my marriage to Will."

Carrying two cups back into the living room, he asked, "Aside from writing, what, if anything, did Willard let you do?"

She sighed and drank some of the coffee. "I want you to know there's no truth to anything Janet said this morning. I was never unfaithful to Will. And I've never tried to take Laurie away from her. I do love him, though. Do you know him, Richard?"

"I vaguely recall meeting him after the funeral. I knew Janet had a son, but that's about it."

"Laurie is the only member of the family who has ever loved me without equivocation or qualification. His mother has despised me since the day we met, and has never missed an opportunity to make that clear to me. Initially she came up with the silly fiction that I'd allowed myself to become impregnated in order to force Willard to marry me. Then, when a child failed to materialize, she did a complete about-face and accused me of refusing to have his children. My God!" she exclaimed. "How could I have forgotten?" Putting down her coffee, she went to the bedroom to get the letter from the pocket of her dress. Another piece of her stationery, or an exact duplicate. "I'd better read this," she told Richard, sitting again at his side.

"Maybe you should wait," he advised.

"It's that bad, is it?"

"Let's say it's not the most complimentary thing I've ever read."

She looked down at the letter, then back at Richard. "What do you think of me, Richard?" she asked, the pulses in her throat and injured arm in tempo, her whole body palpitating.

He seemed taken aback by the question. Then, a canny glint to his eyes, he said, "Let me ask you a question first then I'll answer yours. Was I just handy, or was what happened last night a result of some feeling you have for me?"

"You *believe* Janet's accusations!" she said in a hurt whisper.

"No, I don't." He shook his head.

"Then how could you possibly think that I'd use you simply because you were, as you say, handy?"

"I apologize if I've offended you, but all of a sudden I seem to be involved up to my ears. I need to have some idea where I stand."

"You're afraid I'll make a fool of you," she guessed correctly, seeing the accuracy of her assessment register in his eyes. "I can't think what I've done to give you the impression I might be capable of such reprehensible behavior, but please accept my apology for involving you. I think it would be best if I go home now. I'll get dressed and telephone for a taxi." She went to pick up the bag with her clothes, saying, "It will only take me a moment or two to change, then Calla and I will be on our way." Stricken, she turned and walked away to the bedroom.

Why did you do that? he asked himself, watching her draw her reserve around her like armor. The matter of the letters notwithstanding, why was he trusting one moment, suspicious the next? This was Dell's legacy. But it wasn't written anywhere that he had to subscribe wholeheartedly to the implication that he was directly or indirectly to blame for her evolution into a lesbian. "Not only are you not to blame," Dell had asserted repeatedly, "but, first of all, I resent the idea that this is something so monstrous that somebody has to be held accountable, and, secondly, if you keep on with this endless analyzing, I'm going to start believing you think you're more important than you are. You *are* important, Rich, but not *that* important. So stop beating yourself up, and stop treating me as if I've signed on with a coven of witches. I'm exactly the same person I've always been. I just finally, thank God, found out something significant about myself and my preferences. Okay?"

The truth was he was afraid. Emma had roused him out of the benumbed emotional state in which he'd been living since his initial disbelief at Dell's announcement had been replaced by grim acceptance. If you cared, you got hurt. It was that simple. So he'd pulled on a protective overcoat of numbness and buttoned it securely to make sure nothing got past the outer layer. Emma had snipped off the buttons, the coat had fallen from his shoulders, and the rusty cogs of his emotions had once more started turning. Instead of being grateful, he was responding with mistrust. And if he didn't make some show of faith right now, he'd be back in that heavy overcoat before the end of the day. Maybe it did hurt to care, he thought, but wasn't feeling preferable to numbness? A few hours earlier he'd been prepared to commit himself to seeing Emma through the present confusion, or whatever it was. Given time to think about it, he'd started pulling back. Either he was involved, or he wasn't. Which was it going to be? And how important was it anyway, being safe?

Emma was dismayed to find the bag contained the new blue jeans and a sweater. Since she'd put on pantyhose and a slip to wear under the now ruined dress, her shoes and underwear were all wrong. Still, she had no choice but to put the jeans on over the hose and wear the sweater with nothing under it. It would only be for the half hour or so until she was home.

Shrugging off the robe, she struggled out of the slip. The pain of lifting her arm made her eyes water. She placed her hand over the bandage, feeling heat radiating through the gauze. Remembering the way Janet had come at her, her stomach went tight, as again the key ripped downward into her flesh. Initially she'd felt nothing. Then, like sharp pointed teeth, the pain had bitten into her. She squeezed her eyes shut for a few moments, then opened them and reached for the sweater. She'd go home and telephone Dr. Fisher, ask for an emergency appointment. Then she'd clear the kitchen and spend the rest of the day working. With luck she'd complete the second chapter and make a start on the third. The writing was going well, coming quickly. She'd concentrate on her work. It was the one thing that never let her down, the one thing upon which she could rely; it was the place where she could hide. No one would enter her paper world without invitation. She alone was in control of it; she oversaw every aspect of its administration. She could decorate the rooms as she chose and move about freely in them; she could select the people who inhabited that world and engineer their thoughts and actions. She knew precisely why things happened and could predetermine every event. In her world no one acted arbitrarily, or struck pointless blows. Everything happened for a reason and she took great pains to supply a cause for every effect. The paper world was the only safe place she knew.

"Please don't go," Richard said from the doorway.

Folding her left arm over her breasts, she turned her head to look at him.

"I got scared," he admitted sheepishly. "A lot's going on. I mean, things seem to be happening pretty quickly."

"Life," she said coolly, "is sometimes like that, Richard. Things rarely happen when it's convenient."

She wasn't going to make it easy for him, and maybe he deserved to sweat a little. He had two choices: he could give it up, go back to being her lawyer and maintain his distance. Or he could stay open to the possibilities and try to deal with events as they happened. He was tempted to take the simpler route and bow out. But his inner voice was telling him this might be the last chance he'd have to jump back into life and splash around with everyone else.

"Last night was like a fantasy," he said, reaching deep inside himself for the truth. "It was probably the most exciting thing that's ever happened to me. I think I'm fairly much like most people in that there are things I think I might want, but I know the chances of my having them are slim to remote. Last night I wanted you. I got what I wanted, but I discovered that getting what I want doesn't come for free. We always have to pay. I'm beginning to see that maybe you, more than most of the rest of us, know that. The cost in this case is my putting aside my defenses. That's kind of hard for me. I got burned and now I'm gun-shy about committing myself. The thing of it is, I don't seem to have a choice because I'm already committed.

"You asked me what I think of you and I didn't give you an answer. I used the classic lawyer's defense and countered a question with a question because I got a little panicky. That was childish, and kind of stupid, and I'm sorry for that. I envied Willard from the day the two of you came to the office to revise his will. I wondered why he'd been lucky enough to find the one woman I'd have wanted. You want to know what I think of you, I'll tell you. I think you're the most exciting woman I've ever met. You're certainly the most magnanimous in terms of what you gave of yourself last night. And since I'm dealing with the truth here, I might as well go whole hog and tell you that what scares me the most is the possibility that I'm falling in love with you. What you said the other day about losing your independence rang a bell because in a lot of ways I did the same thing with Dell. I didn't depend on her per se so much as I depended on the marriage. But I just don't see how you can care about someone and not surrender at least a small part of your independence. That doesn't mean you turn yourself over to the other party for safekeeping like some sort of human safe-deposit box, but I can't see how it's possible to care, to be involved, without giving up a part of yourself."

"I don't think it is possible," she allowed. "I haven't asked you to do *anything*, Richard. Oh, yes, I've made a few practical requests. But I've asked nothing of you, beyond questioning your thoughts about me."

"People don't just blithely ask each other to hand over parts of themselves, Emma," he said sagely. "It's been my experience that caring prompts us to *want* to. I can feel myself getting ready to do it and my instincts for self-preservation have started the alarm bells going off in my head."

"I see," she said, still cool. "You'd like to keep an intellectual hold over your emotions to guarantee you don't lose control. You make it sound as if I'm some sort of swamp you might drown in."

"That's unkind, to both of us," he argued.

"But true nevertheless."

"I'd like you to give me, to give both of us, a chance."

"At what, Richard?"

"I don't know. At whatever's going to happen, I suppose. Unless last night satisfied all your needs."

"Not even remotely. It was never my intention to make love with you in your automobile. Or at all, for that matter. It wasn't a notion I allowed myself to entertain. I apologize again for my unseemly behavior." She paused a moment, then asked, "Did it satisfy all your needs?"

Crossing his arms, he leaned against the doorframe and gave her a smile. "It just whetted my appetite."

"Is that so?" she asked, her shoulders losing some of their rigidity.

"That is so," he confirmed.

"And what do you propose to do about that, Richard?"

"What would be permissible?"

"Taking my recent injury into consideration, I should think anything short of arm wrestling would be acceptable." She smiled, very relieved. They'd gone about it in the most circuitous fashion possible but they'd managed to arrive at an understanding. "You know," she said, "Will would never have admitted to the majority of things you've just said."

"I'm not Will," he said.

She wanted to say, Thank God for that, but instead said, "I know," and allowed her arm to fall. "Unless you want Calla to participate, I suggest you close the door. I need to use the bathroom, if I may."

"Of course."

She heard him close the door as she reached into the medicine cabinet for the aspirin bottle. She took three more with several handfuls of water, then, keeping her back to the mirror, worked off her pantyhose. She came out of the bathroom to see him draping his slacks over the back of the chair by the desk. She sat down on the edge of the bed, admiring his body, struck by the contrast between Richard's healthy, still-firm flesh and her memory of the way Will had looked just prior to the discovery of the cancer.

After they'd been married about eight years, Will had taken to making love to her in the daytime because, although he'd never have admitted it, by nightfall he was simply too tired. It had been on an afternoon in January, two and a half years earlier, that he'd interrupted her in the office with a direct invitation to the bedroom. Annoyed at being caught midthought, she'd said, "I'll be along in a few minutes," then tried without success to complete what she'd been saying. Defeated, she'd given up and gone to the bedroom to remove her dress. She'd felt like a whore.

Overly aware of the mechanics, there'd been a moment when she'd looked at him kneeling between her legs and had seen him clearly, without benefit of the prior redeeming gentle glow of her affection. She'd seen the way his flesh sagged, the bony prominence of his knees, the slackness of his pale belly, the ludicrousness of his erection, and she'd had to close her eyes to the sight of him. He was old. By comparison she'd felt almost indecently young. Every nuance of her construction sang of her comparative youth. She'd felt healthy and limber, aware that she was very near the peak of her life as a woman. She'd allowed her mind to go traveling while he claimed her body, and she'd wondered if that was how prostitutes managed to survive the constant assaults on their flesh. It had been the last time they'd made love properly.

Richard came to sit down beside her, and she said, "You have a good body. You've taken care of yourself."

"I swim. There's a pool here. They'll be closing it up for the season any day now."

"I don't know how to swim," she said, placing a hand on his thigh.

"I could teach you. I used to teach a beginner's course at the Y, while I was at law school.

I'm worried about your arm. Please humor me and call your doctor. If he can see you this afternoon, I'll take you."

She picked up the receiver of the telephone on the parson's table, punched out Dr. Fisher's number from memory, then looked at Richard as the ringing started. In view of the fact that it was Saturday, she was a bit surprised when the nurse answered. She'd expected to get the answering service.

"It's Emma Bellamy here," she said, her eyes remaining on Richard. "I'm afraid I've had a bit of an accident and I was hoping Stephen might possibly be able to see me this afternoon."

"Hang on, Emma. Let me see what he says."

"I'm on hold," she told Richard.

Caring was the damnedest thing, he thought. Once you'd made up your mind to it, it took you over. Your entire being became directed outward, focused on the object of your caring. Common sense slid to one side, and emotion and instincts assumed control. Either you battled it—as he'd tried briefly, unsuccessfully, to do—or you succumbed. He slipped off the bed and knelt in front of her.

"Emma, four-thirty," the nurse said. "Okay?"

"Yes, thank you. I'll see you then."

Richard put both hands on her knees. She lowered the receiver into its cradle. "Four-thirty," she said, a daunting fondness for this man overtaking her.

"Good."

Her knees had started to quiver. She allowed her legs to relax. Richard's hands moved slowly up her thighs. She laid her hand on his cheek, her breathing accelerating. He gently maneuvered her forward, kissed the side of her knee, parted her legs, and lowered his head. She fell back, whispering, "Oh, my *God!*"

Eyes tightly closed, she felt as if she were giving birth to him, laboring determinedly to complete the process. Then suddenly, too close to the edge, she had to pull away, raising his head with both her hands. "Richard, stop!"

He looked up at her, asking, "Why?"

"I'm not good for more than once. This isn't the way I want us to be just now."

"Dell preferred this. She didn't like having me inside her."

"Listen, Richard!" she said feverishly. "You're not Will. And I'm not your former wife. I want you inside of me. Come up here!" She tugged at his arm. "There are only the two of us here. No ghosts!" Pushing aside the pillows, she stretched out, urging him down on top of her, relishing his weight upon her. His flesh fit snugly to his bones; it had elasticity; the muscles underneath flexed under her hands. God, the difference, the exquisite novelty of holding life tightly in her arms! "I can't get pregnant," she whispered, "and neither of us has been with anyone else for far too long." Guiding him forward, she lifted, shifting by slow degrees until they'd joined. Had she thought of Richard, ever, during those guilty late-night investigations of her own body? Had he been the one she'd projected on the darkened screen of her eyelids? For such a long time she'd felt gutted, hollowed, like a canoe carved from the denuded trunk of a tree. Richard slipped into the hollow, filling all the emptiness. She sought his mouth like a blind woman in the desert searching for moisture.

Anything can happen, he thought, battered by sensation and by his volatile emotions. You can hide out and be numb and unscathed, or you can take risks and find solace where it's least expected. Better by far, he thought deliriously, to take the risk.

Chapter Thirteen

Richard's head rested on her belly, his hand slowly stroking her breast. Drowsy, but kept awake by the constant throbbing in her arm, she absorbed his warmth, wishing she'd never have to move. She heard a door slam and instinctively turned her head, then looked up at the ceiling, perturbed, as heavy footsteps passed directly overhead. A moment or two of silence was followed by the sound of a radio announcer's voice giving the weather.

"How can you bear to live here?" she asked, appalled. Richard laughed softly and kissed her navel. "I told you."

He smiled up at her.

"But it's frightful! Doesn't it drive you mad?"

"It's irritating, all right. Fortunately, as I mentioned, he's not here that often. How are you?" He leaned on his elbow at her side, thinking again how very pretty she was.

"Aside from a punctured arm and a rather tender cheek, I've rarely felt better. You make love wonderfully well."

"I was inspired."

"Inspiration is no guarantee of satisfaction," she said. "You're too modest."

He studied her dark eyes a moment longer, then looked slowly down the length of her body. "You're beautiful, Emma, positively beautiful."

"I'm not at all," she disagreed with a shake of her head. "If anything, I'm misproportioned."

"You can't seriously believe that!" He saw no indication that she was fishing for compliments. Her features had taken on a grim cast.

"My shoulders are somewhat too narrow for my breasts, and my breasts are rather too large for my frame. I fully expect to wake up one morning soon and find them in my lap, like my mother's. I always envied my sister, Vivian. She had lovely small breasts. She, for some absurd reason, was desperately envious of me because mine were on the large side. It was most embarrassing at twelve to be the only fully developed girl in my class, as well as the tallest by several inches. The boys made obscene faces, waggling their tongues at me, and the girls circulated a variety of scandalous sexual rumors, none of which were true. My mother was no help. She sighed a good deal and peppered her conversations with words like 'curse,' and expressions like, 'woman's lot,' and men wanting 'only one thing' from a girl."

"From twelve to about nineteen, we do want only one thing," he joked, seeking to distract her from her self-deprecating litany. "I remember in high school the guys all sat around like drooling cretins, swapping lies about our prowess and speculating on whether or not it was true that Virgie MacDowell blew her dates."

"Poor Virgie," Emma said. "She was probably innocent."

"Nope. She blew her dates. I called her up and we went out a couple of times. It was her way of saying thank you for the evening. I don't think she liked it much. The whole thing lasted no more than two minutes, and I felt rotten, as if I'd taken advantage of her. It didn't stop the guys, though. Virgie had more dates than any other girl in the school."

"Do you know I had no idea people did things like that, until I met Will. I was fairly dazzled back then by what I perceived to be his inventiveness. It took me quite a few years to see that his repertoire was of a decidedly repetitive nature. One afternoon I suddenly had a profound sense of déjà vu and I realized that everything was happening precisely as it had every other time for years. He even said the same things, smiled or laughed at the same moments. Quite an alarming revelation, actually." She was telling too much, she thought, feeling an icicle of fear piercing her rib cage. "Don't you find it inhibiting knowing the fellow upstairs can very likely hear you just as clearly as you do him?"

"Until today it didn't matter. Where is your doctor's office?"

"Greenwich, the medical building next to the hospital. I'm going to have to go home first, get proper underwear and shoes."

He said, "Okay, we'll allow extra time," and she was again struck by his considerate instincts.

"I can telephone for a taxi, Richard. There's no need for you to chauffeur me about."

"I'll come with you. Unless you don't want me to."

"No, I want you to," she said, then, her eyes drawn to the ceiling, she felt the silence taking her over, pulling her away, and she was in the dining room of the house in Richmond with her parents and sister.

It was the summer bank holiday weekend in late August 1975 and she'd come down on the train for one of her Sunday visits, intending at an appropriate moment to make her announcement that she was going to be marrying Willard Bellamy. He'd already been with her to the American Embassy in Grosvenor Square to file her application for a visa.

She chose her moment carefully, after the dessert but before they moved to the lounge for coffee. "I have wonderful news," she told them, and at once had their complete attention. "First of all, my book is going to be published."

"Well," her father beamed, "isn't that splendid, Emma!"

"Are they paying you pots of money?" Vivian asked avidly.

"Very nice, I'm sure," her mother said dubiously.

"I met someone, you see, who's helped me tremendously," she told them. "An American publisher. He put me on to an agent some months back, and the agent rang me a week ago Tuesday to say he'd had an offer."

"Is it a lot of money?" Vivian asked.

"Quite a lot," Emma hedged, reluctant to discuss the terms with them. She doubted she'd be able to make them understand that she'd have accepted almost anything in order to be published, and that the twenty-five hundred pounds was, to her, a veritable fortune. "There's something more," she said, nervous of their reactions but hoping they might be happy for her. "I'm to be married."

"*Married*?" Her mother appeared shocked.

"Who to?" Vivian wanted to know.

Her father simply stared at her.

"His name is Willard Bellamy and he's the American publisher I told you about."

"Crikey, Em!" Vivian exclaimed. "You're going to live in America? That's super. Is he rich?"

"Who is this man?" her mother demanded. "How long have you known him?"

"Isn't it rather sudden, Emma?" her father said.

"I've known him almost a year," she told them. "He's divorced and has four children. He lives in Connecticut, about forty miles from Manhattan."

"Just how old *is* this man?" her mother wanted to know.

"He's somewhat older."

"Divorced with four children. I should think he's a fair bit older," her mother declared.

"He's forty-five," Emma admitted.

"What does a man of forty-five want with *you*?" her mother asked, aggrieved. "He's far too old! It's completely unsuitable! What *can* you be thinking of?"

"Forty-five." Vivian made a face. "That's ancient, for God's sake, Em!"

Emma looked at her father. He avoided her eyes.

"We're to be married in London on the fifth of December. We'll be leaving for New York on the sixth. I wanted to invite you to the wedding," she said, doubting now that they'd come.

"It's an outrage!" her mother cried. "Why on earth would you take up with a man old enough to be your father? And what, I'd like to know, is he doing with a girl your age?"

"The difference in our ages doesn't matter, not to him or to me. We get on wonderfully well. We love each other. He's been very good to me."

"I think it's disgusting," Vivian said, her lips curling. "An old man."

"You can't go through with this!" her mother said. "It's simply not right. You're far too young to know what you want. He's taking advantage of you, of your innocence. I've a good mind not to allow it."

"It's a mistake, Emma," her father said, looking as if he'd tasted something bitter. "You're throwing your life away."

"I'm not doing anything of the sort! And you can't stop me. I'm not a child," she defended herself, angered and, hurt that they'd condemn Will without ever meeting him. "I love him and we're to be married. I had hoped you'd come to the wedding, but whether or not you do won't change my decision."

There was a silence. Vivian looked at her long, lacquered fingernails, then worried a hangnail with her teeth. Her father kept his eyes lowered. And her mother glared at her, her mouth working.

At last her mother declared, "If you insist on going through with this, I can't see how we can continue to be friends."

The statement was so preposterous Emma

couldn't respond. The words were all there, crowding her mouth, but she couldn't get them out. *Friends? You're not my friend; you're my mother.* Was that actually how her mother viewed their relationship?

"I thought you'd be happy for me," she said finally, their animosity and anger fogging the air in the room.

"You're living in cloud cuckoo land," Vivian said. "It's pathetic, really, Em. Just the thought of someone that old touching me makes me sick at my stomach."

"Watch your tongue, young lady!" their mother barked.

"You could do better for yourself, my girl," her father said, looking saddened.

"He's probably only after live-in help for his children," her mother said cruelly.

"Oh good God! His children are grown adults!" Emma said hotly, which only exacerbated the situation.

They argued and cajoled, pleaded and threatened, until Emma said quietly, "I'll be going now. I'm sorry you feel this way." She looked at her sister a final time, disappointed most by Vivian's failure to support her. She wondered why she hadn't seen it sooner: Vivian, the rebel, secretly subscribed to all their rigid beliefs. And she, Emma, who'd always been the good child, the well-behaved obedient child, was in their eyes the true renegade, the ne'er-do-well.

On the train headed back to London, she'd gazed out the window, her throat aching. She'd refused to reconsider. She'd married Will. And she'd never seen her family again. They hadn't replied to her letters and in time she stopped writing. She'd never missed them.

Without warning, as Richard watched, she went off somewhere. Her face acquiring an expression of infinite sadness, her eyes turned opaque, her body went slack and she was no longer with him. He spoke her name. She didn't hear. He waited for her to snap out of it, but as minutes passed and she remained in this abstracted state, he began to feel frightened. It reminded him too strongly of those visits to the nursing home when suddenly, in mid-conversation, his mother would drift off, lapsing into an impenetrable silence. Initially he'd been unnerved by these episodes, but with time he'd come to accept them as an indication of her preoccupation with the panoramic interior display of the long life she'd lived. He'd put it down to her advanced age and deteriorating physical condition and to the many years she'd lived alone after his father's death.

To see Emma slip away into a state so strongly reminiscent of those trances of his mother's unnerved him. He wondered if while in this state she might have penned those damned letters. It seemed distinctly possible. After more than five minutes had passed, bothered by the completeness of her absence, he began trying to bring her back. Rather than attempt to converse with her, he applied himself instead to her body, deciding it was a subtler and somehow more direct route to her attention. It was also admittedly self-indulgent, since he was enchanted by the beauty she so strenuously denied.

He took his time examining the prominence of her hip bones and the smooth soft concavity of her belly, the taut flesh over her ribs leading to the satisfying rise of her breasts, the warm swell of her inner thighs, the polished curve of her shoulders. He kissed each of her fingers, the cool dry palms of her hands, the out-pushing knobs at her wrists; he traced the veins running from the bends in her elbows to her upper arms, tracked them to the hollow at the base of her throat. At last he could feel the rhythm of her breathing begin to alter.

For a moment, as his fingers slid over her, he was overcome by the staggering realization that he was in bed with Emma Bellamy, the wife of the late Willard Devlin Bellamy, a woman he'd long admired and had even coveted, but had never dreamed he might one day embrace. It was nothing short of incredible that he should now be in the process of acquainting himself with every aspect of her anatomy as well as with the many facets of her mind and personality.

Her hips began a subtle undulation, and resting his hands flat over her belly, he looked up to see her gazing at him.

"How," he asked, "did you ever get the idea you're not good for more than once?"

"Because I'm not," she said, then thought of what he'd confided to her about his sexual encounters with his former wife and felt compelled to elaborate. "That is to say, we didn't . . . he couldn't . . ."

It was becoming increasingly clear to him that the admissions she made about Willard were spontaneous, and that whenever she tried to respond explicitly to direct questions she usually failed. To put an end to her struggling, he said, "Shh," and laid a finger on her lips. "It's all right. I understand."

Fervently, she said, "I wish *I* did."

His hand slipping down again, her eyes grew round, and he felt her strain towards him. She made an indecisive move as if to prop herself up on her elbows then fell back, her eyes closing as she bit down on her lower lip. Stirred by her responsiveness, he lowered his head.

This time he didn't stop. It was, she thought, like a gift, something he wanted her to have entirely for herself. Generous Richard, giving simply because it gave him pleasure, not because somewhere he had a hidden agenda. All that was required of her was to accept the gift, to give herself over to it. She forgot entirely about the man upstairs, a brief cry escaping as her body froze for a moment, then convulsed.

Dr. Fisher looked at her cheek without comment. Then he asked her to remove her sweater and hop up on the examining table. He cut away the gauze bandage and bent close to look at the wound, straightened, shook his head and asked, "Emma, how did you do this?"

"I'd rather not say, Stephen."

"Okay, we'll skip the how part. But I need to know what did it."

"A key."

"A key?" He bent to take another look, and again shook his head. "That's a nasty lesion. I'm going to have to clean it out. It'll need a few stitches, otherwise it won't close properly."

"All right."

"I'll give you a local, but I'm afraid it's going to hurt some."

"I understand."

"You just lie down here while I get Judy in to assist."

The local anaesthetic seemed to have no effect at all. When he began probing, tears poured down her cheeks. She closed her eyes tightly to the instruments that seemed to be reaching deep into her muscle. She felt Judy's hand smoothing her hair, heard her murmuring comforting phrases. Then Stephen said, as if to himself, "There're bits of fiber in here. It's a good thing you came in. You'd have had a nice case of septicemia in another day or two."

Vicious pain. Something that felt as if it might be a needle piercing the heart of her injury aroused a sympathetic reaction in her legs. They twitched, and she tried to keep herself still, telling herself it would be over in a few minutes, just another minute or two. She willed herself away and, with relief, heard the sounds fade.

She and Will were on the Pan Am flight to New York. There had been no time for a honeymoon, but he had promised they'd take a week or two away after the first of the year. "Maybe Bermuda," he said. "Or somewhere in the Caribbean. Someplace warm with miles of white sand beach."

"I love the seaside," she said, "but I'm afraid I can't swim."

He looked at her as if she were joking. "You can't swim?" His expression implied he found this unthinkable.

"I've never had an opportunity to learn."

"Didn't you have a pool at school?"

"No. I expect pools are quite common in America. They're not in England. Very few of my friends know how to swim."

"Well, you'll have to learn," he said with finality, once again causing her to feel inept and doltish, just as he had in wiping off her makeup.

When they were in the limousine en route to Connecticut, he held her hand and said, "The kids're going to be crazy about you."

"Perhaps they won't. They may very well resent me, for any number of reasons. You shouldn't expect that they'll like me just because you do."

"You're so serious," he said with a smile, leaning across to kiss her. Then, sitting back, he said, "First thing we'll do is take you shopping for some clothes, and a decent winter coat. You'll freeze in that thing. Plus, we'll have to open a checking account, get you some credit cards." He went on for several minutes, listing countless things that would have to be done. Then, as if remembering her, he hugged her to his side. "I can't believe it's finally done, you're finally here. No more phone calls and letters, no more too-short visits. You're going to be right with me in the same house." He pressed a kiss to her temple. "Christ! I'm so in love with you. Tonight I get to make love to you in my own bed. And in the morning, we'll be able to have breakfast together. While I'm at the office, you'll have the entire day to yourself to write. There's already strong interest over here in *Strangers*. I've got an agent lined up for you to meet. I think we may even get into an auction situation, with half a dozen houses bidding. Are you excited, Emma?"

"Oh yes, very," she answered, looking out at the passing landscape, at the enormous automobiles speeding on the wrong side of the motorway, and the large garish billboards advertising cigarettes and beer. Snow on the ground, and houses with green and white plastic awnings over the front doors. "It's very ugly," she said, and at once feared she'd made another gaffe, for which he'd again cause her to feel witless.

He looked out the window. "It is," he agreed, to her relief. "But once we cross over into Connecticut, you'll see it's beautiful."

It was beautiful. And uncrowded, with no sidewalks, no shops nearby, nowhere to walk except along the abbreviated crescent of their private beach. She who'd relished each moment of her life in London, who'd loved the theaters and the restaurants and the museums and art galleries, found herself effectively cut off from those things. No shop windows, no custard tarts, no friends to ring up, no films to see on the spur of the moment, not even any quality radio programming of the sort to which she was accustomed. She had given up everything—her friends, her family, and her way of life—to live in isolation on the edge of the sea with her husband, a man she was coming to understand she scarcely knew, but to whom she was deeply indebted. She did love him, very much. And he was incredibly good to her, visibly proud of her, determined to protect her in every way. With time, he'd protect her so effectively she'd come to wonder if he hadn't managed, in the course of overseeing every aspect of her existence, to render her purely decorative and essentially useless.

"All done, Emma!" Judy was helping her sit up.

"You'll want to put some ice on that," Stephen

said, indicating her cheek. "I'll give you a prescription for Tylenol three, just in case. Judy will set you up with an appointment for next week so I can take out the stitches."

Judy assisted her off the table and handed Emma her sweater, saying, "Come on out when you're ready."

Richard put aside the *Newsweek* he'd been reading and came over, asking, "How was it?"

Emma shook her head and went to the hatch. Judy flipped through the appointment book, grabbed a card and filled in a date and time, then passed it through the hatch. Emma took the card, reached for Richard's hand and walked through the waiting room with him.

"Bad, huh?" he said as they headed across the parking lot to his car.

She nodded, determined to contain herself.

"I'm sorry." He put his hand on the back of her neck.

She turned, hid her face against his shoulder and cried noisily.

"Poor Emma," he crooned, and smoothed her silvery hair.

She wiped her face with both hands and stood back from him. "I feel better now." She gave him a weak smile. "For some idiotic reason I never feel it's my right to let it show when something hurts. One must be stoic, endure at all costs. Bloody nonsense! Thank you for waiting. I know it took ages."

"I didn't mind. I got caught up on all the news I missed back in eighty-six," he said with one of his beautiful smiles.

"Richard," she said soberly, "I like you so very much."

196

"Is it that terrible?" he teased.

"I'll begin relying on your kindness."

"And you think that'll lead to losing your independence."

"It's how it begins."

"Listen," he said, laying a finger across her lips. "You're not Dell, remember? And I'm not Willard. Remember?"

"You do understand that I need time to myself, that I have to work, and be alone to think?"

He stared at her for a moment, then laughed and kissed her on the forehead. "Emma, my dear," he said, "we all do."

"No." She shook her head. "That's the point, you see. It's what I haven't had for seventeen years."

He again stared at her, considering, then said, "I understand," and took her hand. "Come on. I'll take you home now."

"You're not hurt?" she asked anxiously.

"I'm not hurt," he assured her. "I do understand and everything's perfectly all right."

She exhaled slowly and went with him to the car.

Chapter Fourteen

The message indicator on the answering machine showed five calls. She pressed the play button and stood listening.

"Hi, Aunt Em. It's Laurie. I'm probably too late to warn you but Mom's a fire-breathing dragon because of that letter you wrote. She called me at the crack of dawn this morning, threatening me with death if I so much as phoned you. As if I'm about to listen to anything she has to say. Anyway, I'll be in my room all day working on this bullshit essay we have to turn in tomorrow. So call me. Okay? Talk to you later. Bye."

"This is Shawn. It's a goddamned good thing you're not home, because the mood I'm in, I'd be tempted to come down there and tell you to your face what I think of you and your charming letter. You've got nerve calling *me* a hypocrite because

I'm willing to stand up for what I believe in, but you're so full of shit. You'd have *loved* to go out sporting a nice coat of little dead animals, only Dad wouldn't go for it. You'd better watch what you put on paper, you bitch. You might find yourself slapped with a lawsuit. I hope *you* get cancer so we can sit around and watch you rot, the way poor Dad did."

"Em, it's Linda. Where are you at twenty to nine in the morning? Did you stay out all night, you naughty girl? Call me the minute you get in. I want to hear all about your date with the hunk. Gotta go. Call me! Love you, Bye."

The sound of someone taking a breath, then hanging up.

"Aunt Em, it's Laurie again. Call me, will you? I'm getting kind of nervous, imagining a bunch of weird scenes. Mom was so crazed this morning when she phoned, she sounded capable of murder. I really want to talk to you. Okay?"

She reset the machine then went into the bedroom to take off the constricting jeans and the rather itchy sweater. Relieved to feel the cool air on her skin, she started the tub filling and sat down on the side of it to read the third letter.

Janet,

Why do you imagine it's your ordained right to deprive other women of theirs? What noble cause do you believe you're espousing when you harass pregnant women, picket clinics, and try to intimidate doctors and nurses who are performing a valuable service? What purpose do you imagine you're serving in publicly demonstrating your private rage, selecting troubled women and teenagers as the focus of your amorphous anger?

It might be wiser to seek psychiatric assistance that would help you deal with your long-term anger, rather than targeting vulnerable women (as you were once vulnerable) and using them as an outlet for your great and abiding antagonism. It might also improve matters were you to use all that energy to become a better mother. In view of your ongoing failure to direct your son to your satisfaction, perhaps you should have found some way to have that abortion you so desperately wanted sixteen-odd years ago.

While it is fortunate that Lawrence has life, it is unfortunate that you've been exacting payment from him for the privilege since he drew his first breath. It would be infinitely wiser in the long run, and less debilitating for both of you, if you would give up attempting to coerce him into performing as you would wish and allow him simply to be the fine young man he is. It's certainly not too late to salvage your relationship. It might even be possible for the two of you to establish a healthy interchange of thoughts and feelings, something more appropriate to parent and child than your present dictatorial stance over an unruly subject.

Perhaps you should take some of these

facts into consideration before you next set out on one of your self-righteous, misguided stints in front of yet another clinic.

E.

Emma folded the letter and put it beside the sink before turning off the water and climbing into the tub. Calla came trotting in and with a little jump rested her front paws on the tub's rim. Emma scratched behind the dog's ears. "Someone's impersonating me, Calla, writing letters. It's obvious Shawn's also received one, as did poor Janet. Very puzzling and most distressing. Why're they doing it? Who can it be? It's eminently possible, although somewhat unlikely, that Susan or Edgar could be the culprit. Susan's rather too lazy, though, to go to the trouble of duplicating the way I write. But Edgar's neither lazy, nor without imagination." She withdrew her hand, thinking, and Calla curled up on the bath mat, head on her paws, eyes on her mistress.

"Why would Edgar do it?" Emma wondered. "We've always got on very well. Next to Laurie, I've been closest to him. It doesn't fit. Mind you, it's always the least likely suspect, isn't it? The one with the sublimated hostility, the long-festering injury. It's that ability to conceal the anger well below the surface, that talent for duplicity that makes for a first-rate villain."

Keeping the bandaged area of her arm out of the water by twisting slightly to one side, she sank lower, reviewing possibilities that overlapped into the plotting of her narrative and that finally took over her attention. Reaching for the soap and a washcloth, she began scrubbing herself, sort-

201

ing out some of the climactic details, envisioning scenes between her characters.

By the time the water was chugging away down the drain and she was quickly toweling herself dry, she was in a hurry to dispense with the telephone calls in order to get back to the word processor.

Throwing on underwear and one of her loose dresses, she stepped into a pair of old flat-heeled shoes, then went to the office.

She had to wait several minutes while the boy who'd answered the telephone at the dorm went to get Laurie. She could hear echoey laughter in the distance at the other end of the line, then a snippet of conversation as several boys went past the telephone. At last, Laurie came on.

She smiled automatically at the sound of his voice, and said, "Hello, darling. It's Emma."

"*O-kay!*" he said with audible relief. "I had visions of Mom chopping you up with an axe. Is everything all right?"

"She did pay me a brief visit this morning. It was rather awkward. She was very overwrought. But no harm's been done. How are you, Laurie?"

"I'm okay. The work load's unbelievable, though. We're not even two weeks into the semester and already they're assigning two-thousand-word essays. I've got one due tomorrow for history and another due Thursday for English lit. The lit's cool. We're doing *The Epic Of Gilgamesh*. We've only done the first chapter, but so far I'm really into it. So what're you up to?"

"I've started a new book."

"You have? Excellent! You're going to let me read it, right?"

"Absolutely. You know I rely on your feedback. You'd make a first-rate detective."

"Damn straight! So, tell me about the scene with Mom. It was major league bad, right?"

"Luckily, I had a friend visiting for breakfast. Otherwise, it might have been worse. It appears that someone's taken to writing rather hateful letters and signing my name to them."

"No way!"

"I'm afraid so, and your mother received one of them."

"Oh, man! What're they, like poison pen-type things?"

"Something like that. So far, I'm aware of four people who've received them. There are probably more. It's unnerving to say the least, but it has provided me with the basis of a plot."

"Well, that's good. Who d'you figure it could be?"

"I honestly have no idea. It's lovely to hear your voice, Laurie," she said. "I do miss you."

"I was thinking maybe I'd hop on the train and come see you the weekend after next."

"Laurie, I'd hate to have you antagonize your mother. I know you wish she'd show it in a somewhat more acceptable fashion, but she does love you. She's had a very difficult time of it."

"That's what you always say."

"Only because it's the truth. Your grandfather made very bad decisions, Laurie. He took frightful liberties with her life. He drove your father away, made it impossible for him to see your mother."

"So now she's trying to do the same thing to me."

"She means well."

"No," he argued. "She's jealous of you."

"All the more reason, my darling, not to antagonize her."

"Okay, so I won't say anything. I'll tell her I'm spending the weekend with a friend, and get Carl or one of the guys to cover for me. No way I'm going to let her stop me from seeing you," he said strongly. "I miss you too, you know. Say, who was over for breakfast anyway?"

"Richard Redmond, my attorney."

"Oh, yeah. I met him at the funeral, right? Tall dude, sharp suit and a moustache?"

She laughed. "That's Richard, yes."

"You're having breakfast now with your lawyer?" he asked with a wicked laugh. "Is he an item, or what?"

"An item, Laurie?"

"You know, like is it a *thing*?"

"Very possibly."

"That's cool, Aunt Em. Seriously. He's decent, and you deserve to have some fun."

"You're very sweet."

"No, I mean it. You really do. I know you had a pretty rough time the past couple of years. So, my Mom and Uncle Shawn finally give up that nonsense about Grandad's will?"

"Finally, yes."

"About time. So is it okay for the weekend after next?"

"Of course. I'll have Bernice ready the guest-room. Would you like to bring a friend, Laurie?"

"Really?"

"Yes, really."

"I'd like to, but if I do, then I won't get to spend as much time with you. Let me think about it, okay?"

"Certainly."

"I'd better go," he said. "I'm not even halfway through that lousy history assignment. I love you, Aunt Em."

"I love you, Laurie. You know to ring me if you need anything, don't you?"

"I know. Bye."

She put down the receiver and sat for a few moments, then lifted the receiver again to call Linda.

"Tell me everything!" Linda said at once. "Was it great, or a disaster?"

"It was eventful," Emma said carefully. "We went to dinner in Greenwich. A charming French restaurant with very good food. You might want to tell your new friend about it."

"I sure might. So then what?"

"We talked. He's a lovely man, very kind."

"You're not going to tell me, are you?" Linda said disappointedly.

"I like him enormously, and it would appear he likes me. More than that I don't care to say."

"Are you going to see him again?"

"Oh, I think so."

"Well, that's something."

"I'm working at the moment, Linda, so I'm not going to stay on the line. You understand."

"Sure. I'm happy as hell to know you're back in harness, sweetcakes. You even sound more like yourself. We'll talk during the week, huh?"

"Yes. I promise."

"Okay. Go work. Take care, Em."

* * *

She wrote without pause until eight-forty, when the telephone rang. Reluctant to talk, she let the answering machine take the call, and waited to hear who it was.

The outgoing message played, then Richard said, "I'm only checking in to see how you are."

She picked up and said, "Hello, Richard."

"Playing possum, huh?" he laughed. "Are you working? If you are, I won't keep you. I just wanted to hear your voice, and tell you I'm behaving like one of those drooling sixteen-year-olds."

"Are you? Not a very pretty picture."

"It's not all that bad. I'm mildly fixated, somewhat distracted, but generally in great spirits. How about you?"

"Well, let me see," she said, pushing back from the desk and stretching her legs. "I'm in a highly productive state, which is very good. And the sound of your voice has had an interesting effect on certain erogenous portions of my anatomy."

"Have you eaten ?"

"I have not."

"Are you hungry?"

"I believe I am."

"Would you like to eat?"

"I have an idea," she said. "But first, is your noisy neighbor in residence?"

"Can't hear a thing."

"Good. Why don't I collect some of the Colonel's chicken and bring you dinner? Do you fancy that?"

"I don't want to take you away from your work."

"I've put in three very productive hours, so neither of us need feel guilty." She looked at the desk clock. "I should be there in about half an hour."

"You remember the way?"

She smiled. "Like a homing pigeon. Oh! And I should warn you. I'm wearing one of those dresses I know you don't like."

"Okay. I've been warned."

After storing the nearly completed chapter on the disk, she switched off the machine and went to the dressing room for a sweater. About to leave, she remembered the cosmetics in the bedside table drawer and took a few minutes to apply a bit of eyeshadow, mascara, blush and lipstick. She viewed her face in segments in the tiny mirror, then returned everything to the drawer, picked up her bag and keys and went down to the kitchen to top off Calla's water and food bowls.

"I won't be late," she told the dog. "I'm going to see Richard. I know you dislike being left alone, but this is important. I can talk to Richard. He's very good for me. Being with him accelerates the review. Somehow now I don't have to go all the way back to the beginning every time. It's going more quickly. You be a good girl and look after the house while I'm away."

She coded the alarm, made sure the outside lights were on, then went out to the car.

"We seem to have covered a good deal of territory in a very short time," she said, wiping her fingers on a napkin.

They were sitting on the floor in the living room in front of the coffee table. Richard reached into the bucket, saying, "One last piece," as he pulled out a drumstick. "Does that bother you?" he asked, feeling very alive and exceptionally alert.

"Not at all. It's as if everything's accelerated. The feeling I have is of—compensation, I suppose. A great deal happening very quickly to make up for so many years when almost nothing did. So much has occurred in the last twenty-four hours that by rights I should be tired, but I'm brimming with energy. And not just sexual energy, but creative drive as well."

"The curative powers of lust." He grinned at her, brushing crumbs from his moustache. He'd decided finally that if she was a little crazy, then it was a craziness he admired. One way or another the issue of the letters would be settled, and with luck, long after it was an entirely forgotten issue he'd still be close enough to go on admiring her.

"I had no idea you were so profligate."

"I wasn't. It's a recent trend. And I could say the same about you."

"Oh, but I was," she said. "It's curious, really. Will took great pains to make me sexually aware. Very aware. It's as if I were the personification of some long-held secret craving he had to see himself in an omnipotent light. I came along, this relatively inexperienced eighteen-year-old, and provided him, all unwittingly, with an opportunity to educate me to his satisfaction." She paused to drink some of her wine. "He succeeded to an extent that I think frightened him, because having unleashed whatever latent sexuality I possessed, he was not capable of coping with it. I perfected an ability," she said softly, lowering her eyes, "to masturbate without making a sound and without noticeable movement. There were many, many nights when he lay—possibly asleep, possibly not—on one side of the bed, and I lay on the other, relieving myself quickly and efficiently without so much as a change in my breathing, all the while listening for any hint that he might be aware of what I was doing. He never knew.

"It made me feel grotesquely guilty. And deeply angry. I had to resort to furtive acts of self-gratification while the man responsible for my heightened awareness lay only inches away, of no use to me whatsoever. I felt ashamed, and cheated in the most terrible fashion. Because if he'd left me alone, if he hadn't gone to such lengths to stimulate me in the first place, I'd have been better off by far. But he'd taught me everything in his personal lexicon of concupiscent practices and then backed away because I'd so far outstripped his fantasies that he actually found me—or rather he found his *image* of me—frightening. It was as if he believed he'd created a monster.

"So," she said, returning her eyes to his, "you're very graciously enabling me to work off, as it were, a considerable head of steam. You're very giving and marvelously attentive. And I find you surpassingly attractive."

He shook his head. "All those adjectives. I'm wildly flattered, and completely smitten."

She smiled. "And very humble."

"I feel lucky, most of all."

"As do I."

"You do?" He appeared surprised that she'd say this.

"Richard, I'm beginning to believe your ego's almost as deflated as mine."

"Probably more."

"Probably not. At least Dell saw you as a separate individual, a person in your own right."

"And Willard didn't?"

"I was his creation. By the time I realized that, it was too late. Had enough?" she asked, lifting the lid for the bucket.

"More than enough, thank you."

"I'll just put this in your refrigerator," she said, and moved to get up.

"Don't bother." He put his hand on her wrist to stop her. "I'll do it later. If you get up you'll break the mood, and I love talking to you. You're remarkably candid. It inspires me to be equally open, something I haven't been since college, when I lived for spontaneous confessional conversations that would keep five or six of us up for an entire night. Until Friday evening, I'd forgotten how good it is to talk without holding all kinds of things back."

She looked at his mouth, then down at his hand on her arm, and felt again that excessive fondness that seemed to want to crack open her chest. "I've never talked to anyone the way I have to you. It feels almost dangerous, but I'm not willing to give it up. You bring me out of myself."

"Good. I'm not willing to have you give it up. I feel as if I want to do whatever I have to to hang on to you."

"Would you fight for me?" she asked.

"Fight who? Fight how?" A little shiver of alarm darted across his consciousness. Did she know about the letters after all?

"Ghosts," she said, feeling imperiled. She was flirting closer and closer to harmful facts. Putting her hand on his chest, she amended it. "Ghost singular, actually." She slid her hand down his chest to his lap and saw an immediate response in his widened eyes. "I've been thinking about doing this," she said. "And you've been thinking about having me do it."

She kept him constantly off balance, constantly alert, because he simply couldn't anticipate what direction she might suddenly go. Once again he was held captive by his fascination.

She deftly freed him from his clothes, and began stroking him with her cool fingers, all the while closely watching his eyes. She leaned forward to kiss him on the lips, and he held her face in his hands, trying to read her eyes. He couldn't. Nor could he keep a firm grasp on what he perceived, from moment to moment, to be her essence. She closed the distance until he could no longer focus and kissed him, as she had in the car, one, two, three times quickly, then slipped from his hold, dropping down over him.

"You taste sweet," she said after a time, sitting up to kiss him again on the lips.

"Jesus!" he said thickly, tugging at the zipper in the back of her dress.

"Not yet, Richard." Slowly, she kissed his eyes, his forehead, his chin, and then his lips again. "Wait." She ran her fingertips over his mouth. "It will be wonderful, if we can wait a bit longer." Once more she bent her head to his lap.

The pleasure was maddening. She was someone delivered intact to him from a dream he couldn't recall having. How could her husband have treated her as he had? Had Willard been a madman, he wondered, or the biggest fool who'd ever lived? What was madness, anyway? He no longer knew. And he didn't especially care. Everything was a matter of degree, and he wasn't qualified to judge. He didn't want to have to. He wanted only to keep hold of her, to keep learning more and more of her.

Chapter Fifteen

She drove home along the dark deserted streets, the window rolled halfway down, admitting the crisp night air that was fresh and contained hints of wood smoke. The radio was tuned low, faint violin music underscoring her thoughts. Her body felt easy and supple, powerful but at rest. Her mind was clear, uncluttered, and all at once her freedom was something real, something that could, if she trusted it, fill her with a sense of euphoria. *She was free.* No one was waiting at home for her. There were no demands to be met, no obligations to fulfill, except those she chose to set up for herself. She might do anything, go anywhere. If she could only believe with her emotions what her brain insisted was true. She yearned to pull her thoughts and feelings into accord, but was held back as if by unseen shackles.

Calla was curled up in her bed beside the stove, asleep. Emma made herself a cup of tea, wishing she could see Shawn's letter. She'd told Richard over dinner about the message and the existence of a fourth letter and his response was, "Someone's been busy." Considering that response now, she couldn't help wondering if Richard hoped to spare her additional pain by refraining from further comment. All in all, he didn't appear overly concerned about the proliferating number of letters. Was it remotely possible he was writing them? "No, that's ridiculous," she said aloud, getting a box of arrowroot biscuits from the cupboard before going up to the office.

She ignored the answering machine that indicated two messages had been left, and turned on the lap-top. A quick trip to the bathroom to get the third letter, then she settled in front of the machine and recalled the second chapter from the disk.

After rereading all three letters, she reviewed the index cards and sat for a moment thinking the letter Shawn had received might have provided her with some clue to the identity of the sender. Still, she didn't actually need to see what he'd received in order to create, for the purposes of the work-in-progress, a prototype based on those aspects of his character that might prompt criticism. She looked up at the screen, pressed the Return for a new paragraph, indented, and began.

Should she telephone the police? she wondered. What could they possibly do? The letters contained no threats, but merely pointed out certain salient truths. In all likelihood the police would advise her to take practical actions such as informing her friends that someone had embarked upon a letter-writing campaign on her behalf, but without her knowledge and consent, and that they should disregard any letters that appeared to have come from her. Or they might suggest she order new stationery. If the writer were someone close to her, the change of paper might prove discouraging.

Neither of these things was likely to have any positive effect, she decided. Words committed to paper constituted an act of finality. Once the letters had been received and read, they would exist for all time in the memories of the recipients. Unlike one's thoughts or ideas, they could not be altered or embellished. And what was most alarming about these letters was the degree to which they were truthful

Emma held down the Correct button and backed up.

And what alarmed her most was the truth of these letters. Each one of them clearly and succinctly stated private long-held views she'd had on any number of matters. She *was* strongly attracted to Edward Evans. She *did* believe Lillian had abilities she was failing to put to good use. Julia *was* an appalling mother. And Stewart *was* an outrageous hypocrite who on crowded streets at times of peak pedestrian traffic crept up behind women wearing expensive fur coats and blasted the unknowing women with bright yellow or acid green spray paint. He was convinced it was his ordained role to serve as an avenging messenger on behalf of all four-legged creatures who were slaughtered for their pelts. He had no compunctions, however, about wearing leather shoes or belts, or about using certain skin-care products and fragrances which were routinely tested by the manufacturers on laboratory animals. He ate meat. He also argued vociferously that the purported hazards of his secondhand cigarette smoke were nothing more than a part of the manic mythology proferred by self-indulgent fanatics determined to deprive him of his freedom of choice. He could not and would not see that his zealous defense of animals was a convenient device to reinforce his belief in his own importance.

Both he and his older sister Julia, the rabid antiabortionist, had little regard for the sensitivities of others. Only their views were right; only their actions were sanctified by a higher power. They alone knew that those who chose not to have unwanted babies, or to wear fur coats, were doomed to an eternity in hell. It would never have occurred to either of them that they, rather than their victims, were far more likely to end up as fuel for the ovens of Hades. Like all people who doggedly adhered to one rigid viewpoint to the exclusion of every other possibility, they were smugly blind to their own failings. Their causes gave them justification, elevated and ennobled them.

She wished she knew what to do. The situation was very frightening. Yet it was also oddly rewarding. The truth, regardless of how it was aired, was always welcome. Naturally, she had no desire to see anyone hurt. But it was good to have certain facts out in the open. The writer, however, seemed bent on destroying whatever credibility she had with family and friends. Was the idea to segregate her, to cut her off so effectively that she was rendered defenseless? What was the point? And why was it happening?

She walked from room to room of the house feeling an invisible but pervasive menace. Someone who very possibly had access to her home was bent on harming her. This person had chosen a most insidious means to accomplish his or her ends . . .

Her fingers skipped over the keyboard. Her eyes on the screen, she watched the narrative unfurling and stopped only to change a word or to shift a phrase. Her stomach grumbled and she grabbed one of the biscuits, then gulped some of the now-tepid tea to wash it down.

. . . "And you shall know the truth, and the truth shall make you free." Yes. But free to do what? Where? She stared into the blackened well of the fireplace, at the mound of gray-white ash beneath the grate, and saw her life in the ashes, something that had burned so long ago she could scarcely remember its warmth. The housekeeper would come along tomorrow or the next day and shovel the waste into a bucket, leaving in its place kindling and twists of paper to ignite the next fire.

Suddenly, contemplating the specter of her former self, she was stricken by a craving for Golden syrup, for lemon curd spread thickly on a doorstop of toasted white bread, for plaice and chips in a newspaper cone slightly damp with vinegar, for sweets from the tall glass jars in the tobacconist's shop at the top of the road, for a Cadbury's Flake bar, and an ice lolly; she hungered for Cornish clotted cream and strawberry jam on a fresh-baked scone, for puffy Yorkshire puddings and baked parsnips, for gooseberry tarts and summer pudding and treacle tart with custard.

What was she doing in this alien place, surrounded by people who hadn't her memories of the Number 7 bus to South Kensington or the escalators descending into the depths of the Victoria underground, of bank holiday weekends and Boxing Day and pubs that reeked of spilled beer? She'd all but inverted herself in her efforts to assimilate into the culture, learning to drive on the wrong side of the road, to say zee instead of zed, to take elevators and not lifts, to refer to lorries as trucks and motorways as highways; she'd learned the terms of reference, the vocabulary, and knew to refer not to petrol but gas, not to macs or anoracs but raincoats, not jerseys but sweaters, not jumpers but pullovers.

She participated in the easy credit, the drive-through banking, the touch-tone-telephone access to information, the fast food, the automated teller machines, the acquisition of clever household appliances to save her time in a kitchen she scarcely used. She'd immersed herself in the jargon, the conveniences, the catch-phrases, and the accelerated pace of the nation in which she was still, and would always be, a foreigner.

But she was free. She could leave. Could she leave? It was common knowledge that one couldn't go back, because inevitably, "back" no longer existed except within the confines of one's carefully hand-tinted memories. The past was a photograph album with yellowed pages and a cracked binding that contained referential images. If you allowed your eyes to travel beyond the deckle-edged boundaries of the snapshots you might see details—the nosy next-door neighbors, perhaps, leaning on the common fence between the properties, eavesdropping on the family picture-taking in the garden—better left forgotten. There was nowhere to go back to, and no one except one's self left to remember.

Tears ran irritatingly down her cheeks, dripped from her nose, and finally distorted her vision so that she was forced to stop. Blotting her face on her sleeve, she reformatted, then stored the text on the disk. Turning stiffly, she saw by the desk clock that it was after three. She was tired now, her neck ached and it was chilly in the office. She switched off the lap-top and walked across the hall to the bedroom.

The master's bedroom. Will had slept here for years before she came to live in the house. He'd kept his shirts and socks and underwear in that chest of drawers between the windows. And the box on top of the chest had nightly received his deposit of loose change, wristwatch, wallet, and keys. His various prescription bottles had stood in a cluster to the left of the segmented box. Later, when the bottles and boxes had multiplied, when each of the three nurses came for eight-hour shifts, the chest was no longer used. The battery having died, the watch hands stood frozen at two-eighteen. The credit cards in the wallet had expired and the new ones that arrived automatically in the mail were returned for cancellation. Thank you, but Mr. Bellamy no longer requires this credit line. Mr. Bellamy will not be purchasing hand-embroidered cotton undergarments, or Laura Ashley dresses, or L'Air du Temps cologne, or any of the dozens of other things his wife never wanted in the first place.

"Mrs. Bellamy," she told the rather too-cool room, "has poured the cologne down the sink and purchased a pair of quite tight bluejeans that chafe against her unaccustomed skin but which represent in no uncertain terms her right to make unilateral decisions. Mrs. Bellamy is considering making a bonfire, into which she will throw the shoes and the dresses and the childish underwear. Perhaps she'll celebrate Guy Fawkes day by incinerating the complete contents of the dressing room, with the exception of her recent acquisitions. In fact, Mrs. Bellamy is giving serious consideration to making another excursion to another department store to purchase even more items of which Mr. Bellamy would have disapproved. She has recently developed a fondness for the feel of silk next to her skin, and an interest in finding a fragrance that appeals to her in a way L'Air du Temps never did. She is thinking of allowing her hair to grow long again and of giving up shaving her underarms. After all, Mr. Bellamy never felt the need to shave his underarms on her behalf. Mrs. Bellamy is thinking about cashmere sweaters and lacy undergarments and a one-piece swimsuit. She is also thinking about Mr. Bellamy's Mercedes Benz, which has been sitting collecting dust in the triple garage for many months, while she has been driving the small Renault he thought suited her purposes and her all-important image as a simple, unaffected Englishwoman.

"And Mrs. Bellamy is now leaving her clothes on the floor and preparing to sleep in Mr. Bellamy's bed, her flesh strongly redolent of her quite recent and rather strenuous but exquisitely satisfying lovemaking with her newly acquired lover, the late Mr. Bellamy's highly competent attorney. She wishes Mr. Bellamy could know all these facts, could smell the scent of sexual congress on her skin."

Her arm aching, she turned out the light and closed her eyes.

She fell into a depression immediately upon waking. It was there waiting to embrace her. More potent by far than Richard's gentle ministrations, it entered through her pores and seemed to thicken her blood. She went reeling into the bathroom to take three aspirins before brushing her teeth.

Then she pulled on the heavy pink terrycloth robe Will had bought and which she hated, and went barefoot down the stairs to the kitchen.

Calla at once approached her, seemed to scent the darkness of her mood and settled into her basket, head on her paws, to watch Emma dump yesterday's coffee grounds before preparing a fresh pot. She watched Emma clean the dried blood off the floor with a wet sponge, and then throw the remains of the previous day's aborted breakfast into the trash.

While the water dripped through the filter, Emma rinsed the pots and dishes in hot water and loaded them into the dishwasher. Then she wiped the counters, tossed the sponge into the sink and sat down to wait for the coffee.

Once she'd consumed a cup of black coffee and had poured a second, she felt somewhat better, and looked over at the dog.

"I'll bathe, Calla, then you'll have your run on the beach."

Calla stepped out of her box and came over to rest her head and one paw on Emma's knee.

"What a good girl you are!" Emma praised her, stroking the well-shaped little head as she looked into Calla's intelligent eyes. "My dearest friend, my one true confidante. You know I love you, don't you? Shall we go up now? Come along and keep me company while I shower."

As if comprehending every word, she waited for Emma to pick up her cup, then followed as Emma headed back upstairs.

"Dreary bloody place, isn't it, Calla? Portraits of dead ancestors and ugly oil paintings Will bought as investments. I've a good mind to turn the lot of them over to Sotheby's, buy some lovely moody pieces like Richard's. He has very good taste, you know, Calla. You saw those paintings. Weren't they lovely?

"The Town Center's open today, from noon to five. Perhaps I'll drive down and buy a new robe, something that doesn't feel as if it's smothering me. I think I'll do that. I know I won't be able to write. It's gone again. I can't count on it the way I used to. I won't be long, Calla. Then we'll go down to the beach."

She stepped under the spray of hot water and was immediately lulled by the heat, made vulnerable to the lure of the retrospective.

Will said, "Promotion's invaluable, Emma. And it's damned hard to get for people who write fiction. We've got a great hook and we have to use it. You're only twenty and you've written a book that sold damned well in England for a first novel."

"But I didn't have to do any of what you're proposing there and, as you say, *Strangers* did well. Why . . . ?"

"This isn't England," he interrupted. "Do you trust me, or not?"

"Well, yes, of course I do. But I'm not comfortable with the idea of being marketed, as if I were some sort of product."

"If you want a future, you're going to have to get comfortable with it. I've spent an entire year grooming you for this. You're distinctive now, a unique *type*. It's going to be worth a fortune to you."

"Will, I really don't want a fortune."

"Then what the hell's the point, Emma?" His eyes had turned cold. She'd never seen him this way, so angrily insistent. If she continued to refuse, he'd probably grow even colder, angrier. And she couldn't bear the idea of it.

"I'm sure you're right," she said softly.

"You'd better believe it. I've spent my life in this business. If I don't know it, nobody does. I've been working up to this for the past year and a half. I want you to be a success. It's what you deserve. If you don't go along with the promotion, you'll never be more than a mid-list author."

"You're always saying the mid-list authors are the ones who put bread and butter on your plate. They're the backlist backbone of publishing, you said. Surely that's not so dreadful."

"Not if you don't mind having each new book sell between ten and twenty thousand in hardcover and a hundred thousand or so in paperback. Why would you want to settle for that when you can sell upwards of fifty thousand in hardcover and half a million to a million in paperback?"

"I don't know," she said almost inaudibly, filled with dread at the prospect of the promotional plans he and the agent and her publisher had decided upon. She found it difficult meeting new people and knew, as a result, that she came across as cool and aloof. Instead of protecting her from situations he was well aware made her nearly sick with apprehension, he was pushing at her to agree to an entire series of media interviews.

"Do you know what an appearance on 'The Today Show' is worth in terms of sales?" he went on. "Or an interview in a syndicated newspaper, or national magazine?, If it wasn't for me you'd never in a million years have a crack at an opportunity like this. I'm trying to *establish* you!" His voice was rising and for each decibel of volume it gained her fear mounted proportionately.

"Isn't it possible to allow my work to do that for me?" she asked, knotting her hands tightly together in her lap.

"Yes! *After* people have read about you in the papers and seen you on television and heard you on the radio. And *after* they've made their next trip to the bookstore and picked up a copy of your book and taken it home to discover you're not just a pretty face but a damned good writer. *Then* the work will back up the promotion. Jesus!" Exasperated, he grabbed a cigarette, lit it and took a hard drag. "Look, Emma! Will you just, please, *trust* me? I want the world to know that my wife isn't just a hot young number I married because I was having some kind of mid-life crisis. I want people to know you're a hell of a lot more, that you're gifted. And they *can't* know that if you don't *show* them. *Can* they?"

"I see," she said. "All right, Will."

And she did see. He was proving what a hell of a clever guy he was to have found himself not only a hot young number, but one who was a clever performing seal to boot. She owed it to him, didn't she? It was the least she could do, wasn't it, to repay some small measure of all he'd done for her?

"Good girl!" he said, giving her one of his warmest smiles. "That's my girl. Trust me," he said, patting her knee. "That's all I ask—trust me."

* * *

She made the water a little hotter and reached for the shampoo. "God!" She sniffed back the tears. "He talked to me the way I talk to the bloody dog! *God!*" she cried, wishing she could break something, kick in the glass stall door with her bare foot, or put her fist through the tiled wall. "GOD!" she raged, furious with herself now as she realized she'd soaked her bandaged arm. "You're an idiot," she told herself. "Have been for years."

Slowly calming down, she reminded herself that good things had come as a result of that initial promotion. The best thing had been Linda. And she'd had to fight him all over again for the right to have Linda as a friend.

"She's nothing, less than nothing," he said scathingly. "She looks cheap, dresses like a goddamned fifty-dollar hooker. She's got a smart mouth, a big mouth. You can't *afford* to associate with someone who'll have a negative effect on your public image."

"I don't have a public image," she'd said evenly. "It's all in your imagination."

"You damned well do!"

"No, Will. It isn't the public that has an image of me. It's you. I've let you tell me how to do my hair and my nails, let you choose everything from the clothes I wear to my automobile. I won't allow you to shop for my friends. I won't allow you to refer to Linda in those ugly terms. And I won't discuss it further."

Whatever it was he saw in her eyes caused him to back down. "Okay, baby," he relented. "I'm only trying to do what's best for you."

* * *

What was best for me, she thought, was that room on the fifth floor of the house in South Kensington, with the bath and toilet one floor below, and the telephone extensions on every landing. That cozy, elongated room, with an oversized wardrobe occupying the entire wall to the left of the door . . .

Chapter Sixteen

Upon returning home from the Town Center, Emma went up to the dressing room and methodically emptied it of almost every item Will had decided she should wear. Into sturdy green plastic trash bags went all the hated Laura Ashley dresses, the schoolgirlish white cotton underwear, the flat-heeled shoes, the quaint pastel-colored cardigans, the lumpy bathrobe and the long-sleeved flannel nightgowns.

She kept several shawls and handbags and all the jewelry. Everything else went into the trash bags, including the winter and spring coats he'd deemed suitable for her. She then dragged the bags, two by two, downstairs to the foyer for eventual collection by the Salvation Army.

That done, she unpacked her purchases and put them away in the now relatively empty dressing room. Three pairs of comfortable slacks, several

long-sleeved silk shirts in vibrant colors, jackets of
tweed and of black velvet, cashmere cardigans—
one dark brown, the other buttercup yellow—
pullovers in navy, plum, and emerald green, one
skirt of basic black and another of neutral brown,
a variety of lace-trimmed undergarments, half a
dozen pairs of knee socks, pantyhose, three pairs
of shoes, a magenta silk robe with a matching
nightgown, and a calf-length winter coat of chocolate brown melton wool, with epaulettes and a
belted waist. To go with the coat there was a vivid
orange scarf with matching gloves.

Now, instead of looking like a repository for
a collection of characterless, nunlike garments,
the dressing room contained color and texture
and reflected the rediscovered personal taste of
the owner.

Pleased, she went down to the kitchen to
have some toast and tea while reading several
pages of a recently published biography of Emily
Dickinson. Then she went to the wall phone to
call Richard.

"You sound very chipper," he said.

"I spent this afternoon shopping. I now understand why so many women enjoy it. It's highly
restorative. It was also the first time I've spent
my own money on things I actually wanted."

"Speaking of money, I meant to bring up the
subject of the estate on Friday evening. We really
need to sit down together and review the final
accounting and decide on the disposition of the
net proceeds."

"Let's see. It's just gone five. I'd like to put in
a few hours on the manuscript. Would you be
interested in meeting me for dinner, say at eight
or so? We could go over it all then."

"Sounds fine. How about Mexican?"

"Tell me where and I'll meet you."

She wrote down his directions, then said, "I'll be there at eight-fifteen."

"Great!"

After listening to the messages on the answering machine—two hang-ups, one with breathing—she set the alarm on the desk clock for seven-thirty, reviewed what she'd written so far, then settled in to complete the second chapter and begin the third.

"Willard's illness ate pretty badly into his capital," Richard told her.

"Yes, I had realized that."

"There are other assets, of course. The stock he received as part of the takeover, and his company pension plan, as well as his IRA and the contributions he made to the KEOGH account after he stepped down as CEO and began consulting. The major asset in terms of his holdings is the house, which, conservatively speaking in today's fairly depressed market, has an approximate appraised resale value of three point nine million. The accountants have drawn up a schedule, and I've got a copy of that for you, as well as copies of statements on the various plans and accounts. All told, the cash on hand amounts to just under ninety thousand. When we begin cashing in the various pensions, not including the insurance money already received, the estate'll gross another three hundred-odd thousand, for a grand total of four hundred and ninety-two thousand. That's after deducting the expenses above the major medical coverage, which ran to more than two hundred thousand. One of these days somebody's going to have to start making some serious changes in the health-care system in this country instead of just complaining about it," he declared.

"Janet and Shawn would be distressed to learn they'd been battling for very little," she said.

"That's the truth. After the costs and the disbursement of the bequests, with fifty thousand going to each of the four children, and an additional ten thousand each to the four grandchildren, plus twenty-five to Bernice, the net to you is one hundred and forty-four thousand, six hundred and twelve dollars. Not a hell of a lot. The annual taxes and maintenance expense alone on the house will eat that up pretty fast."

"I do have my own money, Richard."

"Do you really want to spend it all on a house that's impractical in every way for your purposes?"

"I know you think I should get rid of it."

"Absolutely," he said. "You should. Even after the capital gains tax, and even after you bought something on a more human scale, you'd have enough capital to provide a very nice interest income for the rest of your life."

"I don't think you realize just how much of my own money I do have," she said. "Will never allowed me to pay for anything of a personal nature. Aside from my own contributions to personal pension plans, I have investments of just under two million dollars."

He sat back and stared at her for a moment, then drank the last of his Margarita. "I'm impressed," he said at last.

"It's never seemed completely real to me," she said thoughtfully. "From the beginning I've found it fairly astonishing that people were willing to pay me very large sums of money for something that gives me the greatest pleasure, and which I'd have happily done for far less. Aside from writing checks for charitable donations and sundry items for my office—the copier and the telephone answering machine for example, as well as that useless fax machine Will insisted I have—today was the first time I've gone on a spree and indulged myself. I even bought perfume." She held out her wrist saying, "Smell. Tell me what you think."

He sniffed her wrist, then kissed it, and released her with a smile. "Smells sinful."

She smiled widely, holding her wrist beneath her nose. "It does, doesn't it? It's called *Ma Folie*."

"Hang on," he said. "Let's see how much of my high school French I remember. My Foolishness?"

"Yes. Or, My Madness."

"I'll run out tomorrow and buy you a gallon of it."

"You like it," she said. "Good. So do I."

The waitress came to remove the platters, asking, "Coffee?"

Deferentially, Richard asked, "Emma?"

"Yes, please."

"Two coffees, thanks," he told the waitress, then turned back to see that Emma had, for the second time, slipped away from him.

Sitting with her chin propped on her left hand, her eyes had turned inward and her expression had melted again into sadness. It disturbed him, raising again the question of how well she might be mentally. There was nothing he could do but wonder where it was

she traveled to that grieved her so, and wait for
her to return.

Will's nose wrinkled and he removed his arms
from around her, asking, "What is that you're
wearing?"

"Chanel Number 5," she answered, with a smile
breathing in the flowery fragrance on the inside
of her wrist.

"It's completely wrong for you. Too heavy and
far too—mature. I've given you the perfume you
should be wearing."

"It isn't at all wrong for me," she protested
mildly. "It's lovely. Reminds me of my grandmother. She used to wear it. I don't care especially for L'Air du Temps."

"This is too old for you, all wrong."

"Oh, Will," she smiled, "it's just perfume. And
I like it."

"Wash it off, Emma. And please don't wear it
again."

"There's not a thing wrong with it. Tons of
women wear it."

"Another good reason why I won't have *you*
wearing it!"

"Tons of women wear L'Air du Temps as well.
Why are you making such a fuss over a bit of
scent?" she asked, confounded.

"I don't like it, and I won't share a bed with
you while you reek of it."

"What are you saying?" she asked, becoming
nervous.

"I want you to go into the bathroom and
wash it off. And while you're at it, get rid of
the bottle."

"This is absurd," she argued, unable to believe

he was serious. Surely any moment now he'd drop the matter and reveal he'd only been joking.

"If you don't, I'll do it for you," he warned, getting up off the bed.

"I would like to keep it," she said. "I've paid for it with my own money. Am I not allowed even to select my own fragrance?"

"Fine. *You* won't do it, I guess *I'll* have to." He marched off into the dressing room.

Jumping up to hurry after him, she said, "Please, Will. You really are going too far with this. I'm not a child who needs you to do every last thing for her. I'm twenty-five. Don't you think I'm old enough and sufficiently intelligent to decide for myself what perfume to wear?"

"*When* will you get it through your head that I know what's best for you?" he said, his eyes blue ice as his hand closed around the small bottle. "Have I been wrong even once? No, I have not. Have I predicted every step of the way exactly what would go over well and what wouldn't? Yes, I have. Why do you *insist* on making everything a battle?"

"That isn't fair. I haven't at all."

He pushed past her and stormed into the bathroom. She ran after him, tugging at his arm as he removed the stopper from the bottle and poured the perfume into the toilet.

"That was cruel and unnecessary," she said quietly, hurt. "I wouldn't dream of usurping your rights in this fashion."

He dropped the empty bottle into the waste-basket, swung around, and wrapped his hand hard around her throat. "I want that smell *off* you!" he declared, his face the menacing mask of a stranger, his powerful hand on her throat propelling her backward toward the shower stall.

Terrified by this first display of violence, she couldn't think how to stop it or how to defend herself. What was occurring seemed so out of character for the Will she thought she knew that she latched onto the idea that this had to be a nightmare from which she'd awaken momentarily.

But she was already very much awake. His features hate-filled, he reached past her to turn on the water, shoved her into the stall, and with his arm rigidly extended held her forcibly under an icy spray, shouting, "*I made a simple request and you've turned it into a pitched battle. WASH IT OFF, EMMA!*"

She tried, using both hands, to remove his hand from her throat. Impossible. His arm's-length stance effectively kept him beyond her striking range. She kicked, but he simply ducked aside with the grace and ease of a skilled torea-dor. In response to her struggles, the somewhat evil light in his eyes seemed to glow more bright-ly, his grip on her throat tightening so that she could scarcely breathe. The combination of fear, his choking grip on her throat, and the gelid water sent a hot rush of urine down her legs. His fingers digging harder, then harder into her throat so that she had to gasp for air, he went on holding her under the punishing blast of water until she'd lost any feeling in her limbs, her teeth were clacking together uncon-trollably, and all resistance had left her. She was convinced, finally, that he intended to keep her there until she died. And in her increasingly lightheaded state, she thought it might just be an enormous relief to die. But at last, looking disgusted, and even possibly contemptuous of her inferior strength, he released her with such abrupt force that she flew against the wall, lost her balance and fell heavily to the floor, her head colliding with the faucet.

She lay there for some time, her lungs working frantically to compensate for the loss of oxygen, her heart racketing like some inefficient machine too small for the body it served. When she recovered from her dizziness and her breathing had steadied somewhat, she labored to turn off the water with her benumbed fingers. Then, her frozen joints reluctant to respond to her commands, she crawled out of the stall. After locking the door with palsied hands, she switched on the wall heater, wrapped herself in a bath sheet and sat huddled on the floor in front of the blowing warmth. Finally thawed out, and grateful this once for the terrycloth robe, she belted its bulky warmth around her.

Will was sitting in bed reading, his features once more recognizable, looking as if nothing at all unusual had happened. She stood trembling on her side of the bed, fists clenched at her sides, and in a voice so husky with animosity that she scarcely recognized it as her own, said, "I may be your wife, and I may be young, Willard, but you have my solemn promise that if you even so much as *think* of treating me in that despicably brutish fashion ever again I will kill you. You know very well that I'm not in the habit of making threats, let alone idle ones. So you'd best pay very close attention. *I will kill you!*" Drawing a painful breath, in a small way rewarded by the shock enlarging his eyes, she said, "I am going now to sleep in the guest room, and I intend to lock the door. I can't bear the sight of you at the moment. I'm not entirely certain I'll ever again be able to bear the sight of you." Too distraught to trust herself to say anything more, not in the least interested in the explanations that were already springing from his lips, she walked on unsteady legs out of the room, smartly slamming the door.

Richard had finished his coffee. And her cup, she saw, sat untouched in front of her.

"I'm sorry, Richard," she said. "What were you saying?"

"Emma." He took her hand and held it between both his own. "Where do you go when you tune out that way?"

"Tune out? Is that how it appears to you?" All at once she was frightened. Was she actually absenting herself during these sojourns into the past?

He nodded, seeing her apprehension, and said, "Uh-huh."

"How awful of me! I really am sorry." She wondered how she must appear when she "tuned out," as he called it. Did any of it reveal itself on her features? She very much hoped not. God! What was happening to her?

"No need to apologize. We all get distracted now and again," he said in the hope of allaying her nearly palpable fear. "But I would love to know where you go."

"It's the interminable retrospective," she explained, thinking it sounded woefully inadequate.

"Ah!" He nodded again. "I see. Emma," he said, gently chafing her hand, "if you find it so painful, why not stop?"

"It is painful," she admitted. "And I wish I could stop, but I can't. I'm afraid it's not voluntary. I seem to be trying to get to something and this, evidently, is the only way I'm able to do it."

"I understand."

She tilted her head to one side, asking, "Do you?"

"I think so. It hasn't been all that long since Willard died, after all. When my Dad died, it was a good year before my mother started picking up the pieces."

"Are you an only child?" she asked, eager to change the subject.

"I have a brother ten years older. I was a little 'surprise,'" he told her with a smile. "My mother was forty-two when I was born. Forty-one years ago, that was considered a highly risky age for a woman to be having a baby. But my mother often said she couldn't understand why everybody made such a fuss. She didn't have any problems with the pregnancy or the birth. She used to say her only regret was that she didn't have more kids. She was a great mother."

Emma smiled reflexively. "And what is your brother like?"

"Lionel's a good guy. He took over the business when Dad died, and when it was acquired by a conglomerate five or six years ago, he signed a phenomenally lucrative contract to stay on and run things for ten years. When his contract expires, he plans to retire to Arizona with his wife Anne."

"What sort of business is it?"

238

"They manufacture an exclusive line of bath-room fittings and accessories. Good-looking, very expensive stuff—towel racks, soap dishes, hooks, shelves, that kind of thing. You look tired," he said with concern. "Let me get the check and we'll get going." He turned and signaled to the waitress.

"You know," Emma said, "one of the reasons I can't do anything yet about the house is that I don't know where I'd go."

"Are you thinking of moving away?" He hated the idea that she might leave when they were only at the beginning.

"It's more that I've been trying to think where I belong."

"After so many years, don't you think you belong here?"

"That's what I don't know."

"Well, from a completely selfish point of view, I hope you're not going to go very far."

"You really do like me, don't you?" She smiled at him as the waitress arrived. "I'd like to buy you dinner, Richard."

"You got the chicken. It's my turn tonight." He glanced at the total, pulled some bills from his wallet and laid them on the table. "I more than like you," he said, getting up. "I hope you'll bear that in mind during your decision making. No offense, Emma, but doesn't it bother you living alone in that house?"

"Not so far. And I do love the beach. So does Calla."

"There are other beachfront properties," he said, holding her hand as they headed across the street to the parking lot, "less forbidding ones, too."

"You find it forbidding?"

"To tell you the truth, I think of that place as Queen Victoria with her back to the sea."

She laughed gustily and spontaneously, bending almost double with amusement at the image. "That's too marvelous!" She threw her left arm around his neck and kissed him. "You're so good for me, Richard. You make me laugh, and it feels ever so long since I found anything funny. Queen Victoria with her back to the sea," she repeated appreciatively. "I swear if I could think of some way to use it, I would."

"Where's your car?"

She pointed across the lot to the Mercedes. "I had doubts it would start after so many months in the garage. But it did. First try. Edgar last drove it to the dealership to have it appraised soon after Will died. Will only drove it for a few months before he became housebound. It suddenly seemed a frightful waste to leave it sitting in the garage."

"Good for you," he said. "It is yours, after all."

"Yes, it is." Her chest felt empty in the aftermath of the laughter. "So, Richard. Thank you for dinner, and for making me laugh. I am tired, now that I think about it. It's been quite a hectic weekend."

"Feels more like several months than only one weekend. Drive carefully, and I'll call you tomorrow."

"You don't mind that we're not going to make love tonight?"

"Of course not." He looked taken aback by the question. "It isn't something I automatically assume is going to happen, Emma."

"No," she said slowly, searching his eyes. "You

wouldn't assume, would you? You're *very* good for me. Do you know that?"

"So you keep saying. You're very damned good for me, too." He kissed her and said, "Now, get in the car and go home. You're falling asleep on your feet."

"Wherever I do eventually go, I don't think you'll be far away. Goodnight, Richard."

He waited until she'd driven off before heading to the BMW. He must, he reminded himself, make a trip to the library on the way home tomorrow after work.

Chapter Seventeen

"Looks like all kindsa things been going on here this weekend," Bernice said, putting a plate of bacon and eggs in front of Emma before settling at the table with a mug of coffee. "How'd you get that bruise on your face? And what're you plannin' on doin' with all them bags in the front hall?"

"I'm going to call the Salvation Army, have them come for the clothes," Emma said.

"Don't break my heart none," Bernice said. "I notice you went and bought yourself a whole bunch of swell new stuff. I sure do like that silk robe. That's real pretty. So tell me how you got the bruise."

Emma decided it was time Bernice knew about the letters. "It's complicated," she began, eating slowly but steadily. "Someone's been writing letters." She quickly filled in the details, tracking, as she did, Bernice's reactions, which ranged from surprise to bewilderment.

"Well now," Bernice said when Emma finished. "That's strange all right, but it still don't explain that bruise."

Emma spread marmalade on a wedge of toast. "Janet," she said, "got one of the letters. She burst in here Saturday morning, and was rather, shall we say, physical—simply wouldn't listen to reason. She had that key on the counter. I've no idea where she got it."

"That sounds like Janet," Bernice said wryly, "using her fists 'stead of her brain. So far as that key goes, she could've taken it from her daddy's key ring."

"No. I have Willard's keys. I used them last night when I took out the Mercedes."

"Ohhh!" Bernice grinned. "Aren't you the bold one? Must've been some weekend. How was the dinner with Mr. Lawyer?"

"It was fine," Emma said, chagrined by a sudden flush.

"Fine, huh?" Bernice folded her arms on the table and kept grinning. "So you had yourself this fine evenin', then bright and early Saturday mornin' Miss Janet comes chargin' in here with her fists flyin' on account of how she got this nasty letter. And sometime after that you cleared out your dressin' room and went shoppin'. What else'd you do?"

"I worked on the new manuscript." Emma put her knife and fork down across the plate. "How were Cedric and June and the children?"

"They were all just fine," Bernice answered, deciding that in spite of the bruised cheek Emma looked better than she had in a long while. She looked, in fact, as if she been up to some loving with that Richard Redmond. Which, all things considered, would probably do her more good than anything else Bernice could think of. "What about Miss Linda?" she asked, wondering how much Emma would admit to. "She get one of them letters too?"

"Yes, as a matter of fact she did." Emma held her coffee cup with both hands, thinking about the direction of the third chapter. One small, almost unnoticeable clue would nag at Roger Hurley—the cellist detective who figured in all her books. She'd introduce him in this chapter. . . .

"I know you're anxious to get up to the office," Bernice said, interrupting Emma's plotting, "but you want me to call the Salvation Army people to come for those bags?"

"If there's anything in them you want, please help yourself," Emma said. "I can't imagine you'd care to, given how much you've always disliked those clothes."

"You're right about that. It's a treat to see you in something different for a change." Emma looked a whole lot less childish in her new black slacks, with one of the stripey cotton shirts they'd bought the other day, and a yellow cardigan. She even had on black socks and a nice pair of brown loafers. "What was Miss Linda's letter like?" Bernice asked, striving for a tone neither too serious nor too casual.

"What's odd, you know, is that every letter I've seen so far has basically been true. Hers was rather a cruel indictment of her novels, but I couldn't disagree with any of the comments. Fortunately, I was able to convince her I hadn't written it. I'm worried about who else may have received them."

"What're you goin' to do?"

"I don't think there's anything I can do. I'm sure Richard would have advised me to go to the police if he'd thought it would be of any use." She looked over her shoulder toward the doorway. "Bernice, would you think I was mad if I got rid of most of the paintings and some of the larger antique pieces?"

"I'd think you were showin' some sense," Bernice said. "They're plain ugly, those pictures. And most of that furniture's too big to fit anywhere else but this house. You gettin' ready to sell the place?"

Emma turned back. Bernice didn't appear worried by the prospect. "Richard thinks I should."

"All of a sudden I'm hearin' a lot about Mr. Richard." Bernice smiled, her green eyes very knowing. "I'm gettin' the impression you two had your heads together real close."

"We talked about a number of things. The house was just one of them. You'll be getting your check in a week or so, by the way."

"It was decent of Mr. Willard to do that," Bernice said, looking slightly uncomfortable now at the mention of the money. "I've promised some to each of the kids."

"I hope you'll keep a sum back for yourself."

"Oh, I will."

"What would you do with this house?" Emma asked.

"If it was mine? I'd have to think some on that."

"But would you keep it?"

"No, I sure wouldn't. I'd get me something more homey. But I'm not you."

"So you agree with Richard that I should sell it."

"I guess I do."

Again Emma looked over her shoulder. "It is far too large for just one person. Would you come with me if I moved?"

"Sure," Bernice said at once. "You kiddin'? Course I would. You're family. I'd go right along with you."

Emma smiled at her, relieved. "That's good to know. I'm going up now. It would seem Calla didn't care to wait for me this morning."

"That pooch's been down to the beach for better than an hour. You go on ahead to work. I can tell you're itchin' to get to it."

Emma had been at the word processor for slightly more than an hour when Bernice rang up on the intercom to say, "That Mr. Colsen's on the phone for you." Emma glanced over to see that the first line was indeed lit up. She had turned off the ringer on the desk extension before starting in to work. She thanked Bernice and picked up the receiver.

"Jack Colsen here. Emma, I have to tell you I'm pretty upset by your letter."

The bottom seeming to drop away from her stomach, her mouth suddenly dry, she said, "My letter?"

"To say this was unexpected is an understatement," he said, his voice rather shaky. "If you had a problem with my representation you should have talked to me about it. I'd have done my damnedest to straighten things out. But to be—dismissed this way, with no warning, it's quite a blow."

Good God! The phantom writer had fired her agent. Was that what she was hearing? "Jack," she said, scrambling to think how to handle this, "when did you receive the letter?"

"It was waiting for me when I got back this morning, after being in Los Angeles for a few days."

"I wonder," she said, eyeing the fax machine, "if you'd be good enough to fax me a copy of it. I, ah, wrote it in rather a hurry. Perhaps I should take a second look."

"You didn't keep a copy?" He sounded perturbed by her inefficiency.

"I'm afraid not. I would appreciate it," she said, and gave him the telephone number to which the fax was hooked up.

"Well, all right," he said dubiously. "You'll call me back?"

"As soon as I've reviewed the letter," she promised, and hung up to switch on the Panasonic fax, which Will had adored and had used constantly, but for which she'd never found a need.

In no more than two minutes paper began to scroll through the printer. When it had stopped, she removed the page and sat down to read it.

Dear Jack,

    After thinking it over for quite some time I have decided to seek representation elsewhere. During the many years of our association I have found you to be a skilled negotiator but a disappointment in all other areas. Primarily, I've been irked by your consistent failure to return telephone calls, especially those originating with me rather than with my husband. It has always appeared as if you deemed me secondary to Will, and therefore not worthy of inclusion as an involved party in the decisions made regarding my work.

You have rarely responded to my direct questions but have been evasive and have jollied me along as if my intelligence were limited to writing and I was neither sufficiently well informed, nor cognizant of the subtleties of publishing to merit more than vague allusions and fragmented answers that invariably failed to satisfy my questions.

Since you were Will's choice as agent, I have gone along for far too long with a situation I find less than salutary. You've been more than happy to accept your commission throughout the years without ever bothering to determine whether or not I as the author—and not Will who was merely the husband of the author—found your efforts to be commensurate with the sizeable annual income you garnered as a direct result of *my* efforts. I am no longer willing to tolerate your blithe disregard, nor your patronizing attitude.

You are, naturally, entitled to continuing income from those contracts you negotiated. But as of the above date your services are hereby terminated. Sincerely,

Emma Dalton Bellamy.

Jack must have had a seizure when he received this, she thought, reading the letter for a second time. As well he should have. He'd been roundly upbraided, taken to task for his sins. And what made the letter truly terrible was that every word of it was irrefutably true. She had for years tolerated his condescending disregard while watching him fawn over Will, hanging on his every word. Over the previous two and a half years she'd become almost daily more displeased with Jack's highly cavalier attitude and his continuing failure to return her calls.

Will had refused to hear any negative comment about him. "He's good, and that's all you should care about," he'd said countless times. "He's your agent, and he's done damned well by you. Don't go stirring things up."

Clearly, she didn't have to stir things up. Someone else had undertaken it on her behalf. She imagined a figure furtively slipping away from the clusters of mourners gathered in the house, gliding up the stairs and along the hallway. Checking to be sure he/she was unobserved, he/she ducked into the office, slid open the drawer to her desk, removed a supply of letterheads and envelopes. After tucking these into a pocket or handbag, the figure again checked the hallway, then made his/her way next door to the bathroom. God! she thought with sudden fear. Was it even remotely conceivable that Richard could be writing these letters? He was an admitted fan of her work, and had had access to the house for years. He was clever enough to guess her susceptibility in the aftermath of Will's death, clever enough to send the first of the letters to himself in order to focus her attention in other directions. No! It was too preposterous. What possible motive could Richard have for so arcane an enterprise? No. It was simply inconceivable. Richard would never take advantage of her. Would he?

The intercom went again, and, agitated, Emma said, "Yes, Bernice?"

"There's a Dana Brown callin' for you."

"The name sounds familiar, but I don't know any Dana Brown."

"That's what I said, and she says she got the letter you sent her."

"Oh good God!" Emma exclaimed. "Not another letter."

"You gonna talk to this woman?"

"Please tell her I'll be with her in just a moment."

On a hunch, Emma pulled open the bottom drawer of the desk and got out her copy of *The Literary Market Place*, found the section on agents and ran quickly through the list. There she was, under The Stanley Group, Dana Brown.

Overheated, she picked up the receiver and said, "Sorry to keep you. Emma Bellamy here."

"Emma, it's Dana Brown," said a strong, positive female voice. "I have to tell you your letter was a hell of a surprise. A delightful one, I might add."

"Yes?" Emma said neutrally.

"Everybody's always thought you were signed to Jack Colsen for life."

"Yes, well, so did I," Emma admitted, liking the humor underlying this woman's tone, as well as her directness.

"Naturally, I'd jump at the chance to represent you. I'm also a big fan. I thought lunch would be a good idea. We sit down, look each other over, see how we like what we see."

"May I ask you a favor? I seem to have misplaced my copy of your letter. Could you possibly fax me yours? I have rather an urgent call to return, and then I'll get back to you."

"No problem. Let me give you my number."

Emma made a note of it, in turn gave Dana Brown her fax number, promised to get back to her shortly, then swiveled to turn on the machine for the second time. In about five minutes it went into action. When it had stopped, she tore off the page.

Dear Dana Brown,
    My good friend Linda Thurman has always spoken very highly of you and since I have recently terminated my relationship with Jack Colsen I am now seeking a new agent.
    If you would be interested in undertaking my representation perhaps you'd be good enough to ring me and we could make arrangements to meet.
    I look forward to hearing from you.
    Sincerely,
                    Emma Dalton Bellamy.

Emma snatched up the receiver and punched out Linda's number.

"It's Emma, Linda. Will you tell me a bit about Dana Brown?"

"Dana? Why? What's up?"

"I'm, ah, thinking of changing agents and I recall you speaking very well of her."

"Dana's the best," Linda declared. "She has as much time as you need whenever you need it. She's one of the toughest, most respected agents in the country. She's smart, thorough, and knows contract boilerplate like you wouldn't believe. Are you going to go with her?"

"It's possible," Emma said, wondering why she was responding to a series of letters written by someone else and allowing her life to be changed as a result.

"Do it, Em. She's got great editorial ability, plus she'll work her ass off for you. I've never understood your sticking with Colsen. He's famous for never returning calls. That alone would drive me nuts. And never mind all the other stuff he's famous for."

"What stuff?"

"You don't want to know. I've heard through the grapevine he's into some pretty weird things."

"I'll keep you posted, Linda. Is everything going well for you?"

"Peachy keen, sweetcakes."

"Oh, good. Look, I must go now. I must ring Dana Brown back."

"This is great news, Em. Seriously. Don't forget to call me."

"I won't. And thank you."

She dialed Colsen's office and was told by his assistant that he was on another line. "Could he call you back?"

"That won't be necessary," Emma said. "Just tell him, please, that I've decided to abide by my letter."

"Oh. Okay."

Next she called Dana Brown's office and was put through at once.

"Mrs. Brown, I think we should meet as you suggested. When would be convenient for you?"

"Let me just check my diary." Emma could hear her turning pages, and a telephone ringing in the background. "Look," Dana Brown said, "I've got a lunch date Wednesday I can cancel if that'd be a good day for you."

Emma said, "That would be fine. I'll come to your office."

"You have the address?"

Emma said, "Yes, I do."

"I'm really looking forward to meeting you."

"And I you."

"Good. I'll see you Wednesday, say, noon?"

"Yes."

She put down the receiver and the intercom went off.

"Yes, Bernice?"

"There's a delivery down here for you, Emma."

"What sort of delivery?" she asked guardedly.

Bernice chuckled and said, "You come on down and see."

Emma got up feeling frazzled. "What now?" she said aloud.

On the table in the kitchen was an arrangement of long-stemmed red roses, with baby's breath and ferns.

"Somebody likes you," Bernice said, arms folded across her chest as she watched Emma open the gift card.

The words triggered an echo in Emma's mind of Richard saying, "Someone's been busy," and she looked closely at Bernice for a few seconds before reading the card. It read, "I can't stop smiling, and you're responsible. With love, Richard."

"Mr. Lawyer?" Bernice guessed.

Emma nodded, too choked and guilt-filled for a few seconds to speak. How could she have suspected Richard? What was wrong with her?

"Man's in love with you," Bernice said matter-of-factly. "I sure do like his style."

"I need some air," Emma said, beckoning to Calla. "Would you please put the roses in the office?"

"Happy to," Bernice answered, thinking Emma's reaction to the flowers was kind of on the peculiar side. Instead of being pleased, she looked confused, even upset.

"I'll only be ten or fifteen minutes. Come, Calla." She started toward the back door as the telephone rang. Freezing in her tracks, she looked with consternation at the wall phone.

"You go on," Bernice said, picking up on her mood. "I'll take a message."

"Thank you," Emma said gratefully and escaped out the door.

Having already taken herself out this morning for a run, Calla was content to settle on the pebbly beach with her head in Emma's lap. Emma petted the small dog and looked out over the water. "I can't think why I did that, Calla," she said softly. "I behaved as if I'd actually written those letters. I've *fired* Jack Colsen after sixteen years. Not that it isn't something I've thought of doing a hundred times, but to allow myself to be manipulated this way . . . Dana Brown's done very well for Linda. And if we don't hit it off, I'm under no obligation. Suddenly there's almost more going on than I can handle. Did you see those exquisite roses? With love, Richard. He sent me flowers, Calla. Never once in all those years did Will ever send me flowers. Not once. Every last thing he gave me was intended to be displayed on my person. Clothes and jewelry, bags and expensive silk scarves. But nothing as ephemeral as flowers. Don't you want to run, Calla?" She held the dog's head with both hands and looked into its eyes. "Don't you need to reinforce the territorial claims you've made all over this beach? No? Well, then, let's go back to the house. I want to call Richard and thank him. How could I have thought such things about him? Those letters are beginning to impair my judgment." She got up and with Calla springing along at her side went running through the tall grass back to the house.

"God, Calla!" she said, as they ran. "The bloody letters are overturning my life. I wish I knew who was doing this, and why."

Chapter Eighteen

"The situation's getting out of hand. Every time the telephone rings now I'm certain it's someone else calling to say they've received a letter. Is there anything I can do?"

Feeling guilty but playing along nonetheless, Richard said "Nothing I can think of. If you walked into a police station with copies of those letters they'd assume—as does everyone else— that you'd written them. There are no threats, real or implied, in any of them. And the fact that they've been written on your letterhead and that at least the two of them with envelopes show cancellation marks for your zip code tends to corroborate the impression that you're the one who wrote them."

"That's fairly much what I'd concluded," Emma said. "But I thought I should ask your professional opinion."

"Well," he laughed, "you've got it. I know it's upsetting as hell, but I'm afraid I have no idea what you should do. Damn! That's my intercom. Will you hold on for a sec?"

"Certainly."

He came back on the line very quickly, asking, "When will I see you?"

"Dinner tomorrow?"

"Great. I'll pick you up at seven."

"Richard, thank you again for the roses. They're beautiful."

"So are you. Tomorrow at seven," he said.

On impulse, she opened the bottom drawer of the desk and went through the various contracts until she found the last one Jack Colsen had negotiated with her longtime publisher, Regent Press. Quickly locating the clause she wanted, she read it through carefully.

If the Author fails to deliver the manuscript within ninety (90) days after the above date or if the manuscript that is delivered is not, in the Publisher's judgment, satisfactory, the Publisher may terminate this agreement by giving written notice, whereupon the Author agrees to repay forthwith the amount specified in Paragraph 16.

It was now some fourteen months past the stipulated delivery date. Nowhere in the contract did it state her position with regard to terminating the agreement. Still, if Regent agreed to go along, and if she refunded the seventy-five thousand dollars she'd received on signing the contract, she should find herself free of any contractual obligations. But a letter wouldn't accomplish what she wanted. And aside from that, her personal dealings with Jim Finney, the president and publisher of Regent, had always been most amicable.

Unlike Will, Jim Finney wasn't interested in absolute control but rather in the long-term growth and contentment of his authors. And unlike the recent majority of publishing executives who'd come to the business via various acquisitions and mergers and who had little if any knowledge of or feeling for books or the people who read and wrote them and were interested almost exclusively in the bottom line, Jim was devoutly dedicated to books and to the fiercely loyal nucleus of writers whose careers he'd built over a period of years. He was also a shrewd salesman who regularly started word-of-mouth campaigns for forthcoming books, which resulted in top-dollar reprint sales and battles between the book clubs over rights. It wasn't unknown for Jim to let one of the clubs or a reprinter sneak a look at a novel he was considering buying. If the club showed interest, or if the paperback house did, he'd then make an offer on the book. He'd successfully hedged his bets in this fashion for years. He was fairly notorious for hanging on to manuscripts for as long as seven or eight months before either making an offer or turning them down. And without fail he came in with offers so low that agents simply laughed upon hearing them. Over weeks of haggling, he'd eventually come up with an offer that, had it not been preceded by at least a dozen exchanges of telephone calls, would have been refused outright, but which, finally, sounded reasonable by comparison to his initial bid.

He had from the outset treated Emma with respect. He'd also always taken the trouble to involve her in every aspect of the publishing process, from consulting with her on the covers to seeking her input on flap and advertising copy. It was that involvement and his overt regard for her intelligence that was responsible for her staying with Regent even when Jack Colsen and Will had argued that she could get far larger advances from another house. They'd wanted to reject Jim's offer on the second to last book she'd done and hold an auction. Emma had flatly refused, and the two men had treated her as if she were an unruly and slightly retarded child. Their behavior at the time had only served to make her even more determined not to leave Jim Finney.

She dialed her editor Kathy's direct number. Kathy picked up on the first ring.

Upon hearing it was Emma, she said, "How *are* you? It's been months since we talked."

"I'm getting along. Look, Kathy, I'm coming into the city on Wednesday and I know it's very short notice but there's a matter I'd like to discuss with you and Jim. It has to do with the contract, which, as I'm sure you're aware, has not been fulfilled. I have rather an unorthodox proposition to put to Jim with regard to that contract and I was hoping we could talk about it Wednesday afternoon. I'm having lunch with Dana Brown and I expect to be free by three at the latest."

"Are you signing with Dana?" Kathy asked excitedly. "You're leaving Colsen?"

"I've terminated my relationship with Jack."

"I think I'm getting the picture," Kathy said. "The delivery date's long past due. And why should Jack get a free ride? Am I warm?"

"Very."

"I hear you. Let me run down the hall and talk to Jim right now. I won't call you back unless Wednesday's no good. Okay? Otherwise, I'll see you then. And Jim, too, if I have to nail his feet to the floor." She paused for a moment then cautiously asked, "You're not thinking of dumping us, are you, Em?"

"I wouldn't dream of it. Besides, I'm used to working with you." Emma laughed, saying, "You've got to be the only editor in New York who's stayed with the same house for twenty-odd years. Do you know I've been through five different editors with my London publishers? No," Emma assured her, "I'm not going to leave you. Please tell him that. I simply want to clear the slate, as it were."

"Makes sense," Kathy said, "especially if you're going to go with Dana. She's a good choice, Em. You'll find her quite a change from Jack. Are you writing again?"

Emma debated telling the truth. But Kathy was a friend as well as her editor, and would never betray a confidence. "Actually," Emma said, "I've just started. Which is why, as you can imagine, I'm most anxious to clear up matters with regard to the last contract."

"I can't see there'll be a problem. I'm going to talk to Jim right now. When will you have something to show me?"

"Not for a month or two, I shouldn't think."

"Just a few chapters," Kathy begged. "Anything. I'm desperate for a new Emma Bellamy title. Not to mention the market. If you could deliver by, say, January, we could schedule for the following September. That'd make it just over two years since your last book."

"We'll discuss it Wednesday," Emma promised.

"It's great to talk to you, Em, and great to know you're working again. Take care."

Emma turned back to face the word processor screen. The many interruptions had taken their toll on her concentration and she couldn't remember what her next point was to have been. She went over the index cards, took yet another look at the five letters she now had, then scrolled back to the start of the chapter. Getting caught up again in the unfolding scenario, she was able to continue from where she'd left off, immersing herself in the mood and the interplay between the characters.

Roger Hurley made his initial appearance as an old friend of Edward Evans, the man who had a burgeoning romantic interest in the heroine. On a visit from London, Roger was in New York to attend a four-day conference of international law-enforcement officers. He'd retired from the London CID the previous year and was in great demand as a security consultant. So much so, in fact, that he had precious little time for his beloved music or for his continued reading of the classics. He had, prior to his retirement, reread all of Dickens, Wilkie Collins, Henry James, Jane Austin, and Trollope. However, since embarking upon his career as a consultant he'd had even less free time than before and as a result was stalled midway through his rereading of the Brontes.

His friend Evans had, at Roger's request, secured tickets to three concerts. Roger was looking forward particularly to a performance that evening at Lincoln Center of the Haydn cello concerto No. 1 in C major and the Monn concerto in G minor, two of his all-time favorite works, and anticipating a few hours of undiluted pleasure. The young Israeli cellist was reputed to be profoundly gifted, and had already, at only eighteen, played with many of the world's finest philharmonics.

When Evans introduced the subject of the letters during an early dinner before the concert, Roger's initial reaction was irritation. This visit to New York was proving a disappointment on a professional level and he hoped that disappointment wasn't going to spill over into the personal area. He disliked large gatherings in general, but had been willing to put aside his dislike in the hope of being brought up to date on the latest surveillance products as well as renewing acquaintanceships with foreign colleagues he'd encountered over the years. The conference so far had proved tedious, with the exception of the seminar on plastics—handguns and explosives—and the development of new equipment to detect them. For the most part, it seemed to him that the conference was nothing more than an opportunity for a number of middle-aged men wearing stick-on identification badges to drink too much and to swap crude jokes or to argue vehemently about gun control. The European delegates tended to band together, as if for protection from their American counterparts, so many of whom were almost incomprehensibly chummy immediately upon introduction. Now, on top of everything else, his old friend Edward wished to involve him in a situation having to do with poison-pen letters.

"They're not quite that," Edward was saying as he twirled lobster pasta around his fork. "I'm not sure exactly how to describe them. I've seen five of these letters and, as bizarre as it might sound, it's almost as if they'd been penned by an alter ego. In one sense you could say they're directives, as if whoever is writing them is attempting to reroute the course of Elsa's life."

His curiosity aroused, Roger asked if he might have a look at the letters. "I'm not promising anything," he said. "But I will take a look."

"I was hoping you would. I'd value your opinion. I'll get copies made and sent to your hotel by courier tomorrow."

Mildly annoyed with himself for his perennial inquisitiveness, Roger took another bite of his chicken breast in a raspberry sauce, marveling over the ingeniousness of the food offered in American restaurants . . .

She wrote steadily, completing the chapter just before noon. After reading it through and referring several times to *The Synonym Finder* for alternative verbs and adjectives to substitute into the text, she stored it on the disk, then went downstairs to the kitchen.

Bernice said, "I was about to come get you. I fixed you some of them salmon sandwiches you like, with the sliced cucumber. Gotta get a little meat back on them bones."

Crossing the room to put on the kettle, Emma said, "In case I forget to mention it later, I won't be in for dinner tomorrow evening."

"Out again with Mr. Lawyer, huh?" Bernice flashed her a smile as she brought the knife blade down on the diagonal through the sandwiches.

"Are you making fun of me?" Emma asked, hesitating with her out-held hand holding the kettle's plug.

"Go easy, woman!" Bernice gently chided. "Can't you tell when someone's teasin'?"

"Actually, I can't." Emma finished plugging in the kettle, then got down the teapot and cups. "I come from a family that rarely found anything amusing."

"Yeah?" Bernice asked interestedly. Emma had never talked much about her background, and Bernice was curious to know what kind of family she'd had, what kind of people they were to break all ties with their child just 'cause they didn't cotton to the man she'd married.

"My mother was—or is to this day, for all I know—a very proper middle-class matron who was perpetually concerned with what the neighbors might think, with appropriate dress, and with appropriate behavior. She was the living essence of rigidity, and dictated endlessly to my father, sister and me on everything from our table manners to the way we walked. She had an opinion on every subject, whether or not she actually was familiar with it. Vivian, my oldest sister, left home at seventeen. I left when I was eighteen."

"Your mother must've had fits when you took up with Mr. Willard," Bernice said, thinking her mother and Mr. Willard sounded a whole lot alike.

"She refused to have anything more to do with me," Emma said, scooping tea into the warmed pot. "I've had no contact with any of them since shortly before the marriage. My mother forbade my father or sister to communicate with me."

"I know you haven't been in touch with them. But don't you wonder how they are?"

"Now and then," Emma admitted.

"What about your daddy? What was he like?"

Emma gave her a sad little smile. "He had more generous instincts than my mother. I remember when Vivian and I were tots he'd take us up to London to the Regent's Park zoo, and the planetarium, Madame Tussaud's, the pantomime at Christmas. Mother would never come. These outings were too frivolous to suit her. She shouldn't have had children. She wanted us to be miniaturized adults, even dressed us like tiny matrons. I think Father simply got tired of resisting her year after year and surrendered. In the end he fell into line with whatever Mother laid down as law. And Vivian, whom I'd admired exorbitantly for taking charge of her own life, was in reality very much her mother's daughter. She may have left the house but she took Mother's values with her. I do sometimes wonder if Vivian married and had children and, if she did, was she as dreadful a mother as ours had been. I always thought if I had a child I'd make every effort to be as different from my mother as humanly possible."

"You'd've made a real good mother," Bernice said judiciously.

"You think so?" Emma asked touchingly.

"Yup, I do. So you don't have any secret wish to go lookin' for them," Bernice said, settling with her arms folded in front of her on the table.

"When Will and I were in London a few years ago, just before he became ill, I rang directory inquiries to see if they were still listed. They were. I thought about telephoning, realized I hadn't anything to say to them after so many years—especially when they'd never responded to my letters or seasonal greeting cards—and that was the end of it." Emma brought the teapot and cups to the table. "I'm sure it sounds heartless of me, but I've never really missed them. We weren't at all close. If anything, we were like a trio of painfully polite tenants in rather an upscale boarding house who met for meals and talked about the frightful weather, or the rising costs of public transportation. The only exceptions were when Mother decided either Vivian or I had breached one of her many rules."

Emma looked at the plate of sandwiches. Talking about her family had agitated her. Her stomach was roiling and there was an acidic burning at the back of her throat. She held the strainer in one hand and poured the tea through it into the cups with the other, watching the English breakfast blend stain the milk.

"How come that upset you so much?" Bernice asked incisively, helping herself to a sandwich.

Impressed as always by Bernice's acuity, Emma said, "Perhaps because it revives too many unpleasant memories." She had only to contemplate the eighteen years she'd spent with her family to feel depression begin pulling her down.

"That's a shame," Bernice sympathized. "Seems like as if not too many people had any kind of a happy upbringing."

"Did you?" Emma asked, glad to direct herself outward.

"Pretty good. We didn't have much money, but we were close. My folks were hardworking people, always taught me if I was gonna do a job, to do it right or not at all. They were real bothered when I dropped out of school to marry Joe. They'd been savin' so I'd go to college, you know. But I was pregnant with Cedric and crazy for Joe and stubborn as a mule, so they gave us the college money to help us get started. They took Joe right to their hearts, and never said another word about bein' disappointed. And Joe, bein' an orphan, you know, they loved him like a son. When me and Joe started workin' together, my mama looked after the kids as they come along. We paid her every week so there'd be no hard feelings, and there never were. My four and Joe took it real hard when Mama died. So did my Dad. He just couldn't get along without her. Two years later he was gone, too. Then, just when we were gettin' over all that upset, Joe had his heart attack. One, two, three, they died."

"I'm so sorry," Emma said.

"It's how things happen sometimes," Bernice said philosophically. "You gotta go on, doin' what needs to be done."

Emma looked at Bernice's appealingly round, untroubled face, at her clear green eyes, and envied her ability to deal so admirably with life. "Why," she said, "can't I be as sensible as you? Why am I so bloody mired in the past?"

"You're comin' along," Bernice said. "Take a sandwich. You're a whole lot better than you were even a couple of weeks ago. That Richard's doing you a world of good."

"You called him Richard! Not Mr. Lawyer or Mr. Richard, but simply Richard."

Bernice's shoulders lifted and fell. "Seems to me like we're gonna be seein' a lot of him."

"I hope you know I'd be lost without you," Emma said, at last taking a sandwich.

"That's a fact," Bernice agreed. "Grown woman who can't even cook."

"You know why that is," Emma said.

"Uh-huh. Indeed I do."

"I think I'd like to learn."

"What? To cook?"

Emma nodded, chewing.

"Any time you want a break from that writing machine, just come on down here and I'll show you."

"You're a good friend, Bernice."

"I do my best. And you're not bad yourself, you know."

Back upstairs in the office, Emma sat in front of the word processor, her eyes fixing on the far wall as the familiar silence, like the muffled hush of a snowfall, fell around her. And like one of the figures caught within the glass of a paperweight, she floated weightlessly in the liquid interior of the globe.

They were at a large house party in Westport given by one of Will's authors. As was his custom, Will had begun circulating within moments of their arrival, so she'd dredged up a social persona to help her get through the evening. She made herself smile when necessary but instinctively remained on the perimeter, watching and listening, intrigued, to snippets of conversation. She preferred to be an observer rather than a participant, especially when confronted by large groups of strangers. On those occasions when Will insisted she make a special effort to join in, she disliked herself for the falsity of her behavior and for her failure to be secure enough to be herself. There were many situations that required her to be more outgoing, more conversational than she was naturally. And she did her best to meet the requirements of those situations, even though, afterward, she felt exhausted and even jaded for having once again misrepresented herself. It was yet another part of Will's ongoing work at her "image," and the aspect she disliked most. Effecting a social exterior was so at variance with her instincts, required such a concentrated effort on her part, that she was never entirely certain at these times which of them—herself, or her husband—was the more deserving of her contempt.

She felt someone staring at her and looked around, catching sight on the far side of the room of a tall, elegant woman who looked to be in her late forties. Her side-parted blonde hair failing precisely to her jawline, she was impeccably turned out in a smartly cut black evening suit, adorned by a circular diamond pin on the lapel. Emma smiled uncertainly, finding the woman vaguely familiar. The woman smiled back, and Emma moved through the crush of other guests toward her.

"Have we met?" Emma asked, admiring how well put together she was. Her makeup was sparingly but effectively applied, her long fingernails painted a bright red that matched her lipstick.

"No, but I think it's time we did. I'm Alexandra Lowenstein, formerly Bellamy." She extended a slim hand.

Jarred, Emma shook hands with her, and said, with an awkward smile, "Oh, dear. How very foolish of me."

"Not at all. And call me Sandra. I've been curious about you for a long time. It's fairly surprising, all things considered, that we haven't run into each other before." With a disarming smile, she said, "Please don't take this the wrong way, but I would guess the reason you thought you knew me is because we look an awful lot alike."

Emma studied her feature by feature, noting the large brown eyes and strong chin, the well-defined mouth and realized it was true. Sandra was a more sophisticated, older version of herself. They looked enough alike, even to their height, to be sisters.

"Scary, isn't it?" Sandra said. "Please don't take *this* the wrong way, but it looks as if Willard found himself a young duplicate."

"It would seem so, wouldn't it?" Emma had to concur. "He's spoken very rarely of you, but from the little he has said, I certainly wouldn't have expected you to be so immediate."

Sandra laughed. "I doubt he's had anything nice to say. Emma, isn't it?"

"Yes."

"Your husband, Emma, is not a very nice man. But you must have figured that out for yourself by now. After all, it's been, what, ten years?"

"Nine," Emma said, looking around nervously.

"Don't worry," Sandra said. "He's way over on the other side of the room. You know, the moment I saw you I knew who you were. I've been watching you since you arrived. You seem a little lost. I take it you don't care any more for these things than I do."

"I'm not fond of large parties, no."

"Don't let him bully you," Sandra said compassionately. "Because if he sees you'll put up with it, he'll turn you into a puppet. These past twelve years since leaving Willard have been the happiest of my life. It took a while to get used to buying what *I* liked, and it took even longer to believe that Tom—he's my second husband—wasn't conning me, getting me to trust him before he launched into full-scale mind control. We've been married almost ten years and he's never once tried to tell me what to think."

Emma felt nearly sick with disloyalty listening to this woman speak but was anxious to hear more. It was as if she'd suddenly been shown a series of photographs depicting her husband in extravagantly compromising positions.

"You're so young," Sandra said, with a kindhearted smile. "Very sweet and very shy. For some reason, I thought you'd be more formidable. I should've known better. After all, I was only nineteen when I married Willard. And if you're going to repeat history, it makes sense you'd repeat it as closely as possible." Taking hold of Emma's hand, she said, "Don't let me upset you. I have a tendency to say more than people want to hear."

Prompted as she rarely was to give voice to her intuitive impressions, Emma said, "I know you're not a cruel person. It's simply that I'm unaccustomed to people who say what they actually mean. I'm also not in the habit of discussing my husband. Especially not with someone who's known him intimately."

Sandra smiled. "Well," she said, "if nothing else, now you know that I'm not the hostile, aggressive, castrating bitch Willard told you I was."

Emma flushed painfully. That was precisely the way Willard had described her. "No," she agreed. "I'm pleased to have had a chance to meet you, to form my own impressions."

"Me, too. And by the way, I like your books. You're a damned good writer. It's hard to believe you're so young. But I think you've got an old 'head.'" She smiled, her eyes shifted to the side and she said, "You'd better move on now. Willard's radar just kicked in." Releasing Emma's hand, she said, "Good luck, Emma. I'm happy we met."

Emma said, "Thank you, so am I," and slipped away, hoping Willard hadn't seen the two of them talking.

But he had. And on the way home in the car later that evening, he said, "I see you met my ex-wife. I'm sure she must've given you an earful about me."

"Actually," she said cautiously, fearful of incurring his wrath, "she was very gracious. I liked her."

Will snorted and she tensed, anticipating a scene. But for a change he allowed the matter to drop.

Emma was saddened to read in the paper just a few months before Will's death that Sandra and her husband had died in a plane crash. She'd always meant to get in touch with her, talk more. But somehow there'd never been an opportunity.

She found herself back in the present and with a sigh switched on the word processor.

Chapter Nineteen

She left off working only long enough to go down-stairs to eat dinner with Bernice, who, well aware of the signs, didn't interrupt Emma's thoughts with attempts at conversation. After the meal, which she scarcely tasted, Emma bade Bernice goodnight and rushed back to the office, anxious to return to Roger Hurley.

Over the years she'd come to know Roger so well that there were times when she fully expected him to arrive at the front door, or to telephone to talk to her. She was constantly having to remind herself that Roger wasn't real, but during the months when he was the primary focus of all her energy and attention he was more real to her than anyone she'd ever known. She was intimately acquainted with his habits, his likes and dislikes, his instincts, his powers of deductive reasoning, and his weakness for a certain type of outwardly strong but inwardly vulnerable woman. She knew the way the cello felt when positioned between his legs, and the degree of pressure he applied to the strings with his fingers and the bow in order to produce the rich sobbing music he so loved.

Roger was forty-six, six feet tall, brown-haired and blue-eyed. He had a lean nose and a long jaw and smiled infrequently. He was highly intelligent and not at all embarrassed to rely on his experience-honed intuition. He was by nature a caring man whose greatest fear was of that very ability to care. He'd learned early on to conceal his compassionate side, aware it had a place well near the bottom of the list of requirements in police work. But occasionally he was drawn, almost helplessly, to some woman whose combination of intelligence and need he found powerfully compelling. At those times he'd do battle with his ingrained reservations and common sense, reminding himself of the many reasons why he preferred—since his youthful marriage and divorce—a life alone.

Roger was a man of taste and learning and discrimination. On clement days he tended to his garden while listening to one of his favorite recordings through the open french doors at the rear of his house in St. John's Wood. He was a man of specific pleasures who was happiest with an open book, a glass of good wine and Mozart or Vivaldi or Mendelssohn on the stereo.

He loathed violence in all forms, the abuse of any substance, waste either of time or resources, and stupidity. He was occasionally abrupt, most often scrupulously polite—to everyone, even those whose stupidity seemed like muddy shadows they dragged about with them—and, at heart, decidedly romantic. He frequently fell in love with children whose faces or antics charmed him, with elderly people in possession of exceptional grace or dignity, with teenagers whose troubled eyes starkly contrasted to their metal-studded leather adornments and outrageous hair styles. He preferred dogs to cats, British chocolate to Swiss or Belgian, chicken or fish to red meat, and had a secret lifetime passion for the fine older models of Rolls, Bentley, and Daimler.

Roger was, according to the fan letters she'd received over the years, the ideal of many women and an almost equally large number of men. He excelled at his work, knew how to make the best of his leisure time, and never discussed personal matters with his associates. He had a wide number of acquaintances and a handful of close long-term friends, among whom was Lady Gillian St. Alban-Smythe, the widow of his childhood friend Adam, who'd died more than a decade earlier in a boating accident.

It was to Gillian he confided the majority of his concerns, and with whom he had an ongoing although intermittent affair. Gillian was the embodiment of all those qualities he deemed most valuable in a partner: warmth, wit, intelligence and foresight. She was a well-respected journalist who often provided insightful feedback when he was stuck on a case and couldn't decide in which direction his inquiries should go. She was, so far as Roger knew, content with the on-again off-again indirection of their relationship and was invariably delighted to see or hear from him. Gillian was, to all intents and purposes, Roger's second self.

For Emma, playing out these roles on paper was her greatest pleasure. She had Will to thank for this because it was he who'd latched onto Roger in that partial manuscript she'd given him back in 1974, declaring, "Make this man your hero. He's too well-drawn to be a secondary character. Reshape what you've written around him. Flesh him out some more and you've got the makings of a series."

Since she'd felt a fondness for Roger Hurley right from the start, it hadn't been difficult for her to move him into the spotlight and endow him with all the qualities he insisted to her he must have. She'd found it far harder to get into the rhythm of writing a mystery than she had to shift Roger from the supporting cast into the starring role. She'd done many rewrites on *Strangers* before she'd understood where and how to introduce characters and clues. And Will had gone over every page with her line by line, pointing out where she'd overwritten and where she'd failed to say enough. Starting her in her long relationship with Roger had been Will's most significant and lasting gift to her. She'd reminded herself of this fact whenever she had doubts about the marriage, which, as the years passed, occurred more and more frequently.

Strangers ran to three hardcover printings in its American edition, and the paperback sold upward of two hundred thousand copies. Roger's next appearance in print, *Delayed Arrival*, ran to five hardcover printings and more than half a million paperback copies sold. The third book, *Generations*, put Roger on the *Times* best-seller list, and each of the four subsequent books had achieved best-seller status within weeks of publication. She'd completed the last book during the first stages of Will's illness and it had been published thirteen months earlier.

Under normal circumstances she'd have had a new manuscript finished roughly at the same time the previous book was being published. But she'd been too busy and far too distraught even to think of writing during the final months of Will's life. Now she was writing again, back in close contact with her beloved Roger, and was being led by him through the tangled underbrush of the plot like a child entrusting her safety to a favorite uncle. So enamored was she both of Roger and of the process itself that to leave them, even for an hour, was similar, she was sure, to feeling pain in a phantom limb.

She sat with Roger in his Manhattan hotel room as he read the letters purportedly written by Edward Evans's friend Elsa, then leaned back in his chair to consider the whys and wherefores of the matter.

What bothered him most was the lack of a discernible motive. He couldn't get a fix on what it was the writer hoped to accomplish with these letters. There was nothing for it, he thought, but to meet with the lady in question. Only by acquainting himself with the victim could he possibly gain some insight into the puzzling issue of why the letters were being written.

Certainly there was nothing in any way threatening in the letters. They were, as Edward had aptly suggested, more in the nature of directives. That, in itself, was most curious, not at all in keeping with traditional poison-pen letters. He couldn't help wondering what sort of woman this mysterious Elsa must be. . . .

Just before midnight she stored what she'd done to the disk, then spent another half hour writing up additional index cards. At last she turned off the desk light and stood listening to the silence of the house. She looked up and down the length of the hallway before going down the stairs. Switching on lights as she went, she moved from room to room, studying the configuration of walls and furniture and shadows.

The large living room with its formal placement of sofas and chairs grouped centrally before the fireplace struck her as disagreeable. No aspect of the person she believed herself to be was reflected by the room. She lived only in a few of the photographs grouped on the mantel. Otherwise, she might be nothing more than a guest in this house. Soon after the young Willard Bellamy and Alexandra, his first wife, had come to live here, he'd hired a decorator to fit out the rooms. The result was that the taste reflected throughout the house was that of the decorator, not of the inhabitants.

The bedrooms that had once contained Will's four children had long since been converted to guest rooms by the simple expedient of removing all personal touches. A change of linens and curtains and the rooms lost their idiosyncrasies. The library was a classic reproduction of Victorian style, with heavy leather armchairs, brass fireplace tools, and dark wood paneling. The only modern note was the stereo, which she now saw had been left on since Saturday morning.

She crossed to stand before the impressive array of stereo equipment, scanning the various controls and levers and, as nervous as if Will were liable to appear at any moment to demonstrate his displeasure, she pressed the eject button and the compartment popped open. Removing Richard's cassette, she then pressed the power switch and the red indicator light went off. She smiled. Then, backing away to gaze at the shelf of components, she was suddenly very angry. She'd been obliged to ask Will's permission whenever she'd wanted to hear recorded music, and eventually, bridling at the ongoing implication that she was too feckless even to be allowed access to a piece of machinery, she'd listened exclusively to the radio.

Now she wanted the stereo, as well as the racks of compact disks and cassettes. Certain there had to be instruction manuals somewhere, she began a methodical search of the room, going through the storage compartments of the built-in wall units and then through every drawer of Will's desk until she found the manuals in a file marked "Appliances." Tucking them under her arm, she went up to the bedroom, leaving the manuals and Richard's cassette on the bedside table. She read through all the instructions before settling down to sleep. If and when she ever did leave this house, the stereo system was now among the few things she intended to take with her.

Closing her eyes, she grimaced, seeing Will as he'd been near the end. He'd looked to her like an albino spider. The chemotherapy had given him a bloated face and grotesquely distended belly, while his extreme weight loss had turned his arms and legs spindly. His skin had been almost the same shade as his colorless hair, and his eyes as well as his teeth had acquired a yellowish tinge from years of cigarette smoking. He'd taken shaky steps with the aid of a walker, refusing to remain in his bed waiting to die. His arachnoidal figure bobbled toward her across the chambers of her mind and she felt again the horror and repulsion that so heightened her guilt then and now.

He would not die. Transmogrified, he'd spun a viscous web inside her brain and then positioned himself at its axis, from which point he oversaw the impulses traveling through her limbic system or flooding her thalamus. He sank his fangs into the defenseless spongy gray hemispheres, injecting a virulent poison that paralyzed the ventricles at the middle of her brain, causing her to lose control of her emotional responses. In an effort to combat the poison and prevent the brain cells from dying, she had to take in huge amounts of oxygen.

Brought fully awake by the malignity of these images, she sat up and turned on the light, her heart tripping over itself with anxiety. Her arms wound around her bent legs, she rested her chin on her knees as she looked over at Will's chest of drawers.

She'd had such an abundance of love for him and he'd glutted himself on it, gorging repeatedly at the banquet table of her affection until nothing remained but the fragile carcasses of what had once been birds of paradise, and the dusty residue of spun-sugar dreams. Blinded by his greed, he'd sought dominion over every aspect of her existence. And still she'd loved him; still she'd believed he'd earned her loyalty and respect; still she'd complied with his wishes. Because he'd managed to convince her she had nowhere else to go, that no one else would ever tolerate her multiplicity of inadequacies let alone love her as he did. Without Willard Bellamy's benevolent despotism she would flounder and then die. He'd managed to convince her she was basically unlovable.

He took an admittedly naive but happily independent girl of eighteen and turned her into a diffident, morbidly dependent woman, whose only avenue of freedom existed in the exploits of a fictional male counterpart she'd named Roger Hurley. Roger said and did all the things she was not permitted to say or do: he made his opinions known, stated his preferences without embarrassment or apology; he lived as he wished and refused to tolerate incompetence or asininity; he dressed according to his own tastes, indulged his gentler passions, and lived up to his decisions right or wrong.

She'd put into Roger every last one of her thwarted instincts and saw them come right. And Willard Bellamy, clever as he was, never realized that in keeping Roger alive she was ensuring her own survival. It never once occurred to Mr. Bellamy that she was slowly and steadily writing her way to freedom by permitting Roger Hurley to espouse the majority of her innermost values and beliefs, thereby giving them a permanent reality. Everything she believed in and valued was there, on a shelf in the library, for all—including Mr. Bellamy—to see. That he'd neglected to perceive the truer meanings underlying the obvious ruminations of her central character was her greatest success. She'd sneaked her philosophies right past her husband, and he'd never noticed. Willard Bellamy was Roger Hurley's most devoted fan.

"It's amusing, Will. And very bloody ironic. You never appreciated irony, though. It was lost on you; you were too graphic, too linear to relish the subtlety. Well, what do you think of this? I'm going to sell off your prized possessions, Mr. Bellamy; those dismal oil paintings and the massive pieces of furniture you so treasured. And I think I'll donate the proceeds to the homeless, the desperate and the disenfranchised. You remember, Will. All those people who cluttered up Grand Central, whose bodies blocked your passage. The dispossessed who so irritated you by their blatant refusal to help themselves. Yes, I like the idea of that."

Eased by this decision, she turned off the light, and within minutes was able to glide out of range of the late Willard Bellamy.

Richard sat at his secretary's desk in the now-empty office and rolled a piece of stationery into her Selectric typewriter. Then, slowly, painstakingly, his eyes on the keyboard, he began striking one key after another. It took quite some time but at last he was done. A few more minutes and the envelope had been addressed, the letter folded into it, a stamp moistened with tap water affixed in the envelope's upper-right-hand corner.

After dropping the letter into a plastic bag, he peeled off the lightweight latex gloves, exhaling slowly. He'd drop it into the mailbox on his way home, along with the one he'd written the night before. Taking care to turn off the typewriter, he got up and reached for his briefcase.

NO! Emma told her dreaming self. He wouldn't ever do anything like this. She was determined to escape the dream, fighting her way free of it, swimming blindly upward into a waking state.

She came gasping out of her sleep as if she had, in fact, been submerged in deep water. Slipping out of bed, she went into the bathroom, the tile floor shockingly cold beneath her bare feet. Good! The penetrating cold would ground her in reality. Bloody hell! she thought, filling a Dixie cup with water. Richard had nothing at all to gain from tormenting her. Her anxiety was simply spilling over into her subconscious.

"I thought you'd better know Emma made another trip to the mailbox late last night. Looked to me like as if she was carrying only one letter, but it was hard to tell."

"I appreciate the call, Bernice. But I think about all we can do now is wait to see what happens, and hope the situation resolves itself soon. The feeling I have is that to confront her would be kind of like waking a sleepwalker—it might be dangerous. Best to leave things alone and just wait."

"Otherwise," Bernice said with a smile in her voice, "she seems a whole lot better. Thanks to you, I'd say."

Richard laughed. "I never realized you were into matchmaking."

"Never was," she said. "I hear her coming. I better run."

"Thanks for letting me know, Bernice. I really do appreciate it."

"You're welcome, Richard."

"I liked that book," Bernice said over breakfast. "It was real good, made me cry when the grandmother died."

"I cried, too," Emma said, pleased. "I'm delighted you liked it."

"I hope you don't mind. I gave it to my Marla
to read."

"I don't mind in the least."

"The Salvation Army people're comin' Thursday to pick up them clothes."

"Good. Thank you for taking care of that."

"You're out tonight, right?"

"That's right."

"You say that like as if you think maybe I'm
gonna say you can't go. Stickin' your chin out all
stubborn."

"Did I do that?"

"Uh-huh."

"Oh, dear." Emma smiled. "I was wondering
if you'd help me move the stereo after breakfast."

"Where to?"

"Up to the office, I think."

"Sure. You know how to hook it all back up?"

"I'm confident I can sort it out."

"Okay. That's fine." Bernice grinned suddenly.
"Boy, wouldn't Mr. Willard just shit he knew you
were fussin' with his fancy stereo?"

Emma laughed impishly. "Wherever he is, I
hope he's positively diarrhetic."

"That mean what I think it does?" Bernice
wanted to know, not sure if she should laugh.

"It certainly does."

"You're *bad!*" Bernice declared with a bark of
laughter. "Gettin' badder every day, too."

"I certainly hope so. Oh, before I forget. I'll be
going into the city tomorrow. I'm interviewing
a new agent at lunch. Then I'll be meeting with
Kathy and Jim Finney."

"You're gettin' a new agent? What about that Mr. Colsen?"

"Mr. Colsen is no more."

"Well, you don't say! You're just full of surprises these days."

Emma smiled. "Believe it or not, Bernice, I used to be quite a feisty young thing. I had no qualms about sailing into offices filled with total strangers and introducing myself all around. I often ate alone in small restaurants, went by myself to films and the theatre. It's time, don't you agree, that I started doing some of those things again?"

"Maybe so," Bernice agreed. "Looks to me like Richard's doin' you a world of good."

At the mention of his name, Emma colored, filling with anticipation for the sight and sound and feel of him. "Let's go move that stereo." she said. "Then I'll come back to take Calla for her run."

Crossing each item off her list as it was accomplished, Emma washed and ironed Richard's handkerchief; she changed the dressing on her arm, noting with relief that it was healing nicely; she telephoned Sotheby's and made an appointment to have an appraiser come to the house the following week; and she called Linda to tell her how much Bernice had enjoyed *Glass Houses*.

"I always knew Bernice had great taste," Linda chortled. "So how did you make out with Dana?"

"We're having lunch tomorrow."

"You'll love her. She's the single most important person in my life, next to Chris. And long after Chris is nothing more than a delicious memory, I'll still be with Dana."

"Why do you say that about Chris?"

"Common sense," Linda said unemotionally. "A guy that young's bound to move on sooner or later. While he's around I intend to enjoy the hell out of him, but I'm not kidding myself. So what's up with you and that hot lawyer?"

"We're having dinner this evening."

"This is great!" Linda said. "Seriously. He's probably one of the few surviving heterosexuals."

"Probably," Emma said cautiously.

"Lighten up, sweetcakes! I'm the last person on earth who'd come down on you for enjoying a little romance. I really do think it's great. And how goes the new book?"

"It's coming very quickly. I'm about to start the fourth chapter."

"Must be a nice change not having anyone hanging over your shoulder," Linda said meaningfully.

"It's odd more than anything else. But I'm enjoying it."

"I'm happy for you, Em. Honest to God. You more than most people deserve to get a little pleasure from life while you're still young enough to enjoy it. So speaking of pleasure, when'm I going to see you?"

"I'm not sure. Let's talk toward the end of the week. Perhaps we could have brunch on Sunday."

"If you can tear yourself away from the stalwart Roger Hurley and the seriously sensual Richard Redmond."

"That's right." Emma smiled. She always felt better for talking to Linda.

"Okay. I'll call you. Have fun tonight!"

"Thank you. I intend to."

With all the items on her list accomplished, she popped Richard's cassette into the machine, smiled—pleased with herself—as the music emerged from the speakers, then returned to the desk. She switched off the ringer on the telephone and recalled from the disk her latest chapter. She felt better than she had in many years—and younger. It was fairly remarkable that a few simple acts, like taking possession of a stereo, for example, or laundering a handkerchief, could be so beneficial. She just wished she hadn't had that very detailed dream of Richard. Every time she thought of it, and she seemed unable to stop thinking of it, she felt decidedly uneasy.

Chapter Twenty

After lunch the next day, Emma took Calla for a short walk to the bottom of the driveway to collect the mail from the box. There was another of Regent's manila envelopes that arrived every few weeks with a batch of fan letters; bills from Southern New England Telephone, NorthEast Utilities, American Express, and one from the local bookstore; the usual advertising flyers, and a letter addressed to her. Upon seeing the envelope—recognizably one of her own—she was seized by a fear so immediate and overwhelming that her body turned cold, and she was unable to move.

Calla was dancing about at her feet, looking up at her as she turned in half circles, eager to get going. That feeling that she was being watched was very pronounced. Her heart beating far too quickly and making her feel rather ill, Emma surveyed the road in both directions. No one.

She glanced down at the dog then looked again at the letter, trying to calm herself sufficiently to retrace her steps to the house. She wanted to tear the thing to pieces without opening it, but was unable. She was going to have to read it to know what else the mystery writer had learned of her secrets.

"Okay, Calla." Her voice was thin, without volume, just a shaping of the air expelled by her constricted lungs. "Come, girl."

She ordered her legs to move and they obeyed, propelling her forward but in so robotlike a fashion that she was aware of the bones grinding in her hip sockets, the creaking of her knees. The sight of the letter had robbed her joints of their lubricity. Calla kept running ahead then stopping to look back as if to ask why Emma was taking so long.

It seemed hours before she made it up the front steps and into the house. Calla bounced off to the kitchen and Emma stood gazing up the stairs, hearing the noise of the vacuum cleaner overhead. Feeling crippled, she made her way up the stairs, one hand gripping the banister for support as she progressed stiffly from one riser to the next.

The cord from the vacuum cleaner snaked from the outlet in the hallway along the carpet, disappearing inside the master suite. Emma made it to the office and fell into her chair, spreading the day's mail on the desk. Setting aside the letter, she attended first to the bills, opening them one by one, discarding the envelopes, taking quick notice of the totals due before setting them to one side. Then the envelope from Regent. Fourteen fan letters. She stacked them neatly beside the typewriter. The letter. Her heart pumping crazily, she slit open the envelope.

Emma,
    You know what you did. And you lied. You made promises you never intended to keep. You lied again, and again. Did you really think you'd get away with it? Did you really think no one would ever know? Be very careful. The truth will be known.

There was no date, no signature, just the alarming accusations, the warning, the implied threat.

Her heart was beating so fast, the blood galloping at such a frenzied pace through the valves and ventricles that she felt nauseated and had to put her head down on the desk, closing her eyes and trying to control her breathing. *You know what you did.* Oh, God! Who was behind this? Why did someone want to cause her additional suffering?

This letter-writer was inverting her world, creating havoc, forcing her to accommodate insults and assault, revealing things to friends and enemies that were better left unsaid. How long was this going to go on? How many more of these letters were going to come to light? She wished she could run away, go somewhere so remote that nothing could possibly touch her. But where? And again she had to wonder if was this the intent of the campaign: to drive her away.

"What're you doin'?" Bernice asked from the doorway. "Somethin' the matter?"

With a mammoth effort, Emma lifted her head.

"You sick?" Bernice asked, concerned. "You look awful." Emma's face had turned dead white, making the fading bruise on her cheek stand out. She'd gone kind of green around the mouth and her eyes looked hollow. "You wanna lie down?" Bernice said, approaching the side of the desk. "Come on with me." She took Emma by the arm, leading her to the bedroom. "You're not gettin' enough sleep, I can tell. You close your eyes for a while, try to rest, and I'll go make you a cup of tea."

Emma was relieved to have her take charge and docilely stretched out on the bed, whispering, "Thank you."

Bernice wasn't in the habit of snooping but as she was passing the office on her way down to the kitchen she glanced in, saw the mail arranged on the desk and stepped over to glance at the open letter. After scanning it hastily, she hurried along to the kitchen to fill the kettle. While she was waiting for it to come to the boil, she wondered what it could mean. *You know what you did.* What was the woman accusing herself of? Emma never did a thing to anybody, and she sure as hell never lied. If anything she was, until the past week or so, the least adventuresome woman Bernice had ever encountered. It was like as if Mr. Willard had made her afraid to say or do things, the way he was forever hustling her out of the kitchen, or talking to her like a small child, telling her not to touch this or that, picking out what she should wear if they were going out of an evening or if Emma had to go into the city to meet with her publisher.

There was this one time when Bernice was cleaning the guest rooms after they'd had a bunch of Mr. Willard's friends to stay over a weekend and she heard him go interrupting Emma in her office to recite this list of all the things she'd said and done wrong while his friends were visiting. Bernice could still hear the schoolteacherish way he'd told Emma that a woman in her position didn't offer to go running out to the car to fetch something one of the women had forgotten to bring in. And when was she going to learn not to talk about politics, let alone go getting angry and disagreeing with his important associates? And would she, please, stop helping with the food when they had a housekeeper who was paid to look after that? On and on he went, listing every last little thing Emma had said or done that he didn't like.

It had been one of the many times when Bernice couldn't understand why Emma didn't just pick up and leave. He was so mean-minded, watching her every move. But Emma let him talk himself out. Then she said, "Have you quite finished?" and went back to her work. Bernice thought Emma was smart not to argue and make matters worse. Because sure enough it seemed like as if once he'd got everything off his chest, he forgot all about it and went back to being sweet as pie and real interested in what Emma was writing.

And that whole time the man was sick, Emma was at the hospital night and day, and right there to help him when he came home again. Bernice would come into the kitchen of a morning to find Emma sitting drinking tea, having sat up with him the whole night because he wasn't happy with the nurses, and couldn't sleep unless she was nearby. So what was it she was supposed to've done? Bernice wondered. And why was she looking to punish herself with these letters? It was exactly like as if she'd split into two people—the one she'd been up 'til Mr. Willard died, and the one she was becoming now. Or was she going mental? Bernice didn't know what to think.

When she carried the tea into the bedroom, Emma was just coming out of the bathroom.

"I think I'll come downstairs to have my tea," she told Bernice. "I need a biscuit, or a slice of toast."

"You throw up?" Bernice asked, worried.

"I actually feel better for it. How can I possibly go out with Richard this evening?" she said, more to herself than to Bernice.

"Best thing in the world for you," Bernice advised. "Better than sitting around here fussin' over them letters." Bernice realized she'd given herself away and tried to think how to explain.

"I'll be terrible company."

Relieved that Emma didn't seem to suspect her of snooping, Bernice said, "So call the man up and warn him."

Emma appeared bothered by the idea. "I couldn't do that."

"Why not?"

"He'll be angry." Emma was confronted by a mental montage of Will displaying his anger in dozens of instances, all overlapping each other, to form an endless tirade. And the main point of this particular montage was that one did not change plans at the last moment, no matter how valid one's reasons might be.

"You're gettin' him confused with Mr. Willard," Bernice said bluntly. "Besides, Richard's in no position to go gettin' mad if you change your mind. He's got no claim on you, woman. He's just a man you're seein', aside from bein' your lawyer."

"No," Emma acknowledged, seeing the wisdom of Bernice's logic, but intimidated by even the remotest possibility of unpleasantness.

"Go call him," Bernice ordered, determined not to allow Emma to backslide into her former timid ways. "See if he don't say it's perfectly okay."

While Bernice fixed some toast, Emma used the telephone in the kitchen.

"I thought I should warn you," Emma said rather worriedly when he came on the line. "I'm not going to be very good company this evening."

"Another letter?" he guessed.

Shifting so her back was to Bernice and lowering her voice, she said, "Yes. And this time it was addressed to me." *Was* it possible Richard was responsible for these letters? That dream had been so vividly detailed. But it was only a dream. She had no real cause to suspect him.

"I assume that's why you sound as if you've just been sandbagged. Would it help if I had a look at it?"

"I don't think so," she said quickly, anxious to keep the contents from him. "But thank you for offering. Perhaps it would be best if we arranged to meet some other evening."

"Come on, Emma," he coaxed. "Let me try to cheer you up."

"It's hardly fair to you . . ."

"Sure it is. If the situation were reversed, wouldn't you want to cheer me up?"

She smiled, feeling the knot in her chest loosening. "I would want to, yes." Her doubts were totally unfounded. Richard cared too much for her to want to cause her undue pain.

"So, okay. I'll pick you up at seven. You do have to eat, after all. And so do I."

"All right," she relented. "It's very kind of you."

"It's selfish. I've really been looking forward to seeing you."

"And I you. Thank you for being so understanding."

"I know it's probably useless advice, but try not to think about whatever was in the letter that's upset you. And if you change your mind and decide to let me see it, I'll be glad to give you my opinion, for whatever it's worth. Okay?"

"Yes, okay. Goodbye, Richard."

"He said he'd go with you anyway, didn't he?" Bernice said, reheating the tea in the microwave. "He's not a man's gonna be put off all that easily. So, are you ready to tell me what's got you so worked up?"

Emma stared down at the tabletop, her hands clenched together in front of her. "It's these letters, Bernice, as you said."

"Another one?" Bernice asked casually, bringing over the plate of toast and the cup of tea.

Emma nodded and wrapped her hands around the cup, allowing its warmth to penetrate her. "It's as if every time I take a step or two forward another letter turns up to set me back."

"I don't know. Seems like as if they're clearin' up a whole lot of things," Bernice said. "Gettin' rid of that Mr. Colsen can't be a bad thing. I never did care much for him, the way he was always actin' so important. Those times he came for dinner, he struck me as real cocky, like as if he thought he was the smartest fella ever lived. Who's this new agent you're meetin' tomorrow? What's he like?"

"He's a woman," Emma said. "She represents Linda. And she certainly sounds likeable over the telephone."

"So, see! That's a good thing that's happened."

"That's true, but it's probably an inadvertent bonus." Emma took a sip of the tea, then bit into a piece of toast. "I've always had a horror of confrontations, you know, Bernice. I might never have fired Jack if it hadn't been for that letter. But I was anxious to be rid of him. It's a great relief to think I don't have to see or speak to him again."

"Is that why you put up with Mr. Willard forever telling you what to say and not say, what to put on your back, what to do?"

Eyes widening, Emma looked across the table. "You must think I'm a dreadful coward."

"You want to know what I *really* think?"

"Yes, I do."

"I think you were afraid of the man, that's what I think. I've known some women got beat up by their husbands. They had the same kind of look to their eyes I saw you get plenty of times."

"Will never struck me."

"Didn't have to, did he?" Bernice said shrewdly, folding her arms in front of her on the table, her posture revealing her anger. "He just kept you on edge all the time. Maybe he never meant you no harm. I truly don't think he did. But he sure liked to keep you down, keep you relyin' on him, keep you a child. I never could figure out why you put up with that, why you didn't leave. And don't go tellin' me again how you loved the man. Tell me how come you stayed."

"I wanted to leave," Emma confessed, her eyes filling. She ran both hands over her hair then sat hunched forward. "For years, it was all I could think of. But every time I made up my mind to go, he seemed to sense it, and he'd become very solicitous, very attentive. He'd bring me gifts, and praise me, praise my work, until I was convinced our only problem was that I was stubborn, I wouldn't give in when I probably should have. It was my fault because I made things difficult. And he'd been working too hard and was venting his stress at my expense." Hesitantly, she said, "When I say I loved him, Bernice, I did. But it was a memory. It was obligation and indebtedness and gratitude; it was once upon a time, years ago. It wasn't last year or the year before that, or even five years ago. He killed my caring, just as he trampled Janet's spirit when he told her that in his opinion the boy she loved had only been using her and that she was never to see him again; and that she'd be a murderer if she got rid of the baby, as well as a fool if she allowed the boy access to the child. And he shattered any hope Shawn might have had of finding some measure of happiness by scoffing at his dreams of becoming an actor. The only Bellamy, Willard said, who had any place on a stage was Ralph. Shawn had no special talent, and Willard certainly wasn't going to subsidize him while he tried to get a foot in the door. They were too vulnerable to him. But I protected Susan and Edgar, cautioned them not to reveal their aspirations to their father. I protected Laurie, too. Will simply couldn't see how damaging, how damning his judgments were. The best and worst thing about him was the extent to which he was prepared to go when he believed he was right."

"I could see that," Bernice said quietly, her eyes narrowed. "Man liked to have his own way."

"It was much more than that," Emma told her, uniquely able to discuss her late husband with this woman because Bernice had known him, had so often been a witness to his tyrannical posturings. "He *had* to be right. Sometimes he was. Certainly he was right about the direction of my writing. He put a tremendous amount of time and effort into helping me. And once he was satisfied that I could take instruction, he arranged everything—getting me my British agent, then putting me together with Jack Colsen. He worked every bit as hard as I did to make me a success."

"It made him look good, too, don't forget," Bernice put in.

"He treated his first wife the same way, you know." Emma picked up the piece of toast and gazed at it, as if debating whether or not it was edible.

"Is that right?" Bernice's shoulders relaxed slightly.

"I met her once. I've never told you about that, have I? We met at a party. We looked enough alike to have been sisters. It was eerie. We kept staring at each other as if we were looking into a freakish mirror that reflected her as she'd once been and showed me how I'd appear in another twenty or so years. I liked her at once. She was understandably cynical but very well intentioned. And she managed in only a few sentences to let me know that Will had done precisely the same things to her he was doing to me. At the time I felt sinful merely listening to her. But it was all too obvious she was telling the truth, and it frightened me. I knew if I didn't stand my ground, he'd eventually render me incapable of being anything more than a performing doll. Nevertheless, I still couldn't leave him." She put down the toast and dusted the crumbs from her fingers. "Then," she said, "it reached a point where I realized that if I didn't go, if I didn't salvage whatever I had left of my instincts and self-esteem, I'd be trapped with him for the rest of my life. And that frightened me more than the prospect of trying to make a go of living alone. For years he steadily chipped away at my confidence, implying in one way or another that I wasn't competent to handle my own affairs, that I had no concept of how to comport myself, and that without him I'd undoubtedly make a hash of everything. I clung to my memory of those five months in London when I'd managed perfectly well on my own, when I'd been sublimely happy and completely in charge of myself. So I worked on what I wanted to say to him, and planned when I'd make my announcement and where I'd go when I left him. I was profoundly afraid, but what helped me maintain my determination was the realization that once I was free it was unlikely I'd ever again be so fearful. After being married to Willard for close to fifteen years I felt equipped to deal with almost anything strangers might do. Plus, it was doubtful that any stranger would be cognizant, as Will was, of every last one of my weak points.

"He hadn't been feeling well during his last trip to Europe. Remember? He kept complaining but he wouldn't do anything about it. I finally telephoned Stephen Fisher's office and made an appointment for him. Of course, my doing that prompted another exhausting argument that only firmed my resolution to go. Will kept the appointment. Stephen booked him into the hospital that same night. And I knew it was serious, that something was dreadfully wrong. But *still* I planned to leave. I'd go as soon as the tests were completed and Stephen and the other doctors had taken care of whatever was ailing Will. I'd even booked into a hotel in the city and changed my reservation to coincide with Will's projected release from the hospital.

"You know what happened, Bernice. They didn't release him. They made a preliminary diagnosis, then scheduled the exploratory surgery. After that they bombarded him with chemicals. I couldn't possibly go off and abandon the man to his terminal cancer. Whatever he was, whatever he'd done, he didn't deserve to be left to cope alone, to die alone. And even if I'd gone earlier, I know perfectly well I'd have come back when I learned he was ill. It was too late. For both of us."

"Damn!" Bernice said softly.

"Yes, damn. I felt guilty for not leaving sooner, guilty for wanting to leave in the first place, and guilty for staying to minister to this man out of ancient gratitude and pity. And now, just when I'm beginning to see a bit of light at the end of the proverbial tunnel, someone's decided to play this evil prank. Every so often, you know, I wish I was the one who'd died. It would have been such a *relief*."

"It's hard bein' the one who gets left," Bernice agreed. "In lots of ways it seems easier for the one who dies. It's over for him. He's free, while we've got to try holdin' on to all the pieces."

"That's it exactly! I thought I was the only one who felt this way."

"Well, you're not. Okay? You know your problem, Emma? You don't talk about how you're feelin'. You keep everythin' bottled up inside, and that's the worst thing you can do. If you talk, you find out other folks feel the same exact way you do. Then you don't have to sit around worryin' that you're crazy, or bad, or wrong, because you're only human after all, like the rest of us, with good feelings and bad ones and all that comes in between."

"That's true," Emma said, thinking again of that letter upstairs on her desk. *You know what you did.* Sadly, there were some things that couldn't be confided, because to admit to them was far too dangerous. Perhaps it would never end. She'd spend the remainder of her life grimly anticipating more poisonous letters that would destroy her small store of hard-won equilibrium.

"You bet it's true," Bernice said forcefully. "Don't be afraid to tell how you feel. You've got friends, people who love you."

"Thank you, Bernice," she said thickly. "I love you, too."

"Eat up that toast now and finish your tea so you can get back to work."

"Yes," Emma said distractedly, thinking Roger was there, waiting to help her pick her way through the treacherous tangle of her thoughts. Roger was ready to provide sanctuary. He would permit her to speak through him, to clamber through the tightly coiled chambers of his agile brain in order to assess the often bewildering behavior of others, and to hide behind his valiant shadow. Roger was, more than anything else, a humanitarian, and would understand perfectly why she'd done what she had. And he would never presume to judge or condemn her.

Chapter Twenty-One

For a time Emma studied Richard as he drowsed at her side, gazing with an ache of fondness at his sleeping features and wondering how some men, like Richard, managed to grow to adulthood with so many of their best qualities intact while others, like Will, grew to become men still firmly clutching the least attractive attitudes of small children. Regardless of, or perhaps because of his losses and disappointments, Richard remained an optimist, a man who cared about giving, about reciprocity. Smiling to herself, she imagined the boy Richard sharing his sweets with his friends. He'd have been a child unable to enjoy his treats unless his friends partook of them too. His generosity was ingrained, somehow spiritual, an essential part of his character. It was paired with an awareness of others. When he made love it wasn't an arduous

304

exercise aimed at personal gratification but an attempt to demonstrate a *feeling* and to share it. Had she always suspected he'd be the way he was? Had she actually thought of it? Some things were simply *known*. The sense one had of certain people was one of completeness. You knew that person instinctively and knew, too, how they'd behave in certain situations. And she'd known, without ever having done more than shake hands with the man, that when he gave his heart it was without reservation. Now, incredibly, he'd chosen to open his heart to her, and each time they lay down skin to skin, each time they touched, she felt something frozen at her very core begin to thaw. His affection, the all-but-reverential manner of his slightest caress, were reviving the vital, hope-filled eighteen-year-old who'd been in hiding inside her for almost half her life. Like some cryogenically preserved being, the girl she'd once been was again showing signs of life.

She looked lazily over at her discarded clothes, recalling her Sunday-afternoon shopping expedition, and the kindness of the young woman in the Ralph Lauren department of Saks, and of the one at Rodier. With unfettered enthusiasm they'd suggested styles and colors and sizes, and she'd tried things on, managing to see in the mirrors only the clothes and not her face. She'd made her decisions based on what could very well have been a headless manne-quin's reflection. Now each time she donned one of the new outfits she suspected that her head was very possibly an atrocious mismatch to the items she put on her body. She felt caught midway between the past and the future, like some creation only partially metamorphosed: half what she'd been and might again be, and half what she'd become in the course of the marriage and wished no longer to be.

Gradually awakening, Richard noticed the worried furrow between her brows, and wondered with a pang of misgiving if he was not only expecting too much of her, but also placing unwarranted hope in his mounting affection for her. He told himself it was unreasonable to assume responsibility for her mood when it likely had nothing to do with him. But he'd decided to see this through, regardless of what the resolution might be. So there was little point to anticipating the blame, and considerable value in making every effort to maintain the level of communication they'd established. He reached over and touched the tip of his finger to the middle of her brow.

She reacted with a start. He moved to withdraw his hand but she took hold of it, lacing her fingers through his and bringing it to rest on her midriff.

"What were you thinking, Emma?"

"Does your head ever feel rather too small to contain all your thoughts?"

"Frequently," he answered with a smile. "When I've got too much on my plate and I bring files home to work on in the evening, but the guy upstairs happens to be home for a change, and he's got the dishwasher *and* the washer and dryer going, plus he decides to start vacuuming at ten o'clock at night. And given the construction of this place, it sounds like a jet taking off, which kills my concentration. Then, on top of all that, I get sidetracked and start daydreaming about a certain woman, about how she looks and feels, the things she says and does. At that point, my head feels like a small sandwich bag I'm trying to stretch over a watermelon."

She laughed. "How is it I've been your client all these years and never knew you had such a good sense of humor? Most everything else about you I've surmised, but not that. Why, do you think?"

"Consider the circumstances," he reminded her. "Most of the time we were involved in legal matters, and Willard was usually with you. He wasn't someone who inspired me to toss off witticisms. And, aside from everything else, he was my first big client."

"Did you have a great satchel of gratitude, too, Richard?" She shifted to face him.

"Not a great satchel, more like a small box."

"Until last weekend, I hadn't realized how rarely I'd laughed during the years of my marriage. And when I did, it was usually with Laurie. He rekindled my sense of fun, which, in turn, aroused my guilt. I expected Will or Janet to come in demanding to know what was going on. I think Laurie's one of the prime reasons why I'm even remotely rational. And there's another bit of irony. Janet desperately wanted to abort the baby, but Will made it impossible for her. Yet he'd have insisted on my having an abortion if I'd managed to get pregnant."

"A tad contradictory."

"I keep trying to understand his behavior, as if it would change anything now." They were so close, she thought, savoring Richard's warmth and his instinctual supportiveness. Would he understand? She had the letter in her bag. All she had to do was slip away for a moment and get it. He'd ask what it meant, and she'd confide at last the harrowing details. He might absolve her. Or he might be repelled. She couldn't summon the courage to take the risk. Sliding down so they were even closer, she said, "If you were free to go anywhere at all and start fresh, where would you go?" Of its own volition her hand stroked the broad, smooth expanse of his chest. People were miraculous constructions, when you thought about it. Fiber and sinew, tissues and liquid, a construction that could cease, so alarmingly easily, to exist.

He took a deep breath and considered the question while exploring her eyes, searching for some clue that would dictate his answer. But that was cowardly, he thought, ashamed of the impulse. "I don't know," he said, feeling as if he'd just skidded away from the safety of the shoreline into the treacherous center of an iced-over pond. "I guess I'd want to go wherever you were."

"Would you, Richard?" she asked. "Why?"

"You seem surprised by that," he said, noting the way her pale eyebrows had lifted at his reply.

"I am, rather. Why?" she asked again.

"Why?" he repeated, giving himself a few seconds' extra thinking time. "Because when I told you Saturday morning I was scared, it was the truth. What scares me more, though, is the idea that I'd miss out because it's too easy being safe. And I'm tired of that. When you're safe you're only halfway alive at best.

With you, there's no doubt I'm fully alive." As if to emphasize the fact, he molded his hand to the rise of her hip and applied a gentle pressure.

"The lives we lead inside our heads are so much less complicated than the reality all around us." Her fingers tightened around his and she gazed off to one side. "I'm not quite so truthful as you."

"I think you're way beyond me in that department."

"There are things I've done I'm not proud of."

"We've all got those memories, Emma."

She returned her eyes to his. "I keep thinking I'm bound to frighten you with my peculiarities, my lurid revelations. But I so hoped you'd say you'd want to be with me. I'm starting to believe in possibilities again because of you." She smiled slowly. "You're having a profoundly positive effect on mc. In fact, Roger Hurley's starting to sound rather like you."

"He is? What's old Roger been saying?"

"He's been ruminating in your tone of voice, so to speak. I'm having to watch him closely, to stop him going out of character."

"That's flattering," he said happily. "I can't wait to read this book. How's it coming?"

"Very well, much more quickly than usual. I think it's because this one is entirely mine. It won't bear Will's imprint, and I won't be fighting his usual suggestions that I add more 'juice' to whatever sexual scenes there might be, or that I heighten the male characters at the expense of the females. For the first time ever I'm free to work at my own pace, in my own way. On the last book, I extended him the courtesy, as I always had, of giving him the chapters as they were completed, but I merely pretended to consider his comments. By then I resented his interference, his constant attempts to contravene my editor's judgment. I resented *him*," she admitted, suddenly seeing again the albino spider with its hirsute legs spraddled over her brain.

"What is it?" he asked, seeing her fleeting look of horror, feeling the sudden tightening of her muscles.

"It's nothing," she said quickly. "I'm going into the city tomorrow to meet with a new agent."

"And that gives you the willies?"

It was a convenient explanation to cover her brief spasm of revulsion, and she took advantage of the opening he'd provided. "Somewhat. Embarking on a new era, with a new book and a new agent. It's unnerving." Feeling she'd managed to stop herself from saying too much, she kissed his shoulder, then let her head rest against his chest. "I'm going to have to go home shortly. I want to get a bit more work done tonight."

"Is it," he asked carefully, "within the realm of possibility that I might visit you at home one evening?"

"You could come to dinner. Bernice is a splendid cook, as you know." For a few moments she remembered the occasions when Richard, as their attorney, had brought Dell to dinner. Such stilted occasions they'd been, with Will expounding on something or other while she and Richard and Dell, but Richard primarily, exchanged glances, listening usually without comment. A dozen or so dinners over the years and each time, without fail, she'd suffered a low-grade embarrassment at her husband's need for an audience. "Would you like to do that? Or are your memories of previous dinners such that you'd prefer not to?"

"I don't have any particularly unpleasant memories," he said. "Name the night and I'll be there."

"Thursday," she said, pulling back slightly. "I do realize that you're asking if I'll make love to you somewhere other than here or in your automobile. I'd like very much to offer you free access to the house, to take you into my bedroom and make love to you in my bed. I have thought about it. I've even imagined how it would be to have you living in the house. I've pictured you in every room, and the pictures pleased me. I just can't be premeditated about the things you and I do now." The resident ghost might shake down the walls if she invited Richard into his marital bed. She had a vision of the windows shattering, the plaster rupturing, the floors heaving upward. Wrapping her arms around Richard with sudden ferocity, she whispered, "I want to keep you forever! I'd like to be able to see you every day. I like the sound of your voice, and the way you smile, the way you make love. But I don't know the protocol, and I can't help thinking perhaps it's wrong to admit my feelings for you. One's supposed to hold back, play out one's emotions like a fishing line. I never had an opportunity to learn how the game's played. You've socialized, led a relatively normal life. Tell me, is it gauche to confess I've thought about what it might be like to share my life with you?"

"If there *is* a protocol, I'll be damned if I know what it is. All I do know is it's a damned shame we have to be so afraid that if we show we care we'll be laughed at or rejected. It's a hell of a thing, isn't it, that the older we get the less willing we are to take chances with our emotions. You get burned, so you swear you'll never do it again. I've thought about it, too, imagined what it'd be like to live with you."

"Do you ever regret having loved Dell?"

"No. I could never regret that. We had a lot of good years. What about you?"

She was silent for a long moment. Now was the perfect opportunity. She could reveal what she'd done, then release him while it was still possible for them to separate with relatively little pain. The more time she allowed to pass, the more desolated they both would be at parting. At length she said, "I made a commitment and I honored it. In that, I have no regrets. But with the exception of the opportunity to form an attachment with Laurie, and to a lesser degree with Susan and Edgar, I regret every last minute of those seventeen years. Will loved power and control and possession. He loved what he perceived to be the status of having an adoring child bride, and he very definitely loved my writing ability and the reflected glory that brought him. But he never loved *me*. He had no idea who I was. His only concern was shaping me to suit his *idea* of who I was. And finally," she whispered fervently, "I despised myself for ever having loved him, for having allowed him to do the countless demeaning things he did to me."

"And that's why you covered all the mirrors, isn't it?"

"That is precisely why," she said, and in one swift motion disengaged herself and swung her legs over the side of the bed. "I really must go."

"It's a mistake to blame yourself," he said, disturbed by the way she could, so abruptly, sever herself from him. "Especially since no one else would."

"That remains to be seen." Not bothering with her undergarments, she pulled on her clothes, then stepped into her shoes. She and Richard were swimming in dangerous waters. It was important to beware of the undertow. Once dressed, she waited with visible impatience for Richard to follow suit.

Crossing the room to stand in front of her, he placed his hands on her shoulders, asking, "Are you angry with me or with yourself for admitting that?"

To his consternation, tears welled up in her eyes and she appeared unable to speak. "I have this freshly laundered handkerchief," he said lightly, picking up his trousers and pulling it from the pocket to blot her cheeks. Then tilting up her chin, he gave her a smile. "We'll work it all out," he promised. "You have my word."

"Please forgive me. My erraticism has nothing to do with you." She looked at him with a touchingly childlike defenselessness, her eyes revealing a wealth of hope and fear, and asked, "Do you love me, Richard?"

The question and the innocence with which she asked it stabbed directly into his solar plexus. "Yes, I love you. It's something that's always been there but never had a chance to happen. You know?"

She nodded. "I've known it since the first time I saw you. For the briefest instant of time I wished with all my heart that I'd met you first, and not Will." He'd said what she'd wanted and needed to hear, and now she felt positively corrupt for coercing him into declaring himself when she was utterly unable to reciprocate. It was all at the ready inside her, but there was a needlelike stabbing in her brain, as if the spider's fangs were injecting their venom into the sensitive lobes. "Please, will you take me home now? I really must go." It seemed the more she grew to care for this man, the more the fear spread, the more piercing the pain.

The slightest, all but unnoticeable flinch. Then he responded with one of his beautiful smiles, saying, "Sure. Let me just throw on some clothes."

Roger stood at the top of the driveway and surveyed the formidable gray stone edifice of the manse-like dwelling. Feeling somewhat chilled, he walked with Edward to the front door.

"You say your friend lives here alone?" he asked Edward.

"With the housekeeper," Edward replied.

"The house puts me in mind of Queen Victoria," Roger said wryly. "Ruling her dominions with her back squarely to the sea."

Edward laughed appreciatively and rang the bell, anticipating Roger's surprise at meeting Elsa. He was certain Roger had already formed a mental picture of her based on the letters and on what Edward had told him of her late husband and his children. It was Edward's experience that people were rarely prepared for their first view of this woman he found so compellingly contradictory. He'd witnessed a variety of reactions and never failed to be fascinated by the ways in which people responded to Elsa.

The housekeeper directed them to the solarium at the rear of the house, and Roger glanced into rooms as he passed. The funereal atmosphere was compounded by the sterility of the furnishings and by the mirrors, all of which were concealed behind lengths of black cloth.

"How long did you say it's been since her husband died?" Roger asked.

"Seven months," Edward replied. "I don't know why the mirrors are shrouded. Unnerving, isn't it?"

Roger was forced to agree. "Very religious, is she?"

"Not particularly," Edward said. "I think it's strictly personal. I haven't had the heart to ask."

A slender woman, perhaps seven or eight inches over five feet, was standing by the glass wall gazing fixedly at the splendid view, a small dog at her side also seemingly preoccupied with the panoramic expanse of wild grass running down to the shore. Everything about her, from the somewhat rigid set of her shoulders to the flex of the fingers curled at her sides, bespoke sadness. In one glance, Roger took in the pleasing shape of her head with its boyishly cropped hair, the graceful line of the exposed nape of her neck, the delicacy of her small, well-formed ears. He could only guess at the body concealed by a rather shapeless cotton frock in a style suited only to very young girls. Edward spoke her name and she turned with a start, as did the dog. She stared at them for a moment with large, deep-set brown eyes, then came forward with her hand extended, and Roger felt equally startled and somehow wounded by the sight of her disfigurement. . . .

"So how did you like Dana?" Kathy was asking.

"I liked her very much," Emma answered, looking from Kathy to Jim, who was slouched in his chair with his crossed ankles propped on the edge of the desk. She felt as if she'd been running full-tilt since very early that morning. A jittery excitement kept her on edge, and she was longing to be on the train on her way back to Connecticut. Perhaps Will had been right. Perhaps she really had lost the knack—if ever she'd had it—of coping with her own affairs.

"She's good," Jim said astutely. "Dana's smart, and she's tough, and she'll kill for her authors. So what's your idea?" he asked. "We dump the existing contract on the grounds of nondelivery, then renegotiate with Dana?"

"Basically, yes." Emma opened her handbag, withdrew an envelope and placed it on the edge of the desk. "I've written you a check for the full amount of the advance. This way, Jack gets

316

to retain the commission he's already received. And since he wouldn't dream of returning it, I would think that gives us a decided edge should he consider litigating at some future date. He can scarcely claim lost income when he's benefited from a canceled contract."

"Dana will try to hike up your advance," Jim said shrewdly.

"No. We've discussed it and she'll abide by my decision on the matter, which is to go to contract under the same terms. Her suggestion is that we document everything and then wait until I've completed the current manuscript before we write up a new contract. That will add another three months or so to the term of nondelivery, which will further support the cancellation of the existing contract."

"Well," said Jim, folding his arms behind his head as he mentally calculated the possible risks, "I don't foresee any problems. Colsen could make a fuss when word gets around we've re-signed you. But since he's only the agent in this case and not a directly injured party, I can't see him pushing to litigate. Especially not when he gets to keep the seventy-five hundred he took up front." He ran a hand over his unruly hair, then lifted his feet down and swung around to lean with both arms on the desktop. "Pretty sharp," he said with a mischievous grin. "You think this up all by yourself, Em?"

"All by myself." She smiled back at him, elated by the day's events, despite her uneasiness. She'd hit it off at once with Dana Brown, and Jim, as she'd hoped, was disposed to go along with her proposition.

"Who'da thunk it?" he said, using one of his

favorite expressions to indicate his satisfaction. "Colsen's out. Dana's in. And you're finally back in the saddle. Looking good too, cookie. Sharp duds. No more homespun and gingham, huh?"

"Thank you. No. I've done with all that lot. You look very Finneyesque." Of medium height, with a perpetually worried expression creasing his tidy, perennially youthful features, he wore trousers with fancifully figured suspenders over a white shirt; his tie loosened and askew, the top button of the shirt open; argyle socks and wing-tip oxfords. Aside from the addition of a jacket, she'd never seen him dressed in any other way. Even at the funeral he'd given the impression he'd just stepped away from his desk.

His telephone rang. He put his hand over the receiver, asking, "Have we covered everything?"

"I believe so," Emma said. "I'll visit with Kathy for a few minutes, then be on my way."

"Okay. I'll check in with Dana and I'll be calling you. Nice work, Em. You done good, cookie." He winked at her, then picked up the receiver, hooked it under his ear and barked, "Finney!" into the mouthpiece as he waggled his fingers at Emma.

She waved, then turned to follow Kathy out to her office.

"Come on in and sit down," Kathy said, lifting a pile of manuscripts off the visitor's chair, then looking around to find someplace to put them. Her desk was layers deep in cover proofs, galleys, partially edited catalog copy, and more manuscripts. Giving up, she plonked the pile on the floor, slid around behind the desk and sat back beaming at Emma. "Jim's right. You look great."

"Oh, I've bought a few new things," Emma said,

looking down at the lap of her black skirt.

"I have to tell you," Kathy said. "I owe you a big one."

"For what?"

"Your letter really shook Jim up."

Emma swallowed, a sudden buzzing in her ears. "Letter?" she said, a coppery liquid filling the floor of her mouth.

"I thought he was going to have a stroke," Kathy laughed, looping her long auburn hair behind her ears. The laughter lightened her somewhat heavy features, illuminated her hazel eyes and stripped years from her age. A physically unprepossessing woman in her mid-forties, when Kathy emitted one of her mellifluous, cascading peals of laughter, people nearby inevitably turned, smiling. Her good-heartedness was so manifestly evident in her laughter that she was universally liked, as well as respected for her editorial acumen.

Emma dredged up a wobbly smile as Kathy went on. "I don't think anybody's ever had the balls to tell Jim that if he didn't start paying his editors what they're worth, not only would he lose them, but that his biggest author would personally hire away his senior editor. He came in here with this *look* on his face, and I thought he was going to keel over. What did I know about this? he asked me, slapping the letter down on my desk. He was suspicious as hell, as if maybe you and I had cooked up a plot. Anyway, I said it was the first I knew of it but I wouldn't mind getting twice the money and doing one third the work. He stood here snapping his suspenders—you know the way he does?—and finally he growls, 'Five thousand more. That's my limit. That's *it*.' Then he waits, snapping away on his suspenders, and scowling at me. I was enjoying it, so I pretended to think for a few minutes, prolonging the agony. At last I said, 'Okay, it's a deal.' He exhaled so hard I swear the windows shook, said, 'Fine,' and off he went. It was," Kathy said, winding down, "a moment to remember. So, thank you for going to bat for me. I'm finally going to be able to pay off my Visa card."

Emma again saw herself encased in a paperweight that, when shaken, sent a storm of snow cascading over a tiny town. But instead of snow, dozens of letters swirled around her like armed missiles. "I'm, ah, glad it was of some help," she said, making a show of looking at her watch. "I don't suppose you still have the letter?"

"I think Jim's got it," Kathy answered, appearing confused. "Why?"

"It's not important. I must fly if I'm to catch the three-thirty train." She stood up, her legs feeling too stick-like to support her weight, and Kathy came out from behind the desk to give her a hug and a kiss. "I can't wait to see the new manuscript," she said. "It'll be quite a change working directly with you."

"I know," Emma said. "Without Will running interference. I'm looking forward to it, too. We'll talk soon," she said and hurried off.

As she walked toward Grand Central she felt enormously tall at one moment, shrunken and doll-sized the next: a Wonderlandish eat-me drink-me sensation that was extremely unpleasant. Someone was trying to drive her mad. And if they kept on with it, they might very likely succeed.

After checking the big board for the track

number, she made her way through the station, pausing once to put five dollars into the cup of a wheelchair-bound middle-aged man, and once to give another five dollars to a young woman with a small child clinging fearfully to her hand. The young woman said, "God bless you." Emma smiled, embarrassed, and wished she'd given the woman more.

At last seated on the train, she held her hands tightly together in her lap and ran again down the list of possible suspects. Now that she'd excluded Richard on the grounds that he had nothing at all to gain from the enterprise, that left only Janet. She'd had a key, and therefore access to the house. Undoubtedly she also knew the alarm code. She bitterly resented Emma's closeness to Laurie, which compounded her long-term resentment of Emma's closeness to her father. Poor Janet, Emma thought, would never believe that her father had been incapable of giving the approval she'd so passionately sought.

Chapter Twenty-Two

"Hi, Aunt Em," Laurie said. "How's everything?"

"Ah, Laurie, everything's fine. How are you, my darling? Isn't this rather late for you to be calling?"

"I didn't wake you or anything, did I?"

"Not at all. I was just about to stop working."

"Okay," he said, with relief. "It is pretty late, but this is the first chance I've had to get to the phone. These essays are *brutal*. I'm finishing the Gilgamesh one now. Anyway, I had a couple of things I wanted to discuss with you. I've been thinking it over about my visit the weekend after next, you know, and I've decided I'll come by myself this time. I'd really like to spend the time with you, and if I bring another guy, I'll have to entertain him, sort of. So I won't bring anyone. Okay?"

"Of course, Laurie. Whatever you decide is perfectly all right."

"Great. The other thing is I've got this let-ter . . ."

Emma felt as if her lungs had collapsed and she were choking. She had to put the receiv-er down and close her eyes, concentrating on breathing slowly in and out, in and out. Was this never going to end? After a few moments she was able to return the receiver to her ear and say, "I'm sorry, my dear. I missed what you were saying."

"You okay, Aunt Em? You sound kind of spooked."

"I'm fine," she said, dreading what he might say.

"Okay. So, today I got this letter from my mother you wouldn't believe. Totally insane, full of all these orders underlined five or six times. I'm not to phone you. I'm not to write to you, or visit you, or set foot anywhere near you. And if I don't *obey* her—do you love that?—she'll be forced to take drastic action and not only will she cut off my allowance but she'll notify the school that I'm not to leave the grounds without her *written* permission. She's out of her brain, Aunt Em. I mean, I'm a junior for God's sake, not some kid in eighth grade. It'd be unbelievably embarrassing if she starts trying to pull shit like that. Can you imagine what the headmaster will think? And the other guys?"

"Frightful," she sympathized, fairly light-headed now that her fear had been alleviated.

"Exactly. So I was wondering if maybe when I come down I could talk to your lawyer friend and find out what my legal position is, what kind of rights I've got. You know? To stop all this garbage once and for all."

"I'm sure Richard would be happy to talk with you," she said. "And you know there's no need for you to worry about money, Laurie. I'll be more than happy to provide whatever you need."

"I kind of want to talk about finding a way to make like a legal break from Mom, be in charge of myself. I've read stuff in the papers about kids taking their parents to court. She's hopeless, Aunt Em, really off her head. All she ever does is hassle me. She hates every friend I've ever had. And forget about my girlfriends! She's forever threatening to cut off my money, which isn't even hers to mess with but happens to be my inheritance from my grandmother; she says she won't pay my school fees, one bullshit thing after another. But all the money's from my trust, and I'm getting nervous thinking maybe she's helping herself to it. I mean, she talks about it like it's *hers*. And that's definitely got to be illegal. The whole purpose of her life is to mess up mine. I want out of it. What do I need her for, Aunt Em?" he asked plaintively. "She hates me. She always has. Okay, I can handle that. I mean, it's no big surprise or anything. But when she starts threatening to blackmail me with my own money, that's too much."

"I'll have a word with Richard. I know he'll be able to advise you."

"Would you ever maybe adopt me, Aunt Em?" He gave an uncertain little laugh. "I know I'm kind of on the old side, but the thing of it is I won't be eighteen for another year and a half. And if I could get myself legally free of Mom and have you as my guardian or whatever, I'd be covered for all the contingencies, you know?"

Deeply moved, she said, "Laurie, I don't know the law but I suspect you can't have two mothers. And while I'd be honored to be your guardian, I think it would simply be fueling the fire were I to agree to that. We must take great care, my dear, not to exacerbate the situation with your mother. I'm well aware how trying this is for you, and I'll speak to Richard tomorrow. He may very well be able to come up with some solution with regard to your funds. After all, at sixteen you're no longer legally a minor. He might petition the court to make you responsible for your own assets. Or perhaps Richard might act as your guardian. Just please don't say or do anything that might make matters worse. I realize how difficult your mother can be, but I think she's attempting to strike out at me through you. She wouldn't consciously harm you, Laurie."

"It harms me when she tries to use me to hurt you, Aunt Em."

"I know, and I'm very sorry. If I thought it would help, I'd ring her up, try to talk to her. But I doubt she'd listen to a single word I had to say."

"You can believe that," he said bitterly.

"Do you need money now? I could send you a check by courier first thing in the morning."

"No, I'm okay. But I might have to come back to you for the train fare."

"Just call me and I'll take care of it."

"All right. I guess I'd better let you go," he said reluctantly. "You're not mad at me for calling so late and saying that about being my guardian?"

"There isn't anything you could do that would

325

make me angry with you. I've always told you that nothing you could ever confide to me would stop me loving you, Laurie, no matter how bad you might think it was. Go to bed now, my dear, and we'll talk again in a few days. And if you receive any additional letters from your mother, as hard for you as it might be, try not to overreact."

"Okay, I'll give it my best shot. I love you, Aunt Em."

"I love you. Goodnight, my dear."

Beginning to recover from the panic that had gripped her at Laurie's mention of a letter, she stared blankly at the word processor screen for several minutes before reformatting the several pages she'd written that evening.

Roger sat contemplating the list of names, deliberating his options. If he chose to hire on for this case, his return home might be delayed by as much as a month. It would take quite some time to make satisfactory inquiries. It would also entail his relocating after the conference from Manhattan to Connecticut, which, in turn, would necessitate his hiring a car. He'd already been given to understand the expense involved would not be an issue. But what was an issue was his inclination to proceed. He'd undertaken cases where there'd been just as little to go on as there was in this instance, but he'd been obliged as an officer of the law to do his utmost to unravel those. This one was being left entirely to his personal discretion.

Setting aside the list, he went to stand

by the window and looked out at the rain-drenched streets fifteen stories below. The lights were blurred, and little of the street noise penetrated the double-glazed window. He felt stifled by the heat of the room but neither of the windows opened. It wasn't possible to get fresh air unless he left the hotel, which was one of the aspects of American architecture that dismayed him: almost none of the high-rise buildings afforded the occupants unprocessed air. He also disliked being so far from safety in the event of a fire. He had, of course, taken the trouble to establish the location of the fire exits upon his arrival, but that knowledge in no way ameliorated his concern.

Removing his jacket and placing it over the back of the chair by the desk, he thought again about that afternoon's meeting and about that bleak dwelling on the waterfront. Edward was clearly emotionally involved with the woman, and Roger could readily understand why. It was difficult to resist the plight of a delicate, grieving young woman, living to all intents and purposes alone in that cheerless, sprawling house; difficult not to feel her all-but-palpable confusion and sadness despite her attempt to put on a brave face.

Her face. Remembering now the clear, intelligent eyes, the fine underlying bone structure, and the tragic disfigurement, he knew all his debating was academic. The instant she'd turned from the window and he'd seen her face, he'd known he would take the case. . . .

Once she'd stored the pages on a freshly prepared disk, she turned off the machine and went down to the kitchen.

Calla stirred when Emma switched on the light, half opened her eyes, then went back to sleep. While waiting for the kettle to boil, Emma held her hands out in front of her. They were still afflicted by a visible tremor as a direct result of her immense and sudden fear that her darling Laurie had received one of the letters. Good God! she thought, letting her hands fall to her sides. Was she destined to have some sort of seizure each time in the future someone casually mentioned being in receipt of a letter? This simply had to stop. But how did one stop a shadow?

As she prepared tea, she reviewed what Laurie had told her and was offended by Janet's presuming to threaten to withhold the income from Sandra's legacy. Sandra may have been willing to surrender her children in order to gain her freedom from Will, but she'd cared enough about them and about her four grandchildren to make financial provision for them. Janet had inherited a sizable sum from her mother, and would shortly be receiving Will's smaller bequest. She also had the settlement made on her by Willard at the time of Laurie's birth, in return for which she'd signed binding documents that prohibited her or Laurie from ever having further contact with Laurie's father.

As a small boy, Laurie had often speculated on the identity of his father but when confronted repeatedly by Janet's refusal to divulge this information, he'd come to Emma, asking why he couldn't know who his father was. Stricken by the boy's plight, she'd taken the then-ten-year-old Laurie down to the beach on the pretext of walking Calla and, swearing him to secrecy, told him about his father. "I'm trusting you as I would an adult," she'd told him that day. "Were it to become known that I'd confided in you, the repercussions for both of us could be extremely serious."

"I understand," he'd said soberly. "But if you tried to help her, how come my Mom hates you so much?"

"That's complicated, my darling. In truth, I think she's angry with your grandfather but feels she can't blame him because he is her father, after all. And more than anything else, she wants his approval. You can't blame someone and at the same time seek his approval. The two serve to cancel each other out, if you see what I mean."

"I think so."

"And I think," she'd gone on, "because she so badly wants his approval, she's redirected her anger to me. I came along and replaced her mother, or so she thinks. And to make matters worse, not only was I her new stepmother, I was also a year and a half younger than she. She's been convinced all along that my motives in marrying your grandfather were considerably less than honorable. It's been easier altogether for your mother to lay her disappointment at my feet. But I think she's been wrong to withhold this information from you. You have a right to know who your father is."

"What was he like?" Laurie had asked.

"A very pleasant, very bright and caring young man." Emma had smiled. "You favor him in looks. He had sandy brown hair like yours, and the same dear, lopsided grin. I believe he truly did love your mother. And she him. He tried a number of times to see her, but your grandfather had made his position clear, and your father was not allowed in the house. Nor was he permitted to speak to your mother on the telephone. In the end, he returned to college, and your mother dropped out without completing her junior year." With a sad shake of her head, she said, "If she'd made any attempt to defy him, I'd have gladly helped her. But she accepted the laws your grandfather handed down. Which is why, today, she's such a deeply unhappy woman. Still, she does have you, Laurie. And that's a great consolation."

"She doesn't act like it."

"I know. But please try to be understanding."

Thoughtfully, Laurie had stared out at the water for a time. At last, he'd turned to Emma, asking, "How come Granddad was so mean to her?"

"I have no idea, my dear. I wish I knew how to answer that."

"Is he mean to you too, Auntie Em?"

The question grabbed her by the throat. Dredging up a smile for his benefit, she said, "No, of course not."

"If he was ever mean to you," he'd said fiercely, "I'd make him sorry."

She'd always taken pains to assure Laurie of her love. And he'd responded so strongly to her affectionate displays, to her repeated declarations of caring, that they'd consoled and bolstered each other. Janet, who'd always been at odds with her motherhood, had been all too happy to surrender Laurie into Emma's arms almost from the moment of his birth. She'd first brought him to the house when he was only a week old, and Emma had held the baby with a sense of wonder and with spontaneous love.

It was only when Laurie turned thirteen and began resisting his mother's arbitrary orders and ignoring her frequent and explosive diatribes against any number of people and issues—that Janet restructured her existing antagonism toward Emma into full-scale loathing. Janet was the only person who hated Emma enough to want to cause her pain. Perhaps she'd written that letter to herself to deflect attention away from her as a likely suspect. Fueled by jealousy and rancor, Janet would go to any lengths to retaliate for the many sins Emma had purportedly committed against her. And it wouldn't be all that difficult for someone of Janet's undeniable intelligence to emulate Emma's writing pattern.

"She's what you made her, Will," she told the master's bedroom. "She drank from the cup of hypocrisy you poured for her and then you couldn't bear to have her near you. 'She's a bitch,' you'd complain. 'She's so unkempt, so lacking in pride.' Sad but true, Mr. Bellamy. You'd have had all of us behaving like performing dolls if you'd been given your head. When I defended Susan and Edgar because they trusted me from the outset and saw me as a friend and a peer rather than their new, classically wicked stepmother, you exacted payment from me as well as from Janet and Shawn because they viewed me as an additional contender for your limited affections. You rewarded Janet and Shawn with even more of your contempt, and now they reflect you perfectly. Why won't you *die*, Mr. Bellamy? What will it take?"

Wearied, she threw off her clothes and left them on the floor. Climbing into bed, she set the alarm for seven-fifteen, drank the last of the tea, and turned off the light. In the darkness the room seemed to acquire new dimensions, the walls receding, the ceiling rising so that she was enisled in a vast hushed chamber.

Willard lay on his back in the hospital bed they'd acquired to accommodate his special needs. The bedclothes rose precipitously over his mountainous midsection then fell abruptly onto his wasted chest. His bony hands rested outside the blankets, the long twitching fingers revealing his agitation.

She sat beside the bed gazing at the head on the banked pillows, searching for something familiar in the cadaverous face with its sunken eyes and concave cheeks, its thinned lips and prominent, fleshless nose and chin, the yellowed waxy sheen to the features. She was sufficiently distant to be beyond the faintly rotten odor given off by his dying cells. His Adam's apple rode prominently up and down the length of his scrawny neck each time he swallowed or attempted to speak, and she watched with repugnance as that projection threatened to pierce the slack, crepey flesh.

Riding over top of the stench of his decay was a medicinal layer, and above that, the slightly sweet smell of the Lysol the nurses used regularly, as if that household disinfectant might conquer any malignant cells that managed to get free of their host body and take to the air. Everywhere she went these smells seemed to cling to her, adhering to the lining of her nose and throat and making it almost impossible for her to ingest anything more than milkless, sugarless tea or slices of unbuttered toast. She could smell it on her clothes, even on her skin, and had taken to showering two and three and four times daily in an effort to be rid of it.

The nurses appeared not to mind the smell. In fact, Emma was awed by their prosaic practicality, and by the relentlessly cheerful way they administered to the moribund creature confined to the tall, metal-sided bed. All that remained recognizable of Willard Bellamy was the voice and its ceaseless adjurations. And she was as awed by the undiminished strength of that voice as she was by the nurses' fastidious disregard for its querulous edicts. As if addressing a child, and as if sharing a single voice, all three nurses murmured soothing "now, nows" and "there, theres" and weren't in the least distracted by his howls of pain or frustration or anger. Mr. Bellamy had no intention of going gently into that good night. He raged, he begged, he heaved imprecations into the fetid air, he begged some more.

Periodically one of the nurses would place an astonishingly gentle hand on Emma's shoulder and bend to whisper, "Why don't you take a little break now, grab something to eat or get yourself some fresh air?" Then, given license to flee, she'd take Calla down to the water's edge and gulp down quantities of scentless winter air, preparing her lungs for the next lengthy stint by the deathbed, and praying to whatever higher power there might be for the strength to survive the inimitable horror of this experience.

"Callula," she'd murmur to the sweet-natured Jack Russell bitch, hiding her face in its neck. "Little beautiful one, dear little friend. He won't die. He refuses to let go. I can't bear very much more of this."

Fifteen or twenty minutes out of doors sharing

her secrets with the dog, then she'd return to the chair by the bed with its gears and levers and retractable sides, to study the polished metal mechanisms while the voice went on and on and on, drilling at her eardrums, echoing inside her skull.

"Emma, you've got to do it! I insist! Are you *listening*? You're not *listening*! God damn it! Will you *listen* to me!"

"Yes, Will, I'm listening." Her voice bland, noncommittal. "I hear every word you're saying."

"Don't patronize me! There's nothing wrong with my brain. You think I can't tell when someone's not listening?"

"I'm listening."

A pause while those almost-colorless eyes that were once very blue fix slyly upon her, the wasted, desiccated lips rest briefly, the body draws upon its critically depleted reserves of strength to provide volume for the voice.

"Would you like some water, Will?" She extends her hand to the glass with its bent straw.

A curt nod, and she holds the straw to his mouth, averting her eyes from the sight of the creature's collapsed cheeks as it sucks in the moisture.

"I want you to listen to me," he begins again the moment she's returned the glass to the table. "I want you to listen . . ."

In the darkness, Richard slid from behind the wheel of the BMW and stepped out into the road, one rubber-gloved hand holding the plastic bag containing the letters. Opening the chute, he shook the letters into the box, then quickly returned to the car. Stripping off the rubber glove as he steered the car away from the mailbox, he emitted a laugh, saying, "That takes care of that."

"Nice work, kiddo," Linda congratulated him, lighting a cigarette.

God! They'd never act in concert to hurt her. Why did she keep having these dreams? She hated this, and battled against sleep, against her body's need for rest. *I want to wake up!* she insisted, physically pushing as if at the lid of a gigantic pot.

Wet with perspiration, she sat up and threw aside the bedclothes. Resting her head on her knees, she fought off the inclination to sink back into sleep. She could feel the hateful dreams hovering at the edge of her awareness, and she refused to return to them. Turning on the light, she had to shield her eyes from the lancing pain of the brightness stabbing into her eyes. It took a minute or two before her eyes were acclimated to the light. Then, unsteady from lack of sleep, she stood up from the bed.

"I did tell you, didn't I, that Richard will be coming to dinner tonight?"

"You told me." Bernice smiled, thinking Emma looked real tired, with dark areas like bruises in the pale skin under her eyes. It seemed like as if she was so worn out she couldn't hardly sit up straight. "You got anything special in mind you'd like to eat?"

"I'll leave that to you. You will join us, of course."

"Uh-uh, no I won't."

"Why not? You're a friend, after all . . ."

"Listen, Emma. Your friend's gonna eat her dinner out here, so you can be together with your other friend."

"But that's . . ."

"It's real nice of you to want to include me. And some other time when you two know each other better, we'll all three sit down to the table together. Right now, it's not a good idea. You understand?"

"Not really."

"I keep forgetting you don't know these things," Bernice said. "Just take my word for it. There'll be all kinds of time later on for me to eat with you and Richard. So, what'll we give him? Roast lamb?"

"That would be lovely."

"What time'd you go to bed last night? I'll bet it was real late. You got dark circles under your eyes. You don't have to get this book done all in one day, you know. You need your sleep. Why am I wasting my energy?" Bernice wondered aloud. "You're not hearing a word I say." Emma had that telltale look again, and Bernice knew she was off somewhere moving her new story around in her head, working out this and that.

"I'm going up to the office now," Emma said, and left the kitchen.

Bernice watched her go, and with a smile shook her head, telling herself she should know better by now than to try to talk to Emma when her eyes went blank the way they did when she got all involved in her writing. Calla pushed into the room through her door, and Bernice said, "I suppose you've gone and worked yourself up an appetite, chasin' them seagulls."

Calla came over to stand with her head cocked to one side, her eyes on Bernice's face. Bernice laughed and opened the cupboard for a can of dog food. "You'd eat all the day long, I let you. Get to be so fat you couldn't come through that little door anymore. Then where'd you be, huh?"

Setting the dish on the floor, she watched Calla begin to eat, her small hind end wriggling. "I better make a list for the supermarket," she said. "And then, this afternoon, we'll do some housecleanin'. Maybe take down all that nasty black cloth. What d'you think of that, Calla? Get this place to lookin' less like a funeral parlor and more like a house folks live in."

Initially Julia evidenced considerable suspicion of the purpose for Roger's visit. But after studying his several identity cards she allowed him to enter, leading the way into a living room that was spectacularly cluttered. Magazines and newspapers lay on every surface, many of them with passages underlined in red ink. Dust hung in the slats of light admitted by the shades concealing the windows; the rugs were askew, the once-good furniture was shabby, its upholstery worn thin. There were condensation rings on the several occasional tables and two very full ashtrays in view. A number of used coffee cups sat here and there, and the wastebasket next to the desk was filled to the top with crumpled papers. The room smelled musty and faintly damp, as if something had recently been spilled on one of the rugs. It was the dwelling, Roger thought, of someone either beyond or incapable of caring about the niceties of domestic life.

Moving aside a sizable stack of newspapers, she invited Roger to sit down. Seating himself on the edge of a sagging armchair, he withdrew his notebook and pen from his inside jacket pocket and positioned these items on his knee, knowing from long experience that many people were comforted by their perception of these innocuous objects as significant tools of the policeman's trade. While she lit a cigarette, he took in more details of the room, noting the crowded desktop with an open box of stationery, a roll of stamps and an uncapped pen resting atop a letter she'd obviously been writing when he'd arrived at the door.

The woman might have been attractive had her face not borne the prematurely aging creases of a lifetime's dissatisfaction. The room reflected her. It had pleasing dimensions and fair potential but was somehow intentionally neglected, as if its owner were determined to show that the life of her mind was of far greater significance than any consideration of physical comfort. But what it really revealed, so far as he was concerned, were the outward manifestations of an obsessive personality. And while he had no idea in which direction her obsession might lie, those underlined paragraphs and the numerous clippings stacked on the coffee table and held in place by a heavy ceramic cigarette box confirmed a preoccupation with some newsworthy subject. He was, unfortunately, not sufficiently close to scan any of the underlined passages.

Julia was somewhat overweight, her shoulder-length light brown hair was in need of a washing and the dark green track suit she wore was not only less than flattering, it also put on display a badly neglected body. He very much doubted that this woman made any effort whatever to control either her intake of food or to work off the excess calories she ingested. Altogether he found her unappealing.

"I understand you received one of these letters," he began, providing her with an opening. "I don't suppose you've kept it, by any chance."

"I threw it in the bitch's face," she said with a grimly satisfied smirk.

"And what bitch might that be, madame?"

"Elsa, naturally." She gave him a look that said she thought he was incredibly stupid. "Who else?"

"I see. So you haven't a copy of it?" he asked, maintaining the neutral tone of voice he always used when making inquiries.

"No, I don't have a copy of it. Why would I? It wasn't exactly something I'd want to frame and hang on the wall."

He looked around at the walls to which she referred. They were bare, the once-white paint yellowed at ceiling height by cigarette smoke. "Have you any idea," he asked, "who might want to impersonate your stepmother by writing letters in her name?"

Julia laughed, a harsh sound. "Impersonate? That's very good. I love the way you English decorate the language, prettify it. Nobody's *impersonating* Elsa," she said, the

Katharine Marlowe

corners of her mouth turning down. "Since
you say letters in the plural, obviously I'm
not the only one who's received one."

"That is correct. There have been quite a
number of them, actually."

"Actually," she mimicked him, and he
found himself building a strong dislike
of this woman. "Well, it doesn't surprise
me. Elsa's made a lot of enemies over the
years."

"Oh?" he said interestedly. "Perhaps you
could give me some names."

She regarded him blankly for a moment,
then said, "Do you know how old she was
when she married my father? *Nineteen*,
almost two years younger than me. Why
do you suppose a man of forty-five would
take up with someone like her, unless she'd
tricked him into it?"

"And how do you think she tricked him?"
he asked, mentally contrasting this woman
to her stepmother. It was difficult to believe
that less than two years separated them.
Julia looked considerably older, while Elsa
gave the impression of being much younger. Bitterness, he mused, was a potent
aging factor.

"The usual way," she said, her mouth
again turning downward.

"You're suggesting, I take it, that she
claimed to be pregnant?"

"Probably."

"But you don't know that for a certainty."

"No, I don't know that for a certainty.
But what other reason could there possibly

be?" She leaned over to crush out her cigarette in the ashtray and at once lit another.
"My *stepmother*," she said bitterly, "isn't
above lying to get what she wants."

"Could you give me an example?"

"Plenty. She's lied constantly about me
to my son."

"Could you give me an example of what
she's said?"

"Why should I?" she asked petulantly. "I
don't have to prove anything."

"I see. So you believe your stepmother is
in fact the author of these letters."

"Of course she is. Who the hell else would
bother? Or do you think that because she's
a famous author people are out to get
her?"

"All sorts of things are possible," he said,
making a note in his book which, he saw
peripherally, she followed with interest.
"Getting back to the question of your
stepmother's enemies," he said. "Could
you possibly elaborate on that?"

His returning to this matter seemed to
distress her. She worried a hangnail on
the side of her thumb, first with her fingers and then with her teeth. At last, losing
much of her venomous attitude, she said,
"My brother and I are probably Elsa's only
enemies. People just fall on their asses for
Elsa."

"Taken off-guard by this unanticipated
softening, he asked, "Why is that, may I
ask?"

She sighed heavily and said, "I don't
know. It's just the way it's always been.

341

Dad announced he was going to remarry and I supposed we all pictured someone his age. He didn't *tell* us she was our age, for God's sake. He just said he was getting married and let us make our own assumptions. Then he went over to England and came back with this . . . this *teenager*. It was so goddamned *embarrassing!* She looked about sixteen," she said angrily.

"So your enmity towards her was predicated solely on her age?"

Julia stared at him, her eyes widened, as if his statement had cast a new, decidedly unpleasant light on the reason behind her years of hostility.

"Did you," he asked, "ever make any viable sort of effort to get to know her?"

She sighed again, tiredly. "We knew her," she said. "And we didn't like her."

"Why?"

"We just didn't like her," she declared, her angry energy returning. "Okay?"

"Very well. Leaving that matter for the moment, I can't help noticing you seem to be a letter-writer yourself," he said, indicating the desk.

She jumped up, splotches of color appearing on her sallow face. "There's no law against writing letters!" she cried, ash from her cigarette dropping to the rug.

"There is if the letters are written with an intent to do harm," he said calmly, intrigued by the heat of her reaction as well as by her automatic move to position herself between him and the desk. "I'll be on my way now," he said, rising and returning the notebook and pen to his pocket. She'd become so immediately and furiously defensive he knew he'd get nothing more from her. "Thank you for your time. I'll let myself out."

"She's a professional do-gooder," Julia nearly shouted. "Forever trying to prove how nice she is, what a good person she is. She makes an art of playing the aging waif."

"Indeed," he said. "And that, in your opinion, is just cause for condemnation?"

Julia now appeared on the verge of tears, so choked was she by her inchoate emotions. She shook her head mutely, then said, "My son loves *her* more than he does me."

"Does he?" he asked, maintaining his neutral tone. "And why, if I may ask, would that be?"

"All his life she's made a concerted effort to win him over," she said wretchedly, "by making me look bad."

"I expect, madame, with all due respect, you've made yourself look bad by turning your relationship with your son into a competition."

The words struck home with far more force than he'd expected. Her tears overflowing, she wiped her face on the arm of her track suit, and struggling to maintain her defiant stance, she said, "What the hell would *you* know about it?"

"Only hearsay, madame," he said politely.

He broke through the dust-heavy slatted

bars of light as he went from the place.

That evening, upon returning to his room at the Marriott Hotel, he sat down to write up his notes of the day's interviews. He stopped midway through to go to the window. Looking up at the sky, he allowed his mind to open, and stood gazing at the constellations while his thoughts clarified. Then, looking over his shoulder at the desk where his pen lay across the ruled foolscap pad upon which he'd been writing, he thought, the mystery is not *who* is writing these letters. No, the true mystery is *why*.

Chapter Twenty-Three

"Good evening, Bernice."

"Good evening, Richard. Come on in."

Bernice gave him what he thought was an especially welcoming smile and, on impulse, he bent to kiss her soft plump cheek. Her face was illuminated by pleasure, and he was glad he'd acted upon the impulse. He handed her the bottle of wine he'd brought, saying, "For the cook."

"Thank you. I'll open it for dinner."

Calla came trotting out from the kitchen, and Bernice liked the way Richard at once dropped down to pet the dog, saying, "Hi, Calla. Hi. What a good girl." Still playing with Calla, he looked up at Bernice to say, "I'm crazy about this dog."

"Seems she's crazy about you, too. Emma's up in the office. She'll probably stay up there," she said pointedly, "if somebody doesn't fetch her down."

"I hate to disturb her if she's working," Richard said, getting up.

"I don't think you'll be disturbin' her. Go on up. I got pots on the stove." She turned away thinking Emma had done real well by herself, and she was loosening Richard up. He'd always been a gentleman, never one to drape himself in airs and graces, but he was showing a real friendly side to his nature now. And, no doubt about it, he was doing Emma a world of good.

With Calla dancing about at his feet, Richard watched Bernice head off to the kitchen. Then he looked around. The house felt different. It seemed to have come back to life, and as he started up the stairs he wondered how it could have changed so drastically since his previous visits the week before. But, unarguably, it had. Everything seemed lighter, less gloomy. It was no longer a rather sinister place but one that might not be so terrible to live in after all.

He could hear music playing faintly and, beneath it, the distinctively plastic clicking of computer keys being struck. The secretaries at his office all accessed the main computer through terminals and he was often struck by the odd flatness of the sounds.

He couldn't recall the last time he'd been above the ground floor of the house—it might have been after the funeral but he wasn't certain—and couldn't help contrasting his fairly small apartment to the grandiosity of this house. The hallway ran its full length, with rooms on both sides, as well as a doorway at the extreme far end, which undoubtedly led up to the attic. He passed several bedrooms, drawn forward by the music and the constant clicking of the keyboard, and at last arrived at the doorway to the office, which, he noted with a glance, was diagonally opposite what appeared to be the master suite.

Halting in the doorway, he looked inside and saw Emma busily working. Anxious not to disrupt her, but aware she was oblivious to his presence, he took in the details of the large L-shaped desk at which she sat. Atop the lower portion of the L sat a typewriter and a telephone connected to an answering machine. And on the long side was a tidy lap-top hooked up to a printer. There was an old-fashioned brass lamp to one side of the keyboard that cast its light over an array of four-inch by six-inch index cards and several sheets of paper.

Emma's fingers moved steadily over the keys and her eyes followed the words appearing on the screen. She was completely absorbed in her work, and he watched her, captivated and impressed by the visible intensity of her concentration. He was all at once able to connect her to her work, something he'd never managed to do before. Writing seemed to him so esoteric an occupation that he'd long wondered how the reticent, very youthful Emma he'd known prior to the passionately intense Emma he knew now had accomplished it. Not that he'd ever subscribed to the rumor that it was Willard who'd written the books. He'd never believed Willard sufficiently introspective, or observant, or sensitive to have been the author. Yet he'd been unable to picture Emma actually writing. Now his understanding and appreciation of her was greatly enhanced.

He also took advantage of this opportunity to admire again her pale translucent skin and the sweep of her eyelashes, the aristocratic nose balanced by the rounded thrust of her chin, the graceful length of her neck, and the silvery wisps of hair at her temples. She was wearing a long-sleeved royal blue silk shirt with charcoal gray slacks, and her knees were crossed under the desk, one loafer dangling from her foot.

The music was the Bill Evans dub he'd made for her and it was emanating from the stereo system, which, he now saw, she'd relocated from the library downstairs to a white wall unit that occupied the entire wall to the right of where he stood in the doorway. There was a movement, and glancing down he saw Calla going off along the hall, back toward the stairs. Lifting his hand, he rapped his knuckles lightly on the door.

Emma looked up blankly, stared at him for a second or two, then smiled. "Hello, Richard."

"Hello. This is kind of odd." He returned her smile. "I've been reading your books all these years but always found it hard to make the connection between you and the author. Seeing you working away in here finally pulls it together for me."

"You mean, now you know I really do write them. It's real."

"That's right." He leaned against the doorframe, feeling incredibly lucky to know her. She was positively lovely and very talented, and she'd brought her loveliness and her singular abilities into the interior of his existence.

"I feel rather the same way," she said. "I have difficulty sometimes reconciling my two selves. Let me just store this and we can go downstairs."

He waited while she performed several functions on the lap-top, then ejected the disk and,
with a sigh, shut down the machine. Then she
gathered up the index cards, aligned the edges,
and put them, the disk and the several papers
into the top right-hand drawer. Pushing her chair
back, she got up, turned off the cassette player
and came over to hug him, saying, "You knocked.
Will never did. He interrupted me with impunity
whenever he wished. It drove me wild; it was so
disrespectful."

"I'm very respectful," he said, running a hand
over her short silky hair. "It's genetic. I come
from a long line of respectful Redmonds. It's even
part of the family motto." He gave a little laugh,
breathing in the spicy lushness of her new perfume.

"I've been playing your cassette constantly."

"I'll have to make you some more." He extended his arm around her shoulders as they started
along the hallway. "I've got at least five more Bill
Evans albums, and some others you might enjoy.
Charlie Parker, Dexter Gordon, George Benson."

"I like your bay rum," she said, feeling a bit
drowsy and not yet fully returned from her
paper world, but wonderfully secure inside his
encircling arm. "I like *you*. You are such a nice
man."

"Are you always this way when you finish
working?"

"What way?"

"Kind of sleepy and highly complimentary."

"I think I must be," she said. "It takes some
time for me to come back, to release that other place, those people, the events. They're very
real to me. They have to be," she explained. "If

they're not entirely legitimate to me, they won't come to life on paper. There were many occasions in the past when I'd become so engrossed, I'd actually be resentful at having to return—especially at those times when Will would come bursting in, having started speaking when he was still halfway down the hall. It was like a summer squall one could never anticipate. Enough of him," she said impatiently. "How are you?"

"Couldn't be better," he said, taking her hand as they started down the stairs. "Something smells wonderful."

"We're having lamb," she said with the pleased expression of a child. "Would you like a drink, Richard?"

"I'll wait and have some wine with dinner."

"Let's go to the kitchen, keep Bernice company. Are you hungry? I was very nervous about your coming. Now I can't think why."

In the end, at both Richard's and Emma's insistence, Bernice sat down to dinner with them in the dining room. She'd expected to feel uncomfortable, but it really was like as if she was eating with friends or with her own kids. And it struck her that she'd been a part of the household all these years but she'd never have been invited to sit down to table when Mr. Willard was alive. He'd acted friendly enough, and he'd even left her that money, but she'd always known he thought of her as hired help and not someone good enough to eat with, not a real person. Course she'd never expected him to go inviting her to sit down to table with them, but that didn't mean she hadn't thought about the differences between help and

350

the people who hired that help. It was that class thing that Emma wrote about in some of her books, and it didn't matter if it was England or the States: class was class.

Emma had never been like that, had never held herself apart like she thought she was better than other folks. What had held her apart was Mr. Willard. He'd kept on and on at her, never letting up for a minute. It was a real treat to see her now with Richard, who didn't watch her like a hawk all the time but just looked real happy to be there. Now, finally, Bernice knew for sure that when Emma talked of them being friends she meant it. And as they ate the lamb and the roasted potatoes and the baby peas Emma was so fond of, with the mint sauce and the gravy and the sweet-and-sour cabbage, Bernice could feel the three of them drawing close, like family. She had to smile to herself, thinking of a black woman with a white sister/daughter, and she felt a whole lot better about calling up Richard in the first place.

Emma marveled at one moment over the uniqueness of the situation—she, Richard and Bernice enjoying a meal together, talking effortlessly and laughing—then, in the next, she'd remember and her eyes would go to the door, fully expecting an enraged Will to make one of his significantly quiet entrances and lead her forcibly from the room to interrogate her. At these moments she had to ask herself why she'd imagined, even for a moment, that she might actually be able to personalize this house, make it sufficiently her own to discourage the ghost from returning. It was hopeless. At best she relaxed only for minutes at a time. She couldn't remember when she'd last slept through an entire night in this house. It had been years, long before Will's illness, since she'd had a full night's sleep. A guilty conscience, she'd discovered, never rests.

For his part, Richard had actually forgotten the pleasure of having a meal in a family environment. It was something he hadn't done for years, not, in fact, since before his mother had gone to the nursing home more than six years ago. Prior to that time, he and Dell had dined with his mother at least once a month, and often his brother, Lionel, and his wife, Anne, had been there too. Something so fundamental, and he'd forgotten what it was like. The realization led him to wonder how many other simple pleasures he'd lost sight of.

It would have been even more of a pleasure if he hadn't several times looked over at Emma to see her glancing surreptitiously, fearfully, at the door. It was as if she was anticipating another unannounced visit from Janet, or expecting her husband to return home suddenly and catch her *in flagrante delicto* with another man. Just a few seconds, then she'd recover, smile, and continue eating. It was sad to see, and reminded him that she was still very much a fledgling in terms of adapting to a life alone. There was also still the unsettling and unsettled matter of the letters. He sensed something was going to happen but he had no idea what; it was just a nebulous intuition, a certain tension in the air. Things were changing, for Emma and for him, too.

He knew too well the difficulties of adjustment. He'd had three years to establish the patterns and habits of his single life. And he'd persuaded himself he was content until he'd taken

Emma out to dinner and discovered that all his appetites remained intact. Now everything had changed, and in retrospect he had to admit those three years alone constituted a kind of limbo to which he had no desire to return.

When it came time, he automatically got up to help clear the dishes.

"You don't have to do that," Bernice told him, as Emma pushed through to the kitchen with serving bowls in each hand.

"I'd like to help," he said, and carried the platter and the gravy boat out to the kitchen.

"Okay, the two of you helped," Bernice said. "Now get out and let me have my kitchen to myself so I can get organized and start the coffee going. Go on! You've done your good deed, now you're in my way." She laughed and shooed them off back to the dining room, saying, "I need some workin' space."

Emma and Richard returned to the dining room to sit on opposite sides of the table, smiling at each other.

"This room hasn't been used in years," she said, leaning chin in hand with both elbows on the table. "It's rather too lugubrious to suit me."

"It seems," he ventured, "to make you a little nervous."

"And you've changed your mind about this house, haven't you? You're seeing its potential now, aren't you?"

"It strikes me as less ominous tonight," he confessed, amazed at how well she was able to read him. "Maybe I'm just getting used to being here."

"I endured a long-distance romance for a year with Will. For the sake of being sensible, you understand. Then we were married and for all I knew of him we might never have been introduced. The same thing applies, in many ways, to this house. I'll get up in the morning determined to put my mark on it, to do away with every last trace of him. But within minutes I realize that to accomplish that I might have to raze it to the ground because he seems to have seeped into the very walls. Every so often I think I can actually *smell* him." She held her wrist to her nose to breathe in the scent of *Ma Folie*. She couldn't remember ever feeling quite so tired. "What shall I do?"

"Sell it and buy something else. Or strip it back to the plaster and start again. Make it your own."

"It's odd, you know, but I'm quite attached to this house purely for its own sake. I expect that's why I've resisted your exhortations to sell it. From the day I first came through the door, I've felt that if I ever had the opportunity to clear away all the decorator's touches and begin again from scratch, the house and I could be allies. It's a house with secrets. It wouldn't surprise me in the least to find passages hidden behind the paneling in the library. And the attic is a veritable treasure trove of other people's memorabilia, some of it even predating Will's purchase of the house. He had no curiosity. Never once, in all the years he lived here, was he ever tempted to investigate the contents of the boxes and trunks stored in the attic." She grinned and said, "Laurie and I did. We'd play up there for hours when he was a small boy. We dressed ourselves in the dusty old-fashioned clothes; we read the old storybooks we found and looked through the photograph albums. There was even a box of daguerrotypes and a stereopticon with a collection of plates. You know, those cards that have two images printed side by side? When you look through the viewer they become three-dimensional. We moved the furniture about and played house. It was wonderful." Her expression suddenly changing, her eyes took on an almost haunted look and shifted away from him as she said very softly, "Something's going to happen."

"What?" he asked, mildly disconcerted at her echoing his own thought.

"I don't know," she said. "All those *letters*. Every day I dread hearing there have been more. And I can't for the life of me think how Janet got the key." Instinctively, she placed her left hand over the healing wound. "Perhaps she had duplicates made and has additional keys."

"Have the lock changed, Emma."

"Yes," she said vaguely. "I suppose I should. I wish I were purposeful and decisive, like Linda."

"You're getting there," he said encouragingly. "I notice you decided to claim ownership of the stereo."

Her eyes came back to him and she smiled. "Yes, I did."

"And you've obviously thrown out your old wardrobe," he said.

"I did that, too."

"So, you're becoming purposeful and decisive, like Linda."

"Do you like her?"

"Linda? I've only met her once, at a party you and Willard gave a while ago." He thought

355

back, trying to recall which of the women in attendance had been Linda. It was odd that they'd spoken on the telephone several times recently but he couldn't quite recall her features. "She's got an awful lot of hair and wears heavy eye makeup. Is that Linda?"

"That's Linda." Emma smiled more widely.

All at once he remembered very clearly, and said, "She probably doesn't know it, but she gave me quite a boost that evening. We were talking, and she explained her connection with you. I thought she was very vivacious, fun. Out of the blue she asked me if I'd like to have dinner with her sometime, and I was so taken aback by having a woman express overt interest in me that I went dumb. I couldn't come up with anything to say. I think I just smiled somewhat stupidly, but I felt incredibly reassured. Then I got caught up in conversation with some other people and when I finally decided I'd better give her some kind of answer, she was off talking to someone else."

"What was your answer going to be?"

"I was going to thank her but decline. I found her somewhat too energetic. But, yes, I liked her. I thought she was probably very good for you, someone who'd bring you out of yourself."

"She does do that for me. I'm very fond of Linda. Will despised her."

"Why?" he asked, taken aback.

"He found her crude. Not a suitable companion for Mrs. Bellamy."

"She's not at all crude," he said, frowning. "Jesus! It makes me wonder what he thought of me."

"Oh, he approved of you, Richard."

"I'm not so sure that's a compliment," he said. "The more I learn of Willard, the less I care for him."

"He had that effect on the people who were privy to his unguarded opinions. I'm glad you liked Linda. She thought possibly you didn't."

"Maybe I'll have a chance to correct that impression sometime."

"We'll arrange it," she said. "Perhaps I'll give a party and invite all the people I like. There are actually quite a few people I like but Will took exception one way or another to the majority of them. God, what a despicable man he was!" She covered her mouth with one hand, her eyes on Richard. She could almost feel Will's eyes boring into her back.

Bernice pushed through from the kitchen then, carrying a tray with the coffee and a chocolate mousse cake.

After dessert, Bernice excused herself, saying, "I want to get the kitchen cleaned up so I can go watch "L.A. Law." It's been real nice seein' you, Richard. Don't be a stranger. It's a treat havin' folks to cook for."

"It's a treat eating your cooking," he told her, getting up to give her a kiss on the cheek. "You have my promise I'll come back."

"You make sure you do."

When she'd gone, Richard said, "Do you like the show?"

"I've never seen it. I rarely watch television."

"Really? Don't tell me you disapprove."

"Oh, not at all. I like television very much. When I lived in London, I'd sometimes go next door to watch with Mavis. She had a set. My God! Mavis. I've finally remembered her name. I wish I knew what had become of her. In any event, the set is in the library and I don't care for that room. I keep intending to buy a small one for the bedroom but I've been rather distracted, as you know. We could watch the show, if you'd like to see it."

"I wouldn't dream of subjecting you to the discomfort of spending time in a room you don't like," he said seriously.

"Do you spend your evenings at home watching television?"

"Occasionally. How do you spend your evenings when you're not working?"

"This is dreadful," she said. "You're pointing out to me what a dismal life I've been leading."

"Tell me what you'd like to do," he offered, "and we'll do it. It's not too late to take in a movie. Or we could go hear some Dixieland. What're you in the mood for?"

Killing ghosts, she thought. "Making love," she said softly. "Would you like to come upstairs?"

"I'd like to," he said, "but are you sure it's something you really want to do?"

"I think I have to," she answered confusingly, rising from her seat and holding out her hand to him.

As they went up the stairs together she felt a premonitory tremulousness overtaking her. Nothing could be more hazardous than what she was about to do. The bed might levitate; the pictures would start flinging themselves from the walls; the carpeting might turn into a gigantic mouth and swallow them. She clung to his hand, asking, "Do you find this strange?"

"Kind of," he answered.

"Do you feel it, too?" she asked, her eyes widening as she awaited his answer.

"I'm not sure I know what you mean."

"Mr. Bellamy's ghost," she said with such gravity that he felt a darting thrill of fear. All he could do was hold her hand even more securely and smile in an attempt to dispel his sudden uncertainty.

Her body was eager enough, but her mind kept slipping out of gear, her eyes suddenly opening to scour the corners of the room as her heartbeat accelerated. No ghost. Not yet. But her vigilance kept her hovering on the brink while she labored to get to that moment of release. Labor, she thought, binding Richard to her with trembling limbs. If the mind refused to shut down, the body couldn't perform. She was caught at the vibrating apex of completion, striving to lose herself, determined to break Will's hold on her once and for all.

"Let's just rest for a moment," Richard said, demonstrating yet again his extraordinary awareness of her. "This isn't happening."

Straightening her legs, welcoming his weight, she whispered, "Stay in me. Don't move."

"I'm heavy."

"No, no. I like it."

He gazed into her eyes then kissed her forehead. "We don't have to do this, Emma."

Seeing his concern, feeling it like balm on her overheated body, she thought of the babies that would never be born—his and her own—able to see them very clearly. Willard, who should never have been a parent, had fathered four. She and

Richard, who might have been kind, caring parents, would never have any. Those brown-haired, blue-eyed babies sat abandoned, waiting to be claimed.

She looked into his eyes and saw his caring for her shining out at her. She'd seen many things in Will's eyes but never anything as pure as this caring. People who don't have children, she thought, must parent each other, and satisfy the longing with small kindnesses. She and Richard were unfailingly kind to one another. If they had a future together, they'd undoubtedly always be kind. It was enormously comforting to realize that. Her brain lulled, her body already shifting to its particular rhythm, she closed her eyes and fit her mouth to his.

Chapter Twenty-Four

"Richard, could you help Laurie with this?"

"I think so," he said prudently. "Based on what I know and what you've told me, he may very well have grounds to petition the court for the right to control his own funds. Why don't I talk to him when he comes down?"

"I'd be most grateful. Janet sent him off to boarding school when he was twelve so he'd be out of her way, but she plagues him with endless letters and telephone calls. Some days he's received as many as three letters from her. Pages and pages of admonitions, threats. It's very difficult for him. He's such a good boy. He doesn't deserve this. I doubt she realizes the extent of the damage she's doing."

"When you speak to him, ask him to bring along as many of those letters as he can find, as well as any financial statements on his trust fund. They'll help support his case.'"

They'd arrived in the front hall and he held her hands in both of his asking, "Will you be all right?"

"Yes, I'm fine."

"Would you like to spend the day together Saturday?"

"If the weather holds we could take a drive through the countryside, perhaps have a picnic." She freed one hand, saying, "Before I forget, there's something I'd like you to have," and reached into the pocket of her robe. "It's a key to the house," she said, pressing it into his hand.

"You don't have to do this," he said, uncertain of the symbolism of the gesture.

"I *want* you to have it," she insisted.

"Is this your way of saying you trust me, Emma?"

She thought about that for a moment. "I expect it is. Please take it."

He looked at the key, then back at her, starting to smile. "I can't imagine that you'd want a key to the condo, but you're more than welcome to have one. I've got a spare someplace."

She shook her head. "That isn't necessary."

"Should I know the code?" he asked. "I'd hate to have the police come charging over if I decide to pay you an unscheduled call."

She recited it, then said, "I'd love to wake up one morning and find you beside me."

"Well, thank you. I may just take it into my head to oblige you." He dropped the key into his jacket pocket. "I'll call you tomorrow. Try to get some sleep. You look very tired."

"Yes." She put her arms around him. "Thank you for this evening. It was such a pleasant change, having you here. You're not becoming bored with me, are you?"

"I don't think that's possible. Tonight made me see there's a lot I've been missing," he said, reluctant to leave her. She felt so fragile in his arms and looked to be bordering on exhaustion. "Family dinners, the company of friends, someone to care about. You and I really have covered a fair amount of territory in a very short time. I hope you're not going to become bored with *me*."

"It appears we both suffer from eroded self-esteem," she said sadly. "Do you feel we're moving too quickly?"

"I don't know what the time limit's supposed to be." He kissed the tip of her nose. "It seems about right to me. I was touched to see you had my roses in the office."

"They keep you close to me," she said, sliding away to open the door. "Safe home, Richard."

She waited in the doorway until he'd driven off. Then she closed the door, coded the alarm and went to the kitchen to make a cup of tea.

Roger went to the local police station. After presenting his credentials he asked one of the duty officers if he might see the accident report.

"Hang on a sec," said the fellow from behind the sheet of glass that separated them. "I'll see who's available to give you a hand."

The officer on hand was a Sergeant Anthony DeMillo, who looked, with his thickly curling black hair and wide brown eyes, to be no more than twenty-five, but who was in all likelihood closer to thirty-five.

DeMillo said, "The report's part of the public record. Have a seat and I'll scout it out. Shouldn't take more than a couple of minutes. What was that date again?"

Roger told him, and DeMillo went off to pull the file.

While he waited, Roger looked around the ultramodern police station, marveling at its sterile efficiency. Quarry-tiled floors, timbered ceiling, even a thriving plant in one corner. It looked nothing like the constabularies at home, had none of the atmosphere of urgent energy. The two officers behind the glassed-in reception area seemed relaxed, even jovial, as one manned the switchboard and the other responded to the query of a teenaged boy looking for a release from a ticket placed on his car in the high school parking lot.

DeMillo offered Roger a desk at which he might peruse the file that consisted only of the accident report. It took but a matter of minutes to read, and contained only one fact Roger found of interest. The crash had killed Elsa's husband on impact. Upon arriving at the scene the responding officers had found her attempting to free her husband from the wreck. There had been no skid marks, which meant there'd been no effort made to apply the brakes. Judging by the condition of the car, the officer at the scene estimated that the speed on impact had been in excess of seventy miles per hour. On a residential street.

"Anything else we can do for you?" DeMillo asked pleasantly when Roger returned the file.

"Not a thing, thank you. You've been most helpful."

"Any time," said the youthful sergeant. "Always glad to help a fellow officer."

During his drive to visit Elsa's younger stepdaughter, Sally, Roger considered the accident, wondering if the officers on the scene had viewed it as a suicide. According to the hospital records he'd studied that morning, the husband's blood-alcohol level had been well within the normal range, so driving while intoxicated had been ruled out. Daniel Manning had not collided with the tree accidentally but had done it with intent. And his intent had been not only to kill himself, but to kill his wife as well. Yet when police and rescue vehicles had arrived, they'd found her struggling to pull her husband from the wreck. Bleeding, badly injured, she'd nevertheless tried to save him.

Obviously she hadn't realized he was already dead. Or had she? What precisely had she been doing? It was possible the officers had simply assumed she'd been trying to save him. There was an answer here, if he could untangle the motives. Without question the accident was the key. Somehow everything hinged on it. The letters had to be tied in to it despite the fact that not a single one of them referred in any way to the fatal crash.

Glancing at the clock on the dashboard, he saw it was getting on to one o'clock. If he completed his interview by two he'd be able to catch Gillian at home. He wanted very badly to discuss this with her. Gillian was bound to see something he was missing or point him in another direction. And aside from that he wanted to hear her voice.

Sally was the antithesis of her older sister, Juliet. Slim, meticulously turned out in smart navy trousers and a matching pullover atop an immaculate white blouse, she was a relaxed, easygoing young woman who evidenced great fondness for her stepmother.

Seated opposite Roger on one of a pair of chintz-upholstered sofas, she offered tea or coffee, which Roger declined, then settled back with interest to respond to Roger's questions. His notebook and pen caused her to smile, and she said, "I thought those were just movie props. I didn't think policemen actually used them."

Returning her smile, he said, "In some instances you're quite right: they're nothing more or less than props. But I do tend to take notes now and again. You don't mind?"

"Not at all."

Having ascertained in advance that Sally had not received one of the letters, he showed her the ones received by Edward Evans and by her older sister. Reading them through quickly, Sally returned them, saying, "Elsa wrote them. I haven't the fog-giest why, but I have no doubt that she wrote them."

"What about them convinces you that she wrote them?" he asked.

"I can *hear* her talking when I read them. You've met Elsa," she said. "Don't you agree they sound exactly like her?"

"I do agree," he said. "Have you any idea why she might do something like this and then deny it?"

"If she says she didn't write them, I'd believe that," she said confusingly. "She's probably completely unaware of having written them. She's been terribly dis-traught since the accident, not herself at all. I mean, Elsa's always been very different, but in the past months she's become positively reclusive. She's had a very rough time," she said sympathetical-ly. "My father was a very difficult man, Mr. Hurley. He drove my mother away, and I think in time he'd have driven Elsa away, too."

"Difficult in what way?"

"In every way," she said with an apolo-getic smile. "He knew only one way to do everything: *his* way. If any of us went up against him, there was hell to pay. Did you know he was terminally ill?"

"There was some mention in the autopsy report of metastasized carcinoma in the liver and spleen," he answered.

"He was dying," she confirmed. "And he knew it," she added significantly.

"Could you elaborate?"

"To put it bluntly, I don't think the accident was an accident. But what makes it even more horrible is the fact that Elsa was with him." Placing the manicured fingertips of one hand over her mouth, she gazed at him for a moment, then lowered her hand, saying, "She's never spoken of it, never talked about what happened that night. Perhaps you could get her to talk about it."

"Perhaps," Roger said. "I do intend to try."

"How can you doubt she wrote the letters?" Gillian asked. "You've had confirmation on all sides, darling. I don't see your difficulty, frankly."

"My difficulty, Gilly, is the motive. Why on earth do something like this and then deny it?"

"Oh, I don't doubt she has no recollection of writing them," she said confidently.

"You don't?"

"Not at all. Think, darling! You're not considering who the woman is, what she does. Once you've thought about it, you'll see the logic. It makes perfect sense."

"Frankly, at this moment it makes anything but."

"I've *told* you, Roger. Consider the woman. Give it some long serious thought. I must run, darling. I'm due at the Hendersons' in fifteen minutes and they're all the way out in Chiswick."

"Run along, then. I'll try to ring you in a day or two."

"Are you ever coming home? I'm starting to forget what you look like."

"I expect to be home very shortly, three more days at the outside."

"Good. Must go. Lots of love, big hug."

"And to you," he said, and put down the receiver.

Consider the woman, he thought. Who she is, what she does . . .

She was so worn out she simply had to rest. Getting up from the desk, she went to the bedroom. The state of the bed—the blankets and spread hanging over the foot, the pillows bunched together—stopped her. Then she remembered. She'd brought Richard in here. They'd desecrated the Bellamys' marriage bed, and she'd derived a gritty sense of accomplishment from the act. But with Richard's eager assistance, she'd done it: she'd prevailed over the ghost.

She picked up the alarm clock, surprised to see it was only just after midnight. It felt later, but when she reviewed the evening she knew the clock was correct. They'd finished dinner at about nine-twenty. She and Richard had come upstairs a few minutes later, and he'd left shortly before eleven. She'd only put in an hour or so at the lap-top, yet it seemed as if she'd been in the office for far longer.

Setting the alarm for five, she dragged the blankets back over the bed and lay down.

"Why won't you *listen*?" Will ranted, small clots of sticky white stuff in the corners of his mouth.

"I really don't care to hear this," she said almost soundlessly, her hands so tightly knotted that her knuckles were white.

"You owe me at least this much," he maintained, "after all I've done for you over the years. You know damned well that without me you'd never be where you are now."

That was true. Without him she might have led a relatively serene life as one of those midlist authors he used to love to talk about. She wouldn't have minded in the least, and could readily imagine herself in a small comfortable flat in London she'd paid for with the modest income from her novels. A garden flat, she thought, not unlike Roger Hurley's, with french doors at the rear of the living room affording a view of the flower beds and shrubberies and a tidy kitchen just large enough to hold a plain white table and two chairs. The bedroom had Wedgwood blue walls and deep blue carpeting with draperies to match, tied back over sheer white curtains. In the living room a pair of comfortable wing chairs flanked the fireplace, and her desk sat before the windows overlooking the street. Every so often, she'd look up from her work to watch people passing by outside.

"Will you for Christ's sake pay attention? I'm *talking* to you."

She lived quietly in her ground-floor flat. Occasionally she entertained friends, preparing simple meals for them on her gas cooker, and engaging them in lively conversation. There was her agent and her editor, several fellow writers, Brenda, her one-time supervisor at the temporary agency, and Linda, her American friend. Their talk was of politics, and religion, and nuclear disarmament; of the rights of the individual, of the latest fads, of holidays they'd taken abroad. No one berated anyone else for his or her opinions. Everyone wore the clothing of his or her choice. Her hair was very long and she wore it in a single plait that hit lightly against her spine when she went out, carrying her string bag, to walk to the shops each afternoon, and stopped at the off-license to collect a bottle of wine to have with dinner.

"Without me you'd have been *nothing*!"

"No, I'd have been someone," she said very softly, feeling battered and weakened. Day after day of his badgering had worn down her resistance. "Why do you keep on at me when I've made it clear every way I know how that this is something I simply cannot do?"

"You *can*!" he argued. "There's not one fucking reason why you can't! Not one! Are you *enjoying* this? Please don't tell me you're enjoying this! If you'd just pay *attention* to what I'm saying!"

"I've paid attention to every word."

"You're still refusing to listen!" he shouted.

"All right, Will," she sighed. "Stop bellowing at me, please. I'll do it. I'll *do* it."

"Why did you have to put me through this all these weeks?" he asked accusingly, his immensely distended belly quivering as his head fell back against the pillows.

"I'm sorry you feel I've made you suffer," she said, her hatred for him reducing her voice to a whisper as she got up from her chair. "I'm sorry I cannot demonstrate to your satisfaction my gratitude for the countless things you've done to me."

"Just hurry up!" he urged, his bony fingers clutching the bedclothes. *"Hurry up!"*

She got up and went slowly to the door. Wait! This wasn't part of the retrospective, not part of a dream, nothing of the past. This was happening. She could feel the pile of the carpet under her toes, could hear the sound of her breathing. Real. She was awake, moving. And there in the hallway was a woman staring at her with deep, haunted eyes. Someone in the house, *real*. She screamed, her heart ballooning inside her chest, and leaped back into the office, slamming the door.

"Oh, God, oh God!" She was terrified, images flying through her brain, her body trembling. *That woman!* She knew her, only too well. What to do? God! Richard. Call *Richard!* He'd come; he'd help. Grabbing up the receiver, she punched out his number, her knees wanting to unlock so that she had to hang onto the edge of the desk for support.

He answered and she cried, "Richard! You've got to come! Please come right away!"

"Emma, what's wrong?" He sounded as frightened as she felt.

"*Please!*" she begged, and put down the receiver.

Calla was barking in the hallway but Emma was afraid to open the door, couldn't speak. Richard would come. She squeezed into the corner between the side of the desk and the window, sitting with her arms and legs tucked up close, her eyes on the door.

Bernice was gradually roused from a deep sleep by the sound of Calla whining and scratching at the guest-house door. "What on earth?" Feeling around on the floor for her slippers, she stepped into them and went to the door, wondering how long the dog had been creating such a commotion.

The instant Bernice opened the door, Calla began racing in frantic circles, barking urgently.

"What's the matter with you, dog?" Bernice said, watching Calla for a moment before deciding something must've happened over at the house. Going back to the bedroom for her robe, she said, "Just hold on there a minute, pooch. I'm not goin' out in the cold in my nightgown."

After pocketing her keys she followed the dog to the rear of the house and let herself in, pausing to feel along the wall for the light switch before coding the alarm. Calla danced halfway across the kitchen, looked back to see if Bernice was following, then went skidding across the linoleum toward the door. "Gimme a minute," Bernice said. "Never saw you act so crazy," she told the frenzied little dog, arriving in the hallway to hear a car approaching up the driveway. "Now who's that?" she wondered, going to the front hall to turn on the outside lights before peering out through one of the glass panels on either side of the door.

As she watched, the car screeched to a halt, the driver's door flew open and Richard, with a raincoat over his pajamas and his feet bare except for boating shoes, came running up the walk. She opened the door to him, asking, "What's goin' on?"

"Emma called me, sounding hysterical. Where is she?" he panted, hurrying inside.

"Upstairs, I imagine. Calla come barkin' and scratchin' at my door," she told him as they went quickly up the stairs. "Somethin's wrong, that's for sure."

Bernice went to the bedroom. Richard opened the office door, at once seeing Emma hunched up in the corner.

"Emma," he said gently, going over to her, "what's wrong?"

Bernice came to the doorway and stood watching, trying to make sense of what was going on. Calla was attempting to push past Richard to get to Emma. Bernice scooped up the dog and held her, asking, "She all right, Richard?"

"I think she's just had a bad scare." He looked over his shoulder. "Would you mind putting on some coffee, Bernice? We'll be down in a minute or two."

"I don't mind. Sure she's all right?"

"I think so."

Bernice went off with Calla to make the coffee and Richard turned back to Emma, asking, "What happened?"

Clutching his hand, her eyes and nose running, she said, "I was *dreaming*, Richard. Then, suddenly, I *wasn't* dreaming. I was in here and I opened the door. The hall lights were off but my desk lamp was on. As I stepped into the doorway I saw a woman standing in the hall looking at me." Squeezing her eyes shut, she bent her head to her knees so that when she next spoke her words were muffled. "There was a woman standing there with a *letter in her hand!* Richard!" she cried, raising her face to him. "It was me! There's the letter! I'm the one who's been writing them." With her free hand she pointed to the far side of the room. "There it is! How could that *be?* Why wouldn't I *know* I was doing something like that?" She sobbed broken-heartedly, overwhelmed by fear.

"It's all right, Emma," he said in that same gentle tone. "There's nothing to be afraid of. Why don't you come downstairs with me and we'll talk about it."

She allowed him to help her up, saying with despair, "I killed him, Richard. I had no choice. It's better that you know it now, before you become too attached to me."

"We'll talk about everything downstairs," he said placatingly, his arm around her.

"I'm so cold," she whispered, shivering.

Not wanting to leave even for the few seconds it would take to get her a sweater, he slipped off the raincoat and draped it around her shoulders. Then, his arm again encircling her, he led her down the stairs to the kitchen, where the air was already fragrant with coffee. "Sit down here," he said, directing her into a chair. "We'll have some coffee, and we'll all talk. Won't we, Bernice?"

"Sure we will," she said, putting a box of Kleenex down on the table in front of Emma, then standing with one hand curved protectively over the back of Emma's head. "There's no cause to be afraid," she confirmed. "Everything's gonna be perfectly all right."

Chapter Twenty-Five

"How could I have done that?" Emma asked mournfully. "I don't understand."

"No harm's been done," Richard said.

She looked at him in disbelief. "How can you say that?"

"It's true," he asserted. "Granted, Janet did attack you. If I'd been quicker off the mark, maybe I could've stopped her. I'm really very sorry about that. I never dreamed she'd stab you with the key."

"Stab?" Bernice exclaimed. "What?"

"She injured Emma's arm with the key."

"Why didn't you *tell* me?" Bernice asked her, her round face creased with upset.

"I'm quite recovered now," Emma said dully. "Stephen's removing the stitches tomorrow afternoon."

"Stitches," Bernice repeated, her lips thinning. "She hurt you so bad you had to have stitches, and you don't say a word to me about it. But you tell me we're friends. I *am* your friend, Emma. Don't you think I'd wanna know?"

"I'm sorry," Emma apologized, wondering if it was all a dream. Dreams within dreams. She'd awaken to find herself in the solarium or down at the beach, having traveled off again to that hushed place. She couldn't have written those letters, especially not that lewdly suggestive one to Richard. But she had. She knew she had. Was she insane? Had Will succeeded in pushing her right over the edge? What did all this mean?

"If you think about it," Richard said persuasively, "you accomplished a lot of good with those letters."

"What," she asked, "aside from demonstrating I'm mentally incapacitated?"

"You're not at all," he said with a reproving smile. "You cleared the air with Linda, for one thing."

"How do you know that?" she asked suspiciously.

"I've spoken to her," he confessed. "I've also talked with Bernice a time or two, as well as with Susan and Edgar."

"*Why*?" What was real? she wondered. The dividing line between reality and dreams seemed to have become very blurred. These people had been acting in concert without her knowledge.

"Because I wanted confirmation of a number of facts, not the least of which was substantiation."

"Of what?" She felt angry and betrayed and

impossibly confused. But most of all she felt bone weary, utterly spent. Her head throbbed rhythmically.

"Don't be angry with me," he said, placing his hand over hers. "I've known all along that you'd written the letters."

"You're gonna be mad at him," Bernice put in, "you're gonna have to be mad at me, too. Cause I called him first."

"You called him? I can't take all this in. What is *happening* here?"

"Honey, for weeks and months I'd talk to you and you wouldn't hear me. Your eyes were off somewhere else, not like when you're workin' on one of your books and I can see you're busy thinkin', but *somewhere else*. A couple of those times I saw you goin' down the drive to put letters in the mailbox. That was nothin' unusual, except it was late at night and you were in your nightclothes. Then folks started gettin' those letters but you didn't recollect writin' them. So when finally you tell me somebody's signin' your name to letters, it worries me. And it worried Richard. So we talked about it. And I talked to Miss Linda, too."

"Oh God," Emma whispered, holding a tissue to her eyes. Was she going to spend the rest of her life in some institution? Rational people didn't do things like this.

"There's a piece of paper in the right-hand pocket of my raincoat," Richard said. "Please have a look at it. I think it'll interest you."

"Not another letter," she said apprehensively.

"No, it isn't."

She put her hand into the pocket.

"Look at the part I've highlighted in yellow," he said, finishing his coffee and getting up for a refill.

She rubbed impatiently at her eyes, then focused on the page. She longed to go to sleep. Even the floor looked inviting. She could slide out of the chair and curl up on the linoleum, close her eyes and sleep forever. She forced herself to read.

Fugue: 2. *Psychiatry.* a period during which a patient suffers from loss of memory, often begins a new life, and upon recovery, remembers nothing of the amnesiac period.

"Do you remember writing the letters?" Richard asked, sitting back down at the table, hoping they weren't pushing her too hard, but convinced she was strong enough to deal with the truth.

She thought hard, trying to picture herself at the typewriter, addressing envelopes, writing letters. Nothing. "No," she answered. "I don't remember anything to do with it."

"I did some work at the library," he told her. "I also spoke to my former shrink over the phone. What's happened to you fits the definition more or less accurately, according to him. I'll tell you what I think," he said, again placing his hand over hers. "I think all the pressure built up to a degree where consciously you couldn't see any way out. So you did the only logical thing you could: you tried to escape through a series of letters. You told all the relevant people the truth you'd been withholding for too long and in the process you renewed your friendship with Linda; you got rid of an agent you've never liked and took on a new one who you do; you told Shawn and Janet exactly what you thought of them, after years not only of silently sitting by listening to them expound on philosophies that were abhorrent to you, but also of coping with their blatant antipathy. I'm sure there's probably more, but I can only refer to the letters of which I'm aware."

With a sniff, Emma said, "Evidently, I blasted Jim Finney and pushed him to give Kathy a much-deserved raise."

"See!" Richard said. "All positive results."

"I don't see that the letter to Janet did anything but heighten her dislike of me. And I also wrote one to myself."

"About Willard. Right?"

"I *despised* him!" she cried, the accumulated frustration like a wedge that had been driven into her chest. She felt on the verge of detonating from the explosive force of her combined agitation and self-hatred. "He wouldn't allow me to *breathe*. I was trapped here with him. I had to stay and watch him evolve externally into the miscreation he'd always been internally." She drew in her breath slowly, attempting to calm herself. She sounded quite mad. She wanted them to understand, couldn't bear the idea of their condemnation. She lowered her voice, saying, "During those last few months he began to complain ceaselessly, truculently. Every time the nurses left the room he started in, badgering me. If I had any feeling for him at all I wouldn't sit by and allow him to suffer; I'd help him. Without his intercession on my behalf, I'd never have been the success I was. On and on and on."

"I heard him," Bernice admitted. "I'd be dustin' or carryin' the laundry up the stairs and I'd hear that voice boomin' out of that sick body. I never knew how you stood it."

"I *couldn't* stand it!" Emma exclaimed. "It became so intolerable that the instant he'd begin, I'd concentrate on remembering all the shops at the top of our road when I was a girl and the names of the owners. Then he'd bellow at me that I was merely being stubborn; I enjoyed seeing him suffer. Finally, after months of it," she said thickly, "I had to do it. It was in defiance of everything I believe." Her tears started up again. It was rushing back to her now, overwhelming her with renewed pain.

Richard squeezed her hand, saying, "We understand, Emma. You don't have to do this."

"I think I must," she said, turning to look at him. "If I don't, I may very well go mad. If I'm not already."

"You're *not* crazy!" Bernice declared. "Don't you talk that way! You've had a real bad time, but you're not one bit crazy."

Emma looked at Bernice and then at Richard. They didn't appear to be sitting in judgment of her. If anything, they looked anxious to hear the truth. "I'd refilled the prescription well ahead of time because I had a horror of running out and having him go wild with the pain. So there were spare ampules, you see." She looked at each of them again, willing them to be tolerant. "I'd watched the nurses do it dozens of times. Every four hours one of them would get a fresh syringe and give him an injection. Then, mercifully, he'd be quiet. He'd sleep for

381

a few hours, and I wouldn't have to listen to his ceaseless diatribes and imprecations. I'd come out here, and the silence was like a balm. I'd bathe in it. Or I'd talk with you, Bernice, and the sound of your voice was music, so soothing. It lulled me, enabling me to go back in there and endure more of his tirades.

"So," she took a deep shuddering breath, "I got one of the syringes and did everything I'd seen the nurses do. Except that this time I filled the syringe completely. My hands were very unsteady because I was terrified the nurse would come back at any moment and find me with the weapon in my hand. I'd be arrested, put on trial, sent to prison, all because he couldn't die and was determined I should make him die. It was so dreadful," she cried, the scene too clear in her mind. "I couldn't find a vein. And the smell of him was so foul. He kept on at me to hurry, hurry, use the vein in the back of his hand. *God!* I hated him so much it felt as if I might suffocate from the sheer weight of it. 'Hurry up! Do it!' he told me. 'Hurry!' All I could hear was that voice shattering my eardrums. All I could see was that grotesque spiderlike body. And suddenly I stopped fighting the truth, which was that I wanted him to die just as much as he. So I did it." She shut her eyes tightly against the memory, but it was no use. Her brain had stored the scene down to the last detail and now it was unspooling on her mental screen.

She was back in the guest room they'd converted to accommodate him, with the hospital bed and all the accoutrements of his terminal illness: the bedpan, the sundry stainless-steel kidney-shaped basins, the gauzes and swabs and prescription bottles; the iodine and the alcohol and the omnipresent spray cans of Lysol. She was filled with horror and with loathing for this man who'd devoured her life and turned her into something she'd never been meant to be. He'd taken her emotions and twisted them inside out, and she'd allowed him to do it because he'd succeeded in convincing her that she was little more than an idiot savant whose gift lay in writing. He'd convinced her of any number of hateful things over the years and now, finally, he'd managed to hector her into becoming a murderer.

Gulping down the dry sobs that threatened to choke her, she'd taken hold of his skeletal hand, repelled by the thought that she'd once hungered for the touch of this same hand. Holding it firmly with her left hand, she'd pointed the needle at the prominent vein, telling herself to go ahead, get it over with. Once it was done, she'd never have to see him or hear his voice again. It would all be over. She'd finally be free of his odious influence. He'd be dead. And she'd be a killer.

As if sensing her hesitation, he said, *"Do it! Just do it!"* and his upper body lifted several inches from the bed, demonstrating his impatience.

"I can't!" she protested, unable to look at him, tears rolling down the sides of her nose, distorting her view of the vein.

"Do it!" he said in a threatening whisper.

She turned her head to dry her face on her sleeve, then looked again at the wormlike vein crawling beneath the transparent surface of his skin, telling herself she had no choice. If she didn't go ahead, he might continue railing at her for weeks, even months. It had all come down to this, she thought. There's never been a choice. Her stomach knotted, she aimed the needle at the protuberant vein, her teeth biting down hard on her lower lip.

She knew she was going too slowly. She lacked the skill, the accustomed ease of the nurses who gave the injections quickly and efficiently in order to cause him a minimum of discomfort. But she was slow and could tell from the rigidity of his arm that she was hurting him. God, the nightmarishness of that moment when the needle penetrated his thin papery flesh! The rubbery resistance of the vein below the surface, and its sudden, sickening yielding to admit the needle. Her stomach lurched. She gagged and had to pause for a moment—the needle embedded in the back of his hand—in order to conquer the sickness.

"I injected it all, every last drop," she told them, grabbing several tissues from the box and holding them to her eyes. "Then I put the syringe in my pocket and wiped the blood away with an alcohol swab. Just as the nurses did. He called me a clumsy bitch and turned his head away, whispering under his breath. I'd done what he'd wanted and he *cursed* me." She gave a gulping laugh, shaking her head back and forth, her nails digging into Richard's hand. "I sat in the chair and waited, counting off the minutes, watching the second hand tick its way around the face of my wristwatch. One minute, two, three. Eleven minutes passed before he went to sleep. Then I began counting again, minute after minute. The nurse came back, saw he was asleep, and settled in the armchair with her knitting. I kept counting. Three hours and forty-one minutes later he stopped breathing.

"He forced me to kill him, coerced me in that as he had in most other matters for years. He dictated every bloody aspect of my life, *everything*. And then he used me one last time to get what he wanted, to get me to do what I'd wanted to do all along." She put her head down on her arm and wept brokenly.

"I'd've done it," Bernice said quietly after a few moments.

Richard looked across at her.

"I would've," she repeated, boldly confronting his eyes. "Lots of folks would, in that situation. You think that makes you a murderer, Emma? I don't think so. You think so, Richard?" she asked him, her expression warning him not to dare take a negative position.

"No," he answered, in contravention of all his legal training. He loved Emma. How could he possibly add to her already considerable burden? Besides, if this were a courtroom and if he and Bernice constituted the judge and jury, Emma was bound to be acquitted on humanitarian grounds. "I don't think so," he was able to say with conviction.

"What you need is some sleep," Bernice said as Emma slowly raised her head. "You've been runnin' on your nerve for weeks now. You can't think straight, worn out like you are."

"She's right, Emma," Richard concurred.

"I am so terribly tired," Emma said, feeling emptied, purged; her eyes stinging, her body yearning for rest.

"Go on to bed. Richard'll stay till you fall asleep, won't you?"

"Of course I will," he said at once.

"Yes." Emma latched on to this. "I must go to bed." She got up, the raincoat slipping from her shoulders, and stood swaying slightly. "I'm so very tired."

"Come on," Richard said. "I'll take you up."

It was almost eight-thirty. Taking care not to rouse Emma, Richard got out of bed, and pushed his feet into the Topsiders. For a minute or two he stood looking at her, seeing how her features had been cleansed by sleep. Given what she'd endured, her mental stamina was nothing less than remarkable. A lesser woman would have gone to pieces in those same circumstances. But she'd found a way to salvage her sanity. Granted, it was a most unorthodox way, but she'd succeeded. His feelings for her even stronger now, he tiptoed from the room.

As he was passing the office he remembered the final letter, retraced his steps and went inside to retrieve it from the desk. Reading the address, he began to smile. He was tempted to open the envelope and see what she'd written but didn't dare. With an amused shake of his head he returned the letter addressed to Roger Hurley to the desk top. He had a strong hunch Roger would somehow receive the letter.

Bernice was sitting at the table with a cup of coffee and the morning paper, and looked up when Richard came in. "I'll bet you could use some coffee," she said, going for a cup.

"I've got to make a few calls, and run over to my place for some clothes."

"You have your coffee, then go on and do that. I'll keep an eye on Emma. There's no need for you to worry. She's got all that nasty business out of her system now. She'll be okay. She don't think so, but she's strong."

"Yes, she is," he said. "I think I'll cancel my appointments and come back. There's nothing on the calendar that can't wait."

"That was something, the way you come runnin' over here last night when she called." She smiled her approval.

"I was afraid maybe Janet had found another key. It was the only thing I could think of, even though I really doubted she'd actually come back. Janet scared the hell out of herself attacking Emma that way. She didn't plan it. It just happened. And it scared her. It was very obvious to me that she knew she'd gone too far. It wouldn't surprise me if she made an effort to patch things up."

"You're an optimist," Bernice said skeptically. "Be nice if you're right, but *I'd* sure be surprised. And how come you didn't tell me any of that about Janet?"

"I forgot. I know it sounds lame, but there's been so much going on, I quite simply forgot."

"Well, I can see how that'd happen," she relented. "What with the letters and you two figurin' out what some of us could see for a whole long time."

"What's that?" he asked, lost.

"I'd have to've been blind not to see you had a real soft spot for Emma. Have had for years, haven't you?"

He smiled. "You don't miss a thing, do you?"

"Not a whole lot, no."

"When she's had a chance to think, she may not be too pleased with me." He drank some of the coffee, imagining the negative possibilities.

"Richard, you've been real smart up to now. Don't go bein' stupid now. The woman loves you. She's just got to get her life in order. But she's not gonna go throwin' away someone who lets her do and say what she pleases. Not after all those years with Mr. Willard. And speaking of not bein' too pleased, I was the one uncovered all the mirrors without botherin' to tell her. She was up in the office, busy workin', and I figured she'd notice and be real mad at me, or she'd maybe say it was about time all that black cloth came down."

"For Christ's sake! *That's* what it was. I kept thinking there was something different about the house, but I couldn't decide what."

"Well, that's what it was all right. The way I figure it, she went 'n' saw herself in that mirror in the hall by the office and thought it was someone else. Stands to reason she'd think that. Seven months and more those mirrors've been covered up and in the meantime she went 'n' got herself some makeup and all new clothes. It's happened to me. I've come upon a mirror when I wasn't expectin' it and jumped a mile before I realized I was lookin' at myself."

"It's happened to everyone," he said, then swallowed the rest of the coffee. "I'm going now, Bernice. Thanks for the coffee. If she wakes up in the meantime, tell her I'll be back. Okay?"

"Okay."

He picked up his raincoat from the chair and put it on. "That bastard," he said ruefully. "That rotten bastard."

"Yeah," Bernice agreed. "He was that, all right."

"I feel so odd," Emma said, winding her arms around her knees, her eyes on Calla a short way down the beach. "Perhaps I should consult a psychiatrist."

"If you think it would help, perhaps you should."

"You say that as if you don't think it's necessary."

"Let me put it this way," Richard said. "If you're crazy, I want you to stay this way. I love you just the way you are."

"How can you love someone who's capable of doing such utterly mad things?"

"Easily."

"I'm afraid to go into the office and look at what I've been writing. I keep thinking perhaps I'll find I haven't written anything. I glanced at the last few sentences on the screen, then stored the chapter. Roger had already deduced that I . . . that the heroine, I should say, had in fact been writing the letters."

"He's pretty sharp, that Roger. I'll bet it's probably going to be your best book," he said confidently.

"Why do you say that?"

"Just an educated guess, based on everything you've told me and based on the fact that you did the most logical thing under the circumstances. You used your insight and your talent to get yourself free."

"I truly believed it was Janet." She thought it would be unwise, even unkind, to mention she'd also been suspicious of him.

"I know. If I hadn't already been satisfied you really were writing them yourself, she'd have been a damned good candidate. That scene in the kitchen was pretty frightening. But I think she scared herself, Emma. The impression I had was that she regretted it at once. And as I told Bernice this morning, it wouldn't surprise me if she began trying to make amends."

"I always hoped we could be friends," she said sadly. "I've tried so hard through the years to demonstrate my good faith. For Laurie's sake, as well as for my own, I wanted to show her I was prepared to care about her."

"Speaking of Laurie, I think he stands a very good chance of making a case for being custodian of his own funds."

"I wish he could spend one of his school vacations with me. I could take him on a trip, perhaps to Europe. If only Janet would see that I'm not a threat to her. Perhaps I'll call, try to talk to her."

"I haven't been to Europe for years," he said.

"Are you hinting you'd like to go with me?"

"I was working my way up to a blatant suggestion." He gave her one of his beautiful smiles and hugged her against his side. "Unless you find my skulduggery unforgivable."

"No, I forgive you," she said seriously, craning around to look at the house. "What should we do about the house?"

"We?"

"Yes, we. I did mean it when I said I'd like to keep you."

"I'm very glad to hear that." He also turned to look at the house now. "There's no rush, you know. You'll make up your mind eventually. And whatever you decide will be fine with me. As long as you go on wanting to include me, I'm happy to abide by your decisions. If," he added, "they seem reasonable."

"I haven't consciously made too many decisions in the last sixteen years."

"The few you have made have been good ones."

"God! I don't know how you can say that. I still can't believe I wrote you that embarrassing letter." She flushed and covered her eyes with her hand. "It's positively mortifying."

"Listen, my dear. I opened that letter and thought I was going to have a stroke. There was Carrie, my junior partner, sitting on the other side of the desk and I started to read the letter, trying to be cool. I finally had to tell her I'd go over the work with her later. To be perfectly honest, it was the most exciting thing that's ever happened to me. You wouldn't believe how badly I wanted it to be real. That last paragraph took the top of my head off."

"So you did ask me out to dinner because of the letter."

"I didn't know I was going to," he said. "You seemed very remote, almost unapproachable, when I came by that evening. But then you were so thrown reading the letter, which threw me even more. I thought about how much I've always liked you, and decided to take the chance. You were only human, after all, I told myself. The worst that could happen was you'd say no. So I asked if you'd like to go out for dinner. One of the most intelligent things I've ever done, albeit not one of the easiest."

"I do care very much for you, Richard," she said, threading her fingers through his. "You know that, don't you?"

"Uh-huh. So, are you having second thoughts about the book?"

"Well, no," she answered. "It's such a good idea, I really must keep on with it. Besides, Roger's about to try to discover the reasons why Elsa's been writing the letters."

"Elsa being a thinly disguised version of you?"

"Basically."

"Have you ever done that before, raided your own life for material?"

"Everything I write is filtered through my awareness. I suppose that constitutes raiding, in a sense. But since I'm the villain of the piece, it's not as if it's dishonest."

"Not really."

She was silent for a time, thinking. He and Bernice had acted in concert, but only out of concern for her well-being. At the same time she'd been working through the puzzle of the letters in her own, time-honored fashion, through Roger. Roger had concluded early on that Elsa was in fact the author of the letters. What was strange was that she hadn't made the conscious connection between Roger's conclusions and her own. At some level, she had to have known she was writing the letters. They represented her effort to work her way past the miasmic guilt that had had her floundering for months.

"I wrote my way out," she said. "Even if the letters hadn't accomplished it, the new book would eventually have had the same effect. I've done it before, using Roger to support my ideas and feelings, to bolster my courage. What the hell, Richard!" she said, feeling greatly eased. "I'll use every last bit of what's happened. It's all good material, one way and another."

"Fine, and I'll be very careful in future of what I say in your presence."

"Nonsense! You're obviously my inspiration. I've actually used that letter to you verbatim in the manuscript."

"You're joking."

"I'm not. It's most peculiar, but when I viewed the letters as material, I wasn't at all bothered by them. I've been using each of them as the need arises. I simply failed to make the obvious connection. But I would have, in time." She knew she still had a long way to go in coming to terms with her marriage to Will, and to what he'd obliged her to do. But Richard would help her. Richard knew all her secrets and it hadn't deterred him; he still cared for her in spite of what she'd done.

"Everything really is material to you," he said, somewhat awed.

She lifted her shoulders, gave his hand a squeeze, and with an apologetic smile said, "I'm afraid I can't help it, Richard. I'm a writer, after all."

. . . While he sat in the Departures lounge at the British Airways terminal at Kennedy Airport, Roger considered the strange, sad details of the case. Daniel Manning had attempted to kill both himself and his wife that night of the crash. But Elsa had sensed his intent and had, just before impact, thrown herself from the car. When the responding officers and medical emergency personnel had arrived on the scene they'd misinterpreted Elsa's actions. As she'd tearfully confessed, she hadn't been trying to pull her husband from the car in an effort to save him. She'd been beating at his dead body with her fists, fueled by the years of rage at the psychological and sometimes physical abuse she'd suffered at his hands.

Saddened to think of the pain that lovely woman had endured, Roger opened his briefcase to take another look at the letter—the last one written—that had been delivered to him at the Marriott.

Mr. Hurley, you needn't waste your time seeking a villain. He's long dead. And the mystery author of those letters is, of course, Elsa. Who else could it have possibly been?

There was no signature, but then none was required.

With a sigh, he returned the letter to his briefcase, then sat back awaiting the boarding call. Gillian had promised to meet him at Heathrow. He was longing to see her. She'd help him put the past week into perspective. And she'd mentioned booking tickets to the Royal Philharmonic. He was, all in all, glad to be going home. And glad, too, that no real harm had been done. His old friend Edward was a patient, caring man. Already his affection for Elsa had worked wonders. In time, it wouldn't surprise Roger in the least to receive an announcement of the marriage. . . .

KATHARINE MARLOWE

HEART'S DESIRE

"A fascinating tale...that holds the reader's attention!"
—*San Francisco Chronicle*

Raised by a woman whose obsession with finding "Mr. Right" destroyed her, Alyssa believes herself doomed to repeat her mother's fatal mistakes. Broken and despondent, betrayed by the men who she so desperately craved, Alyssa can only search on for the strength to find the one man who can fulfill her heart's desires.

__3315-1   **$4.99 US/$5.99 CAN**

SECRETS

"Smooth, suspenseful...a satisfying read!"
—*Publishers Weekly*

Struggling to recover from the trauma of her husband's death, Emma Bellamy is shaken anew when her friends and family begin receiving vicious letters signed by her that she swears she hasn't written. Terrified by what she might discover, Emma desperately searches for answers to the secrets that haunt her life and threaten everything she loves.

__3415-8   **$4.99 US/$5.99 CAN**